Prince of Hearts

Book One in The Elders and Welders Chronicles

by

MARGARET FOXE

The characters, places and events portrayed in this book are fictitious. Any similarity to real persons, living or dead, is purely coincidental and not intended by the author. The author has taken liberties with the details of the historical events mentioned in this book.

Copyright © 2013 by Margaret Cooke

ISBN-13: 978-1493585731

ISBN-10: 1493585738

*T*o my BFF Laura.

The Bard, as usual, said it best:

"A friend is one that knows you as you are, understands where you have been, accepts what you have become, and still, gently allows you to grow.".

Books written as Margaret Foxe

Prince of Hearts
A Dark Heart
Thief of Hearts (coming soon)

Books written as Maggie Fenton

The Duke's Holiday
Virtuous Scoundrel

ONTENTS

Acknowledgments

Special thanks to Clarissa Yeo at www.yocladesigns.com for the cover art.

As they took the ski lift up the mountain in pursuit of the evil Lord Rumple, Miss Alison Wren made it a point to ignore her companion. She had turned thirty years of age yesterday, and she could not decide which upset her more: the fact that she had been thirty for several years already, or that Dr. Augustus had once again forgotten her birthday.

Not that she cared in the least. She had her beau, the dashing Captain Standish, to shower her with gifts once this business was through.

"Didn't you turn thirty-three yesterday?" Augustus suddenly remarked.

Miss Wren replied with a superior sniff.

So he had remembered after all. Rather more than she would have liked. Exasperating man! Captain Standish would have never been so thoughtless as to remember her true *age …*

- from *The Chronicles of Miss Wren and Dr. Augustus*, *The London Post-Dispatch*, 1896

1

Gare du Nord, Paris, 1896

"*T*ICKETS, Finch?"

"In my vest."
"Visas?"
"Also in my vest, sir."
"The manuscript?"
"In my walking case."
"Are you certain?"
"Quite."
"Scopolamine?"
"What?" Aline asked, pausing on the train platform, thrown by the question.

"Scopolamine," Professor Romanov insisted, not breaking his stride. "Motion sickness tablets. You know how your stomach was on the airship crossing the channel. Do tell me you purchased them as I suggested."

Suggested? More like ordered. But it was one order she'd forgotten in the chaos of the last week. She was surprised he remembered. She gritted her teeth and hurried to keep pace with Romanov's long, loping stride.

"They are also in my case," she lied.

He pinned her with his peculiar, wolf-like amber eyes over his shoulder.

Damn, she thought. He didn't believe her. The Professor had the uncanny ability to spot a lie from a mile away. She was rarely able to successfully dissemble around him. And even though his head was turned towards her, he avoided running into the throng of people crowding the platform. They parted like the Red Sea for him.

Not only was he an imposing figure in his long, dark, velvet lined cloak, but he was also preceded by his mute, Weldling valet, Fyodor, who controlled the leashes of Romanov's pair of Russian wolfhounds, Ilya and Ikaterina, who, with their unnerving mechanical eyes, were also more automaton than animal. No one in their right mind wanted to go near such a fearsome trio of beasts.

But as usual, by the time it was her turn to cut through, the crowd had settled in again, jostling her elbows and nearly knocking the heavy load of books and documents from her arms. She had to push up her slipping spectacles with the edge of her wireless tickertext and break into a trot to keep pace.

As usual, she felt like the tiny bird that was her namesake, fluttering to stay abreast of an eagle.

Crowds parted for Romanov.

They didn't even *see* her.

When they finally reached their train car, she was winded, her spectacles were perched precariously at the end of her nose, and her arms were on fire from the strain of her burdens. A typical day, really, in the life of Professor Romanov's secretary. But usually she was in London enduring the constant demands of her employer.

They might as well have been in London, she thought wryly as she mounted the steps into the train carriage ahead of an impatient Romanov. They had been a week in Paris – *Paris*! – and she'd not seen anything but manuscripts, notes, and old, stodgy academics the entire time.

She'd hoped to see some of the city, as it was her first time on the Continent, but she should have known the Professor wouldn't allow her any free time, no matter what he'd claimed back in London.

Now he was cutting the trip short and rushing them back to London without explanation. If she hadn't witnessed the Professor receiving the mysterious tickertext for herself last night, she would half- suspect he was returning early just to vex her.

Well, he wouldn't be doing *that* much longer. Little did he know she'd planned on using this trip as a farewell gesture, though she suspected "gestures" were lost on the Professor. She'd aimed several crude ones at the Professor's back over her five years of employment, to little effect. She doubted he'd even care when she resigned. Why she was so nervous about telling him was quite beyond her powers of self-introspection.

She tripped on her hem – of course – and Romanov caught her under her arm and practically tossed her the rest of the way up the stairs. She held back a retort and kept moving forward. He remained on her heels, causing her to increase her already frantic pace, and continued to rattle off his list.

"When you get back to London, you must deliver the manuscript to my publisher," he said. "Do you have the new article?"

"Also in my case."

"Along with the scopolamine?" he asked archly.

"I have the article, *sir*," she said as evenly as she could through gritted teeth.

"Good. Proofread it first thing."

"But sir, it is in Russian."

"Your Russian is nearly flawless now. Written anyway. Can't speak it worth a damn, of course..."

She tossed him a look over her shoulder – a scowl – but it was less than successful, as she bumped into a door handle in front of her and pitched forward.

This time Romanov caught her around the waist. She was aware of iron strength, warm male, and the smell of that spicy, exotic scent unique to Romanov she'd yet to identify in the five years of her tenure as his private secretary.

She'd ceased to be ruffled by these sorts of physical contacts. She stumbled quite regularly trying to keep up with him. She wasn't *that* short, but he was just so much taller than most people, male or female, and his legs were so much longer, that he tended to cover a distance equal to three of her strides.

Though she could detect no outward signs of Welding enhancement aside from his Iron Necklace – a breathing apparatus resembling a metal band, ubiquitous on nearly everyone over sixteen – she sometimes doubted he was wholly human. She had to practically run to keep up with him, and it didn't help that she had two left feet. He was constantly catching her, pulling her along as if she were a clumsy child, all the while never breaking stride or his train of thought.

She often found herself scribbling notes mid-stumble, certain he would right her before she hit the floor.

He didn't break stride now. He practically carried her into their berth with the unfortunately placed door handle, Fyodor and the hellhounds on their heels. Once inside, she tried to shake him off and stand on her own two feet.

After giving him one last glare, she found her seat and pulled out her old-fashioned notepad and pen as Romanov sprawled out on the bench opposite her, rattling off a letter to a French colleague.

Ilya jumped on the seat next to her, plopped his large head in her lap, and began to drool on her skirts. Ignoring the kaleidoscopic machinery of Ilya's enhanced eyes, which never failed to disconcert her, she balanced her notes against the dog's ear and continued to scribble.

When her spectacles threatened to fall off her nose, Romanov reached over and pushed them up for her with one of his long, beautiful fingers, continuing to dictate the letter.

That, too, was a common practice between them, as her hands never seemed to be unoccupied around him. She sighed inwardly. They were way too comfortable in their dysfunction, which was another good reason she was jumping ship and marrying Charlie. Once they were back in London, she was giving Romanov her two weeks' notice, just as she'd promised Charlie.

After the letter was done, Romanov began to rattle off other items of business he wanted her to take care of in London. Around the thirtieth command, her overtaxed brain began to put the pieces together at last, and her heart sank.

"You're not returning with us," she stated.

"I would think that obvious."

She extracted her calendar from her case and thumbed to the schedule for the upcoming week.

"But you have a meeting with the publishers in a week, an interview at Pentonville Prison, an appointment with Inspector Drexler..."

"Cancel all of my engagements," he said swiftly. "For the next fortnight.

She guffawed, which caused Ilya to grumble and her spectacles to slope down her nose again. "But *sir* ..."

He waved an elegantly gloved hand through the air. "Cancel them, Finch."

She glanced at the silent, brooding Fyodor, who just shrugged and turned his attention back to his newspaper. As usual, Fyodor was no help. She'd never figured out what Fyodor did besides lurk about looking scary.

A blond, Viking-sized veteran of the Crimean War, his left side was nearly entirely automated. The Russian Abominable Soldiers had been among the first experiments in human Welding, but their particular technology, which had proven so deadly on the Crimean Front, had been forbidden after the war. His rough-hewn ironwork looked bulky and antiquated to modern sensibilities, but it did its job, enhancing his strength and his life span.

The latter result was one not able to be duplicated by succeeding generations of Welders. The Iron Necklace may have saved Europe from the deadly pollution of the Steam Revolution, but it didn't seem to prolong people's life spans significantly. Nor did the other Welding enhancements that had become so popular these days, despite what was advertised.

Fyodor had entered the Crimean War a young man of twenty. Forty-three years later, he didn't look a day over forty. Not many of his kind had survived the war, nor were they entirely accepted by society, perhaps in large part because of their unnatural life spans. Being a Weldling was one thing, but being an Abominable Soldier was quite another.

And Fyodor was *Russian*, living in *London*. Needless to say, he was given a wide berth for many different reasons, poor fellow.

Not that he was at all scary, once one got to know him. The first time she'd beaten him at poker, he'd smiled at her instead of ripping off her arms, as she'd initially feared he would.

He was, at heart, a soft touch.

And he had about the same fashion sense as Aline herself did. There was no way he was truly a valet to Romanov, whose sartorial elegance was legendary. When the Professor went out for the night, he usually made Aline tie his neck cloth. If the Professor thought she was his best option on that front, she could only imagine the mess Fyodor made when he attempted a straight knot with that bulky mechanical hand of his.

She suspected Fyodor aided Romanov in the part of his life Aline was not supposed to know about.

And she didn't, not really. All she knew was that the two of them always took mysterious trips abroad, sometimes for months on end. And when they came back, there was a new darkness in both of their eyes.

The Professor was more than a criminologist, of that she

was certain.

They would never tell her what was going on now. She'd tried for five years to figure out the Professor's secrets, as she could not help her natural curiosity. But her discreet snooping never yielded anything. Attempting to understand Professor Romanov was like trying to squeeze blood from a stone. He frustrated her like no other.

And she refused to care this time. The Professor, Fyodor, and the rest of Romanov's peculiar entourage would soon cease to be her problem. She was marrying Charlie, honeymooning in the Sahara, and living a normal, respectable life, free of murder investigations, late-night tickertexts, and hellhounds.

She was going to write more, have children, and perhaps plant a garden. In a seaside cottage, like the little one in the Outer Hebrides she'd lived in with her parents, where Romanov would never venture – and far away from the temptations of the East End gambling circuit, her personal forbidden fruit.

There was nothing for it. She was going to have to give her two weeks' notice now, before they reached Calais. She was *not* going to wait until he returned from his trip. She sucked in a steadying breath and released it, preparing to deliver her news, though for some reason the words stuck in her throat.

She couldn't fathom why, when she'd dreamed of this moment for five years.

"You may have your usual chambers at the Mayfair townhouse," Romanov continued before she could work up enough momentum to speak.

She stifled a sigh of annoyance. When he and Fyodor went on his mysterious trips, he always required her to stay at his London residence whenever he left behind the hellhounds. He seemed to think she was the only one on his retainer who could halfway control them.

"You're not taking the hell – I mean, Ilya and Ikaterina, with you?"

"No. Fyodor is coming with me. The pups are staying."

Pups. She always thought this the oddest word to be coming from Romanov's elegant lips. An odd and inappropriate label for two of the most gigantic, ill-behaved mongrels she had ever encountered. But he never called those beasts of his anything else.

"Is that an inconvenience, Finch?" he asked in that teasing manner of his he employed when he sensed her rebellion.

She leaned back in her seat, pushing her spectacles back into place with the end of her pen, and glared at her employer. He lounged on the seat across from her, looking quite comfortable as always, stroking Ikaterina's muzzle with one hand, his intent gaze settled in her direction.

And as always, he looked fantastic. Broad-shouldered and thin-waisted, built like an athlete, not a head doctor. And dressed like a Russian tsar. Beneath his cloak, he wore a stylish chocolate velvet jacket cut tight at the waist and belling out in a bizarre, un-English manner, buff-colored trousers that seemed to fit his over-long, well-muscled legs like a second skin, and tall, foreign-looking riding boots.

She, on the other hand, was *quite* uncomfortable, crammed against her case on the one side, and crushed by Ilya's weight on the other, afraid to move lest the beast growl at her again. *And* she had a giant ink stain on the bodice of her mud-colored gown, which the Professor could plainly see.

She'd almost call the stain an improvement, since the gown, serviceable though it may be, was perhaps the ugliest gown ever to exist in the world. But the stain was directly over one of her ... well, unmentionable parts. It was embarrassing, to say the least. She would have tugged her jacket over the stain, but Ilya was sitting on it, and she didn't want to risk the hellhound's wrath.

The sides of the Professor's devilish lips twisted up at the ends as he surveyed her, as if knowing precisely how uncomfortable she was and how inconvenient he was being.

"You don't have plans, do you, Finch? Some elaborate holiday planned in the next fortnight?"

She narrowed her eyes slightly. She was vexed, but

determined not to show it. She didn't care to be reminded how little of a life she had outside his orbit. But that was all about to change.

As soon as she worked up the nerve to break her news to him.

"Why the sudden trip?" she inquired, ignoring his question and postponing her resignation.

His slight smile faded, and his yellow-amber eyes went dull. It was unusual for him to display even a glimmer of real emotion. Yet, ever since he'd received the mysterious tickertext late last night, which was the catalyst for their abrupt departure from Paris, he'd been acting quite peculiar.

She'd assumed it was from Scotland Yard, calling him home to consult on a new case, but that couldn't be it, since he wasn't returning with her.

"It's personal business," he answered.

She pursed her lips, but said nothing, fighting back her rising curiosity. When it came to Romanov's "personal business", he never revealed anything. And never took her with him.

Weary, annoyed, she took off her spectacles and pinched the bridge of her nose.

"Have I given you a headache, Finch?"

"Of course not," she lied.

His lips quirked again. "Good. Because I need you in top form. No one else can manage the pups like you."

She suppressed a snort. The "pups" managed her, not the other way around. How he'd gotten it into his head that the hellhounds obeyed her, much less *liked* her, was a mystery.

"Sir, I have something to tell you …"

"I want you to meet with the publishers as well, Finch," he continued, ignoring her.

She looked up at him, startled. "Me, sir?"

"I trust you to argue my case, should it come to that. Unless you feel the meeting is beyond your range."

Was he deliberately trying to provoke her? She'd been an independent woman since she was twelve years old. If she seemed like a wilting violet to him, it was only because she kept a firm leash on her tongue around him – most of the time, at least.

Besides, she had publishers of her own that she managed quite well, thank you very much…

Though this was her own secret, and one she was definitely *not* sharing with the Professor.

"I think I shall survive," she said stiffly.

"Good. I wish you to manage as much of my affairs as you can in my absence." He reached into his vest pocket and withdrew a handwritten letter. He handed it to her. She had to grit her teeth and pinch her wrist to keep from rolling her eyes when she saw the letter's recipient.

Luciana Luclair. The mistress.

"Give this to her personally. As well as any trinket you think appropriate." He waved his hand in a vague gesture, as if to say it was of no concern to him.

"Appropriate, as in a token of farewell," she said flatly.

"Precisely." He betrayed not a glimmer of regard or remorse for breaking with – or, more precisely, having *her* break with – his mistress. Not that The Luclair, as Aline secretly called her, deserved the courtesy, horrible harridan!

She was relieved, actually, that she would not be subject to any more of the opera singer's theatrical outbursts at Romanov's office. Somehow Romanov always managed to be "away" when The Luclair came hunting him.

At least he'd taken the time to hand-write a letter, even if he was making her do the dirty work. He had broken things off by tickertext with his last mistress. Low, even for him. The Professor seduced and discarded women with a cold-bloodedness that left Aline feeling chilled.

If not for witnessing first-hand his love for his so-called pups and the closeness he shared with Fyodor, Aline could almost believe Professor Romanov had no heart.

She studied his wolf eyes and sensuous lips critically. She knew him too well to be taken in by his good looks, as other women were. Thank God she had more sense than to ever become Romanov's mistress.

She snapped her attention back to her notes, feeling the blush steal over her cheeks.

As if *that* were even a possibility! As if she would even *consider*...! And as if *he* would ever...! She didn't find him attractive in the least, no, not in the least! He was demanding, impatient, and interacted with lesser mortals – that is, everyone but himself – as if they were scientific specimens under his microscope.

Of course, he was without a doubt quite brilliant and could afford to behave however he wanted. She read his impenetrable work for a living, after all. But he was also insufferable; she'd gleaned that within a few seconds of being in his company five years ago. Brilliant, insufferable, and...

Well, it would be foolish to try and deny it. He was truly, devilishly handsome. He had an unaffectedly aristocratic mien, an animal-like grace. He was like some prince – or villain – *definitely* a villain – out of a fairy tale, with austere features, aquiline nose, and those strange yellow eyes. There was a compelling, exotic slant at the corners of those eyes, and his skin was a rich, burnished, very un-English olive.

And his *hair*.

Thick, curling and black with just a dusting of gray at the temples. Even *she* had to concede he had magnificent hair, but she'd die before she admitted it to another living soul. He was used to women swooning over his exotic good looks, but *she* would never give him the satisfaction. He was too insufferable, and she was too sensible to behave like some ninny simply because the Professor happened to be easy on the eyes.

And, besides, she was getting married to Charlie Netherfield, who was as dependable, steady and accommodating as the Professor was arrogant and demanding.

And if he wasn't as handsome as Romanov, he was quite acceptably attractive.

"What *are* you thinking, Finch?" Romanov inquired, his bored eyes now lighting with interest as he observed her red face.

"You don't want to know," she murmured.

His eyes narrowed, as if he wasn't sure about that.

She squirmed under his scrutiny and once again attempted to break her news about resigning and Charlie. She was grudgingly willing to give him these final two weeks of hellhounds and mistresses. After that, she was out the door.

"Professor, I've something to tell you, and it's rather urgent…"

He held up his hand, cutting her off, and extracted his pocket watch from his waistcoat. At the same time, as if on cue, the steam train began to slow down. He gave Ikaterina one last caress, then stood up, pocketing his watch, and straightening his already immaculate clothes.

"Your news will have to wait, Finch. My transport has arrived." He signaled to Fyodor, who also stood, grabbing up two cases and exiting the cabin with remarkable grace for someone half-machine.

Flummoxed, Aline glanced out the window. They were in the middle of the countryside, not a station in sight. A herd of cattle grazed in the distance, but something suddenly startled them, sending their bulky forms scattering away from the train.

She could see a few passengers hanging out the window staring up into the sky at something she could not see. But she could certainly hear its unique sonic hum, and see its shadow, a giant oblong shape cutting across the rolling green hills above the train.

A dirigible.

She turned back to the Professor, dumbstruck.

"By transport, you mean the illegal dirigible hovering above us?" she asked as calmly as she could.

He quirked his brow. "*Slightly* illegal, Finch. A wonderful way to travel. I was tempted to take you with me on this particular excursion, since you had made it this far, but I know how sensitive your stomach is, even on the airship across the channel. A dirigible is not so tame a conveyance."

Her stomach churned just at the thought. She'd felt as if she might die when she'd crossed the channel a week ago, losing, it seemed, every breakfast, lunch and dinner she'd ever eaten over the edge of the airship while the Professor held back her hair.

It was not something she looked forward to repeating.

A dirigible, a smaller, swifter, and less stable derivative of the airship, with its giant propellers and wings – *and* tendency to crash – would doubtless be a thousand times worse. Besides, most governments had outlawed dirigibles since the end of the Crimean War.

Doing a bit of light gambling in illegal venues of a Friday night was one thing, but traveling by what amounted to a pirate ship was quite another.

She was not surprised Romanov was meeting the dirigible in the middle of nowhere, as they were entirely unwelcome in cities. What did surprise her was how he'd maneuvered the train into stopping here. It must have cost a fortune in bribes, at the very least.

Then again, Romanov was mysteriously, obnoxiously, wealthy. "But Professor!"

"No time, Finch. My flight awaits," he said on his way out the door.

Aline gave the hellhounds a warning look to stay and followed Romanov out the door, shutting it behind her. She scurried after her employer as he made his way to the end of the car. He shoved open the outer door and began to ascend the small, wrought iron spiral staircase that led to the roof.

Aline swallowed hard as she glanced up into the belly of the beast hovering precariously above them. What looked to be an actual pirate, complete with a red kerchief and Welding peg leg, stood on the deck of the ship, unfurling a retractable ladder, but that was all she could discern in the chaos. The wind from the dirigible's propellers was so fierce her hair threatened to come loose from its pins, and she had to hold her spectacles in place lest they blow off her face.

This is ridiculous, she thought to herself, her temper finally snapping completely.

Determined to have her say at last, she started to follow

the Professor up the staircase, calling after him. He stopped at the top, and with his black cloak and hair swirling about in the wind, turned to look down at her, a smile on his face and a spark in his wolf-like eyes.

He looked slightly demonic and entirely too handsome, and her heart stuttered a little at his elemental beauty and … well, her secret jealousy. Despite whatever serious business was awaiting him, he was embarking on an adventure.

Without her. As always. The insufferable man.

"Are you sure you will be able to handle the crossing on your own, Finch?" he bellowed at her over the hum of the dirigible's engines.

Aline highly doubted it, considering her weak stomach and the fact she would have no company but two troublesome hellhounds, but she refused to show her panic. She'd die before she admitted a weakness to this too-perfect male.

"No, but I must tell you something…"

She choked on her words as the propellers blew a hunk of her hair directly into her mouth. She attempted to swipe it away, but in the process, her spectacles went flying. She barely managed to catch them before they fell onto the tracks.

He cupped his ear. "What was that, Finch?"

"I'm giving you two weeks!" she shouted up at him.

He nodded. "Yes, I'll be back in two weeks!" he yelled back, obviously not understanding. He gave her an insolent little wave and turned his back. Aline stomped her foot in frustration.

She was tempted to follow him all the way up the staircase and strangle him, but she'd never make it in time.

Fyodor was already halfway up the dirigible's ladder, two suitcases in one hand, his automaton side quickly scaling upwards.

Romanov started climbing up behind his so-called valet, and as he climbed, Aline stood, glued to her spot on the platform, staring upwards in mingled shock and frustration.

She was not mechanically inclined at all, despite her late uncle's best efforts. Owing to her rare blood disorder, she didn't even have an Iron Necklace—hence a childhood spent in the Outer Hebrides during the worst of the Great Fog. She could operate a wireless tickertext and a steam kettle, but that was about it. As her condition, her sea- and air-sickness – not to mention her poverty – had nipped in the bud any thought of Welding for herself, she had little incentive for studying the subject.

But even without being an expert, she didn't think it was logical that the entirely human Professor could scale the dirigible ladder faster than Fyodor, suitcases notwithstanding.

Her hair whipped into her face again, distracting her from her study, and her frustration with the situation quickly outstripped her shock.

"I quit, Professor! *That's* my news! I'm getting married, you infuriating clod, to someone who lets me *finish my sentences*!" She had no hope he'd heard her, but she felt somewhat better to have yelled at him. Then, for good measure, she made a rude gesture she'd learned from her years in St. Giles at the Professor's retreating back.

With that, she stumbled towards the door to the car before the dirigible blew her to the tracks.

-from *The London Post-Dispatch*, 1857

Genoa, 1896

HE man currently known as Alexander Romanov – Sasha to his few intimates – had grown up surrounded by monsters. His father, Tsar Ivan The Terrible, as he'd come to be called, had been a legendary monster, still reviled to this day. His uncles had also been monsters, as well as the soldiers under their aegis who'd carried out their contemptible orders. And his older bastard brothers, the ones his father had raised alongside Sasha, had been perhaps the worst of the lot, as savage and profane as the worst biblical demons.

Only Sasha had not realized they were monsters for many years. In their company since his birth, he'd thought the behavior of his grand Russian family was normal.

And *he'd* been the heir, Ivan Alexander Ivanovich, Tsarevich of the Russian Empire, his father's favorite – and only surviving – legitimate son. He'd been expected to follow in their footsteps.

But when Sasha became interested in the manuscripts his tutors assigned him when he was around his seventh year and

16

discovered that there were other ways to live, he'd been shocked. It was not normal for his father to beat his mother. It was not normal for a tsar to beat and maim his vassals for amusement, or to rape his serfs. It was not normal to live life with no rules.

It was rather like the moment he realized the earth was round and not flat – a concept relatively new to barbaric 16th century Russia – wondering how such a simple, obvious fact had escaped him for so long.

Of course, the discovery of his family's monstrousness had confirmed his own private fears. He'd always felt different from the others. Even out on the hunt, a sport at which he'd excelled even from such a young age, he'd never felt bloodlust when he took down an animal like his father or brothers did.

His father had called his behavior weak, and Sasha had tended to agree with him. With the help of regular beatings to make a man of him, he strove to overcome his natural aversion to the acts of cruelty that seemed to come so easily to the other males of his family. He'd wanted to fit in. Being seen as weak was dangerous when surrounded by predators.

Then the Novgorod Massacre had happened in Sasha's fifteenth year, and Sasha had decided he would rather die than become what his father wanted him to be.

But Sasha hadn't died, no matter how much he'd wanted to by the end of his life as Ivan Ivanovich. His father had taken everything from him – his wives, his unborn child, his faith, his *very heart* – and given him the one thing he'd never wanted: eternal life.

It seemed a cruel joke that Sasha had lived for centuries, cursed with the mechanical heart beating in his chest, put there upon the orders of his madman of a father.

When he'd left Russia, he'd started living by his second name, Alexander, and his maternal surname, Romanov, in his attempt to leave Ivan Ivanovich behind forever.

Current Welding technology was nothing compared to the device in Sasha's chest. Like the twelve Elders who shared his fate, he was immensely strong and fast, and any injuries he received healed at an accelerated rate. Thankfully, the secrets of Da Vinci's heart were lost, and his fate could not be inflicted on anyone else. All Sasha knew was that he'd not aged a day in the three hundred years since his strange rebirth.

And he'd lived every day of those three hundred years searching for answers to the questions that had plagued him all of his life. What had motivated his father to inflict so much cruelty upon the world? Why had so many followed in Ivan's footsteps, but not him?

Or would there come a day that he, too, would turn into a monster? Was the blood that coursed through his automaton heart tainted with Ivan's evil? Would he wake up one dawn to find some hidden switch inside of him thrown, his conscience extinguished, and the desire to do violence pounding in his veins?

The rage had happened only once before, when, still healing after his unwanted rebirth, he'd been faced with the full scope of what his father had done to his beloved Yelena and their son.

He'd taken exquisite pleasure in killing his father, watching across the chessboard as Ivan Grozny, scourge of Novgorod, had endured the slow, fatal agony of arsenic poisoning – and the agony of knowing it was his favorite son who'd done it.

His father hadn't deserved the honor of dying by the sword.

Reason told him his fears of becoming like Ivan were baseless, and what he'd done to his father was just, all things considered. He'd never felt that bloodlust again, and doubted he ever could. There was no one left for him to lose, after all, no heart left to break.

But a part of him deep inside that was still that frightened fifteen-year-old boy, helplessly watching the brutal sack of Novgorod, could not let go of the past or the fear that his days as a normal, ordinary citizen of the world were numbered.

All those women, he thought to himself, as one particularly powerful memory of Novgorod flitted over his mind, *so long ago, raped, thrown from the bridge into the icy river. The blood flowing like water over the ice and snow...*

To have memories like that seared into his brain was a burden he'd not wish on his worst enemy.

And he knew, deep inside, he'd *never* be normal or ordinary.

None of the Elders had that option.

Yet whatever he was, whatever his father and those awful, long-ago events had made him, he'd been well prepared for his lifelong vocation.

It was useful to be able to bury emotion when solving murders for a living. But that did not mean he was immune. When he looked upon the evidence of a crime and felt that ancient, sick ache in the pit of his stomach, he knew he had at least a drop of human blood left in him, which was perversely reassuring to him.

He would have preferred foregoing the reminder of his humanity if it could have spared him this present moment, however.

All he'd wanted was to stay in Paris with his secretary, the one bright light in his otherwise dark existence. He'd rushed them through a fortnight's worth of meetings and conferences in a single week so that he could surprise Finch with a holiday.

He'd actually looked forward to escorting her to all of the sights she'd studied so covertly in her *Baedeker's* when she thought he wasn't looking. Getting her across the English Channel had been difficult enough with her weak stomach, so he didn't think he'd ever have another opportunity to provide her with the adventure he knew she secretly craved.

But he'd learned the hard way in the past never to ignore a Council summons. Though this time he wished he *had* dared. The scene before him on the basement floor of the Genoa National Museum was so singularly vicious, and so nauseatingly familiar, he was struggling to choke down his usually disciplined emotions.

Above all else at the moment, however, he was furious.

The victim, a woman, had been here for some time. *That*

much was obvious from the stench alone. He clenched his hands at his sides in an effort to rein in his temper before he addressed the smug Italian who still stood at the entrance to the room, arms crossed, staring daggers at Sasha's back.

Franco Salerno had never liked or trusted him. Not that Sasha cared. Like most Italians, Franco was always unbearable company, and possessed of a narrow-minded intellect Sasha had never respected in the three hundred years of their unfortunate acquaintance. But Sasha had never given Franco enough thought to dislike the man in return.

Until now.

It had taken Sasha a good day traveling by Thaddeus Fincastle's dirigible to arrive in Genoa, and he'd received the tickertext the night before his journey, already some time after the body had been discovered. Thus over forty-eight hours had passed, yet here the body remained. It was as if Franco had taken extra pains to ensure Sasha's discomfort – *and* wrath.

"I see you thought it necessary to leave this poor woman where she lay," he said.

"Franco and I both agreed that, though distasteful, it was for the best," the man next to Franco interjected. "We wanted to give you a chance to see the … er, tableau, as it was originally discovered. In case you see something the rest of us have missed."

Sasha narrowed his eyes at the speaker, the dark-haired, aristocratic Rowan Harker, Lord Llewellyn. Of all the Elders, Sasha was closest with Rowan. But he could not miss the glimmer of suspicion lurking deep within his friend's eyes. Sasha knew what Rowan left unspoken, that he and Franco wanted to witness Sasha's reaction to the "tableau", as Rowan so politely called it, for any signs of his culpability.

Franco had already made up his mind centuries ago about Sasha's guilt, while Rowan had always championed Sasha's claims of innocence. But three hundred years of murders without any other suspects could make stronger men than Rowan doubt. Witnessing the doubt in Rowan's eyes for himself, however…

Well, Sasha was not surprised, under the circumstances, but he was disappointed.

Sasha turned back to the body, though he didn't want to. He'd already seen what he needed to, and knew exactly what had happened to the poor woman. The murderer had struck the woman on the head, but not hard enough to kill. Then he'd proceeded to surgically remove the woman's heart while she was still alive.

In that, the villain had succeeded.

From the pattern of burns inside the chest cavity, it was apparent the villain had attempted regeneration, but if it had been the goal of the villain to keep his victim alive, that part of the plan had been grossly unsuccessful.

An experiment, then, and only an incidental one at that.

Sasha rubbed the long scar that had never truly healed on his sternum. He'd been the last successful experiment in Vital Regeneration. But Sasha's transformation had been an illicit one, performed by one of the last of Da Vinci's acolytes – and under great duress.

But that scientist was long dead, and the technology was extinct. Da Vinci's so-called Abominable Knowledge had been forgotten, the manuscripts destroyed by the High Council before the dawn of the 17th century. For those few remaining who remembered and lived with Da Vinci's legacy, that was a good thing.

This murderer didn't think so. He hadn't thought so for three centuries, since that was how long bodies like this one had been turning up, taunting Sasha. He eyed the Cyrillic poem written in blood on the floor next to the victim's head. He suspected it was another one of his father's, just like the ones decorating every other crime scene.

Aside from mass rape and genocide, Ivan the Terrible had loved to write poetry.

It had been a hundred years since the last string of victims, just as there had been a hundred years between those and the first ones. Sasha had his theory about why the cycle had stopped, and why it was starting again. But his theory was one that no one on the Council wanted to hear.

He was convinced it was a Bonded human who'd gone rogue, but the implications of that theory were unacceptable, as that meant one of the Council was, in the end, culpable. Which was an outrageous notion to everyone save Sasha, who shared the Elders' fate, but had never been one of them.

And that was the fundamental difference between Sasha and the Elders. All twelve of the Elders on the High Council had chosen Vital Regeneration. But Sasha had not chosen his fate, had *never* wanted it, something none of the Elders believed. How *could* they, when they couldn't understand how anyone wouldn't crave eternal life like they themselves did? Sasha had been looked upon with suspicion from the moment they'd learned of his existence.

And when they'd learned who his father was, their distrust in his worthiness had deepened. To them he'd always be an outsider. And he'd always be the Council's easiest scapegoat when they found the truth too unpalatable to even consider.

He was about to turn away when the small beam of light shining down from the narrow basement window above hit something shiny tucked beneath the victim's blonde hair. He stopped and stretched out his gloved hand to retrieve it.

He felt Franco start forward abruptly with a growl, as if he suspected Sasha of doing harm to the corpse. Sasha almost – *almost* – laughed out loud at the Italian's absurdity.

"Relax, Franco. What do you think I'm going to do to her? She's quite dead, you know," he murmured, retrieving the object and inspecting it.

Spectacles.

For some reason, his heart, mechanical and flawless though it was, seemed to stop working for the blink of an eye. An unnamed dread began to rise up inside of him, but he couldn't quite put his finger on its source, or why the spectacles should unnerve him so.

He tried to shake it off and spun around to show the others what he had found. He gave Franco his most ironic smile.

"I can hardly harm her any more than she has been. And *I'm* not the one who has let this poor woman rot where she lay for the past two days. Perhaps had you done your job better, you would have found these earlier."

Franco moved to take the spectacles, but Sasha snatched them away and strode out of the room, disgusted with his companions and the entire situation. He brushed rather abruptly past Rowan and stepped out into the hall. He swept down the corridor, towards an exit, needing fresh air.

Not that there was much of that to be found in Genoa these days. The blighted Fog that had swept Europe from the Pale, where the Crimean War had reached its catastrophic conclusion, lingered in this part of Europe. The unstable, quarrelsome Italian Federation had yet to implement any of the clean air measures Great Britain and France had introduced, and anyone without an Iron Necklace would not have survived long in such an environment.

Another reason aside from her tendency to cast up her accounts – not to mention the dead body – to leave the unenhanced Miss Finch behind. She'd had some allergy that had prevented her from being outfitted with the Necklace when she was an infant. He marveled she'd survived her childhood at all, considering how it had been in those dark days after the War.

Of course, with *his* monstrous heart, the toxic air posed no danger, the Necklace around his throat a mere prop to prevent attracting undo attention.

When he finally emerged into the blazing, soot-filled heat of a Genoa summer, he felt marginally better. It was certainly an improvement over the stench of death. He heard Franco and Rowan scrambling to catch up with him as they argued quietly with each other. It sounded like Rowan was trying to calm the Italian down.

But it was too little too late, as far as Sasha was concerned. If Rowan had been a true friend, he would have never let him walk unprepared into this untenable situation in the first place.

Fyodor was waiting for him at the edge of the courtyard, leaning against a pillar amid the gathering of the local gendarmerie under Franco's command. The Weldling looked as out of place as a lion amid a flock of chattering, slightly hostile magpies. He raised his eyebrow in silent inquiry.

Sasha shook his head grimly and turned his attention back to the spectacles, studying them in the full light.

Something about them continued to bother him.

Rowan came up beside him. "So you think the spectacles are significant?"

"The murderer staged the room exactly as he wanted it. I doubt he would be so careless as to leave behind a pair of spectacles, unless he wanted them to be found. As with the poem, the murderer is attempting to play a game with us. And in case you're wondering, it is not I."

Rowan stared at Sasha, not bothering to hide his doubts. "It's hard for me to believe you did this, Sasha. You have never shown the slightest glimmer of the insanity it would take to commit such acts. And even if you did, I would never believe you stupid enough to leave behind such self-incriminating clues."

"Damned with faint praise," Sasha muttered.

"But, dear God, how could I not be suspicious? This rogue has done his best to implicate you, again and again, leading me to believe that, if nothing else, you are hiding something crucial."

Sasha growled in frustration.

"Perhaps you don't even know yourself what you are hiding. But whether you like it or not, you are at the center of this debacle, and you always have been," Rowan finished adamantly.

This was one charge Sasha could not deny.

Rowan eyed the approaching Franco. "Our Italian friend, however, is convinced of your guilt. I would tread lightly. Don't give him any more reason to hate you."

"You mean, stop baiting him? What, and take away one of the few rare pleasures in my long and tedious life? I think not.

And under the circumstances, I believe I will take your advice, my *friend*, with a grain of salt," he murmured.

Rowan clenched his jaw and winced. *Good*, Sasha thought. *Let him stew, the Judas.*

Franco finally arrived at their side. He ripped the spectacles from Sasha's hand and glared at him. "You know," Sasha began conversationally, "I've been in Paris this past week. At the Sorbonne. Dozens of people can testify to my presence there. I could have hardly jaunted down here, butchered that woman, then returned to Paris, without someone noticing my *three day* absence."

"I won't believe you were in Paris all this time without confirming it myself. Even if you were, you could have had an associate who carried out the crime for you. I am well aware of your connections to all sorts of men of science with dubious credentials."

Sasha laughed. "Now I have minions, who go around slaughtering people on my bidding, all to – what, Franco? Throw you off my scent? And I suppose by scientists with dubious credentials, you mean Dr. Freud of Vienna, or Mr. Edison of America? Yes, I suppose anyone with even a spark of creative genius might seem *dubious* to you."

Sasha didn't think it was possible, but Franco's face became redder, and the vessels in his temples began to bulge. Sasha almost felt sorry for the man. Almost. But Franco was so blind. And so, it seemed, were Rowan and the rest of the Elders. Most still held an infuriatingly medieval suspicion of modern science.

Despite its myriad drawbacks – drawbacks that were mostly a result of Elder interference, anyway – one of the few redeeming aspects of the present era was the emergence of the modern scientific method, in Sasha's opinion.

The High Council was still grounded in a mysticism that had never appealed to Sasha. For many on the Council, God had ordained their immortality, but such hubris was downright dangerous.

Sasha's infamous father had also thought God had guided

his hand.

And *that* hadn't turned out well for anyone.

Since the debacle in the Crimea forty years ago and its aftermath, when Elder interference had nearly decimated entire nations, the Steam Age was fast leaving the Elders and their machinations behind. Sasha couldn't help but feel relieved.

He just wondered what would happen when the Elders finally realized they were fossils.

"As I've told you and the rest of the Council for centuries, I am innocent. Someone is using me to distract you, and as much as you don't want to hear it, there are only two possibilities. Either it is one of the other Elders, or one of your Bonded companions."

The incredulous looks they gave him were exactly what Sasha expected. He sighed. Most of the Elders saw nothing wrong with the practice of Bonding – sharing their special Heart's Blood to prolong the life spans of a select few humans. But Sasha had always thought it a morally suspect practice, and above all a risk to their security.

No one had ever listened to his concerns, however. He wasn't a true Elder, after all.

According to the Council, there were rules about Bonding, and those rules were strict enough to prevent any loose ends. But as Sasha had learned the hard way from the moment of his birth, rules were meant to be broken, and often were.

And unlike Rowan, Sasha didn't have blind faith in the virtue of the other Elders. Just because they had Da Vinci hearts did not make them saints. In fact, Sasha's experience with the Council inspired very little in the way of trust – not that he trusted anyone, after the upbringing he'd had.

The few he could have trusted, like Rowan, however, could not imagine the brothers who'd died and been reborn beside them capable of murder – or Bonding a human who was.

It was a failure of imagination that Sasha knew would be the Council's eventual undoing. The outrageous actions of the

Elder Stieg Ehrengard during the Crimean War proved Sasha's point, but somehow Ehrengard's sins had been conveniently brushed under the rug. The High Council had moved on as if nothing had happened and nearly a million human lives had not been lost in Ehrengard's quest for power.

For the Elders, their brotherhood and their belief in their superiority over mankind trumped all.

"And as I've told you before, unlike the both of you, I have never Bonded anyone in my life. How you can consign someone to a fate such as ours is something I will never grasp."

"Leave off with your righteous indignation," Franco growled. "It hardly flatters someone of your lineage."

"By lineage, do you mean the fabulously wealthy and powerful Russian Imperial family I was born to rule?" he asked archly. "Granted, my father was a unique sort of demon, but I am told some of my forebears were quite acceptable company. Saints, according to the Orthodox Church. I can hardly vouch for them, however, since three hundred years has taught me to be wary of history books, and the Church. But at least *my* ancestors could read."

Franco's face turned purple with rage. Everything was a sore spot with the Italian, but he was particularly sensitive about his humble origins. A low blow, perhaps, but Sasha couldn't regret it at the moment. He shrugged. "You started it. And have you ever considered the possibility there is someone out there the Council has missed?"

"Impossible. There were only ever twelve of us," Franco said.

"Yet I make a very unpleasant thirteen," Sasha replied. "Perhaps I'm not the only mistake roaming around out there. But I wasn't thinking of that. I would wager all I owned that this is a rogue Bonded, someone who has fallen through the cracks, despite all of your so-called precautions."

Rowan looked thoughtful. "Why do you say that?"

He sighed. "First of all, an Elder would have no need for such experiments. He is already immortal, and he can Bond a human if he wants the company."

"Unless he is not experimenting at all, merely desecrating human flesh because he is a madman," Franco interjected. "A psychopath like his father."

Sasha merely quirked his brow at the Italian, refusing to respond to such a thinly veiled accusation. "I never said we weren't looking for a madman. That much is obvious. But this is a man who has been Bonded in the past. He is attempting to remove the Elder from the equation altogether by recreating Da Vinci's heart for himself – quite unsuccessfully, I might add."

"If this is true, then that would explain his longevity," Rowan said reluctantly. "But it would also suggest…"

"It would also suggest that there is an Elder out there who is abetting this man," Sasha finished. "And is still Bonding him. That is the reason there are hundreds of years between each string of victims. The Bonding wears off, and the murderer panics as he begins to age once more. He starts his cycle of violence, until the Elder intercedes."

"That is not possible!" Franco insisted. "No Elder would facilitate such a fiend."

"It is entirely possible. You and Rowan here are naïve to think otherwise. I seem to be the only one exempt from your belief in the inherent goodness of your fellow man. Turn some of that distrust upon your comrades and your precious Bonded companions, for God's sake. Surely some likely suspects come to mind. Or did the Crimea teach you nothing?"

For once, he thought he'd gotten through to the Italian, whose face had lost all of its color. For a long time, Franco seemed adrift in some torturous thought, but it didn't last long.

"This is all ridiculous!" the Italian finally burst out, with a shake of his head. "Surely you don't believe him, Llewellyn. He's lying. Spinning this crazy tale, just as he always does, to cover up his madness."

Sasha sighed. "I'm not lying. I'm not hiding anything, and I'm certainly not mad – not *yet* anyway. I have given you my hypothesis, and that is all I can do. As I have never adhered to the Bonding practice, *I* wouldn't know who this villain is."

"Well, he knows *you*," Rowan said darkly.

"Just as he doubtless knows the distrust you have always felt for me. He is using it to distract you. But I have explained all of this before, to little avail. Nothing has changed."

"But it has," Rowan said, studying the spectacles in Franco's hand, his brow furrowed. "You said so yourself. He's never left spectacles before. And, come to think of it, this is the first time it's been a woman."

Sasha could feel the blood pumping faster through his veins with every word Rowan spoke, his resentment receding and that indefinable sense of dread growing stronger. He was missing something crucial. And the answer was in the spectacles, round and dainty, with thin, golden wire. So familiar.

And it was in the woman herself. Small, slight and unenhanced – unusual in this age of mass Welding – with dark blonde hair. She was entirely unremarkable, or at least she should be.

But not to him.

He knew someone who shared all of these characteristics, down to the golden-rimmed spectacles.

His gut was telling him it was not a coincidence.

He'd let Finch go, alone, on a public airship, back to London, thinking it a great lark to see the dismayed expression on her face.

He cursed and started for the exit to the courtyard.

"Where do you think you're going?" Franco demanded, signaling for his guards to cut Sasha off. They raised their weapons, blocking the exit.

A snarling Fyodor stepped between him and the guards, ready to defend his master. Sasha was tempted to join Fyodor in brawling his way through the annoying flock of Italians, but he was already in enough trouble. Sasha touched Fyodor's arm, staying him, and whipped around to face Franco.

"I must return to London," he said, as calmly as he could. "I swear to God, Franco, you'd better let me leave now. You have no right to hold me here, which gives me every right to toss all of these guards on their ears on my way out. And I will do it."

Franco reached into his vest and extracted a familiar, antiquated scroll, sealed with a dab of blood-red wax. Sasha's heart sank – or it would have if it weren't made of metal alchemy.

"I have *every* right to hold you, as the Council has granted me an edict for your arrest," Franco spat. "And if you value your life and the life of the abomination at your side, you will obey Council law."

"Insult my valet one more time, Franco, and I don't care if you have a thousand edicts, I *will* rip your head off, consequences be damned. You have my word on that," he said softly, and with such deadly intent even the restless gendarmerie surrounding him went still.

Franco wisely held his tongue as he repocketed the edict, looking distinctly uncomfortable. Then he dared to extend his hand again. "I will have your wireless, Romanov. Council rules."

Sasha glowered at the Italian before he reluctantly gave over the device. He turned his attention to Rowan. "You knew this would happen, didn't you?"

Now Rowan was the one to look uncomfortable. "It is out of my hands, Sasha. I did all I could to persuade the Council to reserve its judgment. I even went to His Grace."

Rowan referred to the Duke of Brightlingsea, the *de facto* leader of the High Council, which did nothing to reassure Sasha. The rest of the Council thought the Duke a hero for the way he had defeated Ehrengard's misguided metal army at Sevastopol.

Personally, Sasha thought the Duke a mass murderer along the lines of his own father.

"But the good news is the edict is only for your detainment while we corroborate your alibi. It should take a few weeks, nothing more," Rowan finished.

"I don't have a few weeks. Rowan, I *must* return to

London immediately," he growled impatiently.

"The Council will not be gainsaid, Sasha, you know that. If you don't play along, you'll only dig yourself an even deeper hole."

"Does this edict include Fyodor? Is he being detained as well?"

"Unfortunately, yes," Rowan said. "I'm sorry, Sasha."

Sasha groaned in frustration – and panic. He needed to return to London post-haste, if only to assure himself all was well with Finch. To assure himself this was all just an over-reaction. But he was not going to voice his suspicions in front of Franco, who would just twist his words against him. He swallowed his pride, which had been severely wounded by Rowan's betrayal, and faced his former comrade.

"I don't want your sympathy, my Lord," he returned, unable to keep the ice from his voice. "I want to know if you'll stand as my counsel."

Rowan looked surprised, then puzzled. "I hardly think you require one at this point, Sasha…"

"But I am granted one, under Council law, am I not?"

Rowan glanced at Franco, who reluctantly nodded. He sighed. "I am not the best choice to serve you in such a capacity…"

"No doubt, but you are the most expedient. Will you or not?"

"Of course …"

"Then I invoke my right to counsel."

"Here? Now?"

"Yes, damn you. Now." He stepped to the side, and one of the guards attempted to block his way.

Sasha just stared the man down until he lowered his weapon and allowed him to pass. After assuring Franco he was not aiding in Sasha's escape, Rowan followed him until they were far enough away from the others not to be overheard.

Sasha cut straight to the point. "I want you to return to London, as fast as you can."

"I had planned to stay here, and make sure Franco

follows the rules. Despite what you think, I *am* on your side."

"Damn you and damn the rules. You were right to point out the singularity of this crime. Our victim was a woman with spectacles. A petite, unenhanced blonde-haired woman with spectacles."

He allowed a few moments for Rowan to grasp the significance of this, but when the Earl continued to look puzzled, Sasha sighed with impatience. "*Finch*, you idiot! The victim is just like Finch."

Rowan was dumbfounded. "Your ... secretary? Miss Finch? But does she have blonde hair? I confess I hadn't noticed."

"Blonde enough. And those spectacles are identical to Finch's, down to the maker, I would wager. More importantly the woman was unenhanced and gently bred, just like Finch."

"How can you tell she was gently bred?" Rowan demanded.

"The hands. Only a gently bred woman would have hands that smooth."

"You notice those sorts of ... details ... on *corpses*?"

"Damn it, it's my job. Of course I notice."

Rowan shook his head as he took it all in. "But why? Why target *her*, I mean, Miss Finch, of all people?"

"If I knew the why of anything this bastard does, we'd have caught him by now."

"I will return to London as soon as I can to assure myself of her safety, of course." Rowan hesitated. "Shall I explain things to her more fully? Is she more ... intimately acquainted with your activities?"

Sasha barely refrained from punching his friend in the jaw. He didn't know why the insinuation bothered him so much, but it did. "I don't know what you're implying, exactly. I don't think I *want* to know. Finch is my secretary. She thinks I am nothing more than a slightly annoying 'professor of psychopaths,' as she so eloquently calls my current occupation. And I would like to keep it that way. She has a rather overactive imagination, and I would not want to stir the pot, if you please."

"You know, I think you may be right about her overactive imagination," Rowan said thoughtfully. "My sister told me the most incredible tale, that Miss Finch is actually the author of that horrid penny-dreadful everyone reads in the *Post-Dispatch*."

Sasha glared at Rowan. "Are you really discussing a penny-dreadful at a moment like this?"

Rowan sighed. "Quite sorry. I will be discreet when making my inquiries."

"And tell Inspector Drexler to have Matthews resume following her."

Rowan began to nod, then hesitated, his expression darkening. "Resume? You mean you *often* have your secretary followed? Don't tell me you've known about this ... interest the murderer has in Miss Finch!"

"No," he growled. "I have my secretary followed because of her habit of frequenting St. Giles on her day off to wager away her salary at the Automaton Races."

Rowan looked suitably shocked. "Miss Finch? A *gambler*?"

"Inveterate. And with no idea of the danger she courts, the little fool. You don't want to know how many bookmakers she has indebted herself to, or how many arms Matthews has had to break this past month after her last visit."

He couldn't keep the exasperated fondness from creeping into his voice, despite the urgency of the moment. As foolish as Finch was to visit the stews, he couldn't help but admire her audacity.

Rowan shook his head. "I would have never suspected it of Miss Finch. She looks so ... wholesome."

"Never play her in cards, if you value your fortune. She cheats like a sharp in a St. Giles hell," Sasha said, feeling a sudden pang of longing for his quixotic little secretary.

He frowned at himself. It had to be worry he was feeling, not longing. He'd not *longed* for anyone or anything in centuries.

"I wonder if my sister knows this. She plays whist with your secretary every week. I'll have to warn her," Rowan said, interrupting Sasha's strange thoughts.

Franco, his patience expired, began sending the guard in their direction once more. Sasha turned to Rowan. "Give me your word you'll protect her, that I have nothing to worry about while I am detained," he demanded.

"You have my word."

"And your word that, as my counsel, you'll not reveal this conversation to Franco. He'd use this information against me."

"You have my word, as counsel and as a friend, Sasha. How can you doubt it?"

"As easily as you doubt me," Sasha said bitterly, turning back to his fate.

The turmoil within the House of Lords reached new heights of the ridiculous yesterday afternoon when members of the radical Luddite Party stripped down to their Unmentionables when challenged to prove their Persons are as Anti-Welding as their Rhetoric. Opposing parties in various states of dishabille hurled vitriol at each other for an hour before the assembly disbanded. Only Lord L— of the Steam Party managed to say anything sensible at all when he begged the notoriously gouty Lord R— to put his shirt back on…

-from *The London Post-Dispatch*, October 1890

London, 1896

ALINE'S first moments on terra firma once more had begun auspiciously. The hellhounds, as if for once taking pity on her, had been relatively docile during the return crossing, though she'd been just as sick, and with no one to hold back her hair. But she'd refused to surrender her dignity altogether, despite the vomit in her hair, or to allow the hellhounds to have the upper hand.

Perhaps they'd sensed her desperation … or understood her threat to sell them to the Automaton Races for parts if they didn't behave. Battered and dizzy, exhausted to the bone, she'd let the hellhounds nudge and prod her down the disembarkation ramp and onto the air docks when they'd arrived in the London port.

She could have sworn they were trying to keep her on her feet in their own unique and bullying way, and she'd almost decided to give them a reward when they arrived home.

But their good intentions did not last.

35

The moment they spotted Charlie with their mechanically superior eyes, their fur bristled and the growling began. They nudged and prodded her away from her fiancé, who waited for her in the crowd on the air dock. She yanked them back in line, but they in turn yanked her off course again. She was forced to stop altogether and scold them, while Charlie had to come to her.

Ilya and Ikaterina had never taken to Charlie, who often met with her in Hyde Park when she was cajoled into walking them. After the second time the hellhounds had tried to snap one of Charlie's hands off, Charlie had wisely foregone strolling with her when she had them in tow – or rather, when *they* had *her* in tow.

Needless to say, Charlie had never taken to them either. He eyed the dogs with distaste, and turned his attention to her. His expression did not change, and he made no move to embrace her. "My dear, air travel does not suit you at all."

Her fragile spirits plummeted. Of course she looked – and most likely smelled – dreadful. But he didn't have to point it out like the Professor would.

"I don't know what we shall do for the honeymoon. How will you ever make it to Cairo?" he asked, shaking his head in dismay. "You know, I have already told my investor you shall be accompanying me. But I fear our plans may require some adjustment."

Charlie was an archaeologist, and he'd agreed to take her on his next expedition to Egypt for their honeymoon. In theory, it sounded like a wonderful adventure. But now that she'd experienced first hand the effects of the airship on her constitution, she was a little concerned.

Charlie didn't seem the type to hold a lady's hair back while she cast up her accounts. He probably didn't even realize ladies were capable of something so impolite as vomiting.

And she was worried about the air when she got there. Charlie had an Iron Necklace that protected him from the giant sandstorms that had recently plagued the Sahara, but she didn't. Charlie had dismissed her concerns, explaining that if the natives there didn't need a breathing device, then neither did she.

But she remained a bit skeptical. He never said how many of the natives actually survived the suffocating winds of a giant sandstorm. Nor had he likely noticed.

Charlie had many good qualities, but sometimes he could be oblivious to the details, especially if those details weren't British.

But she was determined to go, determined to marry him. She'd not let him see her doubts. She patted his hand, which made Ilya growl. "I shall manage. The Professor suggested I take medicine before I travel. I just hadn't the time to purchase any. I'm sure it will sort me out when the time comes."

Charlie reached for Ikaterina's lead, but thought better of it when she snarled at him. Instead, he picked up the valises the porters had left just beyond the reach of the hellhounds and started to escort them from the docks.

"So did you tell the Professor our news, my dear?"

She sighed. "Not yet. He left so abruptly I hadn't the chance. You should have seen it, Charlie. He had a dirigible pick him up in the middle of the countryside! I think it was a pirate ship."

Charlie looked at her as if she'd sprouted a second head. "You have a vivid imagination, my dear. A pirate ship indeed."

Charlie also lacked imagination. She shrugged. "Well, *I* think it was."

"You've been reading too much rubbish. Why, that sounds exactly like something that would happen in that dreadful serial the *Post-Dispatch* runs."

She gritted her teeth, trying to tamp down her temper. Had Charlie always been so condescending? Or was she just overly sensitive from her exhaustion? Yet to insult her precious *Chronicles* was to insult her person.

Of course, Charlie didn't know she was the author, but still. It *wasn't* dreadful. "Are you saying you don't believe me, Charlie?" she asked quietly, pausing.

Miraculously, the dogs paused with her, but only because

they probably knew she was quite close to arguing with their nemesis and wanted to savor it.

Charlie stopped and gave her a surprised look. "Of course I'm not saying that, my dear. If you say the Professor took a dirigible to Italy, then that is precisely what he did. I just wonder whether it was piloted by pirates."

He made her sound like a child. "Well, there *are* pirate dirigibles, Charlie. If you read the newspapers, you'd know. They are becoming quite the nuisance over the Atlantic these days. And the man had a red handkerchief..." She stopped, hearing how ridiculous that last statement was going to sound. "Anyway," she said, resuming their brisk pace out of the station, "I never said the Professor was going to Italy. Where would you get such a notion?"

It seemed Charlie paused for a few seconds behind her before rushing to catch up with her.

"I haven't the foggiest, my dear. Perhaps it was because of the mention of the dirigible. Genoa is a notorious port for pirate dirigibles."

She threw him a scolding look. "You see, you *have* been reading the newspapers! Though I hadn't read that about Genoa. I don't know why you would doubt my assessment of the Professor's conveyance."

"Perhaps I was just teasing you, my dear."

Now the look that she sent him was one of incredulity. Charlie never teased her. She didn't think he knew how.

She still didn't think so.

"Well, if that was your attempt at teasing me, it was *most* unsuccessful."

Charlie looked contrite. "So sorry, my dear. But we were speaking of the Professor. I proposed a month ago. It is difficult to understand why you've not told him yet."

For some reason, Aline felt guilty. "I *have* tried." Well, she'd tried yesterday.

"We need to begin to make plans for the wedding. Did he say when he'd be back?"

"Two weeks. After that, I'll be free, Charlie. I'd marry you today, but I could hardly let poor Madame Kristeva handle these two mongrels all alone."

"Two weeks, you say?" Charlie said, brightening a little. "Shall we go ahead and have the Banns read? That takes around two weeks, doesn't it? We can be married right when the Professor returns."

Aline smiled a little uneasily at Charlie's enthusiasm, though she knew she had no reason to be apprehensive. This was what she wanted, wasn't it? "Perhaps we might wait," she said. "I ... want to do this properly, Charlie. And I can't do that until I'm completely free of the Professor."

"Yes, I suppose you're right," Charlie said with clear disappointment. She patted his arm. "It's just a fortnight, Charlie. I promise."

$\mathcal{T}$ HREE weeks later, Romanov's latest choice in bed partner was proving to be an exceptionally tenacious case. Aline had been putting off the task Romanov had set for her in regards to The Luclair for as long as possible, but the odious opera singer had stormed Romanov's townhouse, and Aline had no choice but to deal with her.

Aline could imagine why the Professor had chosen Luciana. The Luclair was breathtakingly beautiful. Her lustrous ebony curls were artfully arranged around a visage of alabaster skin and large, luminous sapphire eyes.

Even the Welded mantle that enhanced her voice, covering The Luclair from her neck to décolletage, had been done by a master. Its iron shell had been gilded in gold and set with jewels.

In short, Luciana made Aline feel like a dowdy girl in pinafores.

Luciana's beauty was tempered, however, by her inability to leave her characters behind when she was not on stage. To Aline's immense annoyance, the soprano was currently playing Desdemona in *Otello*, so when she read the letter from Romanov that Aline handed her at the beginning of the interview, she used the bad news therein as an excuse to practice for the night's performance.

Aline tried her best not to roll her eyes as the soprano dabbed invisible tears away with the edge of a lace handkerchief, playing the scorned lover to perfection. Aline half-expected a pit orchestra to rise up from the floor and Madame to break into an aria. She dearly hoped not.

With The Luclair's enhancement, one high C would break every window and chandelier in the entire townhouse.

"How could he do this to me?" Luciana cried, clutching the remains of Romanov's letter against her bosom, which was every bit as spectacular as the mantle above it. "I am singing Desdemona tonight! My nerves cannot take it, Miss Finch. He is cruel and uncaring to abandon me in my hour of need!"

Aline was quite certain The Luclair had not seen Romanov in at least two months, so she didn't add abandonment to the list of Romanov's manifold sins. Poor judgment and bad taste came to mind, however. Aline had to admit that Romanov had outdone himself this time. What was he thinking, to have liaisons with women of The Luclair's ilk?

Perhaps because it makes leaving them so easy, she thought to herself.

Aline glanced across the room where Madame Kristeva, Professor Romanov's Russian housekeeper, stood, rolling her eyes. Apparently Madame Kristeva didn't care for the opera singer either – *and* she understood English better than she let on.

"I am ruined! How can I live another day when I'll never love again?" The Luclair sobbed.

As Aline was quite convinced that no hearts had been broken at any time during this particular relationship, and that The Luclair would doubtless live an irritatingly long time, she counted to ten, summoning up the last reserves of her patience, before answering.

"I know this must be a difficult moment for you, but give it time," she choked out half-heartedly.

Luciana dropped her handkerchief and narrowed her suspiciously dry eyes at Aline. She gave an irritated huff. "And what would *you* know about a broken *affaire*, Miss Finch? What could you *possibly* know of broken hearts? Of *passione*?"

Gritting her teeth, Aline started to count to ten again. The exaggeratedly Continental way Madame pronounced her name, "Meez Feench", was worse than fingernails on chalkboard. Plus Madame was right. What did she know about *passione*? A great deal in terms of second-hand accounts. Very little in the way of actual experience.

But she *did* know a thing or two about the Professor and his mistresses, and the way these little tête-à-têtes always went. It was the time in the interview that the scorned lover decided to take out her frustrations on the secretary, a common refrain. Aline sometimes wondered if these women all read the same script beforehand.

Not wishing to extend the interview any longer, she wrenched open the top drawer of Romanov's desk, pulling out the satin-covered case from the jewelers.

Madame eagerly opened the case, but her face fell as she peered at its contents. "What is this?" she demanded, holding up the garnet brooch Aline had spent hours picking out.

Clearly, Madame was *not* impressed. She was looking at it as one would look at a dirty stocking.

Aline bit her bottom lip to physically suppress a groan. She didn't see what there wasn't to like about the brooch. The gold filigree setting was exquisite, fashioned in the nouveau style, and the garnet insets were of the first quality.

"It's a garnet brooch," she explained, with a dryness Madame did not appreciate.

"I know what it is. It's *brown*," The Luclair huffed. "Like your hideous gown."

"It's quite a unique piece…"

Madame dropped it back in the case. "I don't want *unique*. I want *diamonds*."

Of course Madame wanted diamonds. She should have gone with the gaudiest diamond necklace at the jewelers, as had been her first instinct, but she'd been in too foul a mood over the Professor's continued absence and failure to respond to the thousand tickertexts she'd sent him.

A fortnight indeed!

So she'd purchased the brooch instead, something she'd liked – something she perhaps unconsciously knew Madame wouldn't – even though she didn't think The Luclair had much use for necklaces, with the giant one permanently attached to her chest.

Aline reached for the brooch, as if to take it away. "If you don't want it…"

Madame's eyes grew wide, and she snatched the brooch back, tucking it into her bosom.

Aline rose from her seat, and Madame did the same, but it seemed Madame was not as eager to end their delightful interview. She glared down her nose at Aline, all righteous indignation. "I know all about you, Miss Finch. Sasha's loyal little lapdog. You pant after your master's heels like those two beasts of his."

Luciana was right about the dogs. They *were* beasts. But Aline took offense at the comparison of herself to those two mongrels. She did not pant. She'd never panted in her life.

And *certainly* not after Professor Romanov.

"You English women are so dreary, without an ounce of *passione* in your blood. The women like you are the worst. Bluestockings who insist on working like men and being treated like men, while secretly you are in love with your handsome employers."

"I assure you, Madame Luclair, I am not in love with the Professor. I leave such an onerous task to beautiful ladies such as yourself."

Madame didn't believe her. "Who would not be in love with Sasha? You are not blind. You are not a man. Unless you are one of those women who prefer the company of other women…" Madame's tone grew speculative, her gaze assessing.

Then, gasping dramatically, she clasped her hands over her jeweled mantle and cleavage as if she had discovered her modesty. Apparently she was seeing Aline's ugly brown frock coat in a new light.

Aline bristled. She tried counting again, but only got to three before her patience expired. "My preference is none of your concern, Madame. But should you like to know, I have gentlemen callers aplenty."

Madame looked incredulous at the blatant fable. Aline obviously didn't have gentlemen callers aplenty. But she did have one, thank you very much. One very reliable, entirely respectable, and genuinely attractive gentleman caller. One Charles Netherfield, and she planned to marry him, just as soon as her damned employer returned.

But that was neither here nor there at the moment. What was pertinent was Madame's swift departure from the premises. Abandoning courtesy, she stalked over to the French doors leading out into the back garden and opened it. She stood aside and watched Ilya and Ikaterina lope inside, straight for Madame's skirts.

It had rained, so the hellhounds were quite muddy.

So was Madame by the time she managed to extricate herself.

*S*HORTLY after Madame had departed in tears – real for a change – and the dogs were brought in line, Aline snatched up her reticule and stormed towards the door, telling Madame Kristeva to expect her back in a few hours. She had an errand of her own to run in St. Giles – a distasteful one at that.

She was not going to let the opera singer's tirade dampen her mood, which was already low. The afternoon spent enduring insults had almost been worth it, however, when she saw the look on The Luclair's face when the hellhounds had pounced with half of London's muck on their paws.

Oh, what was she thinking? Of *course* it had been worth it. Aline hadn't felt so perversely satisfied in some time.

Her spirits fell, however, as she exited Romanov's townhouse on Berkeley Square and began trudging towards Piccadilly. It was quite a hike to the East End, her destination, but she was too strapped at the moment to afford a steam hack and had barely scraped together enough coins for the air car that traveled between Piccadilly Circus and Covent Garden, a mode of conveyance that she loathed. Pitching about on the bumpy public transport coaches surrounded by unwashed bodies – as she was always so lucky as to encounter the filthiest Londoners in transit – made her green about the gills just thinking about it.

And just thinking about her upcoming task sent a shudder of mingled shame and apprehension through her. She did not know how she would be received down at Witwicky and Sons, Bookmakers, even though she came prepared to finally settle her debt.

The last time she'd been there, she'd only narrowly escaped being thrown to Witwicky's brutish henchmen. The only reason he'd extended her a grace period had been out of respect for her late uncle, a friend to many in the St. Giles underworld, to whom Witwicky still felt indebted. She couldn't remember ever being so terrified.

Or so humiliated at having sunk so low as to be in debt up to her eyeballs with a St. Giles bookmaker. She'd never thought herself one of those sad cases who haunted the dodgy alleyways outside of a betting house, having lost everything to their addiction, yet still hungering for a few sovereigns and a roll of the dice, a fever in their eyes. She'd not lost everything *quite* yet, but she'd come perilously close over the last few months, unable to resist the siren call.

Usually she had some restraint. But she'd come to find her life so unsatisfactory on so many levels that misery, pure and simple, had driven her to wager more often and in larger quantities. She gambled to feel the thrill of victory, but when she did not win, she kept on playing until she did.

Even when the money ran out.

"Never again," she told herself as she boarded the air car.

Upon reaching Covent Garden, Aline alighted from the conveyance, then crossed to the eastern edge of the piazza until she reached the turn onto Bow Street, crushed with traffic both shod and airborne. She made her way southward, towards the Strand, the street growing shabbier, and the people growing louder and less respectable by increments.

Even so little as ten years ago, when she'd lived with her eccentric uncle in this neighborhood after she'd outgrown boarding schools, Aline wouldn't have dared to wander these streets alone. But since the days of Jack the Ripper and his successors, the London constabulary, led by Inspector Drexler, had gained a foothold over the Cockney stews, despite the Black Market's attempts to keep the police out.

Indeed, many still believed St. Giles was not a place for gently bred ladies to explore, even with an armed guard. Fortunately for herself, Aline had no missish sensibilities or reputation to damage in rubbing elbows with the inhabitants of the East End. As a somewhat anomalous being herself – educated, employed, independent and single in a society that deplored every one of these adjectives conjoined to one of female persuasion – she enjoyed a great deal more latitude than women both far above her station and far beneath.

She turned off a side street, and the noxious fumes arising from the effulgence of the general environment, mingled with the raw tang of the costermongers' wares, hit her like a brick wall. The poverty of the area kept out most of the technological advancements that pervaded the richer sections of the city. So despite the occasional glimpse of an unfortunate Machinist – victim of the early, unregulated post-War factories, whose limbs had been replaced with machine parts – and the militant Luddite preachers – with their eerie white robes and scars, who ranted to the market crowds against the government – life here continued much as it had before the Great Exhibition of 1851 had ushered in the Steam Age.

At least on the outside.

The first time Aline had come here following her parents' deaths, the sensory experience had been overwhelming. But she rather came to enjoy her visits here, and her uncle's reputation had offered her a measure of protection.

One of the pioneers of the Steam Revolution, Thaddeus Finch had turned his back on his career and devoted himself to the plight of the Machinists and other victims of unsanctioned Welding after the War. He'd earned a certain measure of respect in the stews, even among the criminal classes.

Now, years after his death, Aline continued to visit, excited, as always, by the thrill of doing something not entirely without risk. She was, alas, a born gambler. She had, in fact, received inspiration for her column in the *Post-Dispatch* from the people and events she'd witnessed in the narrow warrens near the Embankment.

For instance, she'd based Ping, her hero's valet, on one of the Chinese "doctors" who peddled herbs, roots, and tinctures smuggled from their motherland in the shadows of Fleet Street. She had even set the denouement of her first series in Covent Garden, wherein her villain tried to escape justice in the crowded market place. He had, in the end, been felled by a basket of overripe melons.

That first series of *The Chronicles of Miss Wren and Doctor Augustus* had been wildly popular by the end of its run, surprising the newspapers' editors and even herself. She had fallen into writing the serial novel rather by accident, submitting the half-cocked idea to the newspaper in a moment of desperation – brought on by a bad run at the Automaton Races, her favorite venue, and a particularly draining week doing Romanov's bidding.

She'd been penniless and despairing over her job and wondering why she never made an effort to do something that she wanted to do. So she had written a story and the Post had agreed to run it. Thus A.F. Riddle was born. Despite the column's success, however, the money wasn't good enough to allow her to resign as Romanov's secretary – especially when one factored in her little habit.

Aline passed a fruit stall and smiled wryly at a crate of honeydews well past their prime displayed to one side, a painted sign above them reading "Augustis Melens: 2 p". Horribly misspelled, but nonetheless gratifying to the ego. The cockney street vendors had taken a proprietary view of the Covent Garden melon scene in the Chronicles. Now any overripe species of melon were Augustuses.

Though Aline held no romantic illusions about her current environs or its denizens. She knew exactly how the rouged women loitering at the lamppost she just walked by made a living. She knew that the small, underfed, unenhanced, and often light-fingered boys who hawked oranges were runaways who lived in flash houses along the Embankment.

She knew, from listening to Inspector Drexler recount various misadventures, how very dangerous a place this area of London could be. She knew, for instance, that the Chinese "doctor" she'd used as Ping's inspiration probably earned his money selling opium under the table, not from his boxes of desiccated roots and foul-smelling poultices.

Even worse than the opium blight devastating this part of the city was the all-powerful Black Market, a consortium of underworld gangs who controlled the illegal Welding industry. Horror stories of Weldlings who wandered into the wrong part of the city and were murdered for their parts were not uncommon. The Black Market was Scotland Yard's greatest adversary, and, unfortunately, nearly untouchable.

Aline had little to offer in the way of parts for the Black Market, however, considering her particular affliction, and was therefore relatively safe from its attentions. But Aline certainly appreciated the risk she ran when she went to Witwicky's. The last time she'd come here, having lost it all at the Races, she'd been literally quaking in her boots.

She'd not prayed in years, but after that dreadful meeting, she had returned to her flat, buried her face in her pillow, and muttered an incantation of thankfulness to the Lord on High for the reprieve. She'd vowed before God there and then to leave off gambling for good.

After she paid Witwicky, she was never visiting a bookmaker's or the tracks again. She was about to become a respectable, married woman after all, and if Charlie ever learned about her problem, he would simply faint from shock, then ask for his mother's ring back.

Thank God she'd not gambled that away.

No, she was never even playing a round of cards again unless she wagered in buttons and thimbles...

Well, perhaps she'd put a few quid down on her favorite automaton at Ascot this year, but aside from that, no more betting.

With a huff of decisiveness, Aline slipped into Witwicky and Sons: Bookmakers, a shabby, unobtrusive business on the corner of Aldwych and Fleet Street, the doorbell jangling above her head.

Suspicious eyes fastened on her through a haze of tobacco smoke, Witwicky's lunchtime regulars lounging in the cramped public area talking statistics and studying the charts posted at the back of the house. It was not exactly forbidden for women to come to such places, but neither was it the usual order of things. A bookmaker's was one of the few establishments in the world where Aline *was* noticed.

Her heart plummeted as a hulking figure bounded off a stool and clanked in her direction. The Bull himself, Witwicky's favorite henchman, and more automaton than man. She squinted through the smoke, noticing he looked even worse than usual. His nose appeared to have been recently broken – again – and he was missing an entire mechanical arm. He glared at her venomously from a pair of crude, goggle-like Black Market eyes.

Or at least she *thought* he was glaring. It was hard to tell, since he only had one eyebrow left. He bellowed for Witwicky, who came barreling out of his office at the back of the house.

Witwicky's right arm was in a sling, and both his eyes were blackened. When he caught sight of her, his face drained of color, as if she were a ghost. Or Jack the Ripper.

"Wot're ye doin' 'ere! Are ye wantin' to get me bloomin' 'ead shot off?" Witwicky breathed, taking her by the arm and leading her into the shadows of one corner of the room. The Bull hovered menacingly over his boss' shoulder.

Aline had no idea what had gotten into these men. The last time she had been here, they had been as oily smooth and full of themselves as a pair of snakes toying with a mouse.

"I came here to settle my debt," Aline said, reaching into her reticule for her purse.

Witwicky gasped and stepped away, holding up his hands as if she were about to extract a gun. "I won't be takin' your money, Miss Snitch, so just turn that little rump of yers out the door and don't be comin' back."

"What are you talking about? I am no ... snitch! And I thought you rather wanted my money, since last time I was here, you made that point very clear."

Witwicky's eyes narrowed to slits. "Aye, after that ye sent yer friend from the Yard 'ere to settle yer debt for you," he said, gesturing towards his broken arm, then at the Bull's missing one.

Aline was thoroughly baffled, but deep down in her belly, an awful suspicion was unfurling. "I sent no one. Who came here?" she demanded.

"The Devil Inspector's mutt. Wot's 'is name, you know, the muscle wot looks like a bloody battleship wif' fists."

"Matthews," Aline murmured. Inspector Drexler's cockney prizefighting lieutenant, with literal fists of steel. Aline had met the man on many occasions when she accompanied Romanov to Drexler's offices.

He'd always seemed so nice, despite his bulk ...

"'E came in 'ere, told me we hain't to be doing business with you, little miss, for the duration. In no uncertain terms."

"Bleedin broke me nose," the Bull wailed. "Again."

"Aye, and gave our Reg" – an inveterate gambler who rarely left the premises – "a facer that right popped 'is eye out, just for bein' nearby."

Aline gazed at the two men and almost felt sorry for them. Almost. But it was more out of outrage at her own situation that drove her to exclaim, "But he had no right!"

"'E's the law, Miss Snitch. Right got nofin' to do with it," Witwicky murmured.

"Them two foreign pikers wif 'im weren't no law," the Bull muttered.

Aline's ears pricked. "Foreign pike...? You mean, someone

accompanied Lieutenant Matthews on this … this ridiculous errand?"

"Oh, Aye," Witwicky scowled, scratching the skin under his cast, his look angry and not a little frightened by what he was remembering.

"Describe these men," she said in a low voice.

"Fine *gennellmen* by the look of them. One of 'em were dark, evil-lookin' like one of them Algerians, with yellow eyes. Spoke gibberish, mostly."

Aline's breath seized. Romanov. She was certain of it. Who else on earth had yellow eyes?

"Devil cant," the Bull said, and spat on the floor. She eyed the offending blob, a mere speck upon a floor so filthy she reminded herself to take off her shoes before entering her boarding house tonight.

"The other were a big blond bruiser. One of them Abominables, by the look of him. Made Maffews look like a runt. That one didn't talk. But 'e sure is a fine listener. The dark arab wot's with 'im mumbled somefin in 'is devil's speak, and next fing we knows is me arm's in a cast, and the Bull's 'ere's in the bleedin' Thames."

Aline was outraged. Shocked. A little sickened. "How dare he!"

Witwicky and the Bull both stared at her, nonplussed by her reaction. She gave them a contrite, shame-filled look of apology. Poor sods. They were rascals, thieves, and general ne'er-do-wells, but they hadn't stood a chance.

"I apologize for this high-handed behavior, gentlemen. I did not send these men to you. Indeed, I had no idea they even knew I came here. Rest assured, I shall get to the bottom of this."

"Oh, no ye don't, Miss Snitch," Witwicky snarled, grabbing her elbow and herding her towards the exit. "You'll be getting' to the bottom of nofin', far as I'm concerned. These friends of yourn …"

"They are *not* my friends …"

"Whatever. I'll not be crossin' the likes of 'em. I value me livelihood. And me limbs. You'll be leavin' 'ere now an' not returnin'."

He pushed open the door and shoved her onto the street. "At least let me pay you ..." What was she saying?

"No!" Witwicky cried, paling. "I'll be takin' none of yer money. Debt is settled." He moved to shut the door, but then paused, gave her an assessing glance. "And don't fink to try your 'and at another establishment. Word is your protectors 'ave been up an' down 'alf of London scaring the bejeezus out of me colleagues."

Aline thought she was angry before, but now she was shaking with her fury. "You mean I've been blackballed?"

"Somefin' like that," Witwicky sniffed. "Doubt you'll be placin' another wager any time soon." With that, he slammed the door in her face.

Aline stared at the grimy door in stupefaction for several long moments. Romanov. Damn his eyes! The utter nerve of the man!

She could almost see the scene that must have unfolded in Witwicky's place of business. Matthews pounding his version of the law into the Bull's nose, Fyodor rushing in to underscore the point by breaking a few bones and tearing a few limbs off, and the Professor himself standing in elegant attendance, enjoying himself immensely.

She could see in her mind's eye her employer's smug smile of satisfaction curving one edge of his lips, probably congratulating himself on having tidied up his secretary's little peccadillo.

How did he even know about Witwicky? How did he even know about her habit, full stop? She had been so discreet, so careful.

Oh, oh, *oh*!

Aline stomped her foot on the pavement and whirled around. He thought he could strong-arm her into ceasing her wagering, did he?

She forgot all about her vow to quit gambling as she strode over the threshold of one of Witwicky's rivals. She now had a full purse and a sudden hankering to pick a few winners in the afternoon's races.

She'd show him that she'd not be coerced into developing fiscal responsibility.

She made it all the way to the counter and nearly had her wager lined up when a rather surly-faced bodyguard – also missing a mechanical limb – caught her under the arm, and hauled her to the door.

She nearly fell into a puddle from the force of her ejection. Damn, damn and triple damn!

By the time she'd been thrown out of the seventh betting office and a handful of gaming hells, many of them run by men with plastered or missing arms, her hope that Witwicky's ominous prediction was an overstatement was fast fading.

She'd been marked. Blackballed. Stymied. It was unbelievable. It was not to be born.

Aline trudged back through the throng of Bow Street and Covent Garden in a daze of bafflement and fury, barely seeing where she went. In her stupor, she forgot the cardinal rule of negotiating the vendors' stalls – that is, avoiding eye-contact with the hawkers and their wares – and found herself haggling over various goods and knickknacks she didn't need simply because it was easier to buy the blasted things than walk away.

By the time she reached the opera house at Covent Garden, she was several pounds poorer, in the possession of two bruised apples, a bouquet of wilting daisies, and a quarter pound of turmeric.

Turmeric!

What was she to do with *turmeric*? She didn't cook – she hadn't the barest of inklings what turmeric tasted like or what purpose it served in a dish other than to muddy it with its hideous color. *And* she was probably allergic to it, with her luck. Yet somehow a Hindu spice trader who had hovered at her side in his steam-powered cart all the way down the street had assured her that she could not live without a pouch of his finest spice.

She'd been glaring at the heap of turmeric atop his stall

because in the afternoon light it seemed to match the color of her employer's eyes when he was feeling self-satisfied about something. She had little interest in purchasing a reminder of those devious eyes, but the vendor had convinced her otherwise.

She felt the weight of the pouch in her skirt pocket as acutely as if it were a block of lead.

This was shaping up to be the worst day of her life. She was staring at her feet, feeling so sorry for herself that she didn't notice she was barreling straight into someone until too late. It felt like she'd hit a brick wall. She landed on her arse, her spectacles flying off her face, and cursed mightily. She glanced up.

And up.

To meet Lieutenant Matthews' annoyed glare. A veteran of the underground boxing circuit in St. Giles, he had a battered face that had been patched with crude brass Black Market scraps. He was a handsomer version of the Bull, with both his eyes and eyebrows in tact. But he looked as put out with her as the Bull had. He extended one of his massive Welded arms to help her to her feet.

She took it with great reluctance. "You!" she huffed, as he jerked her upright. "You've been following me!"

"Aye, Miss," he said grimly. "That I 'ave. All bloomin' day."

"Do you often follow me?"

"Aye, Miss. Every time you get the hankering to visit the stews."

"*Every* time!" she cried.

He looked at her like she was a four-year-old child. "Well, it hain't luck that has kept you from getting' yourself raped and killed, beggin' yer pardon, Miss."

She was speechless for a moment at his blunt words. "Nonsense! I have *always* navigated this neighborhood without an ounce of trouble."

"As I've *always* been 'ere to keep the trouble away."

Aline's eyes widened. Perhaps … well, perhaps Matthews was telling the truth. But still, she had never asked for this clandestine bodyguard. To think that nothing about her adventures into London's seedy underbelly had been authentic was quite a blow.

And she didn't think she could handle another blow at the moment.

She pushed her way past Matthews and stomped down the street. He sighed and fell in step behind her.

"So you're not hiding your presence from me anymore?" she demanded after it became apparent he was not going to go away.

"No, Miss."

"And why is that, Mr. Matthews? Decided your cover's blown, as I now know what you and my employer have done to every gambling establishment in St. Giles?"

Matthews shrugged. "Somefin' like that." He held up a coin purse she recognized as her own. "And that blighter spice trader picked your pocket back there."

Blushing crimson with chagrin, she took the purse and thanked him. Perhaps she *was* a hopeless case. "Did you leave his arms in tact?"

He smiled. "Aye, Miss. This time."

"Are you going to follow me all the way to Mayfair?"

"Aye, Miss. Where you go, I go, until the Professor returns."

She stopped abruptly and spun to face him. "You've spoken with the Professor? You know where he is, and why he won't answer any of my tickertexts?"

Matthews squirmed. "Not exactly. But I'm to keep a close eye on you, them's my orders. Straight from the top."

"Inspector Drexler has allowed you to perform this ... *ridiculous* task?"

"'Tis not ridiculous, Miss," he replied stubbornly. "And it goes even higher up than my boss. All the way to the top."

Aline had no idea what that meant. All she knew was the Professor was using his connections to stalk her! And he seemed to have been doing it for five bloody years.

She took a deep breath, pushing through her rage. *It doesn't matter, it doesn't matter,* she chanted to herself. None of it mattered, because she was, as of this moment, done with her employer, whether he was still abroad or not. She was going to Egypt. Far, far away. And she was going to forget the past five years had ever happened.

She was going to forget him and his devil-eyes full stop.

She seethed all the way from Covent Garden to Mayfair, refusing to take the steam car, just to make Matthews have to walk the extra distance. Which was not fair for either of them. Matthews was just following orders, after all, and she was just punishing herself by adding those extra miles. London was not completely pollution-free, after all, and she was feeling the soot in her unenhanced lungs by the end of her journey. She was just too angry to care.

She'd managed to calm her nerves by the time she and Matthews reached Romanov's townhouse.

Unfortunately, the moment she opened the front door, her nerves were once again shattered. The two hellhounds jumped out at her, snarling, and sprinted down the steps and onto the street, their leashes trailing in the dirt. Madame Kristeva barreled out in pursuit, screaming in Russian.

Aline dropped her daisies and turmeric, sighed, and ran to join Madame Kristeva, with Matthews on her heels bellowing for her to stop. Two things she knew for certain: for one, if anything happened to Ilya and Ikaterina, Romanov would start chopping off heads, and hers would be the first to go. For another, she was seriously, irrevocably *done* with her employer.

Madame Kristeva began to flag after the first couple of blocks. Aline groaned and raced past the winded woman, dodging pedestrians and carts, keeping her sights focused on the errant leashes. Matthews stayed stubbornly by her side.

At long last, some fifteen minutes after the chase had begun, it ended. They caught up with the hellhounds, who had found something interesting to sniff. She'd only to reach down and retrieve the leashes.

Which she did. After which, she was yanked off her feet as the two beasts lurched forward, barking excitedly. At what,

Aline would never know, for she was hurtling through the air, the pavement having ceased to exist.

When she landed, she sank into the brackish, churning water of the Thames, and the last thought she had before everything went black was that she was going to marry Charles Netherfield as soon as humanly possible – if she survived the river, of course.

And Romanov could rot in hell.

"You are what?" Dr. Augustus bellowed, though she stood not two inches from him.

Miss Wren sighed in irritation, tapping her foot against the rocky precipice upon which they were perched. Perhaps having this particular conversation with her employer was better suited to a comfortable drawing room and not the top of the French Alps, but it was too late to take back her words now.

"I said, I am returning to England, sir, and marrying Captain Standish." "What utter nonsense," Augustus scoffed.

"Nonsense, sir? I rather think our present predicament – that is, being chased through the Alps by murderous thieves – is ripe with nonsense, not the fact that I am going to marry a proper English gentleman."

- from *The Chronicles of Miss Wren and Dr. Augustus*, 1896

3

London, 1896

AS expected, Franco had taken his damned time corroborating Sasha's alibi. Without Rowan to moderate Franco's grudge, Sasha and Fyodor had seen the weeks drift by behind Council guard, without any great hope of seeing London before the seasons changed.

Unable to contact the outside world, and without knowing what Rowan had found upon his return to London, Sasha could do nothing but stew in his worry and anger in his Genoese jail cell. Only the very real threat of Council retribution, and his growing suspicion the killer would not fulfill his threats while Sasha wasn't in London to bear witness, had kept him from escaping his confinement.

Who knew how long Franco would have dragged things out

had another body not surfaced. When Franco had admitted this development to him as he and Fyodor were being released, Sasha had suffered a moment of desperate panic, believing he had misjudged the situation, and the murderer had already killed Finch. But the victim had been found in Scotland, of all places, on a little island in the Outer Hebrides.

Not exactly a place Finch would have been likely to be, considering the amount of water she would have had to vomit over to get there.

But the facts were bad enough. The victim had been a local woman: blonde, petite, and bespectacled. The killer wasn't through, and Sasha knew that it was only a matter of time before the storm hit London. For some reason, the murderer had decided to threaten those closest to him, on top of framing him.

The murderer had always had a singular vendetta against him – God knew why – but the stakes had escalated in a way that had finally pushed Sasha too far. Sasha's three hundred year vow to temper his emotions was fast fading. He was losing control. Which scared him more than anything else.

Such were his rather bleak thoughts as Fyodor drove him home through the dirty streets of London after three weeks in prison and one week in the Outer Hebrides with none other than Franco himself, investigating another crime scene. Franco had not absolved him of guilt, of course. He was stubbornly clinging to his suspicions that Sasha had accomplices working for him, or some such nonsense. But he had at long last let Sasha and Fyodor return to London, unable to convince the High Council to extend the edict, in light of the events in the North.

Sasha had grown to think of England as his home in the six years he'd lived in London – or as close to a home as he'd ever manage. It seemed an unlikely match for him, having spent the better part of his three hundred forty two years on some part of the Continent, most recently in the cosmopolitan, intellectually sophisticated Vienna.

By comparison, England, despite its claims to be the center of the modern world, seemed rather ramshackle and quaint, populated by eccentrics and puritans. But he liked those eccentrics and puritans. He liked the friends he made and the work he did. He even liked English weather, having always had a partiality for rain.

And he liked the fact that England was about as far away as he could imagine from Russia. In England, it had proved easier to forget who he had been and what he had lost.

He sighed and rested his head against the window of his steam carriage, watching the rain drip down the glass and the gas lit streets of London pass by, impatient to reach his townhouse and see for himself that Finch was unharmed. She'd yet to answer any of his tickertexts, which was most odd. But he'd been assured she was intact by Matthews himself, who was still guarding her. Though from the tone of Matthews' tickertexts, Finch was not entirely happy he'd been gone for so long.

His mood improved in anticipation of the pending reunion with a sulking Finch. No doubt his prim little English secretary would be waiting for him inside with a list of some sort, hiding her exasperation with him behind her spectacles.

He'd not met another like her in three hundred forty two years of life. She was the most fragile human he'd ever met, unenhanced in a world where even the street urchins of her generation had been fitted with Iron Necklaces. How she'd survived to adulthood with her condition was a testimony to her obstinacy. All five foot two inches of her was filled with a proud determination and a fierce wit he'd never encountered before. Hiring her had been the smartest thing he had ever done.

And he enjoyed having her around. After his long life, it was rare for him to find a human whose company he could still tolerate. He liked to provoke her, to test her mettle, and she never failed to delight him when she thwarted his assaults with one of her pointed, schoolmarmish glares. She was immune to him. No other woman was. It was refreshing.

But his little secretary was hardly the pillar of perfection, which made her all the more entertaining.

When he discovered her gambling addiction, he couldn't

quite credit it at first. She seemed so proper, so excruciatingly scrupulous, that dabbling in such a torrid pastime seemed as unlikely as a pig sprouting wings. But it was one she must have developed in the years she'd lived with her eccentric uncle in St. Giles.

He paid his secretary quite a hefty salary, but he suspected she gambled away most of it on a regular basis. Which would explain why, in the five years he'd known her, she'd not scraped together the funds to buy a single new dress.

Not that he cared what she wore. But, bloody hell, mud had never been a good color on anyone.

Finch was a full-fledged addict, courting all sorts of trouble in her visits to the stews. He'd put a stop to that, however, before he'd left for Paris. Matthews' tickertext this morning had informed him of Finch's recent revelations on her last trip to St. Giles.

Finch would no doubt be spitting mad at him for his interference in her private affairs, but she would have to get over it. She'd nearly succeeded in losing much more than her money to that voracious bookmaker.

The Black Market dealt in other things besides automata. She'd no clue how rare she was, or that there were predators out there who craved that rarity. The Clean Air Act did not pass until 1880, so there was a dearth of adults over the age of sixteen who'd managed to survive the Fog without enhancement.

Sasha's old friend, Aloysius Finch, had known his niece's value, and he'd known Sasha could protect her as few could, which was why he'd asked him to hire her in the first place when he knew he was dying. Not that Finch was aware her uncle had ever known Sasha. She'd thought her employment agency had sent her to his door.

Finch had an even bigger secret that, again, wasn't a secret to him at all. It seemed in her voracious quest for more funds to gamble away, she'd taken up another profession. He'd discovered Finch's double life as a sensational novelist quite accidentally while thumbing through the *Post-Dispatch* several years ago.

Drawn in despite himself to one of the popular serials the *Post* published, he began to realize the similarities between the storyline and his own life – or at least, Professor Romanov's life. At first he was alarmed, fearing his secrets would be exposed. But then he'd been amused. It was romantic, fantastic drivel about the misadventures of a heroine named Miss Alison Wren and her overbearing employer, Dr. Augustus. He was convinced Finch was the author.

This discovery had delighted him. He'd not thought her to possess one romantic bone in her neat, gambling-addled little body. He sometimes wondered if there was a real life model for the insufferable Captain Standish, Miss Wren's noble but extremely boring suitor who followed her around the world like a well-trained lapdog.

But inquiring such a thing of Finch would reveal that he knew about her double life.

Fyodor stopped the steam carriage in front of the townhouse, and Sasha strode out into the rain and up the walkway. When he finally stepped into the front hall, he knew something was wrong. Ilya and Ikaterina rushed to greet him, jumping up on his chest and licking his face. His pups were followed by Madame Kristeva. But Finch was nowhere in sight.

His heart sank with disappointment and a touch of apprehension. Then he itched his neck in irritation at his foolishness. Disappointed over Finch's failure to greet him?

Ha! He'd see her soon enough. Doubtless she was buried underneath some mountain of documents, spectacles askew, her fingers stained with ink.

When greetings were dispensed with, however, and Finch had still not shown herself, he grew uneasy. "Where is Finch?"

The normally unflappable Madame Kristeva looked down at her feet and folded her hands over her rotund belly before answering in Russian, as if girding herself. "She has resigned."

He pushed Ilya and Ikaterina off his chest. "Excuse me?"

"She said she was not going to work for you any more. She seemed quite adamant after the dogs knocked her into the English river."

"What?"

"They knocked her into the river. She was quite upset. She left a week ago and has not come back, so I think she was speaking the truth."

Matthews had not told him any of this. Not that the man was much of a conversationalist, particularly over a wireless. "That's ridiculous! The pups were only playing with her."

"I don't think she would agree. And I don't think she liked having to break with your Italian friend," Madame Kristeva continued, coloring.

"Luciana?"

"Yes, your ... er, your Italian friend was quite rude to Miss Finch. Although," Madame Kristeva continued, puffing up with motherly pride, "Miss Finch was the victor in the end. She let the pups loose on the Italian. And they'd just been in the garden. After a rain. The Italian's expensive gown was ruined. It was a wonderful sight, sir."

Well done, Finch! He knew he could count on her to get rid of the bothersome opera singer. She usually left his mistresses on good terms, however. Luciana must have been too much for Finch to manage.

God knew Luciana had been too much for *him*. But none of this seemed reason for Finch to...

To break with him!

He still couldn't quite believe it. And it was a development that could not have come at a worst time, with a murderer on the loose, killing her doppelgangers.

"And," Madame Kristeva continued, still not quite looking at him, "she was very upset about something you did to her. Something about her wagering."

"Upset? Why, she should be sobbing with gratitude!" he scoffed.

"Miss Finch loves the wagering," Madame Kristeva pointed out.

"Loves it too much for her own good. I merely paid what she owed."

Fyodor, who'd just arrived inside with the luggage, arched an eyebrow at this understatement.

"And made it impossible for her to place a bet in London ever again," Sasha added a bit sheepishly.

"Dieu! No wonder she left!" Madame Kristeva breathed, wide-eyed.

"Oh, I'll get her back," he vowed.

Madame Kristeva, however, did not seem to put much stock in his promise, for she shook her head mournfully. "I do not think she's coming back this time."

Well, she didn't have a choice in the matter. "She is. If I have to tie her up and carry her back."

Madame Kristeva looked at him askance, clearly surprised at his vehemence.

Hell, he was surprised himself. Of course he was upset, under the circumstances, but Finch's abrupt resignation got under his skin. Finch's rebellion was the last thing he expected to come home to. Scowling blackly, he strode down the hall, the pups at his heels, and entered his study.

He grabbed a bottle of vodka from the sideboard and threw himself into his favorite leather chair. He stared broodingly into the old-fashioned fire a servant had lit in anticipation of his arrival. With modern steam technology to keep houses warm, fires had become obsolete and illegal without a permit. But Sasha couldn't break three hundred years of habit. He enjoyed warming himself at a fire.

Particularly when he was brooding.

Finch quit? Quit? And in an absurdly underhanded manner, to add insult to injury. He'd been rotting in jail for the past month, terrified she was going to be ripped open by a madman, and all the while she'd been back in merry old London plotting this mutiny of hers.

Why did she have to leave him now? *Now* of all times?

Of course, she didn't know of his suspicion that she was in danger. She didn't know anything about his past and his true identity. And that was just how he'd wanted it to remain, even after Genoa. He'd hoped to be able to catch the murderer and safeguard Finch without having to reveal anything to her. He could have made up an excuse for her to remain here in the townhouse with him, and kept her busy little mind occupied with a thousand tasks while he sorted this mess out.

Which would have been possible, had she not taken off in a snit. She'd made everything a hundred times more complicated.

He jumped up from his seat and paced in front of the hearth.

Even if he told her the truth – which he was never going to do, of course – he doubted she would believe him. He stopped cold. Or maybe she would, which was even worse. Judging from her penny-dreadful, Aline was capable of ridiculous flights of fancy. Learning he was a three hundred year old Russian Prince with a Da Vinci Heart would no doubt give her fits of ecstasy, and fodder for the *Chronicles*.

The latter most certainly could not be allowed to happen. Then the High Council would turn its sights on *her*, as well as the murderer.

No, he couldn't tell her the truth. But he would have her back by his side, where he could keep an eye on her. With a growl, he crossed over to his desk and fumbled around for something to write on. If she wouldn't respond to his tickertexts, he'd contact her the traditional way. He tossed off a note to her, not bothering to mince words.

I am back. I shall give you tonight to come to your senses. Otherwise, I shall be forced to put on the kid gloves. Romanov.

He stuffed the letter into a steel cylinder, sealed it, and sent the cylinder shooting off in the steam- powered post chute.

The network of underground steam chutes that comprised Her Majesty's Royal Steam Mail, seen as such an innovation back in the 50's, were becoming increasingly outmoded with the advent of the wireless tickertext. But it would serve. The letter would arrive at her flat within the hour. He hoped it hit her stubborn head when it flew from her chute.

A few minutes later, Fyodor entered the room to find his master scowling down at the fire, vodka clutched in his hand. Fyodor took the bottle and drank his fill, settling into a chair and gesturing towards the chessboard sitting in front of him.

They usually played together in the evenings to unwind. The custom between them had started when Fyodor had found him wandering the house after an extremely harrowing nightmare. He was often plagued by them, by the dark memories that hounded his unguarded, slumbering mind.

After what Fyodor had endured during the War, he understood Sasha's sleeplessness, his unspoken fear of closing his eyes, even if he did not know its exact cause. Fyodor had poured vodka down his throat and sat him across the chess board, and they had played into the small hours of the morning, until Sasha was too weary to care when his eyes closed, and too exhausted to dream. Since then, they played nearly every evening, the concentration on the intricacies of the game soothing him into dreamless slumber.

Sasha wondered if he should enjoy chess so much, considering how his father had died. But his recent training as a psychiatrist helped him figure out other people's minds, not his own. He would not ruin one of the few consolations left to him with too much self-introspection.

Fyodor moved a knight. Sasha moved one of his pawns. Soon they were embroiled in one of their usual battles, but Sasha's mind was still on the problem of his secretary.

He was not going to sleep well at all.

He groaned when Fyodor managed to steal away his queen with ease, and sat back in his chair.

"I just don't see what her problem is," he bemoaned in Russian to Fyodor when he couldn't stand to remain silent any longer. "I haven't been so terrible to work for."

Fyodor gave him a sidelong glance. "I haven't!" he insisted.

Fyodor sat back in his chair and scrutinized his old friend for a long time. He made a gesture with his hand.

Why do you care?

Sasha reached for the vodka. Why indeed.

THE next morning, a response to his missive finally came as he sat in his library, staring sullenly at a lopsided pile of eviscerated steam cylinders that had accumulated in front of him. None of them were from Finch. He didn't think so many people bothered to send steam posts anymore, with the wireless at hand.

Then again, his secretary always dealt with such mundane matters.

And she was not here. Hung over and exhausted, he retrieved the latest cylinder to arrive from the chute, tore it open, and growled. At last.

Sir, it read in a bold, angry looking scrawl, *you will be waiting much longer than a night for me to 'come to my senses'. As to the threat implied in your third sentence, I believe you have mixed your metaphors. In English, one either takes off kid gloves or puts on boxing gloves in order to fight. Though I have no intention of fighting with you. Ever.*

I quit. Finch.

He balled up her letter with a snarl and tossed it across the room. It didn't make him feel any better.

Damn her eyes! Her rather large, expressive eyes she kept hidden behind those ugly spectacles of hers, eyes that were so often filled with vexation over something he'd done.

What color were they again?

He raked a hand through his hair and returned to his desk with an irritated sigh. He sat down and reached for pen and paper.

Finch, he scrawled, *I would think a proper English gentlewoman like yourself would have done her long-time employer the courtesy of speaking face to face with him when resigning. I would also think a proper gentlewoman would perhaps feel obliged to thank the man who settled her very improper debt owed to a thieving St. Giles bookmaker. This said favor that her employer did out of his generous concern for her dangerous habit would also perhaps sway her into reconsidering the matter of her resignation.*

He dotted the end of the last sentence so hard he nearly tore the paper.

Her reply came later that evening.

I thank you for saving me from myself, she wrote. *I cannot imagine how I could have been so remiss in not doing so sooner. I suppose it was from the fact that I neither wanted nor needed saving. You must have gone through a great deal of trouble with Inspector Drexler to make sure that every gaming establishment in London has shut its door in my face. Forgive me for not kissing your feet in gratitude for such a*

BENEVOLENT feat, and for STALKING me for the past five years.

Yes, I know about that.

In regards to reconsidering my resignation because you went behind my back and did something that distinctly displeases me, let me be perfectly clear: I OWE YOU NOTHING. A.E. Finch. P.S Call off Drexler's watchdog. He is scaring the other tenants.

The imp!

He crumpled the note in his fist.

At what point did Finch develop such a barbed tongue? If he weren't so furious, he'd be rather intrigued.

Oh, toss it, he *was* intrigued. If he'd known this was the result when her temper finally snapped, he would have … well, he wasn't sure what he would have done. Probably provoke her even more than he usually did in the hopes she responded with something more than her customary roll of the eyes.

He was about to toss her latest scathing rebuke in the direction of the last one, but then thought better of it.

He smoothed out the letter, folded it up, and slipped it into the secret drawer in his desk where he kept his most prized correspondence. Though why he wanted to save the blasted thing was quite beyond him at the moment.

He'd not expected to feel so much and so deeply. He'd not expected her to ever quit, full stop, which was ridiculous, in retrospect. One day he would have to move on from this life, become someone else, and leave Finch behind anyway. But she'd been unique from the start, the niece of an old friend, and the only secretary he'd ever had who'd not stormed out after five minutes in his company.

He started to write her another letter, but then reconsidered, sitting back in his chair. Letters were getting him nowhere. And she was safe, for the moment.

He had half a mind to go to the little nest of hers in Bloomsbury and drag her back bodily if he had to.

He growled.

He resented the idea that she was driving him to actually consider seeking her out like some recalcitrant schoolboy. She should be coming back to *him*, groveling at his feet to take her back, not the other way around.

And she would do just that.

All he had to do was sit back and wait. In a few days, she would return, chastened. He paid her too well, and Lord knew she needed the money.

He didn't doubt for a moment she'd find some way to gamble, despite the barriers he'd erected for her own good. And when she'd lost all, she'd have no choice but to come back to him.

He smiled to himself.

Yes, all he had to do was wait it out.

TWO days later, Sasha was through waiting it out. Though he had increased the watch on Finch to five guards, he still had no peace of mind. No murders had been reported, but it felt like he was just waiting for the axe to fall, and his intuition was telling him to keep his secretary close. Which he could not do when she was determined to remain across town in her flat.

And worse than that, his tie was crooked. He stared at his reflection in his bedroom mirror with a mixture of despondency and irritation. He was to attend the opera tonight, having decided that *La Traviata* was just the ticket to end his brooding...or to at least make it look like his life was not spinning out of control. He suspected that was the killer's goal, and he wouldn't give the man the satisfaction.

But as he cast his eye over his evening clothes, he decided that he looked ridiculous. This century's fashion choices were a welcome improvement over the giant powdered wigs and high heels of the previous one. And for once in centuries, he was able to clothe himself without the aid of a legion of servants. But no matter how he tried to knot his neck cloth, it still came out crooked and limp.

Finch had tied them for him for the past five years, and he had grown used to it. For such a clumsy little package, she had remarkably dexterous fingers. His crooked necktie was, quite frankly, the last straw where she was concerned. He'd not be traipsing around London looking like a vagrant. He stalked downstairs and threw open the door to the billiards room. Fyodor was inside playing by himself.

"Bring my curricle around. I'm going to find Finch and drag her back here kicking and screaming if I have to."

Fyodor curved his mouth in a sly smile, as if to say he'd believe it when he saw it, but not before. Sasha scowled at him and strode from the room.

Ten minutes later, he was driving himself across town in his steam-powered curricle, his body thrumming with irritation. This little standoff between him and his secretary was about to come to an end, and he was the one who was going to come out on top, not the other way around.

Perhaps giving her these past few days to come to her senses had not been the best plan. Indeed, it had been the entirely wrong thing to do. He should have marched to her flat the night he'd arrived and sorted out the business there and then, pride be damned.

Oh, she was going to pay for turning his life on its head, that was for certain.

He arrived at the boarding house Finch lived in on the border of Bloomsbury, and jumped down from the perch, yanking off his traveling goggles and gloves. Matthews emerged from the shadows to greet his unexpected visitor. Sasha was too irritated to speak with the man, so he merely gave him a terse nod and continued on his mission. He strode up the steps and rang the bell.

And rang and rang until the door finally opened.

A middle-aged woman he took to be the proprietor stared up at him, her eyes wide. It was not every evening, he supposed, that a man dressed for the opera showed up on her doorstep.

"I am here to see Finch."

She continued to stare up at him in bemusement.

"Finch," he repeated, too vexed to explain further.

"I ... er, you mean Miss Aline Finch, sir?"

He nodded and followed her inside, nearly treading on her skirts in his haste. He stared around a dusty hallway distastefully.

"What room is hers?" he demanded.

"Er ... I ... seven, sir. But if you will wait here." She gestured towards a small parlor to the left, "I shall see if she is available to come down and speak to you. You are...?"

He moved towards the stairs instead of the parlor. "There is no need to bring her here. *I* shall go to her."

"I ... oh, dear! But that is not ..." the woman huffed behind him.

"Proper?" he supplied, striding up the stairs. "I am sure Finch would agree."

"But ... I, er, that is ... sir!" the woman called after him. But she made no move to follow. Useless woman.

He reached the landing of the first floor and located the number seven on a door at the end of the hall. It was a plain, no-nonsense-looking door. A very innocent looking door. He wondered if it knew it stood guard over an ungrateful, shrewish imp.

He pounded his fist against the wood so forcefully the number seven went slightly askew. He continued for what seemed an interminably long time until his knuckles were numb from the effort. He was beginning to think that Finch was not in. Or that she knew who was paying her a visit and chose to ignore the knocking.

The latter, most likely.

Well, he'd make it impossible for her to ignore him. He pounded even harder.

Just when he was about to curse, the door swung open, and the head of an automaton peered furtively around the corner. Or at least that was what Sasha's overtaxed brain told him he was seeing: a metallic head with a glass-covered mask obscuring its eyes, attached to a crude mechanical breathing device, the likes of which he'd never seen before. The closest thing he could compare it to was something an ocean diver wore.

Then a human hand came up and yanked the device off, revealing his secretary underneath. His rebuke died on his lips at the sight of her. Finch's ever-present spectacles were missing, and her hair, usually tied back in a vise-like hold, fell loose down her shoulders in a wavy, tangled heap.

He reassessed several things about Finch in that moment. Her eyes were big, too big for her face, and the color of chocolate, and her hair was not so much mouse-colored blonde as it was the color of a baby fawn, streaked with gold and copper. She looked...

Adorable. Adorable and...

Sick. Her eyes were bleary, and her small, pert nose was the color of a candied cherry. She squinted up at him as if peering through a thick fog.

She sneezed.

Then she shut the door in his face.

Stunned by the unexpected sight of the unsightly mask, followed by her disheveled state and her rather abrupt dismissal, he stared at the door, unmoving.

Gathering his wits, he lifted his fist and pounded against the wood with renewed insistency, the brass number threatening to fall off completely. He'd break the door with his enhanced strength if he was not careful, but he was *not* going away without a fight.

Seconds later, the door reopened as his fist was poised to strike once more, catching him off guard. She glared up at him as she tied a ratty-looking pink robe around her waist. "What are you doing here?" she demanded in a stuffy, miserable voice.

"What was that thing on your head, Finch?"

She held up the mask. "My uncle's invention. It helps keep my lungs clear, if you must know. As you can clearly see, I am sick!" she bit out.

Well, her eccentric uncle must have managed to get one thing to work, though it was hideous. "It makes you look like an aquanaut."

She glared at him. "What are you doing here?" she repeated.

"I am going to the opera, and I can't manage my necktie," he muttered.

She snorted. "Unbelievable."

"No one can tie it like you, Finch. It was the last straw."

"Really," she said dryly. "Why are you truly here?"

"To discuss your desertion, naturally."

"It was a *resignation*," she corrected. "And there's nothing to discuss. You shouldn't be here. It is improper. If anyone should see you..."

"Then you better let me inside before I ruin your reputation."

She debated this for a moment, then reluctantly stood aside.

He strode into the tiny flat before she changed her mind. Books lined the walls in neat rows, and ferns and flowering shrubs in mismatched, colorful pots filled every available nook. He glanced towards the rear of the flat, where a small wrought-iron-framed bed stood near two glass doors leading to an ant-sized balcony overflowing with more potted plants.

It was not what he expected. What he expected Finch's private sanctum to look like was more in line with the stacks at the Bodleian. Not this ... this jungle. Yet despite the apparent clutter, everything was precisely arranged and spotless, just as he expected of the neat little Finch. The only signs of her current indisposition were the tangled nest of blankets atop her narrow bed and a trail of wadded handkerchiefs littering a tidy desk.

She shuffled past him to the desk and snatched up her spectacles. She settled them on her nose and sniffled.

"Well, get on with it," she demanded in a peevish tone he'd never heard before. She extracted a dank handkerchief from her robe's pocket and blew her nose. The noise was loud and unladylike.

Another first for the prim little Finch.

Staring down at that spectacular mane of fawn-colored hair, he forgot his anger, and something warm and completely foreign flooded his chest. It must have been relief. This was the first time he'd seen her with his own eyes since this whole nightmare had begun, after all.

He smiled, earning him a fierce glare over the top of the handkerchief. "Do I amuse you?" she mumbled.

Why, yes, she did. Perhaps too much. But he couldn't help himself. After weeks of nightmares, this was like waking up to a summer morning. He'd always loved bantering with her, and this new defiant backbone she'd sprouted was as delightful as it was inconvenient.

He wanted the delight to last as long as it could. He pasted a stern expression on his face, crossing his arms over his chest. "What do you mean by turning traitor?" he demanded.

Most people caved when he used such a tone, but not Finch. She rolled her eyes and crossed her own arms over her chest, digging in her heels for battle. He almost smiled again, but caught himself.

"My behavior is hardly traitorous. I merely left your employment," she sniffed.

"You are a traitor. You have thrown my affairs into a shambles by your irresponsible behavior."

"Irresponsible! Why you complete, utter... " She sneezed again, knocking her spectacles at a precarious angle.

He reached out and straightened them for her before she could protest. She muttered something that sounded close to a thank you and blew her nose again, looking quite miserable. "You're at death's door, aren't you?"

"No thanks to those ... those hellhounds of yours."

"Hellhounds?" he cried, quite offended. Finch had never called his pups hellhounds before ... to his face. They were a frisky pair, to be sure, but *hellish* was taking it too far.

"Yes, hellhounds. Those unnatural beasts you insist on calling pups. They knocked me into the Thames."

He couldn't help himself. He laughed, imagining the sight of the proper Finch up to her neck in the mud and filth of the river.

"You think it's funny those mongrels nearly drowned me?"

He bit his lip. "Of course not."

She didn't buy it for a moment. She fixed him with her best schoolmistress stare, placing her hands on her hips and squaring her shoulders even more. The effect was ruined by her red nose and watering eyes. Poor Finch. She really *was* quite ill, and he almost felt sorry for her. But not quite. She had caused too much trouble.

He struggled to look contrite, however. One caught a Finch with honey, not vinegar. That much he'd learned. "I'm sure Ilya and Ikaterina are very sorry. They shall apologize just as soon as you come back to us."

"I am not coming back," she muttered, wiping her nose.

"Once you are well...”

"I. Am. *Not*. Coming. Back."

Now the delight was fading. He was not getting anywhere with her. "What has come over you?" he demanded.

"Nothing has come over me, sir. Unless it is my good sense returning at last," she retorted.

"What is it you want? A raise? I'll double your salary."

Her usually full lips settled into a grim, stubborn line.

"Triple it, then.”

Her lips all but disappeared, as did her eyes. "No."

"I'll raise your salary ten times over."

Her eyes widened, her lips parted, but she shook her head. "No. No. No."

"What is this about? The pups? I shall find someone else to exercise them. Though they love you, Finch.”

"*Love* me? Are you blind as well as deaf? Those mongrels hate me."

"If they hated you, Finch, they would have pulled out your throat by now.”

She paled. "The sad thing is that's probably true,” she muttered. “But it is not about the dogs, sir. Not entirely, at any rate."

"Then what is it, damn it?"

"Do *not* curse, sir. I am simply choosing not to be your slave any longer."

"*Slave?*"

"Or serf. Whatever it is you Russians call it."

Oh, if she only knew how sore a subject she'd raised. Or how good she had it compared to the serfs he'd been born to rule. "You are my secretary."

"Secretary. Note-taker. Housekeeper. Accountant. Valet. Errand boy. Dog-sitter." She began to enumerate on the fingers of her free hand. "I run all over London on your invariably bizarre missions. I proofread your work, though I hardly understand a word of it. I solve all the disputes with your servants, despite barely understanding a word *they* say. I buy your clothes. I have even been forced to stitch your ... your ... unmentionables."

"No need for that, Finch. Throw them away. I hardly need to scrimp."

She was not finished. "I make on average ten cups of tea a day for you."

"You've counted?"

Her scowl deepened. "I take shorthand while you interview psychopaths. I grade your students' exams. I... I..."

Her tirade was cut short by a violent sneeze, launching her spectacles to the floor. It was too loud a sound to come from her tiny frame, and she shook miserably from the effort. Belatedly, she wiped her nose and stooped to retrieve her spectacles.

He got to them first and handed them over. "Are you finished?"

She snatched her spectacles from his palm, glared at him, and fixed them into place behind her ears. "No, sir. Where was I? Oh, yes. You even leave me to finish with your mistresses for you!"

"Is that what this is all about? Your maidenly sensibilities are offended by your proximity to sinful women?" he quipped.

She sniffed. "Hardly."

"You're jealous, then," he continued. "It pains you to see the other women in my life."

That was a mistake. Her eyes narrowed, and he heard a low, fascinating growl issue from the back of her throat. "You conceited bas..."

"No cursing, please, Finch," he said with a calm sure to provoke her.

She growled again and started forward with one of her fingers extended. It poked him in the chest. "Ouch!" he said, though it didn't hurt. Not a lot could hurt him.

"I am not one of the 'women in your life'. I am not jealous. I feel sorry for those women." She hesitated. "Well, most of them, anyway."

"Luciana failed to impress?" he said dryly, trying not to

shudder at the thought of his last mistress. What *had* he been thinking?

"That's not the point," she said, poking him again. "The point is, you should be a man about your entanglements and break them off yourself, not have your secretary do your dirty work."

I was being toyed with by a madman, and the High Council thinks I'm a murderer. Do I really have time to deal with hysterical sopranos? he wanted to say.

Instead, he smirked. "But you are so good at it, Finch. And you always know what to buy for them. How should I know what a woman wants in the way of trinkets?"

She threw her hands in the air in exasperation, waving the mask around wildly, then began shooing him towards the door. "You are impossible. I've listed my reasons for resigning, now you may leave."

He didn't budge. "No, you have just listed the reasons why you are irreplaceable to me, Finch."

"I am *not* irreplaceable."

"What is it you want? An assistant of your own? That is easily done."

"I don't want an assistant. I don't want *ten* assistants. I don't want to work for you any longer!"

Well. "That is unacceptable. You shall come back to me if I have to drag you back by your pretty head of hair!

Her eyes widened, and her hand went up to tangle in her luxurious mane, as if she'd just realized she'd failed to pin it back. Her cheeks flushed. Adorably. "You wouldn't..."

He cocked an eyebrow.

She visibly deflated. "All right. You probably would. But it won't make any difference. I'll refuse to work. I am tired of being at your beck and call. You are exhausting."

"I've not even been here for a month!"

"Even your absences are exhausting," she amended. "Now if you don't mind..." She signaled with her mask for the door once more.

He didn't move. Her contrariness was baffling. He'd thought it would be a simple task to win her back, once they'd spoken face to face. Finch had always come around after her rare attacks of pique.

Apparently, he'd thought wrong. This was a side of Finch he'd never seen: defiant. Undone. Angry. Stubborn.

Well, she'd always been stubborn. But he'd never thought she had even the barest inkling of true passion lurking beneath that prim, unflappable exterior. Fire flashed in her eyes behind the lenses, turning the chocolate into coppery embers. Her entire person was poised as if for battle, and her full, rosy mouth quivered with pent up emotion.

The strange, delighted warmth in his chest expanded, and in the back of his mind he knew he should start worrying.

What was happening here? He had the oddest desire to provoke her even further just to see what might happen, though he knew things were getting ... dangerous between them. He fell back on his original complaint, which was sure to nettle her.

"But my necktie," he murmured.

She groaned, tossed the breathing mask on her desk, and approached him. He half expected her to strike him, but instead she stuffed her handkerchief into her pocket and reached up to his collar. She began to jerk his tie into some semblance of order, muttering to herself the whole time.

He caught the words "oafish" and "selfish" and smiled. Unconsciously, he turned his head downwards and caught her familiar scent, masked in menthol lozenges at the moment. She smelled of lemon and mint soap, as always. So fresh, so properly, adorably English.

She wrenched the last knot, nearly choking him. "There."

"It is too tight." It wasn't. He just wanted her to stay where she was for a little longer.

She made an odd, strangled sound, jerked the knots free and began again. He leaned closer, closed his eyes, and breathed in Finch's scent, wondering what in hell's name had come over him. Wasn't he supposed to be angry?

"I am going to *La Traviata*, Finch," he said softly.

She snorted and concentrated on his collar. "You've made amends with your Italian friend, then? After all the trouble I went through? Typical."

"Luciana? I believe she has gone back to Italy. No doubt on the proceeds of the rather extravagant parting gift I left her."

She snorted again.

"What was the gift?" he inquired.

"A rather flashy garnet brooch. But not flashy enough for *Madame*."

"Garnet. Interesting choice."

"I am fond of garnet," she murmured.

"Hmm. The color of your eyes," he mused. Not chocolate after all.

She shrugged, trying not to look affected by this personal observation, but he noted the flare of color creeping up her neck. He smiled.

"*Aida* is your favorite opera, is it not, Finch?"

Her hands stilled for a moment. He'd hit his mark at last. Finch loved opera. He'd once spied her waltzing and caterwauling to a phonograph recording of *Aida* in his office. He'd not interrupted the interlude in order to spare her mortification. But he was not feeling so generous at the moment.

"Come back to work for me, and I'll take you to the opera every week. I have the best box in the house. *Aida* is playing at the end of the month."

She hesitated. "You are jesting."

"I've never been more serious," he said, and he meant it. He needed to keep her close, after all, and he was surprised to find the notion of escorting his secretary to the opera not at all repugnant. He wouldn't mind sitting next to her, breathing in her comforting scent, watching her reaction to the drama unfolding on stage.

He eyed the collar of her robe distastefully. He'd have to buy her some new gowns of course. The brown sacks she wore would never do for the opera. Blues would suit her, and greens. Pink would definitely *not* do. And the less frills, the better.

Finch was tiny, no doubt stunted by what must have been a sickly childhood, barely reaching his collarbone, with a lithe, girlish figure and a graceful way of moving that reminded him of the bird whose name she bore. Frills would make her look like a missish debutante. No, a simple blue gown would do, one that complimented her slender little figure and didn't overwhelm her with bows and lace.

A gown, he amended, with a hemline high enough to avoid getting caught on her slippers.

He wondered how such a small, graceful-seeming creature could be the clumsiest of his acquaintance. He was always setting her back on her feet, retrieving her erstwhile spectacles, rubbing ink off her cheek. But what harm could come to her in an opera box?

She would be sitting, and there wouldn't be an inkwell for miles.

She finished her work and stepped back to survey the results.

"No," she said at last.

"Hmm?" he asked, imagining Finch in a sky blue satin gown.

"I said no to your last absurd bribe." When he didn't respond and continued instead to sniff about her hair, she began to look uncertain. "What is the matter with you?" she demanded.

Her sharp words snapped him out of his trance, and they stared at each other, at a mutual loss.

Indeed, he had no idea what was happening to him, but something had changed as they argued, and she felt it just as strongly as he did. Like him, she didn't understand it at all. Her cheeks turned as red as her nose, and her hand went up to the top of her robe, pulling the collar tighter.

"I ... I think it's time for you to leave..." she began.

Oh, no, he wouldn't, not when he sensed her resolve weakening at last, despite whatever strange path they had wandered down. He cut her off by drawing closer rather than retreating, so that she was pressed up against her desk.

"I can hardly think how you shall occupy yourself without me," he teased.

She blushed even more fiercely. "Contrary to what you

might think, the world – *my* world – does not revolve around you."

"Ha!" he grunted derisively.

"I have a life, you know. I have plans."

"Ha!"

Her eyes flashed. "If you must know, I am getting married."

He felt as if he'd been punched in the stomach. The air went out of him. He wondered if his perfect heart had finally failed him, because he couldn't breathe for several heartbeats. This was the last thing he'd expected her to say.

"You're what?" he choked.

"I'm getting married," she enunciated, as if he were half-deaf.

He scowled and clenched his hands into fists. Now he was breathing rather too hard. "To whom?" And how had he not known, with all of his spies, that she even *had* a suitor?

"That is not your affair, but suffice to say he is a gentleman I have known for years. A nice, *undemanding* gentleman. He has been the soul of patience and forbearance during my employment to you. I have decided to accept his proposal."

He guffawed, shocked not only by her information but his reaction to it. What was wrong with him?

Why couldn't he breathe properly?

And why in hell was he still imagining her in blue satin?

She was looking quite pleased by his discomfiture. Well, he'd wipe that smug look off her face. "So Colonel Standish exists after all," he muttered.

The blood drained from her face. "What did you say?" she whispered.

Victory surged through his veins at the sight of her wide eyes. Finch deserved to be as unsettled as he was feeling at the moment.

Though in the part of his brain that was still rational, he knew he had lost any chance he had of a reconciliation.

"Colonel Standish. Miss Allison Wren's milksop suitor," he said.

She stiffened, her bafflement turning to fury in the pace of a second. "Milksop!" she breathed. "The Captain is not a milksop. He is a noble, generous war hero."

"Who lets his woman run roughshod around the world with a scoundrel."

"He encourages her independence and trusts her implicitly. He is an enlightened, civilized gentleman who is willing to allow her to live her own life."

"He is a milksop. And his romantic drivel is nauseatingly insincere. I usually skip those parts."

She put her hands on her hips and ignored her slipping spectacles. "I assure you, the Captain's words are very sincere. He is deeply in love with Miss Wren."

"If that were so, he would have proposed to her three series back. After that vampire business in the Carpathians. No, he can't care very much for her. Doubtless, he has a doxy in every port he visits."

"He doesn't," she cried.

"Well, I suppose *you* know best," he shot back, pleased by her ire. He pushed even farther. "Or perhaps he's merely a coward. He's too afraid of Dr. Augustus to pursue Miss Wren like a real man."

Her mouth worked, but no sound came out. She sat down abruptly at her desk chair, shaking her head and sniffling. "How do you even *know* about the *Chronicles*?"

He gave her a devilish smile. "I know everything, Finch. Just like your Dr. Augustus. I wonder why that is so."

"You read the *Chronicles*?"

"Avidly."

"And you know that I..."

He nodded.

She swallowed. "When did you discover this?" she demanded.

"About three minutes ago, after your reaction to the Captain's name. Though I've had my suspicions for three years."

She gasped, looking too furious to speak. She looked down at her desk, picked up a glass paperweight, hesitated, and set it back down. He realized she'd considered chucking it at him and guffawed at her audacity. Instead, she threw one of the half-dozen dirty handkerchiefs littering her desk at him, then another and another.

He dodged several, but the rest hit him in the chest. "That's disgusting, Finch."

"No less than you deserve for tormenting me! For ... for laughing at me! It is mortifying that you should know!"

He held up a finger. "That you should know I know, you mean."

She clutched her head in her hands and groaned. "Please stop! You're making me dizzy. Just go away!"

"Not yet. First you mutiny, then you tell me you're getting married. I demand to know what this Standish fellow is about!"

"His name is Charles Netherfield," she moaned.

Oh, this was too good. "Neverfeel?"

"*Nether*field," she corrected. "And he's not a soldier. He's an archaeologist."

"A bone-hunter?" he scoffed.

"An archaeologist," she insisted. She uncovered her face and glanced up at him, her jaw setting at a stubborn angle. "He lectures at the same university as you, in fact, not that you would know because you're *never there*. He's quite well-respected in his field."

He tapped his finger to his chin several times in thought. "Neverfeel, Neverfeel. I think I've heard of him. He's an Egyptian specialist."

"Yes."

"How ... tedious. And dusty. How old is this bone hunter? Sixty? Seventy?"

Her eyes widened in offense, and she shot to her feet. "Why would you think he was old? Do you think me so ... so ... unattractive that only an old man would be willing to marry me?" By the end of her words, she was trembling with rage and humiliation.

Sasha was thunderstruck. He'd not meant for his quip to be interpreted in such a way, or for her to be so wounded. He'd not intended to insult her person. He had not even been thinking about her person, but rather some old fart of an historian sneezing over ancient tomes in the University library.

Of course, his picture of Neverfeel did imply he had certain assumptions about the kind of man Finch would choose for herself. And he was quite sure that Finch had chosen this Neverfeel, not the other way around. Finch loved to manage people, and she was practical to a fault. If she wanted something, she was the type to go out and get it without any nonsensical female falderal. He just assumed that was the case with husband hunting, too. She was not the type to be swayed by superficial nonsense like looks or charm, either.

She was not swayed by *him*, after all.

No, Finch would look for a man of intelligence, integrity, and egalitarianism. A boring old Englishman, who would devote himself to some field of esoteric study and keep out of her way. He thought it an honest enough assumption, all told, to suspect the man to be of advanced years.

The only elements to Finch that didn't quite fit into the formula he had devised for her were her gambling addiction and her moonlight occupation as a writer of romantic serials. *And* her passionate refusal never to work for him again, of course. He didn't know what to make of these aspects of Finch's personality.

Nor did he know what to make of her current pique at being thought unattractive. How very ... *female* of her. How very...

And in that moment, Sasha looked at Finch as if seeing her for the first time. He'd looked at her as a human, as his indomitable secretary, as a prized pet he liked to tease, even as a friend. He'd even looked at her dispassionately as a female, a very interesting, unusual example of her species. But he'd never looked at her as a woman.

He'd not let himself.

But he looked at her now. And looked at her some more. And he could not speak for a very long time. He could hardly manage a decent breath.

Despite the sacks she wore, despite the unfortunate pink robe, despite her red nose and watering eyes, Finch was rather pretty. Not beautiful, not sultry like he usually preferred in the fairer sex. She was like a pretty English tea rose, milky-skinned, with a dusting of freckles across the bridge of her nose.

And when she was vexed, as she was now, she was spectacular.

Those chocolate eyes of hers sparkled like the garnets she'd bought for Luciana, and her full lips quivered with emotion. Quivered and quivered as if they would not stop unless he kissed them.

He staggered back a step at his insane line of thought and the even more insane tightening of his loins.

Kiss Finch!

Kiss *Finch*? Ugh!

He didn't know how long he'd been staring at her like a bloody gape-mouthed fool. But it was long enough that she leaned against the desk uncertainly, uncomfortably. At last, she shoved away and shot to his right with a huff that was supposed to be haughty but came off sounding rather miserable.

"Of course you do," she said wryly, though the anguish underlying her voice was plain to his ears.

He had forgotten she'd asked him a question before until she'd spoken again. He had no idea what his expression must have conveyed to her, but it couldn't have been good. She'd taken it as confirmation he thought her repulsive.

Impulsively, he reached out and grabbed her by the shoulder, stopping her cold. He spun her around to face him, amazed as always at how small she was, how finely made. No wonder he'd never let himself see her as a woman. He'd break her if he wasn't careful. She tried to shrug him off, but he easily held her in place.

"I did not mean ... I did not mean to imply..." Hell, he was stuttering as if he'd forgotten how to speak English, a language he'd learned a hundred years ago! "You're not unattractive. You're quite ... quite..."

"You've said enough," she moaned, her face flushing cherry red once more. "I want you to leave."

"Not yet."

"My humiliation is complete!" She strained against his grasp.

"I did not mean to humiliate you. I mean to rehire you."

"Never, now let me go," she cried.

She was struggling so, it became necessary to hold both of her shoulders to keep her from flying away. Though he couldn't think of a reasonable explanation why he found it necessary to keep holding her.

The only thing he could come up with was that he didn't *want* to let her go.

He *just didn't want to.*

She kicked his shin, and he let out a little yelp of pain. He fell forward, and she fell with him. The desk blocked their descent, wedging Finch against him, with no means of retreat. This didn't seem to dim the enthusiasm of her struggling – or the enthusiasm of his grasping. "Damn it, Finch, hold still. Let me explain."

"Let me go!" She jerked her head back, sending her spectacles flying off her nose and against his chest. He reached for them at the same time she did, and their hands collided. Her's was warm and soft and trembling. He couldn't ever remember touching her hand, though he must have, over the years. But it had never felt like this. Like a lightning bolt had struck him where they were joined.

He caught his breath. So did she. They both froze.

He stared down into her eyes, which seemed so much bigger without her spectacles. They were wide with surprise, and dark and muddy with anguish. He felt his heart – what passed as his heart, anyway – sinking at the sight of those big, hurt eyes. Suddenly he would have traveled to the moon and back, if it could have restored their defiant luster.

She snatched her hand away a moment later, leaving him clutching her spectacles between them, and she stared up at him uncertainly, afraid to move.

"God, Finch," he muttered, shaken to the core. He began to put her spectacles back on for her, but then thought better of it. He folded them up and tucked them in his lapel. "I don't know why you wear those things all the time," he continued, shaken.

"I need them," she murmured, reaching for his lapel.

"You need them for reading. That is all."

"How do you ... how would you..." she sputtered.

"I just know. You wear them all the time to hide from the world."

"I am not hiding."

"Yes, you..." His words strangled in his throat, for he felt Finch's warm fingers against his chest, burrowing inside his jacket for her spectacles, so that all that stood between his skin and hers was a starched linen shirt. So near his secret heart.

Everywhere her small hand touched, he felt branded. As her head dipped nearer to him, the scent of her hair penetrated all of his senses, choking him. The feel of her small, lithe little form pressed between him and the desk, squirming around for her freedom, suddenly registered, making him burn with an aching, impossible desire.

He had never felt such a strong reaction to a woman in three hundred years, even Yelena, and that it was Finch of all people ... Finch! ... it simply boggled the mind. It was because he was so angry with her, he reasoned. It was because she was defying him, and no one defied him. It was because ... because...

Why had he never seen her before? Why had he never noticed how large and luscious her eyes were, how beautiful her tawny hair was, how big and plump and imminently kissable were her lips?

He *must* have noticed. He never missed important details like this.

He stopped her hand with his own. She raised her eyes to his, and she seemed puzzled by what she saw written on his features, for her lips parted tentatively.

The movement sent him over the edge, hurtling into madness.

Sasha never did anything without careful deliberation. He had learned long ago that making calculated choices and avoiding impulsive, rash behaviors preserved sanity and orderliness in one's life. Carelessness with one's mind and body led to chaos, and often, as he had learned the hard way growing up, pain and suffering. Yet from the moment he had crossed the threshold of Finch's little flat, he had done nothing but act on impulse. It was quite an unfathomable state of affairs.

He couldn't seem to help himself as he leaned downwards, knocking Finch's small body flat against the desktop, sending handkerchiefs and drafts of her serial novel flying to the floor around them. He couldn't seem to help himself as he placed both arms above her shoulders, lowered his head and touched his lips to hers.

He was stunned. She was the sweetest thing he'd ever kissed. She tasted of honey and lemons and menthol cough drops. Her lips were warm, as soft as a rose petal, as plush as a ripened fruit.

To her credit, she stiffened underneath him, and attempted to push him away.

To his delight, her protests lasted only from the time it took her hands to travel from her sides to his shoulders. Then she melted, and her fingers dug into his arms, drawing him towards her, not away. The kiss changed. Her mouth parted more, and his tongue seized the opportunity to taste her deeply, thoroughly.

Good sweet Christ!

The kiss changed again as he seized her mouth hungrily, selfishly, until neither one of them could breathe. He leaned into her, trailed his hand across her waist. She was so small he could easily fit his hands around her. Her hips were narrow, her legs slim and long and pressed against his thighs. But her breasts...

Her breasts were surprisingly full, crushed against his chest. He'd never dreamed she had breasts, as they had been unidentifiable in the bags she wore. But there they were, round and heavy and aroused. He ran a very unsteady hand lightly over the curve of one. Finch made a faint moaning sound deep in her throat, and the noise set his loins on edge until he was near to exploding like some green boy.

Dear God, he burned for her. He wanted to take Finch right there and then, no ceremony, no pretense. He'd take her against the desk, quick and hard, like some marauding barbarian. Just to show her who was in charge of this little dance of theirs. And then he wanted to carry her over to that shoddy little cot of hers, throw that pink robe into the grate, and make painfully slow, revoltingly sweet love to her all night long.

He had lost his mind.

He was aware that she had gone rigid beneath him once more, and her hands were now attempting to push him away in earnest. He'd never taken an unwilling woman before, and he wasn't about to start.

Nevertheless, this time he was sorely tempted.

And this realization, that he hovered so very near the line between who he was and who his monster of a father had been, was enough to stop him cold.

He raised his head as if awakening from a dream.

He didn't want to, but he glanced down at Finch. Damn. Damn. Damn! He still wanted her!

She sneezed in his face.

He sobered immediately. Sanity returned completely. He drew back and straightened, then drew back some more. All the way to the door.

Finch raised herself on one elbow and watched him retreat, her lips swollen from his kisses, her cheeks flushed, her hair wildly mussed. She looked dazed. She opened her mouth, but whatever she'd been about to say was swallowed by another sneeze. And another. She looked so miserable and confused and adorable his traitorous body almost returned to her side, enfolded her in his arms, and kissed her again.

He clutched the knob for dear life and fled out the door as if escaping a fire. He didn't stop until he was seated atop his curricle.

Matthews, who had stood guard by his vehicle, eyed him as if he'd just escaped from Bedlam. He certainly felt as if he had. He touched his lips, remembering the damnably sweet feel of her mouth against his. His head started to spin, and he clutched the seat boards for purchase.

Unable to help himself, he glanced up the side of the boarding house to the windows of her room.

Finch was staring down at him from one of them, her eyes wide, her hand pressed against her mouth. He jerked his gaze away, trying to fight down another vexing bout of arousal below the belt.

He had gone utterly mad! He knew this, could trace its pathology as a psychiatrist, could give a hundred technical names for his sudden sexual interest in Finch, yet for the life of him, he could not let the feeling go.

He could not let *her* go. And this had nothing to do with keeping her safe from a killer any more. If it were possible for him to catch her cold, it would serve him right.

-from an advertisement in *The London Post-Dispatch*, 1870

*I*T was common knowledge that the most beautiful woman in England was Lady Christiana Harker. Golden-haired, green-eyed, with alabaster skin, a perfect figure, and giant dowry, she was what every debutante entering the marriage mart wished she could be. Even at thirty years of age, her beauty was the same as it had been at her debut. People were aging at a slightly slower rate than they had forty years ago, but even so, Lady Christiana seemed to be enjoying a remarkably long youth.

Aline hadn't the advantage of longevity or beauty. Standing next to her resplendent friend at the charity ball Lady Christiana and her brother, the Earl of Llewellyn, held every year at their huge London residence, Aline felt all of her thirty-four years in her dowdy blue silk gown she'd purchased a decade ago. These feelings were nothing unusual when in the company of Christiana or most of her feminine acquaintances. She was always the smaller, unenhanced wallflower of the group, and she was resigned to this fact.

She disliked coming to these events. She was an unsurprisingly poor dancer, and found making conversation with the few vapid London society ladies who stooped to speak to her tedious and often painful. And when there was a crush, she invariably got trampled, owing to her size and her amazing ability to become invisible to onlookers.

Now that she was no longer Romanov's employee, she didn't have to attend such functions as his representative. But she couldn't celebrate quite yet; her friendship with Christiana prohibited her absence.

Her nerves were even more fragile tonight for several reasons. She kept glancing towards the door, her blood thick with dread. Romanov never deigned to come to the annual ball, though his financial contributions went a great way towards funding Lady Christiana's charitable ventures. He tended to keep a generous distance between himself and most society functions. His only concessions were his box at the opera and an occasional private dinner with friends.

But one never knew with a magician like him.

Legend had it that Romanov had attended once, six years ago, before her employment. The ladies still talked about it in hushed whispers along the ballroom sidelines when they ran out of recent gossip to pass the time. They tended to bring up the subject when she was around, since everyone knew she was his secretary.

This spurious recounting invariably prefaced an interrogation about her employer, what tailor he used, what mistress he kept, what plans for matrimony he had, and exactly how many pounds he was worth.

Having to endure conversations about Romanov was one of the reasons she hated balls. Having to endure conversations about Romanov while Romanov was in actual attendance, however, would be far, far worse.

"Why do you keep looking at the door, darling?" Christiana asked, glancing down at her in concern.

Aline wrinkled her nose. "No reason."

Christiana looked as if she doubted this, but continued her rather one-sided conversation that Aline tried to follow. Something about orphans and miserly old dowagers. But her attention wandered back towards the door.

She had the oddest feeling he was going to come tonight.

She shivered and clenched her hands into fists. She simply would not let herself think about what had happened. On her desk. To her lips.

"Are you well, Aline?" Christiana pressed. "You look rather flushed."

She murmured she was quite fine and turned her back to the door.

He would not come.

And even if he did, perhaps if she remained turned away from him the entire time, she could imagine he wasn't there at all.

Though this shift in position opened up a whole new can of worms, for now she was facing Charlie.

Charlie and the lovely Miss Theodora Hendrix. They still had their heads together, chatting up a storm. They'd not moved from where they'd stood since Miss Hendrix had arrived with her father, Charlie's old mentor, nearly an hour ago.

Apparently, Professor Hendrix and his daughter had spent the last seven years living in Italy, excavating ancient temples. Seeing them here tonight had been a complete surprise to Charlie.

Correction.

Seeing Miss Theodora Hendrix had been a complete surprise to Charlie, or so Aline had learned when Charlie had expounded for a good five minutes about how lovely Miss Hendrix was looking.

Aline was *not* jealous.

Even though she'd walked away from Charlie and Miss Hendrix's tête-à-tête without being noticed.

Even though Miss Hendrix, with her golden hair arranged immaculately, and her sea foam Grecian gown draped around her tall, curvaceous figure, was nearly as beautiful as Lady Christiana. Even though Charlie had been unable to take his eyes off of Miss Hendrix the entire night.

"Don't worry, Aline. I'm sure Charlie's just excited to see

an old friend," Christiana said, noticing the direction of Aline's present gaze.

"So he said," Aline murmured. She sighed wearily, excused herself, and made a beeline towards the punch bowl.

Unfortunately, she was intercepted by Miss Dahlia Ridenour and Miss Sabrina Eddings, two confirmed spinsters, only a few years older than Aline – or so they claimed. Aside from their Iron Necklaces, they had clearly spent a good part of their fortunes on Welding enhancements to improve their looks. Their busts were both suspiciously rigid, and the metal plates under their skin, meant to keep the wrinkles at bay, made changing their expressions difficult.

Their enhancements had not helped them catch husbands.

They had taken it upon themselves to befriend her when she'd first started making the rounds to such events, seeing in her a kindred spirit. And they meant well. Usually.

She suppressed a sigh, for she knew where this conversation was headed. She'd been avoiding them all night just so she wouldn't have to go through the inevitable rigmarole of explaining her engagement, which had doubtless reached their ears by now.

"My dear, we've just heard! How very thrilling that Dr. Netherfield has asked for your hand!" the nervous Miss Ridenour gushed. "Absolutely thrilling. Isn't it, Sabrina?"

Miss Eddings cast a significant glance across the ballroom at Charlie and his current companion. "Just in time, I'd say, for you, Miss Finch," she said lightly.

Aline couldn't help but feel a bit wounded at the jab. Miss Eddings need hardly point out the disparities between herself and the lovely Miss Hendrix. They were evident enough.

But she and Charlie were engaged, and she didn't doubt his intentions. Once Charlie committed to a course, he tended to see it through to the end. He'd proposed, and she'd accepted. It was no grand passion, but they were fond of each other and committed to building a life together.

"This week has been full of happy endings. You and Dr.

Netherfield, and Miss Wren and Captain Standish!" Miss Ridenour gushed. She grabbed Aline's arm, huffing excitedly. "Have you read the latest *Chronicles*, Miss Finch?"

How to answer *that*!

Miss Ridenour, who rarely paused for responses, barreled on, her face lighting up with a sudden revelation. "I could simply not believe it when Captain Standish proposed to Miss Wren on his boat."

"The Albion Lady is an airship, not a boat," Miss Eddings corrected pedantically.

"Whatever, it was romantic! It was how I always wanted the Captain to propose. Aboard his boat. If I had a beau in the Royal Navy, it is how I would want him to propose."

"Balderdash!" Miss Eddings sniffed. "It's not romantic at all. It is drivel. Standish is a lily-liver. Miss Wren is a fool to think that they suit. Mark my words, Miss Wren will soon realize her mistake. Standish is bound to do something foolish, revealing his true character."

"But that ... that's absurd," Miss Ridenour cried. "Miss Wren and the Captain are soul mates."

Miss Eddings groaned. "Is it not obvious to anyone but me? Dr. Augustus is Miss Wren's true match."

The group of ladies who had gathered around them when the conversation had turned to the *Chronicles* drew a collective breath, including Aline herself. What could she have possibly written that would have led all the women of London to believe that Dr. Augustus and Miss Wren were ... were what? Destined for each other? Ugh!

Standish was Miss Wren's match. Standish, not Dr. Augustus.

"I do not think the author intends Miss Wren for anyone but Standish, Miss Eddings," Aline said before she could stop herself.

Miss Eddings gave her a stare that seemed to ask, *And how do you know?*

How did she indeed, when she was merely the bloody author? Why, she'd half a mind to reveal who she was just so she could put an end to these ridiculous rumors. Really, Miss Wren and Augustus! It was just one more way Romanov was intruding upon her sanity.

Miss Edding's glare changed to one of surprise as she caught sight of something over Aline's shoulder. The nosy woman's face flooded with color, and a silly grin quivered on her normally sour lips.

Aline glanced at her other companions, and she saw that they all wore similar mooncalf expressions as they gazed across the room. With an exasperated sigh, she turned to see what had caught their undivided attention.

Her jaw dropped. Romanov.

She'd once seen him seduce a woman with the arch of a single eyebrow across a crowded opera house. Not that she'd been invited to the opera. She'd been forced to go there to give him an urgent message and had quite accidentally witnessed the encounter. The woman – beautiful, of course, and married to an ancient duke – had stayed Romanov's mistress for a month before he grew bored. Aline had bought the woman a pair of jeweled opera glasses as a parting gift – in case the woman needed help scouting eyebrows in the future.

But that wasn't the point.

The point was that Romanov tended to attract women like moths to a flame even when he wasn't doing anything at all other than standing still and breathing air. That seemed to be the case at the moment. The women around her were positively fluttering. She couldn't blame them for being drawn by superficialities. Romanov's superficialities were, after all, quite breathtaking.

She didn't think it fair that any human being should be so absolutely, stunningly gorgeous. Towering, raven-haired with a bit of grey peppering his sideburns, those outrageous yellow-amber wolf eyes glittering out from his dusky skin, he stood out among the rest of the rather staid-looking Englishmen present like an exotic orchid amid an ocean of hothouse daisies.

She bit her bottom lip until it hurt. What had gotten into

her, comparing him and the rest of the gentlemen in the ballroom to flowers?

She was immune to his charms. She'd had five years of his personal torments to erase any missish sentimentality on her part.

Though she had to admit he was looking particularly ... particularly exhilarating tonight. His evening suit was entirely black, and cut in that slightly foreign, Continental style he preferred to fit his broad-shouldered, whip-thin physique like a glove. The only thing that was less-than-immaculate was his untidy necktie.

Could he find no one in his army of retainers to tie a proper knot for him?

He was scanning the assembly as his friend, the Earl, approached him, clearly surprised by his appearance. The Earl was not the only one. What could he be doing here now?

She soon had her answer. His eyes stopped on her, and a slow, predatory smile settled around the edges of his mouth. Damn, he meant to torment her further! Excusing himself from the Earl, he began to stride in her direction with a distinctly feline grace.

A flurry of feminine excitement pulsed around her.

"The Professor!" Miss Ridenour breathed.

"Your employer!" Miss Eddings practically twittered.

"Ex-employer," she corrected through clenched teeth.

"He's coming this way!" another lady nearly screeched in her ear.

Aline rolled her eyes and sighed. She fought the temptation to smooth her skirts, as all the other ladies around her seemed to be doing at the moment, and squared her shoulders, readying herself for battle. Her pulse had quickened, to her dismay, and the temperature of the room suddenly seemed stifling.

He stopped directly in front of her, wolfish grin firmly in place.

"Miss Finch," he murmured. His glittering eyes left her for a moment, sweeping over her companions. "Ladies," he added. He delivered a perfect, graceful bow that undid the group completely. They were practically falling over themselves as they curtsied back. She heard Miss Ridenour give a nervous giggle.

She wanted to vomit.

"Professor Romanov," she said, bobbing her head, not daring to extend her hand for the obligatory kiss. She would not think about her desk. Or his kiss. Or the fact that it had sent her world up in flames.

His lips curled in a knowing grin and his eyes twinkled roguishly. As if he knew exactly what she was trying not to think about. He addressed the ladies once more.

"You'll forgive me if I steal Miss Finch from you for a moment? We have some matters to discuss."

Having no choice without causing a scene, she took his proffered arm and allowed him to lead her away. It was only a moment later that she realized her error. He was leading her towards the dance floor, where a rather high-spirited Viennese waltz had begun. She made one final attempt to escape, tugging herself in the direction of the punch bowl.

"If you think I am going to dance with you, sir..." she began.

"Smile, Finch. People will think you're having an apoplexy."

She groaned through gritted teeth. "I do not dance."

"I shall make do."

"What are you doing here, anyway?"

"What does it look like? Enjoying myself at one of the season's best events."

"You never come to the charity ball."

"Never? But I am here now, so you are in error."

He pulled her onto the dance floor and faced her. Before she could react, one of his large hands anchored itself to her waist, and the other twined through her fingers.

"I shall step on your toes," she warned.

"You weigh less than a bird, Finch. I think I shall come out unscathed."

"I shall fall on my face."

"Have I ever let you do that?" he murmured silkily.

She glanced up, which was a mistake. His nose hovered a scant inch away from her own. Her heart skipped a beat. She attempted to draw back, but his hands were like iron manacles. He swept her into the throng of dancers.

She hadn't the chance to stumble, as her feet barely touched the floor as he circled her around the room. He continued to stare down at her intently, still much too close. She tried to focus on his collar, but she could feel his breath ruffling the top of her hair, as if he were...

As if he were *smelling* her! Again!

She craned her neck upwards and tried to fix him with her sternest glare. But it was hard to do, as she was winded and dizzy from being tossed about like a rag doll.

"Were you ... were you sniffing my hair, Professor?" she breathed.

He looked much too innocent. "Whatever gave you that idea, Finch?" He changed directions abruptly, pulling her along effortlessly. "But if I were ... Isn't that the point of wearing perfume? For gentlemen to sniff about ladies' hair?"

"I do not ... *wear* ... perfume," she managed. "I am allergic."

He seemed to consider this seriously. "Then you *naturally* smell of lemons and mint? How interesting."

"I do not ... oh! Could you please slow down? I can barely breathe trying to keep up with you."

"It has never been a problem before."

"Yes it has! You were just too ... too thickheaded to realize it! Why do you think you were always having to pick me up off the floor?"

He looked contrite. "So sorry, Finch. We could have solved the problem long ago if only you had said something." He studied her. "But of course you wouldn't have said anything. You would have not wanted to reveal your weakness to me, though I must say it was plainly evident."

"If it was plainly evident, you should have been gentleman

enough to *slow down*!"

"But what fun would that have been? I rather enjoyed keeping you upright. Though in retrospect, I should have made things easier for you."

She laughed dryly. "How? By purchasing a bicycle for me?"

"Again, no fun for me. I should have tucked you under one arm. Kept those clumsy feet of yours permanently off the floor."

"You ... you..." she sputtered, trying to find words, but failing miserably.

His hands squeezed her closer and higher so that he was practically carrying her in his arms. How strong *was* he? She was aware of warm, hard male, crisp tailored silk, the scent of sandalwood and leather and that other unidentifiable musk. She choked.

"Shh, Finch," he soothed. "Relax. See, no need to worry about falling on your face now."

"Put me down," she muttered.

He cocked an eyebrow.

"I *said...*"

He complied abruptly. Her feet hit the floor, and the momentum of the dance propelled her forward, right into the brick wall of his chest. Her cheek grazed his lapel, and her nose buried itself in his collar so that she was breathing his singular, exotic scent. His ruffled necktie tickled her nose, and she sneezed.

"Still sick?"

She felt his voice, rumbling through his chest, and it did strange things to her insides. She straightened and scowled at him. "I am quite recovered. It was your untidy necktie."

"Yes, well, I lost my valet some time ago to a fit of pique."

"Pique!"

"Calm down, Finch. You are ruining my favorite Strauss waltz. Try to enjoy yourself for once. I doubt your Colonel Standish could manage your feet half so well on the dance floor."

"His name is Charles Netherfield."

"Ah, yes, the eminent archaeologist," he said, wrinkling his elegant nose as if smelling something distasteful in the air.

"Yes. And we do not dance together, sir. As I tried to explain earlier, I do not dance."

"You are a liar. I have seen you dance before."

This conversation just kept getting worse and worse. "What?"

"In my office. To the tomb scene in *Aida*. Lovely melody. But hardly appropriate for a waltz. You have no rhythm, Finch."

"You were spying on me!" she breathed, feeling her cheeks flood with color.

He grinned unmercifully at her discomfiture. "Hardly. It was my office. My phonograph. Ergo, not spying."

"It was spying, and you know it. Is that all you've done for the past five years? Spy on me? And don't think I don't see Mr. Matthews following me around still."

"You look very pretty when you are spitting mad, Finch," he murmured, leaning in to her, his cheek nearly grazing her own.

She froze, which necessitated that he pick her off her feet once more. She hardly noticed this time, however, because her mind was suddenly back in her flat, the night he'd barged in, picked a fight, pinned her to her desk, kissed her, and barged out.

She'd refused to let herself spend one minute thinking about that kiss – that wet, seductive kiss, lips and tongue and hands, searching, devouring, touching, that had made her legs turn to jelly and her stomach fill with a million butterflies. But it was suddenly all she could think about.

He seemed to be thinking about it as well, for those strange eyes of his had turned the exact shade of yellow diamonds that they had been that night. She tried to think of something to say, but nothing came to mind. He was mocking her, toying with her, trying to provoke her, and she was being a very easy target.

Suddenly exhausted, she gave up trying to battle with him and allowed herself to be carried across the floor. The dance would have been exhilarating, if she didn't feel so miserable ... if she didn't hate her partner so utterly.

He continued to study her with his eagle eyes, never breaking his stare, and she wondered anew what his game was. Why had he kissed her that night, and why was he here now, staring at her as if trying to divine her soul?

The waltz ended. He stood with her for a moment as the other couples left the floor, setting her on her feet and lowering his hands to his side with deliberate slowness.

"Why are you tormenting me, sir?" she managed in a weak voice.

His eyes narrowed. "You've no idea what torment is, Finch," he replied softly, the barest of caresses. What was she to say to that?

He stepped back and offered her his arm. He led her into the crowd and began to scan the room. "Now, where is this Standish fellow? I assume he's here."

"*Netherfield.*"

"Whatever. Introduce me."

She balked. The last thing she wanted to do was introduce Charlie to her ex-employer. "I don't see him," she lied. "Now go away!"

"Aline! There you are!" came a familiar voice behind her. She cringed and turned. Apparently, the Fates had cursed her this night.

Charlie strode up to them with Theodora Hendrix on his arm – this just kept getting better and better! – and the Earl of Llewellyn trailing behind. Romanov faced Charlie with an impenetrable smile after giving Theodora an appraising look that made Aline grit her teeth.

Despite her intentions otherwise, she found herself comparing Romanov to her fiancé. Charlie was considered a handsome man on most occasions, but standing next to Romanov, he seemed almost plain.

Even the Earl, who was legendary for his good looks, faded away next to Romanov.

"Professor Romanov, may I present Miss Theodora Hendrix, and Professor Charles Netherfield. My fiancé," she said reluctantly.

Charlie smiled broadly and extended his hand. "No need for ceremony, what? I feel like I've known you for ages, Professor. Aline has told me so much about you," Charlie gushed. His obvious pleasure upon finally meeting Romanov made Aline want to scream. She prayed he wouldn't immediately begin to solicit Romanov for funds for the upcoming expedition.

Romanov eyed her as he shook Charlie's hand. "*Has* she?" he murmured. "Only the good things, I trust?"

The Earl snickered. Charlie looked startled. "Of course."

"You come as a bit of a shock to *me*, Mr. Neverfeel," Romanov continued.

"Netherfield," she corrected.

He ignored her. "Fin ... *Aline* ... didn't inform me she had a fiancé until a week ago."

Charlie looked even more startled. He looked at her, and she was struggling not to blush. Romanov had never spoken her first name in the five years she had known him, most likely because he'd forgotten it. Hearing it now, spoken in such a low, languid drawl, made all of her insides knot.

She lifted her eyes to discover the Earl glancing from her to Romanov with a thoughtful look on his face. That thoughtfulness gave way to cunning, however, and Aline groaned inwardly. Rowan Harker's life mission was stirring up trouble.

"I'm sure Aline intended to introduce you at the wedding," his lordship said with a devious smile.

"Ah. The wedding. When *is* the happy day again, Aline?" Romanov asked, turning to her expectantly.

"In a month," Charlie answered for her. "Then we set sail for Egypt."

For a moment, Romanov was silent, giving her an

incredulous look. He clearly remembered their journey across the Channel together. "Ah, an exotic honeymoon. Aline has always dreamed of traveling to outlandish places." A cat-like grin hovered at the edges of his lips.

Charlie was nonplussed. "It's not *quite* a honeymoon. That is, I am heading an expedition to an area just below Luxor."

Romanov's attention never faltered from Aline's face. "A not-quite honeymoon digging for old bones. How romantic." At last he shifted his glance from Aline to the extremely confused Charlie. "Do you know your fiancé quit without notice, sir? While I was abroad, no less. I came back to find my affairs in a complete shambles."

Charlie hadn't known this, since she'd lied and told him she'd informed Romanov of her resignation over wireless tickertext. Which she had done. The Professor just hadn't read it. He swung her a questioning glance. "Is this true, Aline?" he demanded.

"Very true," Romanov supplied for her.

Charlie furrowed his brow. "Well, I don't see why you couldn't finish out the month, Aline."

What? Well, *Aline* could see why. And Charlie had been the one so adamant she resign as soon as possible in the first place. Evidently, Charlie was so unnerved by meeting Romanov that he was spouting nonsense. She glared at Charlie. "I have *much* to do before the wedding, Charlie," she said as evenly as she could.

"Like what?" Charlie asked the same time Romanov did.

"I have … *things* to do," she gritted out.

Charlie looked unconvinced. The Earl looked as if he was about to explode with mirth.

Theodora, of all people, seemed to take pity on her, for she laid a hand on her arm and faced the men. "An engaged lady has many things to do before the wedding. Preparing a trousseau. Planning for the wedding and reception, picking out flowers. Things men have no concept of."

"But we're getting married at the registrar's," Charlie said, baffled.

Theodora's brow lifted in surprise. "Oh, well that certainly makes things ... easier." Aline heaved a sigh. Theodora was not helping.

Aline was saved from further interrogation by the start of another Strauss waltz. Charlie cleared his throat and gestured to Miss Hendrix, who was staring at Aline so intently she didn't see Charlie's gesture.

Aline had the uncomfortable sensation that Miss Hendrix was ... well, *sniffing* her, as the Professor had done earlier. But that was ridiculous. She was just feeling overly sensitive at the moment and must be imagining Theodora's strange behavior.

"My, you smell nice, Miss Finch," Theodora said. "What *is* that scent?"

No, she hadn't imagined it after all. And she wasn't imagining the strength with which Theodora gripped her forearm. It was rather painful. What was the matter with the woman?

"I don't wear a scent," she said, unable to hide her irritation, sending the Professor a glower. Just as she was about to jerk away from Theodora, decorum be damned, Charlie pried Miss Hendrix's hand from Aline's arm. Miss Hendrix seemed to come to herself at last and turned her attention to Charlie, smiling brilliantly.

"We shall continue this discussion later, Aline," Charlie said, after giving Theodora an odd look. "I have promised this waltz to Miss Hendrix."

Aline didn't know what to make of that odd moment with Theodora. But it was, sadly, just one of many odd moments that seemed to be plaguing her life.

And Aline was *not* jealous as she watched Charlie lead Theodora to the dance floor. She *wasn't*.

"An unromantic wedding at the registrar's, followed by an unromantic honeymoon digging up mummies in the desert," came a voice near her ear. Heat raced down her spine. She turned, gave Romanov her most contemptuous scowl, then bestowed it upon the Earl for good measure, and walked away.

Moments later, she was outside in the Llewellyn gardens,

breathing in the night air, and reining in her temper. Charlie was smitten with Miss Hendrix, and Romanov was in rare form at her expense. She tore down the garden path when Matthews, her ever present and unwanted bodyguard, appeared out of nowhere and winked at her before melting into the shadows once more. She barely repressed her shout of surprise.

And then she wished she *had* shouted. The evidence that her life was no longer her own, and perhaps had never been, was fast-mounting. The night could not possibly get any worse.

But it did.

"I believe I have something that belongs to you." She spun around, her heart catching in her throat.

Romanov smiled at her from the shadows and approached her languidly, tapping her spectacles against his lapel.

She snatched at them, but he held them high above her head, out of her reach. She lowered her arms and glared at him. "Give them back."

"Not until we come to an agreement."

She crossed her arms. "No agreement. I am *not* coming back to work for you."

"Inside, you gave me a month."

"*Charlie* gave you a month. *I* did not."

He tsked. "That's no way to begin life as an obedient bride, defying one's husband."

He tucked her spectacles back into his lapel. She leaned forward to retrieve them and stopped cold, remembering what had happened last time she had fumbled about the area of his chest. Heat surged through her, and she backed away, nearly stumbling over the uneven bricks.

As always, he caught her, but she shoved his hand away and continued to back up. A wall stopped her escape. He paced forward but stopped several arms' lengths away. He had grown serious, thoughtful, which was more worrisome to her than his former mockery. She wondered if he too was remembering their outlandish encounter on her desk.

MARGARET FOXE

"A month, and I return your spectacles."

"No." She shook her head and turned away. "I am marrying Charlie and going to Egypt."

"Nonsense. You aren't going anywhere. No, you can come back to me. Of course we shall lighten your load, if that shall make you more ... obedient. And you may marry Standish..."

"*Netherfield.*"

"... if you like, though I have my doubts about him, Finch. Really, a honeymoon spent digging for bones in the desert? It's an absurd idea."

"It sounds heavenly," she insisted stubbornly, hating that he had a point. Charlie hadn't even mentioned the possibility for a proper honeymoon, and she hadn't bothered to ask. She'd been too distracted by her decision to marry at all – and her spectacular irritation at Romanov – to even think what she wanted. At the time, a ceremony at the registrar's office and a swift ticket out of London seemed the perfect solution to her problems.

Now she was not so sure she'd not been hasty. She'd always wanted a church wedding, even though that was rather old-fashioned, embarrassing sentimentality on her part. A small wedding in the quaint country chapel where her parents had married.

But she'd never tell Charlie this. Or the fact that she wouldn't mind a few weeks' holiday settling into married life before digging in the desert for old bones.

Romanov moved closer, his voice grew softly seductive. It was the voice of the devil. "Finch ... *Aline*. What shall you do without me?"

She stiffened, stepped backwards. "I shall manage, sir."

"Sasha."

She snorted. She was not about to start calling him *that*. "I am marrying Charlie and settling down," she insisted.

"How dull. How bourgeois."

She ignored him. "We shall have a cottage together."

"Ten children, three dogs?"

106

"No dogs," she retorted.

"You are not the housewife type," he pronounced.

She bristled. "Some people rather like the idea of having a family. You might think it silly, but I want children."

"You hate children."

"I would love *my* children," she amended.

"You'll be bored to death."

"I will not be idle. I will write full time. But this is getting us nowhere. I will never be your secretary again. Not for all the tea in China."

He was silent, still. The music inside the ballroom hummed in the background. She thought about bolting for the doors, but something made her hesitate. *Romanov* made her hesitate, damn him. For five years, she had watched him waltz through life with one of two masks on his face. One was the intense, absorbed, driven mask he wore when playing his role as the professor. The other was the devilish one he took up when he flirted with women or played with his hellhounds ... or teased her. Rarely had she seen those masks drop away.

But they did now. He looked weary, soul-dead.

It could have been a trick of the light in the poorly lit garden, but somehow she doubted it. He ran a hand over his face, through his hair, and sighed. "Please. Don't leave me now."

It was a mere whisper on the wind.

She clutched her hand against her traitorous heart, which had begun to beat dangerously fast in her breast, and turned away to face the garden wall. Beneath his masks, despite his success and wealth and perfect beauty, he was little more than a lonely man adrift upon a very large sea. And she hurt for him.

Something had happened to him on this last trip.

No, that wasn't right. Romanov's soul-sickness had always been there. He'd chosen to study killers, psychopaths, and all manner of deviants with a singular, unnerving focus. He relished in the hunt of the sickest of society's criminals when Drexler called for his assistance, and spent his days and nights trying to understand what drove men to murder and cruelty. A man like that had to be a little touched.

Or extremely tortured.

But she would not become mired in that world again. He would *not* draw her into his obsessions. "I can't."

She turned back to him and nearly collided with his chest. He had approached her while her back was turned. Now he was much too close. She could barely breathe now, barely think.

"Where do you think you're going?" he said gruffly.

Her lips tightened with stubborn disapproval. "I am going back inside, to my fiancé."

"We are not through, *milaya*," he murmured.

She sucked in a breath. First he called her Aline, and now … this Russian endearment. "Don't call me that," she demanded, feeling her blush rise.

"Yes, my pet."

She growled at him, a fierce little noise that surprised both of them. His eyes widened, and something … *hot* … passed over them.

"Just give me my spectacles, and let me go."

"You'll ruin your eyes, wearing them when you do not need them." He raised both hands and touched her temples, lightly caressing. "It is why you get so many headaches," he said in a low voice. "Trust me."

"That is something I ... will ... not ... do," she murmured. Yet she stood fixed in place as his fingers massaged her temples. What was he doing? And why was she letting him do it? She worried her bottom lip with her teeth, and he stared at the sight as if it fascinated him.

He stepped closer, and suddenly he seemed to be breathing as rapidly as she was. A fingertip grazed her lips, tracing them, pressing them apart at the seam. Oh God, it was her flat all over again. A bolt of electrified lust traveled down her spine, settling low, in unmentionable places.

"If you kiss me," she whispered, "I'll scream."

"I'm not going to kiss you," he whispered back. "You're imagining things, Finch."

She gave him a look that told him exactly how little she believed him and attempted to say something further, she knew not what. But he silenced her by placing a finger on her lips once more. He let it fall down her chin, over her throat, to the top of the high collar of her dress. He eyed the bit of faded lace peeking over the top distastefully.

"I hate your clothes, Finch."

"I don't care," she managed, refusing to be affected by his proximity.

He raised his finger and tapped her on the end of her nose. "I'll buy you a new wardrobe," he said, then leaned close and whispered in her ear, "Better yet, no wardrobe. Not. A. Single. Stitch."

All of her self-possession went up in flames. Her whole body seemed to have lit on fire. Over four words. He was seducing her for some nefarious purpose; she knew this in the last rational corner of her brain. But she was powerless to resist him. She began to wobble on her suddenly boneless legs.

The Professor caught her by the shoulders and pulled her against him, as if he'd been waiting to do just that. Then he let out a ragged breath, and she peered up at him, startled. He was shivering, and his heart was speeding out of control beneath her hands. She'd never imagined a heart could beat so fast. She'd never imagined he'd be as affected as she was. She licked her suddenly parched lips.

He groaned. "What are you doing to me?" he murmured, sliding one arm around her back, raising the other between them, encircling her neck with his fingers, as if he contemplated strangling her. But she was not afraid. She'd never feared him, though she knew she probably should.

"I am not doing anything," she murmured.

His eyes flashed with amber fire. "You're offering yourself up on a platter, Finch. I would devour you whole."

Her eyes widened in comprehension. "You wouldn't!" she breathed.

He held her tight. "I would. I could."

"You wouldn't!" she repeated, less certainly now.

"I could have you, Finch. If you like." he stated. "I could kiss you too. If you like." He tightened his hold around her back to emphasize his claim, and she let out a little breathless yelp. "I dare you," he finally said.

She blinked through her fog of desire. "What?"

"I said, I dare you. Say, 'I'd like that, Sasha,' and I'll kiss you again. Say, 'I'd like that, Sasha,' and I'll ..." He thrust his hips against her crudely, almost brutally, letting her feel the hardness of him. Her eyes widened in surprise, but instead of being revolted, she burned even hotter.

She didn't know how long they stood there, locked together, on fire. They stared at each other, speech forgotten, and for a moment, she thought he looked as startled as she was by this sudden turn of events.

And God forgive her, she couldn't remember ever feeling so alive. It was how she'd felt in her flat, when she'd begun challenging him for the first time, how she'd felt when he'd had her against the desk, reason suspended.

He lowered his head, and his lips brushed hers, light as a butterfly's wings. She craved more. She thought in that moment she would sell her soul for more. And that scared her so much she managed to get enough of a grip on herself to wrench away from him.

It seemed to snap him out of his trance as well, and he backed away. His insouciant mask quickly fell back in place. Though the heat in his eyes remained. They practically glowed with it.

Anger and shame quickly replaced her momentary madness. She'd let him paw her, while her fiancé danced inside, oblivious to her inconstancy. How could she let him overcome her so easily?

Not. A. Single. Stitch.

She shivered, hugging herself. "Why are you doing this to me?" she demanded. "Trying to ... seduce me? I am marrying Professor Neverfeel." Oh, God, and now *she* couldn't get her fiancé's name right. And at such a moment!

He pulled her spectacles out from his lapel. "You

underestimate your importance to me, Finch. *Aline*." He tapped the end of her nose with her spectacles. "I want you." *Tap. Tap. Tap.* "And I shall get what I want."

Tap.

She snatched her spectacles from his grasp and settled them behind her ears. Just then, she spotted two figures approaching over Sasha's shoulder, and her blush returned. The last thing she needed was for others to see her in the aftermath of such a blistering encounter.

She had no time to escape, however. A grim-faced Earl was nearly running down the path in their direction. On his heels was Inspector Drexler from Scotland Yard, limping behind him with his long cane, looking equally serious. The jagged burn that ran from the edge of the gleaming carapace of his Welding eye to his chin was pulled taut by his frown.

Sasha's fierce concentration on her broke, and he turned towards the intruders with unnatural speed, something unsettling flashing through his eyes. His hand reached into his jacket, as if for a weapon. Which was absurd. The Professor consulted with Scotland Yard, but he was no warrior. He was a head doctor. He didn't carry a weapon. Did he?

When he saw who approached, his shoulders relaxed, but only a little. And his expression did not grow any less dangerous. In fact, his mouth tensed at the edges, as if he was holding back intense emotion.

The Earl shook his head as he came to a stop next to them. "Sasha, it's happened."

Romanov closed his eyes as if he'd received a great blow. Aline started to feel very alarmed. She'd never seen the Professor look so ... human. So weak. What was going on?

"Where?" he bit out.

"St. Giles. Where else?" the Inspector said gruffly. "I believe this is what you've been waiting for. You'll never guess the address," he said, giving Aline a wary glance that she didn't understand.

"I think I can." Romanov heaved a great sigh. His expression was so bleak, so ... *hard* ... that Aline started to tremble with apprehension.

"I think it is time Miss Finch knows the truth," the Earl said softly.

It was as if the Professor couldn't bring himself to look at her now. "This is not what I wanted," he said in a low, tortured voice.

"She is stronger than you think..." his Lordship began.

"No one should have the knowledge we do. Nor should she have to face the dark dealings of this night."

Her dread was quickly being replaced by exasperation. *Men.*

"Oh, please! Stop these ridiculously ominous riddles! I don't know whether to be annoyed or frightened. Professor, as I have been your secretary for five years, I have seen plenty of dead bodies. I assume that's what this is about? There has been a murder?"

"This one is different," Romanov insisted.

"More different than even *you* imagined, Sasha," his Lordship said in a low voice.

Romanov looked sharply at his friend. "Something's changed?"

The Earl gave Drexler a dark look. The Inspector stared stoically ahead. "Everything's changed."

Suddenly, out of nowhere, Lady Christiana joined their group, slightly winded, as if she'd sprinted from the ballroom. Aline bit her lip. This was *all* the night needed. Who would join them next? The Misses Ridenour and Eddings?

"Would someone please tell me the meaning of all of this?" Lady Christiana demanded of them all. But she was looking at the Inspector. And Aline had never seen such an expression on the lady's face. She looked ... well, what Aline suspected she herself had looked like about five minutes earlier when Sasha had been whispering naughty things in her ear. Aline gaped at her friend. Lady Christiana was in love with the Inspector. How could Aline have missed noticing such a blatantly obvious thing?

The feeling, however, did not seem to be mutual. Drexler

refused to so much as look at Lady Christiana, his jaw clenching even tighter and his hand gripping his cane until she could see the whites of his knuckles even in the dim, gaslit garden.

When it became clear that the Inspector would not answer her, much less acknowledge her, Lady Christiana's expression changed to one of frustration … and hurt. She turned to her brother. "I saw the Inspector's arrival. You've been gone forever, you know. The guests are starting to notice. What is going on?"

When Aline glanced over at the Earl, he looked so furious at his sister that Aline took an unconscious step backwards. She'd not thought Rowan Harker capable of such anger.

"Go back inside, Christiana," he ordered. "I will deal with you later."

Christiana's eyes widened. "*Deal* with me? What in heaven's name have I done?" she scoffed.

"Elijah has just told me everything."

Christiana froze, and the blood drained from her face. She turned to the Inspector. "Why?" she whispered. "Why would you…"

The Inspector shook his head tersely.

Devastated, she turned back to her brother, rushing to his side and grabbing his arm. She stared up at him pleadingly. "Please don't hurt him. Don't tell the others. They'll … kill him! It was all my fault!"

Now Aline was sure her jaw was touching the garden path, shocked by the turn of the conversation. She took another step backwards, straight into Romanov's chest. And stayed there. She had a feeling something huge was happening, and she needed something to anchor her. Even if it was her nemesis.

The Earl looked down at his sister, his expression arctic. Then he removed her hand from his arm, gently but impersonally, as if she were a stranger. He turned away, as if he could not bear to look at her. "You should worry for your own hide, my Lady. Go inside. You've a ballroom full of guests, and it will look most odd if one of us is not there. We shall discuss this later. I have business that cannot wait."

Lady Christiana stood there, her shoulders stooped as if in defeat, and a heavy silence fell over the garden. Aline wanted to go to her friend and comfort her, but she could not seem to move her feet. She was too stunned, too *confused* to do much of anything but gape at the scene unfolding before her eyes.

"Do as the Earl says," the Inspector said finally, breaking the silence. He was staring at Lady Christiana's back with a bleak expression. "You've done enough. Said enough. We are not alone here, your Ladyship, if you have not yet noticed."

Slowly, as if awakening from a dream, Christiana glanced in Aline's direction, as if just realizing she was there, and her expression grew guilty. "Rowan…"

"Just go, Christiana. I … won't hurt him," the Earl said, still not looking at her.

Finally, she nodded. Then after sending one last worried glance Aline's way, she started back towards the ballroom.

At some point, Romanov had placed his hand on her shoulder. She'd not even noticed, in her shock. He tightened his grip a fraction, and when he spoke, she could feel the fury rising up inside of him, his heartbeat once more pulsing at an alarming rate against her back. "It seems you have much to explain, Harker."

The Earl nodded. "But for now, let us depart and show Miss Finch the trouble we face."

"Professor?" she asked, turning her head in his direction, ashamed at how small her voice sounded.

Her heart sank when he met her gaze. He had that soul-dead look again, nothing remaining of the masterful seducer. "I'm sorry, Finch, truly sorry. But you must see for yourself."

MURDER IN WHITECHAPEL! The hunt for the villainous Ripper continues despite the Metropolitan Police's Inspector E. Drexler's recent violent encounter with a suspect in the case last week. The state of the Inspector's health is unknown, but he remains on temporary leave from the Force...

-from *The London Post-Dispatch*, 1888

6

*F*INCH'S expression was ominously blank as she stared at the woman's nude, butchered body lying in the moonlight on the floor of the condemned St. Giles warehouse Aloysius Finch had once owned. The killer's sense of the profane was evolving. He had placed the spectacles on the victim, who was completely unclothed.

The victim also appeared to be unenhanced, which was telling. Either she was younger than she appeared to be, born after the Clean Air Act barely sixteen years ago, which was disturbing enough. Or this woman was of Finch's generation, which meant the killer had gone to a great deal of trouble to find her. The similarities to Finch were even more pronounced, down to eye color, and Sasha knew there could be little more than a handful of unenhanced thirty-year-old women in this country who fit that description.

And the scene was even more gruesome than usual. It was as if the killer wasn't even bothering to reinvent Da Vinci's Heart anymore. There were no indications of experimentation or finesse. The incisions on the chest cavity were crude, and the heart looked as if it had been literally ripped out. Nor had the woman been bludgeoned. Instead, there were suspicious marks on her throat he'd never seen before, two deep gashes over her jugular.

There should have been a lot more blood at the scene with that neck wound, unless the body had been moved to its present location. But something about the violence of the scene and the position of this woman's limbs told Sasha the killer had done the deed here.

Another departure from the pattern.

If not for one of his father's poems scrawled in atrocious Cyrillic script next to her head, he'd almost believe an entirely different killer had done this.

And had he known what they'd find here, he would have rethought Finch's presence. This was leagues worse than what he'd seen in Genoa. At the very least, the officers could have covered up the woman's nudity. He knew it broke Drexler's stringent protocol, but letting Finch bear witness to that woman's unclothed, butchered corpse just seemed wrong.

It could have been her.

During the ride across the city in his steam car, Fyodor at the wheel, Aline had remained silent, studying him with unnerving intensity. As if she'd never seen him before. He'd not met her glance once, and he'd wondered if he'd ever be able to again. He'd nearly seduced her twice in the past week, and now he was taking her to view a corpse. It should have never come to this.

He'd wanted to keep the truth from her forever. But even Rowan had argued that was impossible now. Only ocular evidence of the truth would convince her – *frighten* her – enough to cooperate. Maybe Rowan was right, but the last time he'd regretted something this much, he'd still been the Tsarevich of Russia.

And when she'd begun to recognize her surroundings and had seen the crowd gathered outside her uncle's former residence, she'd grown increasingly uneasy, as if she'd known something more dreadful than usual was awaiting her inside.

"But this was my uncle's warehouse. I lived here," she'd murmured.

He'd finally looked at her. Or at her shoulder. "I know."

But now … *now*, inside the warehouse, there was no expression on her face, and he felt as if he might do something desperate, like scream. Or cry.

For a few moments, the warehouse was silent, almost frozen in time, as Finch stared at the corpse.

Then she raised her head, looked right at him, and said, "She looks like me."

Of course his Finch would cut straight to the heart of the matter. And though her expression was blank, her eyes were filled with such horror, and such accusation, he nearly *did* cry. But he strangled his emotions into submission and nodded. As if his legs were no longer connected to his body, he started in her direction, to somehow comfort her, as out of practice as he was at such things.

And he *wanted* to be near her, God help him – craved it. He knew exactly how her skin would feel now, feather soft, supple. He knew exactly how her hair would smell, of lemon groves and oceans of mint.

He clenched his hands at his sides, and made himself stop, shaken by this inconvenient desire for his secretary. Ever since he had kissed her, he could not look at her without remembering every detail of the way she'd felt, the way she'd smelled and tasted.

It was getting out of hand.

"Excuse me," she said dully. "I think I'm going to be sick. I'll be outside."

He moved to follow her once more, but she sent him such a dark look he stopped cold. She did not want his comfort, that much was obvious.

"Stay with Fyodor and Matthews," he told her. "Don't leave their side."

She nodded tersely and walked back towards the entrance. He watched her until he was certain Fyodor was with her. When he turned around, Drexler was studying him with a rare sympathy. As if he understood him. And maybe he did, a little. Sasha suspected Elijah had nearly as many demons as he himself, having been born in a gutter – quite literally – and raised in London's worst slums. Something drove the man to pursue the most unholy of England's criminals with a nearly reckless single-mindedness.

Something also drove the man to inject opiates into his veins on a regular basis, a fact that no one else seemed to have realized. But Sasha had trained as a doctor in his last life. He knew an addict when he saw one.

Yet Elijah had never confided in Sasha, and Sasha had certainly never confided his own dark history. Sometimes he wanted to, wondered what it would be like to have a true confidante.

But how could he ever burden another with his past? A past soaked in blood and violence and hate that no one in this warehouse, including Drexler, could ever conceive of? How could anyone truly know him without knowing the unspeakable?

And that *Finch* was here now, in the presence of even this small part of his legacy, made him insane. He turned to Rowan. "Have your associates been informed?"

Rowan shook his head. "Not yet. I'm thinking that perhaps we should keep this between ourselves for now."

Sasha gave Drexler a pointed look. The Inspector shrugged. "None but Matthews and I have seen the victim. The initial witness is in our custody and too scared to speak."

"The crowd outside?"

"Know little of the facts. There will be a thousand stories on the streets by daybreak."

"The Council will have to be told. Eventually," Rowan continued. "But if one of our kind is in league with this madman, keeping our hand close for the moment might be prudent."

"So you finally believe me," Sasha said.

"I have always believed you, Sasha," Rowan growled. "But I still think you know this madman. You just don't remember him."

Sasha shook his head. "It isn't possible."

Rowan sighed. "I know you don't like to speak of your

past, but the few times you have, you said there were holes in your memory."

"I remember too much," he muttered.

Rowan shook his head. "When you were reborn, you said you were out of your head for months – years. I think you need to remember that time. I believe our killer was there, with you. How else would he know everything? He knows you were struck in the head, then cut open while you were still alive. He reenacts exactly what happened to you on the victims…"

"Stop," Sasha demanded, unable to bear another word. He crossed his arms over his chest and glared at his friend. "Now tell me what is *truly* going on, Rowan. Why you are suddenly so ready to consider my theories. *And* to conceal information from the Council." He paused and glanced pointedly at the Inspector. "Moreover, why do you speak of the Council at all in front of this human? We've never revealed ourselves to the Inspector."

The Earl shook his head. "Elijah will have to explain this tangle. I confess I still don't quite understand what's going on. But not here."

Sasha decided to have both Fyodor and Matthews escort Finch back to Mayfair in the meantime, unwilling to take risks with her safety, or to make her stay a moment longer than she had to. After he'd seen to this task, he let himself be led into the bowels of the warehouse by Elijah and Rowan, away from prying eyes.

"Prepare yourself," Rowan warned as he set down the steam torch he'd brought along for illumination on an old table.

Sasha just shrugged at Rowan's dramatics. He was fairly certain nothing could shock him after all the things he'd witnessed in his long life.

Sasha was wrong. He was very shocked indeed when Inspector Drexler tore off his Iron Necklace, revealing a neck that appeared as if it had never been touched by a Welder's blade. It looked just like Sasha's own neck, underneath the fake Necklace he wore to blend in. Drexler then set aside the long cane he was never without and straightened to his full, towering height, his limp miraculously disappearing.

Sasha was even more shocked when Drexler reached up and detached his brass-Welded eye carapace.

"The old Earl gave Elijah the Welding eye when Elijah was just a boy. His real one had been damaged beyond repair. I saw for myself," Rowan said quietly. "But now…" He trailed off, speechless.

Sasha took up the steam torch and approached Drexler for a closer look. Drexler didn't look pleased, but he stoically endured the inspection. Sasha reared back in shock at what he discovered. Like the Necklace, the carapace had been nothing but a facade, for underneath was a very healthy human eye. The only indication that the eye was not quite right was its unusual color. Only the Elders and Sasha had eyes the color of yellow amber, but never just the one.

"I've never seen the like," Sasha murmured. "Your eye … *grew* back?" It sounded ludicrous to say aloud.

Drexler nodded uneasily.

"Even I cannot regenerate," Sasha murmured. "What are you?"

Drexler's expression grew grim. "I'm a vampire," he said bluntly.

Well, *that* was unexpected. Sasha laughed. He couldn't help himself. "There's no such thing," he scoffed. Vampires were the stuff of sensational novels of spurious quality…and Finch's penny dreadful.

"There's no such thing as four hundred year old Elders with Da Vinci Hearts either," Drexler shot back. "Or at least that was what I always thought until I was changed."

"How long have you known about us?" Sasha demanded.

"I've known about the Earl since I was changed eight years ago. Before you came to London. But I knew you were one of them the minute I saw your eyes," he said bitterly.

"I'm not one of them, not exactly," Sasha protested. *They* had never let him call himself an Elder – not that he'd ever wanted to. "I'm only three hundred forty two, by the way. And

I still say there are no such things as vampires. What absolute rot."

With that, Drexler's canine teeth descended into sharp points that gleamed in the lantern glow, and the whites of his eyes flooded with amber fire. He picked up Sasha with one arm, tossing him into a wall ten feet away, so quickly Sasha hadn't time for a single blink. The wall caved inward with the force of his impact.

Shaken, he remained where he'd fallen, leaning against the crumbled wall for support and brushing mortar out of his hair.

"He's nearly as strong as we are, Sasha," Rowan said darkly. "Nearly as fast."

Drexler sneered, and with those fangs still extended, it was a chilling sight indeed. "Stronger, faster, after a feeding," he muttered.

Sasha did *not* want to test either of their claims. He climbed to his feet, but kept his distance from the Inspector. "What the *fuck*, Elijah?"

"Could you put those away, old boy?" Rowan said, eyeing the fangs and glowing eyes uneasily.

"Sorry," Drexler said through clenched...*fangs*. "They'll go away in a moment. I'm just a bit on edge."

"*You're* on edge?" Sasha cried.

"Well, yes. I have just revealed what I am to not one but two Elders tonight. Forgive me for being concerned for my life."

"I am *not* an Elder," Sasha insisted. Though he didn't know why he bothered. "And why would you be concerned? The last time I checked Council law, there was nothing about killing vampires in them," he said wryly.

"Not in so many words," Rowan said. "But what he is ... it's forbidden."

"If I have to say I don't understand one more time tonight, I *will* rip someone's head off," Sasha cried.

"You have always wanted nothing to do with Bonding, so you would not be very familiar with all of its rules," Rowan began.

"I *have* read the rules," he said. "A long time ago," he added a bit grudgingly.

Rowan arched a skeptical brow. "Foremost among these rules – rules that, if broken, are punishable by death, if you'll recall – is that no Bonded may share his blood with a mortal. It is an inviolable rule, one that I thought no one had ever broken. Until tonight. Now I am questioning everything."

"You mean to say, Bonded blood turns people into vampires who can regenerate eyeballs?" Sasha said disbelievingly. "But it makes no sense. Bonded companions have none of our powers, other than longevity and accelerated healing. Even those are limited."

"There must be some property in Bonded blood that is corrupted when passed onto others," Rowan said.

"I feel as if I've fallen into Finch's penny-dreadful," he said, shaking his head in dismay.

"The feeling is mutual. And you've not even heard the whole story," Rowan said. He sighed and leaned against the table. "I know you never approved when I Bonded Christiana. But she was my descendant, and she was dying."

"She was a child," Sasha murmured.

"She was my blood, Sasha!" Rowan cried. "You can never understand, with the family you had. But I couldn't watch her die."

Sasha didn't know why Rowan's words hurt so much, but they did. He *could* understand. Had his child lived, perhaps he too would have been tempted to do what Rowan had done, if it had come to that. But he'd never know. He'd been forced to watch the child and Yelena die, helpless to change their fates.

"Maybe you *were* right to disapprove," Rowan continued in a raw tone. "She has put me in an untenable situation."

Sasha recalled that strange scene in the garden earlier, and the pieces of the puzzle started to come together. He glanced at Drexler, whose fangs had receded. Thankfully. "She did this to you."

Drexler's expression grew bleak. "Eight years ago, during the Ripper case. The little fool followed me into Whitechapel the night the Ripper tore me open. Drank me dry and left me for dead."

"Wait. The Ripper was a vampire too?" Sasha choked out, still incredulous. He couldn't believe he was having such a ridiculous conversation.

"There are many of us out there," Drexler said grimly. "Or so I have discovered. Lady Christiana found me, and she fed me her blood. She didn't know what it would do. She'd never been told that. She just panicked and tried anything to save me." He turned to Rowan with an anguished expression. "She couldn't watch me die, just as you couldn't watch her die. You cannot hold her responsible, no matter how misguided she was."

"What she did is a killing offense. I cannot rewrite Council laws," Rowan said grimly.

"No wonder you don't want to involve the Council," Sasha said. "You're protecting Christiana."

"For now. For as long as I can. But from what the Inspector has told me, it seems there are many of his kind walking around out there. And they can only be made by the Bonded. I don't think we can trust anyone at this point, Sasha. Something strange is happening."

"Obviously." He turned to Drexler. "So you are a vampire. Or a being who perhaps inspired the creation of that fictional creature. Do you ... dear *God*, I can't believe I'm asking this ... do you drink blood?"

"I crave it," Drexler said baldly. "I've found a way to control the ... frenzy to a degree. But when I must feed, I only feed from criminals."

A *frenzy*. That sounded lovely, just lovely. "How noble of you. And the morphine? Does it serve some purpose?"

Drexler's eyes widened in surprise. "How do you know about that?"

"I know an addict when I see one."

Drexler reluctantly took off his jacket and rolled up one of his shirtsleeves, holding his arm under the glow of the steam torch. It was riddled with what looked like hundreds of raw, blistering track marks where he had injected the opiate with a needle. The evidence of Drexler's addiction was hard to stomach – but no harder to stomach than his vampirism, Sasha supposed.

"Dear God!" Rowan said, aghast, obviously seeing this for the first time. "Elijah, what is this?"

Sasha ignored Rowan's outburst, his scientific curiosity piqued. "Why do these wounds not heal like your neck, or your eye?"

"I don't know exactly," Drexler said. "But the morphine suppresses the thirst."

"And is slowly killing you," Sasha surmised.

Drexler rolled his sleeve back down and shrugged back into his jacket. "Perhaps. But if you knew how it feels when the frenzy sets in, you'd be glad of the needle in your arm too."

Sasha gestured at the scar on Drexler's face. "And why has that not healed?"

Drexler turned it away from the light and Sasha's prying eyes. "I don't know that either," he said in a tone that left no room for further discussion. The Inspector apparently had a few secrets he was stubbornly clinging to. Sasha let it pass, for now.

"Why reveal yourself tonight, Elijah? What does this have to do with the madman we seek?" he asked.

"Because I think your madman might be the vampire I've been hunting for months," Drexler said. "This is not the first body I've seen like this. It's the twelfth."

Sasha sucked in a breath, stunned. "Why didn't you say something earlier?"

"Because I didn't know you were after the same killer. And I never tell you about my cases when a vampire is involved."

"You have *multiple* cases involving vampires?" Rowan cried. "How could you keep these secrets from us?"

Drexler rolled his eyes. "*Please.* If your lot weren't so bloody tight-lipped, I wouldn't be what I am now, would I? And you didn't tell me shite about this madman you were hunting, other than he was after Miss Finch and he butchered people. In my line of work, I run into a lot of butchers. How was I to know there was a connection?"

"So all the other twelve victims had their hearts removed?" Sasha demanded.

"More like ripped out. But they were definitely killed by a vampire, like the victim tonight. The wounds on the neck are unmistakable, and the lack of blood. Someone drank that woman to the bone."

"But this is the first victim *we've* seen with wounds on the neck," Sasha murmured, thrown.

"Maybe we just didn't notice them before," Rowan said.

"Maybe," Sasha replied doubtfully. "Was there anything different about this victim and the other twelve you've seen?"

"The strange writing with the blood was new. And I don't think she was raped like the others."

Aline. "The other twelve were raped? All women?" Sasha demanded.

Drexler nodded. "Prostitutes, most of them. Not like the one tonight."

"Another difference. But you seem certain this is the killer we are looking for."

Elijah nodded grimly and extracted an envelope from his jacket. He handed it to Sasha. "I've no doubt. I received this at the Yard earlier tonight by Steam Post."

Sasha scanned the note, his unease deepening.

Your Russian associate might be interested in the little bird waiting for him on Greymarket Street. Give him and his charming secretary my regards. I continue to enjoy our games, Inspector. OSIRIS.

"Osiris?" Sasha murmured. The God of the Egyptian Underworld.

"That is what he calls himself."

This just kept getting more and more absurd. "How melodramatic of him," Sasha murmured.

"I have been reading about this Osiris bloke," Drexler said. "In ancient Egypt, the heart was removed at death and mummified. They believed the heart would be weighed by the gods, to determine whether its owner was worthy to join Osiris in eternal life."

Sasha handed the note back and ran a hand through his hair, sighing wearily. "It always comes back to the heart. And the blood. Elijah, just how many of your kind live in London?"

Elijah shrugged. "Near a hundred, perhaps. There are more now than ever before. Someone is turning people faster than I can kill them. *Someone* is planning something big in St. Giles, and it reaches far beyond this case."

And Sasha wouldn't doubt it for a minute if Elijah claimed an Elder was involved, not just rogue Bonded. After the revelations of this evening, he was more convinced than ever that the perfect brotherhood of Da Vinci's "chosen ones" wasn't perfect and never had been.

As an old friend of his had pointed out quite succinctly, absolute power could corrupt even the best natures. And if there was one thing the Elders had, it was power. Whether they were ever in possession of the best natures was doubtful.

And he highly doubted that he and Rowan were the first of their kind to discover what happened when the Bonded opened their veins to humans. There wouldn't be a rule against it if someone hadn't known exactly what it did this entire time.

"Someone is breaking those precious rules of yours, Rowan," he said.

"I am wondering if anyone ever followed the rules in the first place," Rowan muttered with quiet devastation. Sasha didn't envy his friend and the trouble he'd face with Lady Christiana if the Council discovered what she had done to Drexler.

"There is one more thing you need to know about my kind, Professor," Drexler said. "We can scent the quality of a person's blood from across a room, and the less enhanced our victims, the better the blood – and the harder it is to restrain our compulsion to drink. But when I met Miss Finch for the first time, I had to knock myself out with morphine afterwards to stop myself from hunting her and draining her dry. The scent of her blood is … exquisite." Drexler shook his head.

"If you ever harm her, I will gut you," Sasha growled.

Drexler looked affronted. "I would never hurt her. But she is in more danger than you could ever imagine. Why do you think I make my best lieutenant guard her? It is certainly *not* because she likes to bet on the Races. If any of my kind were to scent her ... well, let's just say I am one of the few vampires out there who knows the definition of self-control."

*A*LINE raised no protest when Fyodor and Matthews delivered her to Sasha's townhouse instead of her flat. She raised no protest when Madame Kristeva fussed over her, insisting on bringing her tea in Sasha's private study. She raised no protest even when the hellhounds licked her face in greeting, then followed her around the house like two giant shadows, as if sensing her disquiet.

For once in their misbegotten acquaintance, she was glad for their company. They would never hurt her, but they *could* defend her, if the need arose. And the need might indeed arise, since apparently she was being stalked by a killer with a grudge against her ex-employer.

She waited until Madame Kristeva had departed after bringing her tea and Matthews and Fyodor took up posts outside the study, leaving her alone with the hellhounds. Then she went over to Sasha's desk and began riffling through the drawers for the key to the door in the corner of the room.

The room behind the door was the only one the Professor made off-limits to everyone on his staff.

She'd never been brave enough – or callous enough – to break his rule, as she had a feeling what was on the other side was intensely private.

Unlike the Professor, *she* was able to restrain herself from meddling in other people's business.

But after the night's events, she was through treading softly where the Professor was concerned. His secrets were threatening her life, and she was convinced he would continue to keep them, even at her expense.

Why, he'd rather *seduce* her than tell her the truth. That she'd been fool enough to believe, for even one moment, that his attentions in the Earl's garden were sincere, was humiliating. He'd made her think he wanted her, and all to keep her under his thumb. Her blood boiled just thinking about it, and not in the wonderfully seductive way it had when she'd been lost – like a ninny – in his embrace.

Damn him.

A woman's *heart* had been ripped out, and apparently this wasn't the first time. He couldn't have explained all of this to her? Explained why he'd set Mr. Matthews on her heels? Explained why he didn't want her to leave his employ instead of playing these stupid games with her? What secret was important enough he'd rather risk her life than reveal it? She was merely his secretary, but surely he valued her more than that.

Perhaps not, she thought to herself. *Perhaps I don't know this man at all.*

One of the drawers was stuck. She pulled on it with no success, until she realized the secret panel at the bottom was jammed in one corner. She found a penknife and began to pry it open. The penknife slipped, slicing one of her fingers open.

"Damn!" she muttered, sucking on the wound. She took a handkerchief from her pocket – one of the only redeeming features of her drab blue evening gown – and wrapped it around her finger tightly. The cut would bleed all night because of her blood disorder, but she had no patience for dealing with it at the moment. She turned back to the drawer, and after a few more frustrated attempts, pried the false bottom open.

Turning up the gas lamp on the desktop, she peered into the drawer. She easily located the key and put it in her pocket, then pulled out a stack of old letters.

The one on top was the most recent, and, with a little jolt, she saw it was from her. It was the one she'd written when she'd been sick with her cold and the Professor had hounded her to return to work. She smoothed the letter out and reviewed her words with a certain amount of pride. She'd certainly held nothing back. Though she was puzzled why he would have kept it.

She sifted through the other letters, her confusion growing. Some letters were addressed to him, from various friends and in various languages. She saw one from Mr. Edison, another from the composer Verdi, who the Professor admired. She snorted inwardly. *Of course* he would correspond with the most famous men alive and keep their letters as his trophies.

But then she caught her breath when she saw two from her uncle. One was dated around the time of his death, but another was dated much earlier, before Aline's birth, and addressed to a man she'd never heard of, not the Professor. Shaken from the revelation that Sasha had known her uncle all along and never told her, she tucked both letters into her pocket to read at a later time, and returned to her search. She felt no compunction at all with her small act of thievery. What other secrets was he keeping?

All of the remaining correspondence was of varying antiquity, and always addressed to different men. Some letters were so old the paper was yellow and brittle to the touch, the ink barely legible.

The oldest letters, towards the bottom, were still written on animal skin, and carefully wrapped in oilcloth. These were the type of old documents historians would kill for. Why the Professor would collect such a motley assortment of letters addressed to dead men was beyond her ken, since he'd taken pains to blot out his own past.

Unable to restrain her curiosity, she carefully unfolded the oilcloth covering the bottom-most document, revealing a single page of what looked like medieval Cyrillic. The page looked as if it had been well-used, folded and refolded hundreds of times. The vellum was hardly in pristine condition. The letter's recipient must have read its contents again and again, and when she translated them – very roughly, because, despite the Professor's prodding, she'd never taken to Russian, much less *medieval* Russian – she understood why.

Dearest Husband, it read, *I have prayed to Our Father, and He has at last granted our dearest wish. In my heart I know we shall have a son before the summer thaw. I pray daily that you do your duty as our great Tsar's beloved son. I beseech you temper your tongue, and tempt not his anger, so that you may come back to me and our child. Your obedient wife, Yelena.*

Now Aline started to feel some compunction. Reading this intimate exchange felt like she was trespassing where she shouldn't, even though both writer and recipient were long dead. She wondered if this could be written by one of Sasha's ancestors. It was the only thing that made sense, considering its origin and age. Whatever the case, the letter had been precious to someone, and perhaps even the Professor found worth in that. But it offered little insight into Sasha's secrets.

She quickly rewrapped the page and replaced all of the letters in the secret drawer. Then she took up the gas lamp and went to the locked door. She opened it with the key and stepped inside, the lamp casting the room in ominous layers of shadows.

She half expected a monster to jump out and devour her, but there was nothing in this room but old, dusty antiques. Ancient books, old atlases, a hundred forgotten objects piled on shelves, and unframed paintings stacked against the walls – the detritus of many past lives.

She was drawn to the painting hanging on the far wall, the only painting the Professor had bothered to display in the whole room. It was difficult to make out its subject in the glow of the gas lamp, so she wandered closer.

After what she'd witnessed tonight at the warehouse, she'd thought she'd grown numb, but the painting disturbed her profoundly the more she studied it. It depicted the aftermath of a violent struggle in some distant, exotic past, the murder weapon, a long bloody scepter, thrown into the foreground atop a sea of opulent Eastern rugs. A young man in golden robes lay dying, blood running down his face from the blow to his head, clutched in the arms of an older man with a horror-struck expression and wild eyes.

A shiver coursed down her spine. Even the Professor's art was a crime scene.

"It is called *Ivan the Terrible and His Son*," a deep, familiar voice said behind her. Her heart in her throat, she spun to face the Professor.

She'd not heard him come in at all, but then again, he *was* a magician. He switched on an overhead electrical light she'd not noticed, and bright light flooded the room. But dark shadows remained in the hollows beneath his eyes, as if he were desperately, bone-achingly weary. He looked like a fallen angel, but Aline fought down any lingering vestiges of empathy. She'd never fall for his tricks again. All she wanted from him were answers.

She glared at the two uncharacteristically docile hellhounds hovering at his side. A fat lot of good they'd been at guarding her.

"November 16th, 1581." There was an atypical wariness in Romanov's voice.

"What?" she asked, not following his words. She'd expected him to demand why she was in his secret room, but he was acting as if he didn't care she was there. As if he were a bit nervous around her, in fact, when she hadn't thought he possessed a nervous bone in his body.

He gestured towards the painting behind her. "The name of the painting. *Ivan the Terrible and His Son, November 16th, 1581*," he repeated. "I bought it from a Russian artist several years ago. Before I came to England."

Aline bit her tongue to keep herself from interrupting. He was talking about his past for the first time since she'd known him, and though it had little to do with what she truly wished to know, she decided to see where this led. For once in five years, he was not teasing her or ordering her around – or seducing her. Clearly, the events of the evening had taken their toll on him, and he hadn't the fight left for anything but plain speaking. She wasn't about to let this opportunity pass her by.

He approached her tentatively, stopping at her side, searching her face. Then he focused on the painting and began to speak.

"The Tsar had just beaten his son's pregnant wife for

wearing the wrong color dress. She miscarried, and later died. The Tsar's son confronted his father in the throne room, and his father struck him in the head, killing him." He pointed at the scepter in the foreground, an odd, haunted look on his face. "He used the same staff to beat his daughter-in-law."

"What a horrible story. Yet the Tsar is embracing his dying son. He looks so sad."

Something dark passed over the Professor's expression. "Does he? When his son was fifteen, the Tsar took him with his army to the city of Novgorod. He made him watch every day for five weeks while he and his army sacked the city, and tortured and raped ten thousand men, women and children. They even killed the dogs. And in the evening, the Tsar would take his son into the cathedral to pray, because he truly believed he was guided by God." He paused, considering something, his hand going out to pet Ikaterina, as if to comfort her ... or himself. "Maybe he *was* sad when he killed his son, in his own way. He was insane, after all."

Aline didn't know what to make of the Professor's speech, or why he seemed so upset by ancient history. She raised her hand to push up her spectacles, and the handkerchief tied around her cut finger slipped off to the floor. Her wound started to bleed even more, dripping onto her skirts. She was normally inured to her condition, but after the gruesome scene she'd witnessed tonight, seeing her blood staining her gown left her a little light-headed.

When the Professor noticed her problem, all the color in his face drained away too. Before she could prevent it, he'd seized her hand. She hated the way her heart jumped at the contact.

"You are wounded!" he breathed. "What happened?"

"Nothing. I nicked myself earlier."

He pulled a fresh handkerchief from his lapel pocket and pressed it to her finger. "This is more than a nick."

When he would not give her back her hand, she glared at him until at last, with a frown, he released her – reluctantly. She clutched the handkerchief to her wound.

"You mustn't go about in public bleeding everywhere, Finch," he said in a hard, furious voice.

"I didn't plan to, Professor," she retorted. "I cannot control my condition."

He was silent for a long time, as if trying to rein in his fraying temper, fisting his hands so hard she could see the whites of his knuckles, his breath coming in gusts, his eyes closed. She didn't know why her cut should upset him so much.

"You have a blood disorder," he said, as if this were a revelation of biblical proportions. "That is why you remain unenhanced." When at last his eyes opened, he looked at her accusingly. As if she'd done something wrong by being born.

She raised her chin in defiance. "Of course. You would know this if you paid attention to anything I say!" she seethed.

"You said you had an *allergy.*"

She paused, surprised he indeed remembered what she'd told him some five years ago. "Well, yes, I have an allergy. To sharp objects." When her flippancy seemed to enrage him even further, she shrugged. "The doctors could never explain my condition." Reluctantly, she tugged down the edge of her high-collared gown to show him the scars on the right side of her throat. "When the Welders tried to fit me with a Necklace as an infant, I nearly bled to death."

He moved as if to touch her throat, but she released her collar and backed away, out of his reach, sending him a quelling look. He was developing an unsettling habit of touching her at every opportunity. And she was developing an unsettling habit of letting him.

"That is why you're always buttoned up to your neck," he murmured, something softening in his eyes.

She refused to answer, having had enough of this uncomfortable conversation. She was supposed to be interrogating *him*, not the other way around. "Why didn't you tell me sooner?" she demanded.

"What?" he asked vaguely, still staring at her throat, as if he could see through the lace collar.

She put her hands on her hips and drew herself up. "Why didn't you tell me that there was a psychopath killing women who look like me? That *that* was the reason you were having me watched?"

"I didn't want you to know," he bit out. "Ever."

She snorted. "Well, that's just idiotic. Don't you think this is information I need to know, so that I can be prepared in case I encounter this madman?"

"I'd hoped it wouldn't be necessary."

"Do I look like I am made out of porcelain?"

He looked incredulous. "Yes," he growled, gesturing at her bandaged finger.

She paused, nonplussed, and hid her hand behind her back. "Well, I'm not! I may bleed more than usual. And I admit I've a weak stomach, and when I saw the woman tonight I couldn't help my reaction…"

"Don't apologize, *ever*, for your humanity," he said, so savagely that she flinched. "And I know how strong you are – on the inside. You are the most obstinate female I have ever met. But no one should have to witness what you did tonight. Or to know that such evil exists."

Now *she* was the angry one. Of all the patronizing, condescending…"Well, that is very *noble* of you, to want to protect my delicate sensibilities, but I assure you, it is not necessary. In fact, it is dangerous. How could you let me walk around in blithe ignorance?" she cried.

His eyes widened at her anger. "What's the good of your knowing? There is nothing you could do to defend yourself."

She scoffed at this. "I know a thing or two about self-defense," she said.

"You wouldn't stand a chance against this killer, even if you were a man of Fyodor's size," he muttered.

"I still have a right to know. But I suspect there is more to it than that. This isn't some killer who targets random blonde women with spectacles. That … poem … next to that woman was written in Cyrillic. Whoever is doing this is connected to you and all the secrets you keep, isn't he?"

"Yes," he admitted, as if to do so pained him enormously.

"And you didn't wish me to know, because you don't want to share your secrets with me. Isn't that true?"

"Yes!" he bit out. "Damn you."

Oh, it hurt to hear him admit it. "You would rather that I am kept in ignorance about a threat to my life, because you value your secrets more?" she whispered.

"That's not it at all. You don't need to know them. I will protect you, Finch," was all he could say.

And he called *her* obstinate! "Yes, I suspect you will *try*. Well, you have achieved your goal for the evening. You have frightened me into moving into your townhouse for the time being, as I have no wish to be *murdered*. I will gladly remain under your protection, propriety be damned. At least until my wedding."

Her last statement certainly raised his hackles. "You're not going anywhere until we catch this villain. Certainly not Egypt," he practically sneered.

She rolled her eyes. "I hardly think this killer is going to travel all the way to Egypt to kill me. I'll doubtless be safer there than I am here."

"You won't. You aren't safe anywhere," he said, tugging at his hair in exasperation. "This madman has spent … *years* tormenting me, long, long before I came to England. He knows everything about me. I'd thought it was over. It had been so long since this madman had killed I had hoped …" He shrugged. "But then the body in Genoa surfaced. He has never targeted someone I care … *employ*. That part is new."

Something tickled her memory. "Genoa? Is that where you went after you left me in France? How odd."

"Odd?"

"Charlie and I were speculating on where you might have gone in the dirigible. He suggested Genoa. Do you know it is a hub for pirates?"

He gave her an incredulous look. "Really, *milaya*. You're talking about *pirates* right now?"

She scowled at him. "I wish you wouldn't call me that.

135

I'm not your sweet. But why were you gone for so long without a word this past month? You never explained that. Were you following a lead?"

His expression grew stony. "I was in jail."

"What?" she cried. "Why were you in jail?"

"As I've said, the killer has done his best to implicate me. Someone thought *I* committed the murder in Genoa, so I was locked up. Until the next murder in Scotland. As I could not have possibly been two places at once, I was released."

"Scotland!"

"The Outer Hebrides. Not exactly on the map. One of the killer's more obscure references. Which means he'd think nothing of traveling to Egypt. And I *hardly* think your bone-hunter capable of protecting you."

She felt as if she'd been punched in the gut. She sucked in a pained breath. The Professor saw her reaction, and his eyes widened. He stepped closer and stopped just short of touching her on the shoulder.

"What is it? What's wrong?" he demanded.

She met his worried eyes. "I lived in the Outer Hebrides for the first twelve years of my life. My parents took me to live there because it was far enough away from the Fog that I could survive without the Necklace. Where in the Outer Hebrides was the body found?"

"Grimsay."

She could feel the blood draining from her face. "That was where we lived. But *how* could he know that? Who is this … this monster?"

"If I knew the answer to that, I would have torn out this bastard's heart by now," he snapped.

She drew back, alarmed by the black fury in his eyes. She believed he might actually do exactly as he threatened. *Dear God*, she thought to herself. She'd worked for him for five years, but she was more convinced than ever she'd never come close to knowing him. Not even a little.

He seemed to realize he'd frightened her, for his expression fell, and his shoulders slumped, as if he carried the weight of the world on them. Then he retreated from her, as if he regretted ever revealing even this small crumb of his true self to her. She could feel his withdrawal inwards, a veil descending over his unnatural eyes, shutting her out.

Suddenly she too was exhausted, tired of fighting him and his secrets. Perhaps he was right to keep them, if the terrifying rage she'd seen in him tonight was the result of revealing them. She wasn't sure she wanted to know who he truly was.

"There is a darkness inside of you," she said, shaking her head. "I've always known that. And I've always known your secrets must be dangerous. I write fiction, but I am not a moon-eyed idiot. So I forgive you for thinking you are protecting me by keeping your secrets. Even though you should have told me. This man knows everything about me. And though you say you can protect me, I wonder. I wonder if I don't need some protection from *you*."

He clenched his jaw as if he'd received a blow. "Aline…"

"Don't call me that," she snapped. Hearing him say her first name was perhaps more painful than anything else she'd endured this evening. "But what I can't forgive you for is attempting to seduce me instead of telling me the truth. I can't forgive you for allowing me to make such a cake of myself, thinking you actually … desired me. When it was all just a ploy to manipulate me."

He said nothing to deny her accusations or assuage her anguish. He just stared at her in stony silence, expression once again carefully controlled.

She nodded, determined to keep her expression equally controlled, though it was difficult. She'd known hours ago how false his attentions had been, but having him silently acknowledge it was still crushing. It was as if he'd ripped the scab off a barely-healed wound. And she had always been a bleeder. Thank goodness, she thought, that it was only her pride he'd wounded, and not her heart.

She wasn't *that* foolish. She *wasn't*. But it hurt. It hurt more than it should.

"I don't know why I ever thought you could feel …" she

began, unable to stop herself. "Sometimes I don't think you even have a heart."

Something that resembled pain, but couldn't possibly be, flickered over his guarded eyes, but whatever it was, it was quickly suppressed. He was silent for so long, watching her with that blank mask, that she grew restless.

Then he surprised her by letting out a short, mirthless laugh. "You are more right than you know, *milaya*. I lost my heart long ago. It was ripped out the night I watched my father murder my wife and child."

What? "Professor …"

He gave her a terrible, mocking smile. "You wanted to know my secrets. There's one of them. Now if you'll excuse me, I think we've both said quite enough tonight. Please, do not leave this house – not even to visit the garden – without an escort. I should not like it if you, too, were to lose your heart. It would be quite inconvenient. And messy."

And with that he gave her an ironic bow and swept from the room, leaving her more baffled – and troubled – than ever.

Dr. Xavier Augustus was a man with a past. But what that past was, no one had ever been able to discern. He had quite literally fallen upon London one afternoon in a deflating hot air balloon he'd piloted somewhere from the Far East, and set up shop as a detective for hire on Bond Street. He had a Chinese valet, Ping, and two small hairy dogs, Kublai and Genghis, from that same country. All three of them pretended to speak no English.

A student of human nature, Augustus had a knack for solving the crimes that left his colleagues at Scotland Yard baffled. Augustus was the consummate trickster, yet he seemed to understand what motivated the darkest villains, and placed so little value upon his own safety in the pursuit of them that Miss Wren sometimes wondered if he was entirely sane. Clearly, he had a few screws loose upstairs, but then again, so did she, to have remained his employee for so long ...

-from *The Chronicles of Miss Wren and Dr. Augustus*, 1893

ALINE couldn't sleep. The events of the evening kept replaying again and again in her mind, from the sight of that poor dead woman, to all of the dark secrets she had learned about her enigmatic employer. She was scared, of course. A psychopath had made her his target. He even knew she'd lived in Grimsay, and she couldn't recall telling anyone this bit of information, aside from Charlie. Even Romanov hadn't known this about her, and she was quickly coming to realize he knew everything.

Whoever this killer was, he was quite dedicated and formidable. Even Inspector Drexler, who dealt with murder intimately on a daily basis, seemed to be scared of this madman. That was *not* reassuring.

The only thing she could be certain of was the fact her life was never going to be the same. Even if the killer were found tomorrow, Aline could not erase the events of the past twelve hours, or their implications.

She knew horrible things happened all of the time, courtesy of the losses she'd suffered in her own life and her career as secretary to a criminologist. Nevertheless she was insulated from much of the world's evil as a gently-bred Englishwoman. Her uncle had seen to that, by shipping her off to boarding school and shielding her as much as possible from the work he did in St. Giles.

And she'd learned the autonomy she'd thought she'd enjoyed these past five years was an illusion. She was not ungrateful for the protection Matthews and others had provided for her when she explored the city, heavy-handed though it turned out to be. But it was hard to accept that she needed it. She knew bad things happened, even documented them for the Professor, but they didn't happen to her.

Nor could she erase the revelations Romanov had made about his past. She'd known very little about his life before he moved to London, only that he'd left Russia long ago and settled in Vienna, where he'd done all of his schooling. Considering his career, the fact that he'd been hounded for years by a psychotic killer should have been mentioned.

And he'd been married, even had a child, who'd been murdered by his father. His *father*. This was the hardest revelation to take in.

The more she thought about it, nothing about the Professor's life added up. When had all of these events taken place? He had a bit of silver in his hair, but he looked younger than she did. He must have married quite young, before he'd left Russia.

Married, had a child, and lost them both, all before moving to Vienna. And he'd been publishing articles since the early 80's. Sixteen years ago. She knew this because she catalogued his work for him. She'd thought nothing of those dates before, but now...

He must have been an infant when he graduated university.

Either that or he was aging extremely well. The Iron Necklace added a few years at most to a lifespan, not decades. No Welding technology was *that* good. Only the unfortunate, hacked up Abominable Soldiers like Fyodor had such mysterious longevity, and Romanov was definitely not an Abominable Soldier.

Aline sat up in her bed, abandoning any hope of sleep. Romanov was a liar, that much she knew was true. But just how much of a liar was he? Perhaps he wasn't even Romanov at all, merely some sort of clever imposter who'd assumed the identity of a man who should, according to the math, be nearing fifty, at the very least.

A terrible, gnawing apprehension started to grow in her gut. Worse than her fear of the psychopath. Whose roof was she under? She had a feeling that when she'd told the Professor she needed protection from him, she'd been more right that even she had realized.

She turned up a gas lamp and crossed over to where she'd draped her soiled gown across a chair.

She'd nearly forgotten about the two letters she'd stolen in the rest of the evening's drama, but she'd not wait until dawn to get to the bottom of one of Romanov's lies. He'd never given the slightest indication he'd known her uncle, a lie by omission if ever there was one. But why? *Why* had he lied about something so trivial?

Sitting down beside the gas lamp, she decided to start with the most recent letter from her uncle, the one addressed to Romanov himself, just a few short weeks before her uncle's death.

She recalled that time too vividly. She'd handled most of his correspondence at the end, but she'd not handled this one. She would have remembered. She wondered how her uncle had hid this from her – and *why*.

With trembling fingers, she unfolded the letter, the sinking feeling in her gut growing with every word she read.

My friend, it read in the familiar shaky scrawl of her uncle's final days, *It has been too long since we have corresponded. I truly meant* to respond to your last, most interesting note to me about the methods of sanitation in the surgery you observed in Germany.

The Teutons always seem to be one step ahead of us in such matters, a state of affairs I can hardly credit, having once had a Bavarian roommate of monstrous proportions at Eton who evinced great glee in throwing me in the privy at every opportunity.

Had I been in better health, I would have played the Happy Host to an old friend when you informed me of your move to London these many months past. I have been following your newest Incarnation as one of these new-fangled criminologists with great interest.

Unfortunately, I have been struck low, and there I fear I shall remain. I have always wanted to show you the fruits of your investment. Nothing can atone for the part I played in Sevastopol, however I take some small consolation in the services I have provided for the poor of London. But alas, the Black Lung that has been my just burden since the Crimea has at last scored its final victory. I will not make it through the summer.

Your friendship has been a precious, undeserved blessing. How maudlin my last sentence sounds, and how insincere you will think it when I beg a final favor. It seems I mean to make a habit of sending strays your way. I leave a niece behind, and I fear for her future, as I've nothing to leave her but a warehouse full of metal parts. Only through your generous support have I been able to provide for her care thus far. She expects no inheritance, and has every intention of earning her living, as she is a proud little bluestocking.

However, she is the last of my family, and I would not be able to leave this world easily without seeing to her future. I would not be so worried, but I hear horrible rumors on the streets these days, as those of her kind are increasingly targets of evil. Did I mention she is Unenhanced?

She knows nothing of our association, and I would rather she were not introduced to those heavy burdens we both bear. However, there is no one else on this earth I could trust to ensure her enduring welfare.

She is currently seeking employment as a secretary in the city, and should you have need of one, I have provided direction to her agency below. Please write me a discreet reply to my proposal, and set this old man's heart at ease. I remain

Yrs.,

A. Finch

Aline wiped the tears from her eyes, shaken on so many different levels. She'd loved her dear, eccentric old uncle, and so reading his words was hard. Every word was just so ... *him*.

And yet not.

She was beginning to think she'd not known her uncle any better than she did Romanov. He'd never mentioned being in the Crimea to her, nor had he ever evinced the slightest concern for her future welfare. She'd thought him too hare-brained for such mundane considerations. But apparently he had been more perceptive than she'd realized.

And if she understood correctly, Romanov had been her uncle's mysterious "patron". Her uncle had mentioned him once or twice when Aline inquired how he was able to remain solvent providing his services as a Welder for free to St. Giles' most indigent. Aline had not pressed the matter.

Now she wished she had. Her uncle's words suggested that the Professor had funded her education and provided for the food in her belly since she was twelve years old. And hiring her as his secretary had not been a chance occurrence. He'd done it as a favor to a dying friend.

But how was it possible? It wasn't, unless the Professor had begun funding her uncle's charity work when he was a teenager.

Aline's heart pounded in her chest as if she'd run a mile, sweat misting her brow and palms. *Newest Incarnation*, her uncle had said.

Something was terribly, fantastically wrong here, and she dreaded what she would read in the second, earlier letter. She wiped her palms on her petticoats and took a deep breath before she took up the older letter.

She felt the same dread she'd felt when the doctors had emerged from her father's Glasgow hospital room, shaking their heads, their shirtsleeves stained with blood. She'd lost both her parents that same day, when the airship from the Islands to the Mainland had crashed. She'd thought herself incapable of ever feeling that level of dread again, because she'd never had anything as precious to lose.

But she was wrong. She was losing her grasp on reality, and it was harrowing.

She fumbled with the letter, but she finally managed to smooth it open across the desk. She recognized her uncle's handwriting as it had been before his final illness, but the letter was in French, a language she hadn't even known he spoke.

Yet another secret.

The letter was dated September, 1855, a good five years before her birth, towards the end of the War, and addressed to Dr. Alexandre Romaine of the French Imperial Forces.

Dear Sir, her uncle had written, *We are strangers, with a mutual British acquaintance, and it is through him I was discreetly provided your direction. Have no fear I mean to expose those secrets you and your associates keep. I have no wish to cause another soul in this world harm, though you may have little cause to believe me when I tell you who I am and what I have done. However, owing to your interest in the matter, I am sure you already know.*

I am Lt. Col. Alyosius Finch, a Specialist under His Grace, the Duke of Brightlingsea, and an architect of the Final Solution of Sevastopol. I make no excuses for what at the time we felt was a Necessary Evil. I still cannot entirely regret it.

However, I will not condone the present policies of the Allied Forces following the resignation of His Grace. You have professed a similar, public opinion, which has earned you such infamy among your compatriots. I am counting upon that infamy, however, to rescue me from my current predicament.

I have come into possession of a certain casualty of war that our superiors have ordered terminated.

However much we have been assured of their inhumanity, I have seen the lie of this with my own eyes. These Russian Abominables have suffered enough at the hands of their own masters, who fashioned them into these wretched creatures of war. This particular model has lost his ability to speak, and communication remains severely limited. As you are originally from that region of the world, or so legend has it, I believe you would have better luck assisting him. I fear discovery, and have not your resources to remove him to a safer location. I await your response,

A. Finch

Aline didn't know how long she sat there, staring blankly at the letter, her mind reeling with its implications. She didn't even know where to begin. Her whole conception of British history had been undermined in a few paragraphs.

What had truly happened during the War? At Sevastopol? She was beginning to think it was not what she'd been taught in school, which painted the British Army and its allies as noble and just victors.

These considerations paled at the moment to the fact that her uncle had been an officer under Brightlingsea himself, and she had never known.

But this was the least of the letter's blows. She was not an idiot. All the clues were there. But the clues added up to an impossible answer. Alexandre Romaine was merely a poor Gallic translation of the Professor's name; her uncle seemed to be referring to Fyodor in the letter; and "legend had it" this Alexandre Romaine was from Russia.

Legend? She thought of that secret drawer downstairs, full of letters to men she'd never heard of, to men who should be long dead. That earliest, precious page had been dated 1581. The same year that horrible painting in the secret room had depicted.

She shuddered. What she was beginning to suspect was too fantastic to entertain.

This is not your penny-dreadful, she told herself. *Whatever you're thinking is just not possible in the real world.*

There was one way to know for sure if the man her uncle had written to in 1855 was the same one he'd written to in 1891. But she had to return to her flat to look through Alyosius' old things for the answer.

She rose and went to the window. It would be dawn soon, hardly the prime time for psychopaths to strike. Surely it would be safe, if she went with Fyodor. The Professor *had* said she could leave the house if she had an escort.

Though why she was paying heed to anything that man said after all she was beginning to suspect, she had no clue.

She pulled her blood-stained, wrinkled gown back on and

struggled to steady her shaking fingers long enough to do up the buttons. Then she repocketed the letters and went in search of Fyodor.

She didn't have far to look. He was standing guard right outside her room with the hellhounds, wide-awake and looking grim as always. Aline studied him with new eyes after what she'd read in the letter. She'd never considered who he'd been before the war, or how he'd ended up an Abominable Soldier.

Clearly, it had *not* been by choice. And according to her uncle, if the British Army had had its way, all of his kind would have been summarily killed.

When she just continued to stare at him, the human side of his face gave her a questioning look. "You knew my uncle," she stated. Because she knew in her heart that much of the letter was true at least.

Fyodor's brow rose, his mouth took on a grim cast. It was response enough, in Aline's opinion. Her heart sank a little more.

"Is the Professor out with the police?"

Fyodor nodded.

She breathed with relief. The last thing she needed was to face Romanov at the moment. "I need to go to my flat for some of my things."

He shook his head and made a few hand gestures she was able to interpret.

He'd send someone for her things, but she wasn't about to trust anyone at the moment.

"I need to go myself," she insisted. "I need some particular feminine items. For a particularly feminine complaint."

As she'd hoped, the word *feminine* had overwhelmed Fyodor. His human side went scarlet, and he looked as if he'd rather be back in the Crimea than listen to her.

"And the Professor said I could leave the house, if I had an escort, did he not? I'm not a prisoner, am I?" she demanded.

Fyodor gave her an unhappy frown, took out and tapped his wireless.

She shrugged and swept past him towards the stairs. "Fine.

Inform him if you must. But let's be on our way."

When he continued to hesitate, she put her hands on her hips and glared at him. "It's dawn, for heaven's sakes. Nothing's going to happen at this hour. And besides, if *you* can't protect me from this psychopath, then it doesn't matter where we are, does it?"

He sighed and followed her.

In the end, with Matthews also off hunting for the killer with the police, Fyodor had her ride in the steam carriage with the dubious protection of the hellhounds, who did more drooling on her already ruined skirts than any actual guarding. She would *not* be wearing this gown again, not that it was much of a loss. The Professor had certainly made his opinion of her gown clear last night in the garden.

Not. A. Single. Stitch.

Had it only been last night he'd whispered that in her ear? It seemed several lifetimes ago, so much had happened since then.

Any fears she had of being attacked in broad daylight faded completely by the time they reached her boarding house. Her landlady, Mrs. Phillips, greeted her at the door with her usual warm smile. When she caught sight of Fyodor, the color left her face, however, and her smile wavered. But she had become accustomed to Aline's strange entourage, so she let him inside only a little reluctantly. The hellhounds were a new addition, and it took a stern look from Fyodor's fierce visage to convince Mrs. Phillips to let them pass.

Fyodor checked her room briefly, and then took up his post outside the door. He'd agreed to give her privacy, if the hellhounds accompanied her inside. They did so, wandering around her flat, sniffing everything in sight. When Ilya lifted his leg near one of her favorite plants, she squeaked out her protest and shooed him away.

"Behave, you beasts!" she cried. "I've no patience left for the two of you. Not now."

They looked unimpressed at her temper and watched her as she went to her closet, pulled out a fresh frock, and quickly changed into it. She'd worry about bathing later. Right now, she had too much on her mind.

She pulled out a small step stool from the back of the closet, mounted it, and reached onto the top shelf. She found the old metal lock-box that had belonged to her uncle and pulled it down. She'd kept it when she'd moved, but she'd never gone through its contents. All she'd known was that it contained the documents most precious to her uncle, and she hadn't the heart to get rid of it.

She set the box on her desk and found the key to it in the top drawer. She unlocked it and lifted the lid. The contents were innocuous enough, mostly old sketches of devices Alyosius had tried to build and notes on some of the procedures he'd performed on his Machinist patients.

She finally found what she was looking for tucked into the back corner of the box. It was a thick bundle of old letters tied with a red string. She closed her eyes as she lifted the bundle out, afraid to look. Afraid to know.

But she couldn't put it off forever. She sat down at her desk with a sigh, untied the string, and unfolded a letter at random. The writing was very familiar. The date was impossible. 1862. The year she was born.

My Dear Dr. Finch, Forgive the full year it has taken to pen a response to your last letter. As you know, I am occasionally required to relocate, for obvious reasons, and it has taken us a good while to settle into our new lives. Fyodor communicated with me the desire to see the New World, so we are at present in New York City. It is a fascinating place, but I fear our tenure here may be short. This country is a land of Luddites and Puritans of the worst sort. Poor Fyodor is made to feel extremely uncomfortable, as there is no hiding his automata.

I must admit this whole venture was poorly conceived all around, as this country is currently engaged in a most dreadful Civil War. As we have just put one terrible war behind us, we have no desire to become embroiled in another.

Or at least, I do not. Fyodor, despite his rather lukewarm reception, has entertained the idea of joining the Union troops. He sympathizes with the African slaves in the Southern States, whose plight resembles that of the serfs back in our Motherland. I hope I can convince him to another course of action, even though his cause is righteous. I am too old, too weary for righteousness. The last time I tried to muster up some enthusiasm, it was in Paris in 1789. How wrong that went!

I believe I might be able to distract Fyodor with the temptation of a dirigible ride to this country's uncharted western regions. He is exhausting, my new companion! But I am grateful for the gift of his company. You saved his life, and I know to you that seems like a small reparation. But it does not seem small to him. That is something.

In your last letter, you spoke of your intention to devote yourself to the unfortunates of your country. You are a better man than I, and to demonstrate my faith in you, I have had my solicitors set up a fund for your endeavors. You'll starve playing the martyr, and that is something I cannot allow. I hope your work can give you some peace. It is something that continues to elude me, alas, but therein lies the fundamental difference between us. You are a good man who once made a terrible choice. I was never a good man, and I never had a choice. And please, call me as my mother did,

Sasha

Aline dropped the letter to her lap, and squeezed her eyes shut, as if to block out the damning evidence. Had she gone insane, or was the Professor some sort of ... well, she didn't know what he was. But this was his handwriting, and she was as certain of that as she was of her own name. She'd been his secretary for five years.

That meant the Professor had been a grown man in 1862. And apparently, he'd been a grown man in 1789. In which case, he was well over a hundred years old. Which wasn't possible. Not in the world that she knew.

Perhaps she was just having a nervous breakdown. She'd been under a lot of stress this past month, and the corpse she'd seen last night was enough to drive most people to Bedlam. God, she rather hoped that was all it was. A nervous breakdown seemed the more palatable option at the moment. None of this was real, but rather some sort of waking dream she'd conjured in her hysteria.

Suddenly, both the hellhounds, who had been dozing at her

feet, jumped to their full height and began to growl in the direction of the door. More than growl. She'd never heard such a terrible sound emerge from them. They seemed fixated in a deadly way on whatever they sensed on the other side, their fur standing on end, their tails tucked under, and their mechanical eyes going red.

There was a heavy thud in the hallway, and the hellhounds started barking frantically. That was a bad sign. The hair on the back of her neck rose, and gooseflesh pricked her arms. Adrenaline coursed through her veins, her heart drumming heavily against her ribcage. A dull roar began in her ears, and for a moment she felt frozen in place.

Hide.

It was an instinctual desire, because she knew, she just *knew*, someone – something – other than Fyodor lurked on the other side of the door. Heart in her throat, legs like calf's jelly, she hurried to the only place she could think of: her closet, pulling the door closed, burying herself as far as she could go in the mound of dresses and underclothes, trying not to breathe.

She heard the door to her flat swing open, and Ilya and Ikaterina's barking turned into snarls. She heard the crashing of furniture, and then two yelps of pain, and then ... silence.

She clutched her hand over her mouth to keep from crying out in dismay. Those yelps of pain had come from the hellhounds. She prayed they weren't injured, or dead, but the ominous silence made her fear the worst. She'd never forgive herself if something had happened to them, to *Fyodor*, because of her foolish mission.

"Come out, come out, my little bird," came a heavily accented voice she'd never heard before. It was filled with such menace, such evil intent, she felt her blood congeal in her veins.

She could hear the owner of the voice moving around the flat, as if he were in no great rush, which unsettled her all the more. He was toying with her. "I can smell you, little bird, no need to be coy. Such sweet blood." She heard the man sniff the air like some animal, and she shuddered, closing her eyes, praying this was all a bad dream. "I couldn't wait a moment longer to have you."

Oh, God. Why had she ever left the townhouse? And how had he gotten past Fyodor? No one could be stronger than an Abominable Soldier.

Aline sucked in a breath and held it, afraid to blink. The intruder was just outside the closet door.

She could hear his breathing, then a low chuckle.

"I know you're in there, little bird. Shall I come let you out?"

No, she wanted to scream. She clutched the knob and held it firm, but any ideas that she could hold it tight against the intruder were quickly dashed when the door suddenly flew off its hinges and landed on the other side of the room with a loud clap, splintering across her desk. She opened her mouth to scream, but when she saw the man who stood before her, her voice died in her throat.

She was too terrified to scream. Tall, built like a brick wall, he was dressed in filthy, bloodstained garments. His skin was pasty-pale, and he panted like a thirsty dog.

But Aline knew one thing for certain: *it* wasn't human. The whites of its eyes were filled with an amber-colored glow, and its canine teeth dipped past its lips to razor-sharp points. An evil smirk turned up the corners of its lips. It lowered its head nearer her and sniffed. Its eyes glowed even brighter, and a look of ecstasy suffused its expression.

"Hello, my little bird. I could resist meeting you no longer. You smell as good as promised. I shall truly enjoy this." It tilted his head, studying her closely. "But first, shall we have some fun?"

Aline didn't know where she found the nerve, but she shook her head. It laughed as if she'd delighted it.

And with that, it tore her out of the closet, tossing her across the room as easily as it had the door.

Aline finally found her voice as she sailed through thin air, and she screamed as loud as she could. Somehow the villain managed to cross the room fast enough to catch her at the other end. The creature clutched her against its unwashed body so tightly Aline gagged – from its hold and from the stench.

She struggled frantically, which only seemed to amuse the creature further. She heard the sound of her gown ripping as it clawed at her, and then its head was descending, fangs growing even longer, as if it meant to bite her in the neck.

Aline screamed, and all she could think, before all hell broke loose, was that she was going to be murdered. By a vampire.

WHEN Sasha heard Aline's first scream, he was at the bottom of the boarding house stairs, having rushed across town after receiving Fyodor's tickertext. Employing all of the super-human speed at his disposal, he was up the stairs and at her door in the blink of an eye.

He spared a glance for Fyodor, sprawled across the hallway, and his stomach bottomed out with dread. Nothing *human* could fell Fyodor. With no small measure of guilt, he turned away from his old companion without checking his condition. He had no time to lose and could only hope that Drexler and Rowan were not too far behind him.

Aline screamed again, and Sasha didn't even bother opening the door. He kicked it inwards and scanned the flat. He saw the hellhounds in one corner of the room, blood everywhere. Only Ilya was attempting to regain his feet, dazed, one of his Welding eyes smashed, its innerworkings dangling out of the metal socket. Ikaterina was unmoving next to him, and Sasha's blood ran cold at the sight. But he forced the hellhounds from his mind.

He could mourn Ikaterina later, if he had to. But he would *not* mourn Aline. He would not lose her.

Sasha was still trying to accept the fact that vampires existed at all, so seeing one with fangs poised to sink into Aline's fragile neck was terrifying. Seeing the monster simultaneously tearing away Aline's gown, exposing her prim white undergarments then the pale, untouched skin beneath, was something else altogether. Rage shot like molten lava through his veins.

He would kill this bastard, and he would relish it. He was beyond caring what that made him.

He didn't even remember moving across the room, so black was his fury. He didn't even remember tearing the hulking animal away from Aline's neck, microseconds before its fangs sank into her jugular. He threw the creature as far away as he could, through the plate glass and wrought iron of the balcony window, knocking over Aline's plant collection outside.

Shattered glass clung to the monster's clothes, and brackish blood oozed from a hundred tiny nicks on his face and forearms, but the wounds, Sasha saw, were quickly closing up, as if they never were.

The monster quickly regained its feet. It grinned at Sasha as it stepped over the remains of the window and back into the room, eyes aglow with their strange amber fire. "My Prince!" it sneered. "How lovely to see you again, in the flesh, after all these years."

Sasha tensed, his eyes flying wide. The creature spoke in a dialect of Russian he'd not heard in three hundred years. It seemed Rowan was right all along and the killer was from his Russian past. A past he'd tried so hard to forget.

"Who are you?" he demanded.

The creature feigned a hurt expression. "For shame, brother. You don't recognize your own blood?"

He searched the vampire's features with dawning horror. Beneath the fangs and the glowing eyes, this man was too familiar. He was one of the monsters who still haunted Sasha's worst nightmares.

"Vasily!" he breathed. His father's oldest and most vicious bastard. He'd tormented Sasha in secret as a child, and it seemed he was tormenting him still. But how? How was it possible that Vasily had been alive all this time as this creature? And why?

"Why are you doing this?" he demanded.

"I was breakfasting, My Prince," Vasily said disingenuously, in English this time, smirking at Aline, who shuddered and backed away from the both of them, clutching the ruins of her bodice against her chest. "Pity we were interrupted, little bird."

Vasily leered at Aline with such a lascivious, thirsty look in his eyes Sasha snapped. He roared his fury and charged. The creature in Vasily was strong and easily blocked Sasha's fist. It was fast as well, stepping around Sasha and moving with inhuman speed towards Aline, as if it could not resist the temptation of her blood. Sasha was just quick enough to seize his brother by the arm and jerk him in the opposite direction so hard he heard a bone snap.

Vasily landed against Aline's spindle bed, and it collapsed underneath the impact. He quickly regained his feet and came at Sasha with blinding speed, growling like the feral creature he was. He barreled into Sasha so hard he knocked both of them through a wall and into the hallway.

Sasha could hear Aline screaming. So did Vasily – he seemed to respond with glee to Aline's terror.

He raised his head and sniffed the air, as if scenting where she was, and shot back inside the room.

Sasha shook off the impact of his landing and leapt in front of Vasily before he could reach Aline.

He shoved him into a corner.

Realizing he was trapped, Vasily hissed and swiped Sasha's face with a long claw-like nail, ripping Sasha's flesh from his forehead to his chin. Sasha's light, acidic blood sizzled down his face and into his collar, momentarily blinding him in one eye. He groaned as he felt the wound quickly, painfully mend itself.

Aline screamed behind him again, and he feared *he* was the source of her terror this time.

The creature laughed wildly. "I think your dear one just discovered how inhuman you are, brother. I was never allowed to call you that, though, was I, My Prince? You were our father's precious heir, unworthy as you were."

"I have never denied my unworthiness, Vasily. I hadn't our father's taste for rape and murder, as you did," he said quietly.

"You were always a coward, brother, to the end. And a liar.

You murdered our father after he gave you everything!"

Sasha laughed wildly. "You think he gave me everything? He took *everything* from me, and then he gave me an eternity to remember what he'd taken!"

Vasily just sneered at this. "You always had a woman's heart. It was an embarrassment to watch you snivel and weep after your whore of a wife died. Father should have let you die then. That heart was meant to be mine, and he made that old man give it to you instead. And then you killed him with poison, coward that you are."

Sasha had no response to this. How could he deny what Vasily said, when so much of what he'd said was the truth? He had been a coward for too long as Ivan Ivanovich, and it had cost him everything. He wouldn't make that same mistake again, even if he lost the rest of his soul in the process.

But he'd never regretted what he'd done to his father. "He did not deserve honor. He deserved a coward's death. And it was a pleasure to watch him pay," Sasha said at length, enraging Vasily further. "Just as you'll pay for all that you've done. I may have been a coward, but I was never a monster like you."

Vasily smirked. "But it has been so much fun, watching you suffer. Especially this time. I always knew one day your weak nature would betray you, and you'd fall in love again. Imagine my delight to learn that your secretary is the sweetest prize of all to one of my kind. Such lovely blood. That was not planned, I assure you." He paused and sniffed the air as if savoring something. "*So* lovely. Shall I tell you what I plan to do to your little bird there? Before I drink her dry?"

Sasha growled at the creature and blocked its line of sight to Aline. "You touch her over my dead body."

The creature laughed. "But I would rather you were alive to watch, My Prince. You've always been so good at *watching*. Sometimes *I've* watched *you* as you study the bodies, but you never seem to suffer enough. But you'll suffer when I take her. And I *will* take her, My Prince. In all ways. You do remember how good I always was with the women back in Russia."

Sasha shuddered with revulsion. He was through with this conversation. Vasily was his half-brother, but even when they'd grown up together, Sasha had despised him and all of the atrocities he'd committed as their father's henchman. When he looked at Vasily, he didn't see family. He saw the blood of dozens of butchered victims and all the women he'd raped, from Moscow to London. He saw Novgorod, and the blood Vasily had shed with such glee in that city in the name of the Tsar. He saw centuries of hidden anguish as he hunted for a phantom.

Moreover, he saw Aline and what would have happened to her had he been one minute later in arriving.

And it was unbearable.

Vasily's eyes widened at the murderous rage in Sasha's expression, as if realizing he had said too much, and backed away. But there was nowhere for him to go.

"You look just like father now. I never thought you had it in you, brother," Vasily breathed with something like awe, and it twisted Sasha's insides to hear those words.

But Sasha just smiled an awful smile. "I've always been my father's son. And watching him die was one of the rare pleasures of my life. I wonder how it will feel to kill my brother."

Vasily saw his intent and flashed to the right. But Sasha had the strength of centuries of fury to give him the advantage. He moved quickly, unhesitatingly. Drexler had recommended beheading as the only sure way to kill a vampire, but Sasha had nothing to use but his bare hands. It would not stop him. He'd studied human anatomy for years and knew exactly what he was about.

He gripped the creature he'd once called a brother by the neck and bore one hand through its flesh to the bone of the spine beneath. There was no point in having inhuman strength if he wasn't going to use it.

And so he used it. He ripped the creature's head from its body in one clean swoop, its brackish blood coating his arms and splattering his clothes and face. He tossed aside the head and kicked the feet from underneath its body, then turned away in disgust before it had even hit the ground at his feet.

It took some time before he was able to come back to himself, and it was like awakening from a nightmare, his vision clearing, his abominable heart slowing. He glanced around the wrecked flat, taking it all in as he tried to measure his breathing.

Gradually he realized he was not alone. Aline stood near the ruined door next to Drexler, Matthews and Rowan, who must have arrived just in time to witness the end, if their slack-jawed expressions were any indication. All of them were staring at him as if they'd never seen him before. But Aline...

Aline looked at him as she had looked at the vampire. As if he were a monster. And would she be so wrong?

He looked down at the unnatural, congealed blood covering his forearms, and it dawned on him what he'd just done in his rage. He'd torn off a man's head – his brother's head – and he wasn't the least bit conflicted about it. The only thing he regretted was that Aline had witnessed his monstrousness, because he had the awful suspicion Vasily had spoken true about one thing.

He loved Aline, and he had for some time, without even knowing it. And he had surely lost her forever.

Drexler finally broke the awful silence by clearing his throat uncomfortably, sheathing the sword he no longer needed back into his hollow walking stick. "Well, I've never seen it done *quite* like that before," he said with the darkest of wit. "Perhaps you lot *are* stronger after all."

Her Majesty made a rare public appearance at the British Museum's latest exhibition, featuring artifacts of Ancient Egypt recovered by a team led by Egyptologist, Dr. Charles Netherfield, recently appointed to the faculty at London University...

-from *The London Post-Dispatch*, 1893

"OH, dear, I confess I forgot how you take your tea. Cream? Sugar?" Lady Christiana inquired, her hand pausing nervously over the sugar tongs.

All of her plants were likely lost causes. And she didn't know whether the fact that she was worrying over her plants at a time like this was a healthy response or another sign of encroaching hysteria.

Just as she and Christiana were sitting down to dine, the Earl arrived after a night spent sorting out the catastrophe in Bloomsbury. He joined them for a moment, looking rumpled and weary and so very ordinary, nothing like what she imagined a four hundred year old immortal would look like.

Except for his eyes. For the first time, she noticed the Earl's eyes were the same unique amber color as the Professor's. A detail so obvious in retrospect. Gooseflesh shivered up her spine as she stared into his unnatural eyes, unable to look away.

He caught her gazing at him and pulled at his collar uncomfortably. He glanced at his sister. "You told her?"

Christiana nodded. "She deserved to know."

"Of course." He cleared his throat. "Miss Finch, surely I don't need to worry about your discretion..."

She snorted and crossed her arms, feeling as if bravado was the only weapon left to her. "Oh, I won't tell your secrets. Even if I did, who would believe me?"

The Earl looked taken aback by her sarcasm. "Well, it is good to see you've recovered your unique wit."

"How is ... Fyodor?" she asked, catching herself before she did something daft and asked after Sasha. She knew precisely how her ex-employer was. Immortal. Probably still trying to scrub the blood from his hands. She wanted to hate him. To fear him, even, after what he'd done. Yet all she kept picturing in her mind was how she'd last seen him. Hunched over Ikaterina, head bowed, so still. So alone.

"He has recovered. We are still not sure how the creature was able to overpower him without a fight. Even Elders have difficulty matching the strength of Fyodor's kind," his Lordship replied.

"And the Professor's dogs?" she asked, dreading the response.

The Earl's expression took on a grim cast. "I don't know. Sasha is ... unavailable at the moment."

That didn't sound good, and Aline's heart ached. For the hellhounds, of course. She was responsible for what had happened to them. If she hadn't been so foolish as to go to her flat in the first place, all of this might have never happened. While she'd thought Sasha's secrets were dark, she'd never imagined *this*.

"The good news is we believe the danger has passed. From what we have managed to gather, that creature was responsible for all of this madness."

"You can say 'vampire', Rowan," Christiana said wryly. "That was what it was."

He gave his sister an unhappy glance. "I am not comfortable with that word, or with the fact they exist at all. I doubt I shall ever be, my dear."

Aline wondered if the Earl knew his sister was half in love with a vampire. She could foresee some trouble there. But she had her own problems to deal with.

"I still can't believe it was Sasha's *brother*, all this time," Lady Christiana said with a shudder. "What a nightmare that must be for him."

"Sasha always claimed his family was an appalling lot."

"I'm sure they were," Aline muttered. "His father was Ivan the bloody Terrible." *This* was one of the hardest revelations to swallow. That Sasha was the former Crown Prince of the Russian Empire, and his father was one of the most reviled men in history. All of those things he'd said when he'd talked about that painting had happened to him. And that letter...

She did not want to think about that letter from his long-dead wife. It made it too real, too heartbreaking.

The Earl stood up to take his leave, fixing his attention on Aline. "Miss Finch, I believe the immediate danger to you has passed. You are, of course, welcome to stay here for as long as you like, and in light of your unique condition, I would recommend it. At least until we come to some sort of solution to ensure your safety."

"I have lived my life thus far without incident. Besides, I shall be married and on my honeymoon within the month..." She trailed off, her stomach sinking, as she suddenly recalled yet another rather crucial part of her life.

"What is it, dear?" Christiana asked.

"I forgot all about Charlie," she murmured. "I left the ball without a word to him. He must be out of his mind with worry."

She'd had a lot on her mind since the ball – the understatement of the millennia – but the fact she'd not thought once of Charlie wasn't a good sign. After breakfast, she checked her wireless to make sure Charlie had not tried to reach her. There were no messages from him, which was surprising ... and disappointing.

Perhaps she was a hypocrite, as she'd not thought of him once in two days, but she'd expected him to be concerned at least a little. She had a valid excuse for her forgetfulness, but what could possibly be his? Mummies attacking him at the museum?

She sent him a tickertext apologizing for her abrupt departure from the ball, but when he didn't even reply to this, her disappointment turned to worry.

What if something had happened to him?

She knew she was being paranoid after her recent experiences, but she couldn't stop her vivid imagination from getting the better of her. Even if vampires or mummies weren't attacking him, however, *something* was wrong. Charlie had never failed to respond to her tickertexts in the past.

When she hadn't heard from him by the afternoon, Christiana offered to accompany her to the museum to check on him. Matthews drove them through the city, still under Drexler's orders to keep an eye on her. Though the threat was over, for once Aline was grateful for the company. She wondered if she'd ever feel completely safe again.

Charlie's offices were located in the basement of the museum. She'd only visited a few times in the early days of their acquaintance, when Charlie was just settling in. It had always been a dim, unwelcoming place filled with artifacts from Charlie's Egyptian ventures, most of them made slightly eerie by the shadowy room.

As she and Christiana entered the large front room, the eeriness seemed amplified from her previous visits. A giant stone statue of the god Osiris, a new addition, loomed over everything else, casting a long shadow that seemed to envelop them like a living thing. She shivered.

She was overreacting, she knew, seeing threats where there were none. The violence of the last few days had taken its toll, that was all. She tried to shake off her misplaced foreboding.

But even Christiana seemed to take a dislike to the office. "Remind me never to come here at night. This place is enough to give me nightmares," Christiana murmured with a shudder. As they passed by a long workbench near the back of the room with a tall shelf above it, Christiana stopped and gasped. "Dear Lord, what is that?" she breathed, gesturing to the shelf.

Nearly two-dozen giant glass storage jars lined the shelves, filled with lumps of ancient-looking stained bandages. Some of the stains reminded Aline of dried blood, which of course was ridiculous. Aline approached for a closer look, and a chill raced down her spine.

"Are those ... human organs?" Christiana demanded from behind her.

A door slammed, and Aline's heart nearly leapt from her throat. She spun around to find Charlie approaching them, his mouth tight with displeasure. "They are indeed mummified organs, my Lady," Charlie answered. "Thousands of years old."

Christiana, her hand to her chest, eyed the jars skeptically. "They don't *look* a thousand years old," she muttered.

Aline cast a final look at the jars, and she couldn't help but agree with Christiana. Some of the contents looked quite ... fresh. Surely those couldn't be mummified hearts. After being threatened by a psychopath intent on ripping hers out, she didn't like the thought of being near mummified hearts, even if they were millennia old.

"What are you doing here?" Charlie demanded in a hard voice that was so unlike him that she forgot all about the jars.

She turned her attention back to her fiancé, and any idea she had of eliciting his sympathy about her troubles the last few days flew out of her mind. He was clearly in no mood for company, even her own. He looked terrible, as if he'd not slept in days, and extremely upset.

"I came to check on you, Charlie. You didn't respond to my messages," she said.

"I've been busy," he said irritably.

Christiana grimaced at Charlie's tone and discreetly moved to the other side of the room to give them a moment alone, sensing trouble.

"What's going on, Charlie?" Aline asked, following behind him as he prowled towards his desk. He began to toss things quite violently into a box.

"I'm packing my desk, that's what," he bit out.

Aline glanced around and noticed several boxes already filled to the brim and stacked near the entrance. "Why are you packing?"

"I'm leaving the museum. The expedition is off, Aline.

I've been sacked from the university, and my funding has been cut."

"What?" she cried. "But I don't understand!"

"Ask your ex-employer," Charlie retorted. "*He* is the cause of all of this."

Aline's stomach bottomed out with apprehension. "Sasha ... I mean, Professor Romanov had you fired?"

"I'm certain of it. I knew he didn't like me when we were introduced at the ball, but this is too much."

Aline's blood began to heat. She didn't doubt for a moment the Professor had done this. He'd made his position on the matter of her marriage quite clear. He'd interfere in any way he could, just as he'd interfered with the bookmaker's. But why? Why now, when she was free of the threat to her life? The Professor had no reason to be so dictatorial now. And he wouldn't be cruel on a whim, would he?

Perhaps he would. The last two days had proven how little she truly knew the man. He was capable of literally pulling a man apart without so much as flinching. He'd have no trouble ruining Charlie's career. She choked on her rage.

"He had no right. Charlie, I'm so sorry." She touched his arm to comfort him as best she could, her mind in a whirl.

He spun around to face her, and there was such fury on his face she backed up a step. "What does he see in you?" he spat. "You're his secretary. Shall he ruin my life over his secretary? Are you sleeping with him, Aline? Are you his whore? Is that what this is about?

Aline gasped, the blood draining from her face at Charlie's vitriol. "Charlie! How dare you!" she cried.

He wasn't finished. He looked her up and down with disgust. "How could he find you so irresistible? *You?*"

Every one of Charlie's words sent a spear of pain through her chest. "He doesn't. But *you* should, Charlie, if only a little. We're to be married."

He snorted and turned back to his packing. "No, we're not."

She froze. "What? You're breaking with me?" she cried.

"Because the Professor did something I had no control over?"

"The only reason I was marrying you was for your secretarial skills. As I no longer have a career, I no longer need you."

What? "So you never cared about me at all?"

"A passing fondness," he sneered. "Don't try to tell me you loved me either, Aline. You know as well as I that would be a lie. You were using me as much as I was using you."

"I was prepared to have a family with you, Charlie," she said quietly. "You said you wanted that."

He laughed caustically at this. "I lied, my dear. Now will you please leave? I must finish packing today, and you are giving me a headache."

Aline stared at Charlie's back for some time as he continued to pack, ignoring her. She was too stunned to move. But at last she felt Christiana's hand on her shoulder, guiding her away.

She didn't come back to her senses until they were nearing the lobby of the museum. Christiana still gripped her shoulder, as if afraid she was going to fall without the support. She came to a stop, and Christiana paused with her, looking at her with concern.

"Charlie broke the engagement," she said, incredulous.

Christiana frowned and patted her arm. "I know. I heard. Not well-done of him."

"He ... he said he wanted me for my secretarial skills!" she breathed.

"Shall I go back and punch him in the face, love? I am quite prepared to do so," Christiana assured her.

Aline shook her head. "He thought I was ... *with* the Professor! He called me a whore!"

Christiana looked furious, balled her hands into fists, and turned back the way they came. "I didn't hear *that* part. I *shall* punch him."

Aline grabbed her friend by the arm and pulled her back. "Perhaps he saw," she cried. "When the Professor and I were in the garden."

Christiana looked at her sharply. "Saw what?"

"When we were ... kissing."

Christiana's mouth fell open. "You and the Professor ... " She trailed off, looking thoughtful. At length, she shrugged. "Of course, it makes sense. I've seen how Sasha looks at you."

"What? *No!*" Aline cried, distraught at Christiana's reasoning. And perceptiveness.

"And how you look at him," Christiana continued. "I always wondered why you agreed to marry Charlie, when you and the Professor seemed..."

"You couldn't be more mistaken. And I do not look at the Professor!" Aline wailed, a sick feeling rising in her gut. Was she so transparent? Did all of her acquaintances assume she was panting after Sasha?

And just when had he become *Sasha* in her thoughts?

Christiana gave her an exasperated look. "No, you just *kiss* him."

Aline sputtered. "This whole discussion is beside the point. The Professor had Charlie fired, ruining his life. Ruining *my* life in the process."

"Well," Christiana said, "in my opinion you are well rid of Charlie. I've never liked him. He showed his true nature today, and it was not pleasant."

Christiana's dislike of Charlie was a revelation, but Aline hadn't the time to ponder it. She shot Christiana an impatient look.

"That's not the point," she reiterated. "The Professor thinks he can do whatever he wants to whoever he wants. But he won't get away with destroying my life. I don't care how powerful he is, he has interfered in my affairs for the last time."

She stalked towards the entrance.

Christiana trailed behind her, shaking her head in dismay. "If I were you, I'd be more angry with that fiancé of yours, Aline, and the way he just talked to you. So what if the Professor had him fired? That is no reason for him to break the engagement with you so callously."

"I don't care," she said, stomping down the steps to the

street. "I'm settling things with the Professor once and for all."

"Well, don't let me stop you," Christiana said wryly. "But I wonder if by settling things you mean to kiss him again."

She glared at her friend as they climbed into the steam carriage.

Perhaps she was being unreasonable, but she *felt* unreasonable. This was truly the last straw.

Charlie's behavior was despicable, but she knew that the wounds he'd given her were mostly to her pride. He was right to point out that they'd not loved each other. Still, she'd wagered a lot on their future together, house of cards though it turned out to be. To have that taken from her was a colossal blow. She couldn't help but blame Sasha, the architect of all of her recent and not-so-recent grief.

All she'd wanted to do was to go her own way, marry a decent fellow, and start living a halfway normal life for once. All of the things she'd never thought possible to attain until Charlie came along and presented her with the opportunity had been so close! No more nights alone, no more lonely wagers at the gaming house in a desperate attempt to fill the void inside. No more emptiness, and though she didn't precisely love Charlie, she was fond of him. And there would have been children...

But now everything seemed wrested from her control. Sasha had taken away all of her illusions. He had shown her a world she was not sure she wanted to know about, and she could never go back to the way it was before. But more than that, he persisted, even now, to try and control her destiny. Just how much power did Sasha and these Elders of his wield, that they could have Charlie sacked and his expedition cancelled at the drop of a hat?

And Charlie had revealed a side of himself today Aline had not known about. It called into question her judgment. Could she have been so wrong about him? Perhaps she'd been so anxious to free herself from the invisible bonds Sasha had attached to her person that she'd not fully thought this through.

Apparently she'd been wrong to think Charlie was any different from most of the male population, who expected a wife to serve her husband unquestioningly.

Secretarial skills indeed!

Well, the one thing Aline would never do was surrender so completely to another soul. Her independence was hard-won. It had taken her twenty years to get where she was today, and no one was going to tell her what to do, how to live, and *especially* where and with whom to invest her heart.

Charlie wouldn't have controlled her.

No man would, including and especially one particular Russian, who had spent the past five years doing exactly that. Sasha had demanded more of her than Charlie ever had, though in subtle ways she could not quite name. He demanded total surrender from his victims. He gave away nothing of himself, yet expected a pound of flesh in return.

And, *oh*, he had taken it. How could she have been so foolish as to let her guard down with him for one second? How could she have let herself think – no, secretly hope – that those few moments of seduction had been genuine? She'd just been an unfortunate victim of his frightening, secret world.

Even in the midst of the most terrible moments of the past few days, when that creature had accused Sasha of loving her, of all things, she had felt her heart leap in her chest. With hope. Which made her perhaps the biggest fool to have ever been born. If a *vampire's* words were giving her hope, it was time to stop lying to herself.

She was infatuated with the Professor, and always had been. She was fairly certain she still was, even knowing what he was.

And she hated him for it.

Now he had succeeded in coming between her and Charlie, on top of everything else. He was going to pay for all he'd done.

"Drop me at Professor Romanov's house, Mr. Matthews," she said primly, and Christiana rolled her eyes next to her. "I have something to discuss with him."

CHAOS IN COVENT GARDEN! Publicans clashed with members of the Salvation Army in Covent Garden today, sparking a riot that forced the Metropolitan Police to intercede. The riot was eventually quelled before it could spread across London. With the Growing Civil Unrest caused by the Economic Decline, officials worry today's Incident is but the first of many...

... Officials are further concerned the Temperance Movement has become a haven for Radical Elements determined to undermine the Post-War government. According to one MP, Luddite Reactionaries have used the Salvation Army's network to sow the seeds of Rebellion...

-from *The London Post-Dispatch*, 1865

9

*S*ASHA sat alone in his study, head against his desktop, nursing a bottle of vodka in an attempt to obliterate the past few days. It was his tenth. He felt the effects of the alcohol, but they didn't last long enough with this blasted heart of his. He had to drink – and then drink some more – to sustain his oblivion, but even then he couldn't stop all of his bleak thoughts.

Ilya whimpered and nuzzled him in the shoulder with his snout, desperate for the attention. Sasha stroked his pup's head, but could not look at him. It was too painful to see the broken eye Sasha had yet to have repaired and Ilya's mournful demeanor.

His pup had been confused and anxious ever since they'd come home without Ikaterina. Sasha could not make him understand that Ikaterina was gone forever. He didn't want it to be true. He'd loved that dog, even though he'd known all too well he shouldn't. Three hundred and forty two years on earth had taught him one thing: those he loved always, inevitably died because of him.

He was afraid that one more disappointment would push him beyond the pale, so he knew what he had to do. He had to let Finch go once and for all, before he destroyed them both – if he hadn't done so already.

And the only way to do that was to go far away from England and the life he'd established here, because he knew that if he stayed, he'd seek her out. He couldn't seem to help himself. He'd allowed himself to feel too much for her, and she would be the one to suffer. Who knew what dark acts he'd be driven to if he didn't cut his losses now and leave her behind?

She was alive, and she had her future with the bone-hunter. There was no place for him in her plans. And after all he'd put her through, he couldn't blame her – or stop her – from pursuing the life she wanted. He'd never be anything but a distasteful memory to her.

He was halfway through his next bottle when he heard a high-pitched, very familiar voice arguing in the hallway with his housekeeper. He raised his bleary head from his desk in surprise. He'd not expected to hear that voice again. His pulse gave a little leap.

He dropped his head back to the desk with a thud when the voice suddenly ceased. He must have imagined it.

Seconds later, the door to his study crashed inwards, and he leapt to his feet rather unsteadily, though he wondered why he'd bothered. He didn't care who it was. Perhaps another of his bastard brothers had come to finish him off. At this point, he would have welcomed it.

He blinked in surprise as Finch stalked into the room, eyes flashing like lit embers with accusation and fury. Either he was more intoxicated than he thought, or she was really here after all. And he'd never seen Finch quite like this before, her body literally thrumming with rage. It was quite a sight. If he weren't so drunk and miserable, he'd be aroused.

Damn it all, he *was* aroused. Inappropriately and pointlessly.

He collapsed back onto his chair, the elation he felt at

seeing her again tempered with his dread.

She'd come to have it out with him, but he didn't think it was a good idea that she was here at all. He felt ... out of control. And drunk. Very drunk. "What have I done now?" he murmured, in Russian, which she clearly understood, for she seemed to grow even angrier.

"What haven't you done, you ... you *impossible* beast!" she shouted. "Why can you not stay out of my life?"

As it was hard to pinpoint exactly which of his sins against her she was referring to – since there were so many to choose from – he scratched his head, perplexed. "I have no idea what you're talking about."

"Oh!" was all she could seem to squeak out. She clenched her hands into fists, her face red with rage, looking halfway to exploding. For lack of a better outlet, she stomped her foot against the floor in a show of petulance that could have rivaled any six-year-old's temper tantrum. Her gown was suspiciously dirty, as if she'd fallen into every puddle between Llewellyn House and his residence. She was a mess. A very furious mess. He longed, in his delirium, to take that little bundle of fury in his arms and kiss away her bad mood.

But he still had enough of his wits left to know that would be a very bad idea. And that she should leave before he did exactly that.

"You know exactly what I'm talking about! Charlie! You had him terminated and the expedition cancelled!"

He was completely baffled. "What are you talking about?"

"Stop playing games! Admit it!" she cried.

He shook his head. He'd done many things to her over the past week, but he was fairly certain he'd not done this. "I can't admit it. I didn't do it!"

"Liar!" she cried, and she flew at him, batting her fists against his chest. He let her, because he didn't trust himself to put his hands on her. He was enjoying her hands on *him* far too much, even if they were raised in anger.

At length, in his effort not to reach for her, and his inebriation, he leaned so far back he stumbled.

This only seemed to infuriate her even more.

Something seemed to snap inside of her, and he watched in growing horror as her hand shot out and grabbed a porcelain vase lying on the sideboard next to her. She heaved it over her head.

The blood drained from his face. That vase was a priceless gem he'd brought back from a trip to China in the 17th century. He held up his hands pleadingly.

"No, not the vase!" he breathed.

She ignored him and threw the vase with surprising momentum. He was too horrified and foxed to dodge it, so it shattered against his head. He felt shards of porcelain ripping into the flesh at his temple, his amber blood sizzling down his face. The wounds closed up as fast as they were made, but it *hurt*, even with all of the vodka in his blood. He cursed.

Then he brushed the shards off his shirt and surveyed with dismay the remains of his favorite vase at his feet. He couldn't quite believe Finch had done it. She'd known full well how much he'd liked that vase.

She seemed to be determined to make him as angry as she was.

Well, it was working.

He glared at her, his ire blooming through the vodka haze. Oh, Finch was going to pay for this. But exactly how she was going to do so was still open for debate. He considered many different scenarios in which he exacted his revenge on the divan behind her. With his tongue.

But as his gaze dropped to her face, his wicked, ridiculous thoughts sputtered out, and his anger faded. She was staring at him with tears streaming down her bloodless face through eyes the size of saucers.

"I keep forgetting ... how could I forget?" she murmured. "You're *not human*!"

Chagrined, he turned away from her and wiped the remaining blood from his temple with the edge of his shirtsleeve. He had forgotten what a shock it must be to see his wounds miraculously disappear in the blink of an eye.

When he turned back to her, she was still sniffling, and Ilya was pressed against her side as if to comfort her. This only seemed to make her cry harder. She raised her tear-filled eyes once more to him. "Ikaterina?"

He shook his head once, sharply, unable to form the words. It was still too raw.

"Oh, dear," she sobbed even harder. "And it was all my fault! How could I have been so stupid?"

He couldn't answer her. It wasn't that he blamed her, precisely. After the way Vasily had overpowered Fyodor, Sasha didn't think Aline would have been safe even had she stayed at the townhouse. Vasily had been determined to have her, whatever the cost. But he couldn't help but feel an irrational surge of resentment towards Finch. She was, after all, the reason he felt as if he were sinking to the bottom of a very deep ocean.

He'd killed without remorse for her, and he was afraid he'd do so again and again until his father's blood boiled like lava through his veins and he'd drown in the darkness. Until he was no better than that ... *thing* Vasily had become. She'd made him lose all control.

She'd made him love her, and he hated her for it.

And he hated her stubbornness, her desire to leave him and marry a man he knew she didn't love, though this was what was best for her.

Above all, he hated the tenderness she engendered in a heart he had long thought pulverized by his ancient grief. It was overwhelming.

"Why have you come here?" he bit out, all of his anger and self-loathing swiftly returning now that the shock of her unexpected arrival had worn off. He stepped over the ruins of his vase and swiped his vodka from his desk, unable to look at her. "You shouldn't be here."

He stumbled away from her and threw himself in a chair by the hearth. She followed with Ilya, wiping the tears away, though they kept falling. He tried not to care.

"You're drunk!" she breathed with some of her usual spark.

"What gave it away?" he muttered.

"You're a wreck!"

He gave her a significant glance, from the top of her tumbledown hair, to the soles of her muddy boots. Her expression began to grow angry again as she caught his meaning.

She wiped her eyes one more time and stalked to the divan opposite him and the chess board he and Fyodor used. She sat down and glared at him, though her puffy eyes and red nose undermined the effect.

She looked terrible. She looked delectable. He had a very real urge to leap across the distance between them and lick her tears away.

Which was why he needed her to leave. Or stay forever.

A dangerous thought, which he immediately quashed. Yet he found himself waving the bottle in her direction, as if he were no longer in control of his actions.

She looked at him as if he'd grown horns.

He shoved the bottle into her hands. "Drink. Trust me. You'll feel better." He groaned inwardly at his behavior. What was he doing?

She gave him a scathing look, but then, to his surprise, she raised the bottle to her dainty lips and took a long swig. She coughed violently and clutched at her throat.

"It's like ... fire," she protested, but then she raised the bottle again. She took another long drink. And another.

He snatched the bottle away from her when she threatened to take yet another.

"Better?" he asked wryly.

She nodded. "I shouldn't have. I'm a poor drunk. One glass of wine sends me reeling."

She'd be on the floor, then, with the amount of liquor she'd just ingested. Wonderful.

"I on the other hand have been drinking for days. To little effect." That was a lie, of course. He was near to full-on intoxication, and he did not feel one inch better for the effort. He tried to focus. "I know I deserved it, but what exactly compelled you to break my vase on my head?"

Her expression fell in renewed horror at her actions. "Oh dear, it was quite valuable, wasn't it?"

He shrugged. "17th century Ming Dynasty. The artist was a friend."

She paled. "Of course he was," she murmured. "A *friend*. From the 17th century."

He scowled at the bottle. "The vase was small recompense to the damage I've caused you. But I swear I've done nothing to the bone-hunter," he said, taking another giant gulp.

She glowered at him. "Why are you lying? Still? Just tell me the truth."

"I know you don't believe a word I say, but it's the truth."

"But he told me..." She broke off, a look of confusion washing over her features. "He's certain you had him fired from the University. He was quite upset about it." Her face collapsed as a new wave of tears gushed from her eyes. "He told me he was leaving! And he made it clear that ... that we're finished!" She broke off with a moan and buried her face in her hands, her shoulders heaving with broken little sobs.

At this unexpected announcement, his heart soared. But he crushed his rising hope. She was not for him. She would never be for him. When he saw how miserable she was, however, he felt guilty for his momentary elation – guilt and something that felt a lot like jealousy. Jealousy that he was not the one capable of stealing Finch's affection as the unworthy bone-hunter had done. And uncommon anger at the absent Charlie Neverfeel for reducing his secretary to this leaky bundle.

"I swear to God, Finch, if you don't stop leaking, I'm going to have to reupholster," he muttered, tossing a handkerchief into her lap.

"I'm not normally a watering pot," she retorted, dabbing at her eyes. "But the past few days have been rather difficult for me."

"I shall overlook it this time, Finch. You really wanted to marry him, didn't you?"

She met his eyes imploringly. "Do you not see how I might

want what Charlie was offering? A chance to have a family of my own? A family I never had?"

A feeling of understanding so raw and visceral it hurt passed into his heart. He understood exactly how she felt, for it was the same thing he felt deep down inside his ruined soul. A desire for family, for normalcy, for ... peace. But he'd never have that.

"I see, " he said. It was a whisper, ragged and heartfelt.

"You *do* see, don't you? You lost your family too." The sympathy in her soft voice was unbearable. He raised the bottle to his lips once more and drank long and hard, the liquid burning down his throat, warming the hollowness of his chest.

"That was long ago. We were speaking of you and the bone-hunter," he said gruffly. "You are well rid of him, *milaya*. Surely you can do better than that. He was such a prude."

"How would you know that?" she demanded, her anger returning.

"Two seconds in his company was enough to determine that. Did he even kiss you, Finch, or does his English propriety warn against such intimacy before the wedding?"

She blushed crimson. "We *have* kissed."

"So I was not your first," he said teasingly, though inwardly he was not so sanguine. "Well, I would doubt his manhood if he hadn't at least kissed you. He tried, perhaps, to go a bit further?"

If she blushed any more, she'd be the color of a cherry. *God.* He loved watching her blush. "Charlie is a perfect gentleman," she said primly.

"He sifted around you like he was looking for old bones, didn't he?"

"He did no ... Oh, *how* are we talking about this?" she cried.

"You wanted to know my opinion of the bone-hunter. I'd wager you planned on keeping the fact you were the author of a torrid penny-dreadful from him forever."

Her eyes went wide. "How could you know..."

He smirked. "I am three hundred forty two years old, *milaya*. I study human nature for a living. And I'm sure he had no idea you have a gambling problem either."

"I didn't need to tell him that, because it's not true, and I don't gamble any more anyway, no thanks to you!" she cried, outraged.

"Care to wager on that?"

She glared at him. At least she wasn't weeping any more. "The point is moot. Charlie and I are through. Now I am stuck here. Just as you wish," she cried. "I know you have the power to have him dismissed. I know you think you can do what you want to me, and you've made it clear you didn't want me marrying him, or going to Egypt. How can I not believe you had something to do with this?"

"It's true I never thought this Egyptian nonsense was a good idea for you. You'd desiccate in the Sahara. *If* you can even survive the journey."

She huffed and stuck out her jaw defiantly. "That is not for you to decide."

Hearing the truth spoken aloud was more painful than he'd thought it would be. But he just shrugged, as if it were of no consequence. "You are right. Now that the madman has been caught, my interference in your affairs is at an end. Owing to your unique condition, however, and the fact that London seems to be crawling with vampires, I doubt you'd be any safer here than in the Sahara."

"How comforting you are!" she cried. She took off her spectacles and polished the tears from them. He noticed she looked a bit unsteady as she did so. The vodka was kicking in.

"The point is, I didn't do anything to Neverfeel," he said. "I'd not do that to you, despite what you might think, *milaya*. I want you to be happy. And besides, I'll soon be gone from your life completely."

Her brow furrowed in confusion. She stuck her spectacles back on her nose and peered at him. "What? You're leaving?"

He gave her a wry smile and finished off the rest of his bottle. He tried to set it on the chess board between them, but he miscalculated in his stupor, and it toppled to the floor. He ignored it, as he didn't think he could retrieve it without falling out of his seat. "It is time, I believe, for me to move on."

Far from looking relieved, she looked a bit deflated, which gave him some twisted sense of comfort.

At least she wasn't reveling in his pending departure. "But where will you go?"

"As far away from here as I can get," he said honestly.

"Oh," she said, faintly. She was silent for a long moment. Then, "I suppose you have to do this often. Leave. Start over. I saw those letters you keep in your secret drawer. They were from all of your different lives." She paused. "I read the one from your wife."

He'd guessed as much when he saw someone had tampered with his drawer. He clenched his jaw and refused to look at her. "Do you *really* want to discuss my wife, Finch?"

"I don't know what I want, Sasha," she said softly.

He froze. He'd never before heard her call him by his name, the diminutive his mother had used that he'd never quite been able to leave behind. The way she said it, so softly, reminded him of the two moments he'd allowed himself to touch her, kiss her. Dangerous, erotic chills swept down his spine at the memory of the softness of her lips, her breast. He tried to shove these dangerous thoughts aside, focusing on his anger over the direction of their conversation.

"I'll tell you about Yelena," he said. "She was beautiful, sheltered, and devout. And I loved her. Then my father killed her, right in front of my eyes, and she took my son with her." He sat back in his seat, still unable to look at her. But she was very still across from him, so he knew she was listening. He continued, unable to stop himself.

He'd make her understand once and for all what he was, and why he had to leave.

"It took me a year to recover from what my father did to me, and to get all my memories back. When I did, I sat down with my father for our usual chess match." He gestured to the table between them. "I put arsenic in his wine, and I watched him die slowly and in agony, and I have never regretted it. Then I left Russia, and I vowed never to love like that again.

Its cost was too great."

He finally looked at her. She was staring at his chest with an unfathomable expression, and he realized he was unconsciously rubbing the scar over his heart. He dropped his hand away.

"You think what you did to your father makes you just like him," she stated quietly. "You think you are a monster."

He was stunned by her perception, the bald truth spoken out loud. He gave her a wry twist of his lips. "Am I not? You saw with your own eyes what I'm capable of. I ripped Vasily's head off."

"Well, he *was* a vampire who was going to rape and murder me," she said, as if it were the most reasonable thing in the world to talk about.

His heart sank anew at the memory of her at Vasily's mercy. He gripped the arms of his chair until his knuckles were white. "I think the vodka has gone straight to your head, *milaya*. You sound as if you're defending me. You came here to throttle me, remember?"

"I do feel a bit wobbly. I should go, I suppose." But she made no move to rise. She just stared at him with that same, unreadable expression she'd been wearing for the past several minutes. It unsettled him, that look. Where was her righteous anger? Her despair over her broken engagement? "The hall was empty when I came inside tonight," she said thoughtfully.

He shrugged. "The servants are packing up the house."

"Oh." She paused. "Already? You're leaving that quickly?"

"Yes, *milaya*."

She clasped her hands in front of her and bowed her head, hiding her expression. "I'm never going to see you again, am I?" she said in a small voice.

She sounded ... sad. Longing. And it nearly undid him. He was as terrified of leaving her as he was of keeping her close. He'd never felt this way before, even about Yelena. He did not know how he was going to bear it. He hardened his heart, and gave her the unvarnished truth, however. "No, I think that's for the best."

At last she raised her head, and he was shocked to see tears coursing down her face again. "But why? *Why* must you leave? Is it really so necessary?" she cried, with such unexpected anguish Sasha's pulse began to race.

It was the vodka. He was drunk, and so was she. She could not possibly mean anything she was saying. But his heart was racing now, as if he stood at the edge of a very tall cliff, poised to jump.

"Aline..." he began. It came out as a low growl. A low, pleading growl. He needed her to leave, or *he* needed to leave this room and escape the madness that gripped him. Before he said something ... or did something ... he'd regret. But he couldn't seem to move.

"You've only been here a few years. Surely there is no need to leave," she persisted.

He shook his head. "I've lived for too long in this life. I never meant to stay here in the first place. But you came along..." he broke off. There. He'd said too much already. The vodka had claimed the last of his discretion.

Her eyes went wide. Something like disbelief crossed her face.

He groaned and buried his face in his hands. Perhaps if he stayed like this long enough, she'd disappear.

"Sasha," she said when the silence had become unbearable. "You needn't leave because of what happened. Because of me..."

He laughed darkly and tugged at the ends of his hair. "It is *precisely* because of you I must leave. You really have no idea, do you?"

She shook her head. "I don't understand."

He lifted his head and met her perplexed, anguished eyes. He'd tell her the truth, then. Or most of it, anyway. *That* would scare her away, as nothing else could.

Or so he reasoned in his inebriation.

"I want you," he said frankly. "It was never an act for me, *milaya*. I think I've wanted you for years, but lately ... I've taken to dreaming of you at night, wondering if you have freckles hidden beneath your clothes. I wonder if all of your skin is as soft as I suspect, if you taste as sweet as you smell ... all over. I want *inside you*. Do you understand?"

She just stared at him, speechless. She licked her lips, and there was something in her dazed expression that fired his blood even more than his own wicked words. Made him grow hard as a rock.

God.

He should stop. The small voice of reason that remained lucid in his head told him to stop. But he couldn't.

"I want to do unspeakable things to you until you scream with pleasure. In the last five minutes, I've imagined a hundred ways to take you on that divan. Fully clothed. Naked. With nothing but your spectacles on."

She made a strangled sound in her throat, her cheeks growing rosy. She couldn't seem to look away from him any more than he could look away from her. He could hear her harsh breathing from across the distance that separated them, second only to his own.

He gripped the arms of his chair even harder, willing himself not to move. "So this is why I'm leaving. Being near you has become unbearable. I have no control left where you are concerned, *milaya*."

Nothing but the sound of their breathing broke the stillness that followed. How close he was to crossing the distance separating them and demonstrating his words!

"You ... you mock me!" she said at last with quiet devastation, dropping her gaze.

His heart sank with disappointment and anger. Why was it so unbelievable to her? He wanted her madly. It was as if he'd woken up one day to find that his parochial little secretary had been replaced by some alluring she-demon determined to make his life a torment. But he supposed Finch had not changed so much as he'd been forced to take the blinders off and see the truth. He was smitten. He'd spent the last five years constantly thinking about what he could say to irritate her, what he now realized was just an elaborate act of foreplay on his part.

Now he couldn't stop thinking about what he wanted to *do* to her.

She only had to look at his arousal pressing against the front of his trousers to see the truth for herself, but she was too innocent, too oblivious, to even contemplate such an idea. Which made him want her even more. But maybe it was for the best she held onto her illusions.

He gave her a bitter smile. "You may believe as you like. But if you don't wish to discover the truth, I would suggest you leave. Immediately. Fyodor can escort you back to Llewellyn House."

Whatever spell his confessions had woven finally snapped. She gave him a sidelong glance as she finally stood up, a bit unsteadily. She looked like she wanted to say something, then thought better of it and started for the door.

He wondered if this was the last time he'd see her, walking away from him, slightly drunk, without ever knowing how much he craved her.

It *hurt*.

He squeezed his eyes shut and settled back into his chair. When he heard the study door open and shut, he released a breath he'd not even known he was holding. He pounded his head against the headrest. He cursed in Russian, then in French for good measure.

What had he been thinking, saying those ridiculous things? He'd poured out his worst fantasies, and she hadn't even believed him. If she didn't despise him enough already, *that* should tip the scales.

He needed more vodka.

When he opened his eyes, however, he saw Finch standing in front of him with a lost expression on her face. His heart lurched. Surely the vodka had conjured her up. *Surely...*

"Five minutes," she said, all too real.

He tried, but couldn't even manage to stand. He fell back to his chair and gaped at her. "Why are you still here?"

She approached him until she hovered inches from his knees, not meeting his eyes. "Just sit there, please, for five minutes, without moving. I must see..."

He shut his eyes again, not daring to believe what was happening. "What must you see..."

His remaining words strangled in his throat as he felt her hand touch the skin just above his false Necklace. The raging lust that reared up inside of him at her touch sobered him immediately. His breath caught in his throat, and his hand shot out to cover her own, to bring it high to his lips ... or lower, to where his painful erection now strained against his trousers. He couldn't decide which he wanted more.

"No moving. Five minutes," she said, near his ear now. Her breath caressed his skin, causing gooseflesh to rise. He froze and dropped his hands to the chair arms and gripped them tight. He was afraid that if he touched her now, he would not be able to stop himself from devouring her whole. He didn't even dare open his eyes.

She brought her other hand up to join the first, and they felt around the edge of the Iron Necklace to the secret clasp in the back. Every brush of her skin against his own was a torture. At last, she worked the clasp free, and she removed the disguise from around his neck. She sucked in her breath as she touched her fingers to his bare, unmarked neck. She stroked his skin as lightly as a feather against silk, and he couldn't help it. He shuddered.

When at last he looked into her eyes, now level with his own, he tried to fathom what was in them.

They were chocolate now, dark and secretive, and filled with uncertainty. And desire.

He could not be mistaken. But what did she want? Did she even know?

He groaned in agony. "What do you want, Aline? What in hell's name do you want?"

Confusion darkened her brow, clouded her eyes. She bit her lip. "I ... I don't know. Just five minutes to see..."

"See *what?*"

She shook her head. "Neverfeel ... Nether ... *Charlie* never made me feel as you did. As you *do*."

He growled at the mention of that loathed name.

"I just want to see..." She stared at him, lost. At length, she glanced down, where her fingers still caressed his neck. Then she trailed them down his shirtfront, pausing over the area of his heart, which had begun to pound against his ribcage, as if it wanted to burst free. "I want to see your heart," she said, placing her whole palm over it.

Her tender touch nearly unmanned him. He wanted desperately to hold her, to assuage this pounding hunger eating away at his battered soul, but he could do nothing but sit there in disbelief as she tortured him with those warm, stroking fingers. She stared down at him, bafflement clouding her features, as if she couldn't believe what she was doing any more than he could.

"Yes, yes, God," he tore out. "*Anything.*"

His words seemed to startle her out of her distant reverie. She shook her head and leaned in closer until he was drowning in her once more. She began unfastening the buttons of his shirt and waistcoat with shaking fingers. She peeled back the edges, exposing his chest to his navel. She stroked her hands tentatively through the dusting of dark, curling hair, as if surprised by the sight of it.

Then she found the raised, jagged scar, running down the length of his sternum. She traced it with her fingertip, and he sucked in his breath, afraid to move. No one, not one of his lovers, had ever touched him there so deliberately.

It had never been like this before. She barely touched him, and all of his resolve began to crumble. It was all he could do to keep his hands at his sides. It had gone far enough. Too far. She was drunk. *They* were drunk. He should have walked away long ago, before he found himself in this untenable position. But it was the last thing his body wanted, the last thing his soul wanted.

"How painful it must have been," she murmured. "But why did it not heal?"

It took him a few moments to focus his brain away from her caresses enough to answer her. "Something went wrong.

The man who ... turned me broke something."

"A broken heart," she said with a wry quirk of her lips, "that never quite healed."

He looked away from her fingers on his heaving chest to her face. She was watching him with such tenderness that he truly began to panic.

"Aline..." he began. But then she flattened her palm against his racing heart, and he groaned.

"How quickly it beats," she murmured, and she melted into him. That was the only word to describe it. Her legs bumped against his knees, her head tilted forward. Their faces hovered inches apart, and he could feel the hot, sweet breath of her against his lips. She trembled all over. "You feel it too. Do you not? You weren't mocking me..."

"Never," he whispered.

"Do you want me to kiss you, Sasha?"

His heart thrummed in gratitude and fear. "Yes, kiss me. Kiss me..."

She closed her eyes and leaned forward, touching her mouth to his. He made himself sit there as her lips, soft and tentative, brushed against his. Then her lips touched his cheek, his chin, his eyelids, his forehead. He'd never experienced anything so sweet, so tender and so terrifying. It shook him to his toes.

Kissing Finch was harrowing.

She stopped, shifted back, studying him like some unsolvable equation. "Even when you don't kiss me back, it's nothing like..."

He surged forward and captured her lips again. If she mentioned the bone-hunter's name one more time, he didn't know what he would do. With a little gasp, she slid her arms around his shoulders, pressing close. When her lips parted, he seized the opportunity to plunder her mouth with his tongue, tasting her, savoring her. *God*, she was so sweet. Every nerve ending in his body clamored for more.

She seemed to feel the same, for her arms tightened their hold, and her mouth widened. Her tongue tangled with his, meeting his onslaught head-on. Their kiss deepened, became nearly brutal in its intensity. He felt her arms slipping from his shoulders, her fingers running over his face, through his hair, drawing him closer, yet he clung to the arms of his chair, afraid to unmoor himself. He was hanging onto his restraint by a hair's breadth.

Then he felt her shift, and suddenly she was sitting in his lap, straddling him. He could feel the warm weight of her legs across his thighs. He could feel her breasts crushed against his chest. She broke their kiss, and her head went down, her hair tickling his nose. He gasped at the feel of her lips against his throat, the feel of her hands sliding over his bare chest again.

His vision went black. His body lurched with desire. It couldn't have been more than a few minutes since that first kiss, yet it felt like a lifetime, as if he'd never known anything but this exquisite torture. He let out a ragged sob and threw his head back.

"Oh, God. Aline ... *Aline* ... You'd better be sure. I won't stop, if you stay another moment."

She stilled, shifted her weight on top of him, and raised her head. She was cherry red and panting. Clearly, she'd felt the very large evidence of his arousal at last, and she'd understood his warning. She'd come to her senses. He nearly cried out in his despair. He didn't know what he'd do if she attempted to leave him now, so bloody unfulfilled.

He dug his nails into the chair arms until the fabric ripped and the upholstery popped out, preparing himself to let her go without a struggle.

But then he nearly jumped out of his skin at what Finch did to him next. He hissed as he felt one of her hands reach down between their bodies, caressing the outline of his cock, her eyes wide.

So much for scaring her off.

She stroked him again. And again, and he moaned, burying his face against her shoulder. She had no idea what she was doing to him. "Stop, Aline. Stop."

"I'm hurting you?" she asked, pausing, her breathing as

ragged as his own, her eyes behind her crooked spectacles bright with vodka and trepidation and a healthy dose of lust. God, she was spectacular at the moment, incandescent to his eyes. A true miniature goddess.

He laughed darkly. "No, *milaya*. You're not hurting me." *But I'm afraid I'll hurt you.* She was so fragile, so dear. And he loved her, God help them both.

She gave him a shaky smile and ran her finger along his jaw, angled his face upwards once more, and began to kiss him again, hard and fierce and hungry. He could feel the warm, hidden place between her legs gliding against the fall of his breeches. Three layers of fabric at the very least separated them, yet he felt the heat of her, the softness of her, as if they were skin to skin.

She rubbed against him, so innocent in her ardor, and the world seemed to shift around him, knocking the air from his body. He couldn't breathe any more. He couldn't seem to do anything but feel her, wrapped around him so eagerly, so earnestly.

His restraint frayed, and he brought one hand down low to her ankle, sliding it up her stocking, past her knee, to the warm, smooth skin of her thigh beneath her petticoat. She was as soft as a flower petal, and he hadn't even touched her ... *there.*

It took her a moment to register what had happened, but when she did, she stiffened. He raised his other hand, brought it to the soft skin of her throat, her neck, then down her back, to her shoulder blades, holding her, bracing her for what came next. A moment later, the tension in her body ratcheted up as his fingers drifted higher, parting the fabric of her drawers, sliding in to stroke her.

He gasped at what his fingers found. She was already wet for him. Wet and pulsing and ready. And so delicate. He slid one finger inside of her as gently as he could, and she arched against the hand at her back, crying out in shock.

He bit back a curse. She was all slick, soft heat, yet so tight. He hesitated at the discovery. He knew in some part of his brain that this was wrong, but he couldn't remember quite why or summon up enough good sense to care. His head was swimming, his body was pulsing with a need he couldn't ever remember feeling.

He had to have her, and nothing was going to stop him, not even his conscience.

In the blink of an eye, he'd ripped open the fall of his trousers, unleashing his painful erection. A few seconds later, he'd pushed her skirts past her thighs and found the warm, soft curve of her backside, urging her up on her knees over him.

He could barely stand to do so, but he paused and met her eyes. She was staring at him with shock and confusion, and something else bright and wild that made him swell even more, his tip brushing her sex, making him moan.

Then, stunning him to the quick, she eased down upon his length with deliberation, something shifting in her eyes, the confusion fading away. He sucked in his breath at the feel of her soft, damp flesh enclosing around him.

Dear *God*, she'd done it.

She did not get very far.

"Please, please," she murmured, her fingers clawing his back for purchase, her eyes wild.

He couldn't hold back any longer. He settled her close and reached between them, stroking her swollen clit until she was gasping for air. Then when he could feel her open to him, he surged upwards off the chair with his hips until he was embedded inside of her to the hilt, rending her maidenhead deep inside of her. Aline whimpered in pain and bit his shoulder hard.

He groaned against her temple, trying not to move, bringing up his hand to cradle her nape. She was so tight, so hot, clutched around him. Remorse tempered his joy at being inside of her at last. He'd not wanted to hurt her.

She bit his shoulder again, but not in pain this time, and moved her hips, nearly tipping him over the edge.

It was the vodka. Or a dream.

They matched perfectly. Gritting his teeth, remembering how delicate she was, he thrust inside of her with gentle, languorous strokes, reveling in the feel of her as he moved inside her, her uneven breath against his neck. The chair jumped across the floor, throwing them off balance, and he clutched her tight against him. She gazed at him in baffled wonder, her spectacles completely askew.

"Dear bloody God," she murmured.

He slid a hand down the top of her gown and easily ripped aside her stiff corset, cupping one of her breasts. How had he missed noticing her breasts all these years, so lush, so lovely? She moaned at the gesture, and he realized in that moment he was the first man to ever touch her like this. Certainly the first inside of her, he'd felt the proof of that. The first ... the last.

"God, you feel better than my dreams, *milaya*," he growled, moving fast now. "I love being inside of you. The first."

"Barbarian," she whispered.

He ripped the spectacles off her face, tossed them away, and focused on her eyes as he pumped inside of her. She was more right than she knew. Like hell he would let another man touch her now. Like hell he would let these breasts, this body, marry some bone-hunting tosser.

This was precisely what he'd known would happen, what he'd fought so hard to avoid. "Mine," he whispered.

Her eyes widened at his word, and she moaned. Then she began moving her hips tentatively on top of him to meet his thrusts, taking him off guard.

She ducked her head, and he felt her teeth on his throat, biting the tender flesh there, the slight pain heightening his already unbearable pleasure. She bit harder, and harder still. He gasped. His control slipping, he slammed into her so fiercely that she gasped and once again raised her head in surprise. He panicked, tried to rein himself in, but then she smiled, a beatific smile that made him nearly come right then.

"Again," she murmured.

His head spun dizzily. This had to be a dream. He slammed up into her again, shuddering from the effort of curbing his unnatural strength, and from the blinding pleasure washing over him.

She cried out suddenly, tightening her hold around him with every part of her body, kissing his face a thousand different ways as he pounded into her, again and again. He felt impaled upon her to her very heart. He'd never been so closely in tune with another person, not even Yelena. Her pleasure was his pleasure, her body his body.

He could feel it when she began to climax, her entire body trembling, her lips uttering an incoherent cry. He grasped her hips with both of his hands and thrust into her, hard and swift, to prolong her release, watching her face grow incandescent with pleasure, as his own body spiraled towards the end.

He climaxed, and it might as well have been for the first time in three hundred years, for it was unlike anything he'd ever felt. His loins exploded with heat, his body quaked with a pleasure as intense as a lightning strike sweeping through him. On fire, he pumped against her, crying out with wonder.

He fell back against the chair, and she collapsed against him. Their pounding hearts pressed together, one of flesh, one of metal alchemy. "Sasha ... lovely Sasha," she murmured, kissing his cheeks, his eyes.

He tried to reclaim his bearings, but the room began to spin around him. He was drunk, but no longer with the vodka. Drunk with *her*. He felt clumsy, blessedly exhausted. He ran an unsteady hand over her silky blonde hair, down the slight slope of her back, breathing her in, never wanting to let her go now.

Yet knowing, deep down, that nothing had really changed.

He shoved that unpleasant thought aside. He wouldn't think about that. Not tonight. Tomorrow would be different, but tonight she was his.

He stood up with her still wrapped around him, and stumbled towards the door. She looked alarmed at this sudden shift. "What are you doing?"

"Taking you to bed," he said.

"I'm not tired," she murmured, burying her face against his shoulder as if embarrassed.

"Neither am I. But I want you again. All night."

"Again?" She sounded shocked.

"Yes. Again, *milaya*. It will be better this time."

"Better?" Her tone was doubtful, and he laughed.

"So much better, Finch. We didn't even take off our boots," he said, pausing at the door, smiling down at her, unable to help himself. She raised a shaky hand, caressing his cheek, pulling him nearer. Their mouths met hungrily, and all rational thought was suspended once more. He spun around and headed for the divan.

It was some time before they made it to his bed.

*W*HEN Aline awoke to the half-light of dawn leaking through a shuttered window, she found herself ensconced in an unfamiliar bed, curled up against something very large and very warm. Something that smelled wonderful, though judging from the pain in her head, it wasn't the most comfortable pillow she'd ever used.

She turned away, seeking a more comfortable position, and felt something wrap around her waist, pulling her back to where she'd begun. She fell against the mattress with a thud and gasped. She glanced down and nearly jumped out of her skin at the sight of a large, masculine hand splayed across her very naked waist. Thinking she was still asleep and caught in some lurid dream, she closed her eyes.

It didn't help. When she opened them again, the hand was still there and she was still very much sans clothes. Reluctantly, she turned her aching head, though she already knew what she would find. Sasha. A very *naked* Sasha, sprawled out beside her.

A jumble of images and sensations began to fill in the gaps in her memory with alarming intensity. She wasn't entirely certain how she'd ended up in such a compromising position, but she knew a vase had been involved. And a great quantity of Russian liquor.

And a chair.

She groaned and attempted to sit up, which was a mistake, as her head began to spin and the slumbering giant beside her stirred to life. The hand on her stomach pressed her back down, and she tumbled awkwardly against a broad, well-muscled chest, dusted with dark hair. She vaguely remembered being fascinated by that unexpected thatch of hair, and the devastating scar that bisected his chest.

And in that moment, she remembered everything. Sweet merciful heavens! Did she remember!

She felt the blush start in her toes and travel the length of her body and down to the tips of her unbound hair. She had been ruined. Terribly and wonderfully ruined by Sasha Romanov. And she had enjoyed every minute of it.

She felt warm, soft lips press against her temple, and she turned her head. She stared into a pair of luminous amber eyes. Wolf's eyes.

"Hello, *milaya*," rumbled a deep, familiar voice.

She froze and turned away, only to feel the same set of lips against the nape of her neck, sending shivers down her spine. His hand was slowly circling higher, his fingers teasing one of her breasts. His other hand moved from his side and began doing the same to the other breast, trapping her against him. She watched with growing mortification as her body visibly responded to his touch. He seemed to be watching as well over her shoulder, murmuring wicked, wicked things into her ear.

She attempted to extricate herself once more as panic began to set in. But she only succeeded in pressing into his hands, which felt too wonderful to be real. She made the mistake of glancing downwards, where their legs – hers pale and thin, his long and muscled – entwined together, then a little higher, where the very large evidence of his manhood settled within a tangle of short, dark hair that thinned out to a peak over the hard ridges of his stomach.

She remembered what that particular organ had been capable of only a short time before, and she felt her face flame even hotter. As if it had read her mind, it began to physically rise to attention. She gasped, and her mutinous body began to practically sizzle in response, centered around the vicinity of the suspiciously sore spot between her legs.

Dear bloody God. What had she done?

She seized his hands by the wrists and jerked them away,

sitting up with a start, suddenly stone cold sober. She tried valiantly to collect her wits, but then he turned over on his side, and the hard length of him brushed against her hip, sending her mind reeling anew. His lips brushed her shoulder blades.

She swatted him away in vain. What had she been thinking?

That she'd wanted to kiss him, touch him. That she'd wanted to do so desperately from the moment that devil's liquor and his seductive words began to unhinge her hidden desires. That she'd wanted to do so for days. Weeks. Years, perhaps. That she wanted to do so still.

She felt him freeze at her back. "Do you hurt? Have I hurt you?" he asked against her shoulder.

She was a bit sore and entirely humiliated, but she could not say he'd hurt her. She shook her head.

This answer seemed to please him, because he growled and nuzzled his head against her neck. The sensations he provoked threatened to overwhelm what little good sense she had left.

"I must go," she murmured, clawing her way to the edge of his vast bed.

She didn't get very far before he pounced, pulling her back against him. "You're not going anywhere, *milaya*. Not yet."

They tumbled against the bed sheets, the length of his large body pressing her into the mattress. She attempted to turn around, but he held her in place effortlessly, his mouth now against the back of her neck.

"Damn, you're sweet, Finch," he whispered. "So small and perfect." He stroked the skin of her neck, lingering on the small scar as if it fascinated him. "You don't know how rare you are. But I do. A rare little bird, and all mine."

"What nonsense," she scoffed weakly.

"It's been over half a century since I've touched a woman without enhancement," he mused.

"You're talking about your other women, are you?" she muttered, trying in vain to swat his hands away.

"So jealous, Finch," he murmured, sounding pleased. "What if I told you I've never felt such soft, delicate skin in all of my three hundred forty two years?"

"I'd say I've listened to your silver tongue for too long already."

He rolled them both over on their sides so that she was settled into the crook of his body, his arousal jutting against her backside. To her everlasting consternation, her reason went up in smoke, replaced by what she now knew to be desire. The tension in her limbs ebbed away, and she instinctively nestled closer against him. The feel of him, so large, so warm, was overwhelming, and the musk of his body engulfed all of her senses, intoxicating her more completely than the vodka had ever done.

She made an embarrassing sound in the depths of her throat, a cross between a cry and a moan, as he toyed with one of her nipples.

"You are the color of the inside of a seashell here," he said, as if it was a revelation. "So pretty." His voice jarred her back to herself. She inched away from him. He promptly pulled her back. "Don't fight it, Finch. Not yet."

"This is wrong. This ruins everything."

"Nothing is ruined. Everything is better now."

"How can you say that?" she cried.

"Because of this." He shifted behind her, and suddenly she felt his tongue tracing her skin, from the middle of her back to the top of her neck. She shivered uncontrollably at his wicked seduction. "Because of how you make me feel here." He moved his hips, thrusting his erection against the small of her back, making her gasp. "Because of how I make you feel. *Here.*"

And he ran his hand down her belly and into the tangle of hair between her legs. She cried out and arched against him, suddenly helpless to her own desire, as his fingers teased her folds open, bringing forth a mortifying slickness from her body.

He groaned at her ear. "So wet, *milaya*, so sweet. I know. I've tasted you."

She moaned at his words. He had tasted her at some point

last night, after he'd undressed her and cleaned away the evidence of their original sin staining her thighs. She remembered he'd not been happy at the sight of her blood, and he'd spent what seemed several lifetimes attempting to make it up to her with his tongue and lips and teeth. Down there.

A wave of mortified delight passed through her at the hazy recollection. Then as he stroked her and licked her neck anew, a fresh wave of ecstasy rose up from her core, spreading like molten lava through every vein and artery inside of her.

She wanted him, even more ardently than before, and she could no longer deny it. Her arm rose up behind her, her fingers sliding through his thick, untidy curls, tugging him nearer.

"Sasha," she murmured, turning her head.

His eyes glowed like two yellow diamonds in the dawn light, and his mouth, full of sensual promise, descended to cover her own.

"You're mine, Finch," he whispered against her lips.

Her mind rebelled even as her body capitulated. "I'm not yours."

"*Mine*. Now and forever. I'll never let you go."

A frisson of unease slid down her spine, disrupting her pleasure. "You'll have to. Eventually."

He grew still behind her. She thought she'd put him off, and she turned her head once more, capturing his gaze. He looked momentarily lost, and so very, very alone. Her heart lurched.

But he shook his head and gave her a wicked grin. "Care to wager on that?" he murmured darkly.

He tugged her leg over his hip, so that his manhood nudged her from behind, then resumed teasing her between her legs.

He shifted his hips, and she felt his hard length penetrating her from behind. She'd not thought it possible.

Well, she'd not thought it possible to lose her virginity in a chair, either, but she'd been disabused of that notion quite thoroughly.

She moaned and clutched his lean thigh, urging him closer.

He let out a ragged breath against her neck as he filled her body. That feeling of perfect completeness she'd felt the first time reasserted itself. How could something so wrong feel so wonderfully right? she wondered.

And then he began to move, and she wanted to scream it felt so good. "Say you're mine, *milaya*," he whispered against her ear.

"Never." She still had *some* sense left.

He grunted and moved faster and harder, taking her higher and higher. His fingers stroked her from the front, over that magic spot he'd found the night before, and her body seemed to implode with heated sensation. Release spread like a drug through her limbs, and she cried out, clutching at his hip to bring him even further inside of her.

He withdrew abruptly and flipped her over onto her back. He shoved her legs wide and settled between them. She stared up at him as if through a fog. His hair was in a delicious muddle and his cheeks were flushed with heat. His eyes were glittering, and his skin glistened with sweat. His chest heaved, his magic heart working so hard she could see it pounding against his ribcage. He had never looked so beautiful, so foreign, so dangerous.

"Say you're mine," he repeated. "If only tonight ... if only this once..."

Something in his tone, something desperate, shook her to her core. But she hadn't lost her soul to him completely. Only her body. She shook her head, and he groaned, his smile vanishing, dark intent replacing it.

He captured her lips in a hungry kiss and slid inside of her, hard and quick, then withdrew slowly, over and over again, taking her once more to that high precipice of pure sensation. He took her to the very brink, then paused, making her cry out in agony for the release he denied her. His hands slid over her breasts, down her arms, his fingers entwining in her own.

"Say it, say it," he murmured between his kisses.

"No..." she moaned weakly.

"Say you are mine," he demanded, angrily now. He began

thrusting again, ratcheting her up to the brink once more until they were both breathless and trembling and clutching desperately at each other.

"You are mine!" she cried, matching his rhythm eagerly now.

He laughed. "You little witch! Yes, God help you, I am yours. I am yours," he said joyously, and her heart melted at his words. His body was so much larger than hers, so much harder and full of its own distinct will, yet it seemed in that moment a part of herself. So much so she could believe what he said.

Lord knew she wanted to.

She climaxed again, and this time he was with her, crying out in ecstasy against her temple. His body shuddered violently against her, and the warmth of his release seeped deep within her.

"You couldn't say it," he murmured into her ear some time later. He tugged her ear with his teeth. "Perhaps you will ... one day. I don't think I can do any more convincing tonight," he sighed, rolling off her, bringing her on top of his chest and holding her closely, tenderly. "I feel I could sleep for an age."

One day, he'd said. Implying this would happen again and again. But that could never be, could it? He was leaving her, and even if he didn't, it was impossible, wasn't it? He was immortal, for heaven's sake, and she didn't think he'd consider the only option for his kind that could keep her with him. Christiana had explained Bonding to her and Sasha's aversion to the very idea.

And he'd made no declarations, other than he'd desired her. It had been enough for her last night, and she couldn't let herself hope for more. This was temporary insanity for both of them. She was sober enough to recognize this.

But she was having trouble remembering anything but the way her body felt joined to his. She couldn't seem to think any coherent thought, aside from the fact that their bodies were pressed together, sweat soaked, sated. And that she would have been happy to remain exactly where she was for an eternity.

As she watched him through lowered eyes, he seemed

entirely human in that moment, and heartbreakingly young, his nose nuzzling her hair, his lips skimming her temples, one hand carelessly covering her breast. His movements slowed, his breathing became even, and she realized he'd fallen asleep, curled around her as if he never meant to let her go.

She wished she could believe it. Because she loved him, with all of her heart, even though he was a vexing, sly, damaged tyrant. She would be a fool to keep denying it. She didn't know when this turn- around had happened, or if she had loved him all along without knowing it.

But she had a horrible feeling there would be no happy ending for either of them.

"Miss Wren failed to inform me of your existence until yesterday, Corporal Standard," Dr. Augustus declared with a haughty lift of his chin.

"That's Captain Standish, Doctor," the Captain said, his patience frayed by the Doctor's impolite behavior. *"I command the Albion Lady, that very same vessel that has interceded on your behalf for years."*

"Do you not remember Zanzibar, Doctor?" Miss Wren asked in exasperation. *"Thomas rescued us from that nest of dirigible pirates."*

"Ah, yes. Zanzibar. But who is this Thomas? I thought we were speaking of the Corporal," Dr. Augustus replied.

Miss Wren allowed herself a very unladylike huff of frustration.

-from *The Chronicles of Miss Wren and Dr. Augustus*, 1895

10

WHEN Aline came awake again, she was alone. She sat up in the bed with a start, and immediately regretted it. Her head felt as if someone had taken a knife and sliced it open. And her body ... she ached in places she could not even name. She lifted the covers and stared down at herself, heat suffusing her from the toes up. She was naked. In Sasha's bed. She very gingerly lowered her head and buried her face in a pillow.

A mistake. Sasha's scent invaded her senses, pulling her under into a deep sea of carnal images forever branded into her memory. Even now she could feel his hands upon her – wicked, wicked hands, doing things no hands ever had business doing. And then his lips and his tongue, revisiting the places those hands had touched. The very thought of it made the secret place between her legs throb.

How had the night gone so wonderfully wrong?

She had been thoroughly debauched by the Professor. Numerous times. She groaned and squeezed her eyes shut. Which was another mistake, for those memories came into sharper focus. How he had looked as he had driven himself into her. How he had felt. Inside of her.

Too good.

With careful movements, she rose from the bed and wrapped the sheet around her – though what purpose it served at this juncture she wasn't quite sure – and crossed the room where her dress lay folded neatly in a chair. Her face flared red as she realized Madame Kristeva had cleaned and pressed it as best she could, which meant the housekeeper would know precisely where and how Aline had spent her night. How mortifying.

How was she to face anyone? Especially Sasha? This was a nightmare. She was engaged to Charlie...

Then she remembered with … well, relief, to be honest, that she wasn't. He'd broken things off with her. That was why she had come over here in the first place, to ring a peal over Sasha's head for his role in the whole debacle of her life.

What had happened afterwards had been a drunken mistake.

It hadn't *felt* like a mistake, though.

She repaired herself as best as she could and crept downstairs, contemplating fleeing the townhouse altogether. She was so wrapped in her panic she nearly collided with Fyodor in the hallway downstairs. He took one look at her, then stared hard at the floor between them, a hint of red suffusing his human side. She blushed too, knowing he knew precisely why she was wearing the same mud-spattered garment she'd worn the previous day.

He gestured for her to meet Sasha in the study. She drew in a deep breath and nodded, and Fyodor walked away abruptly, as if he was too embarrassed to linger. God knew she couldn't blame him.

Aline shored up her resolve and approached the study, the site of her spectacular folly the night before. As much as she was dreading it, she needed to face him now and sort out this whole dreadful turn of events. She pushed the door open before she could let herself think too hard about it.

The growl of Ilya was the first thing to greet her. The dog was agitated about something. The second thing to greet her was Sasha himself, rising up from behind his desk, looking spectacularly gorgeous, damn him.

Her breath caught in her throat as she hesitated in the doorway, her courage having fled through her gelatinous knees. She knew her face was flaming as she struggled for composure.

His gaze flicked over her. She thought something bright and penetrating sparkled in his eyes, but she could have imagined it, for his face was carved in stone, impenetrable, more impenetrable than ever.

She felt her heart drop, and she hated herself for her weakness. She'd held onto some vestige of hope that things would be different between them, even though she'd told herself not to.

I am yours, I am yours, his voice echoed through her memory. Words she couldn't say, words that had come so easily to his lips, as if he'd meant them with all of his body and soul.

Well, he'd always been a liar.

But she didn't want it to mean anything for either of them, she tried to tell herself. She wanted his indifference. She wanted him to pretend as if nothing had happen, because that was what she had planned to do to him.

But it hurt nonetheless.

Then she noticed his gaze flickered to another figure sitting with his back to her in front of the desk. Her hurt gave way to disbelief.

Charlie.

Good Lord. The one person she'd wanted to see even less than Sasha at the moment, and he was here. Both of them, here. In the same room. All it needed was a biblical plague to make things perfect. Charlie rose and faced her, looking none-too-pleased at whatever he and Sasha had been discussing.

When he started in her direction, Ilya growled at him and blocked his way.

Sasha did nothing to call off his dog, just stood there, looking vaguely amused. She glared at him, then attempted to soothe Ilya, stroking his back, before turning her attention back to her ex-fiance.

"Charlie!" she said, hoping her voice sounded halfway normal.

"Darling," he said, still next to Sasha's desk, not daring to cross Ilya. He focused on her less than tidy appearance, his brow furrowing. "Weren't you wearing that yesterday?"

Aline glanced down at the rumpled green dress that Christiana had made over for her. She caught sight of a tear at the waistline and felt herself turning scarlet. She remembered when *that* had happened last night, quite clearly. Too clearly. She glanced furtively at Sasha, who was standing behind Charlie now, hands behind his back, gazing at her with an unfathomable gleam in his eyes, content to let her dig her own grave.

"Well, yes ... that is..." she drifted off, beginning to panic.

She caught a sudden shift in Sasha's eyes. They seemed to darken with intent. She braced herself, for she'd seen that devilish look many times in the past.

"She spent the night," he said matter-of-factly to Charlie's back. He raised one eyebrow at her, as if daring her to contradict him.

Apparently, he was going to dig the grave for her. The beast.

Charlie looked dismayed, and his normally placid eyes now filled with something that almost looked like rage. "You did what?" he demanded.

"She spent the night," Sasha repeated.

When he opened his mouth again to dig her grave halfway to China, she quickly found her voice. "I did," she said with as much dignity as she could muster. "I fell asleep here. I was too tired to return to Llewellyn House."

"Too *drunk* you mean," Sasha murmured.

It took all of her self-control not to rush to his side and punch him in the face. What in hell's name was Sasha about?

He continued. "In an attempt to calm her overtaxed sensibilities, I offered her vodka last night. I can honestly say I have never seen her behave in such an abandoned manner. So I put her to bed."

She was speechless at Sasha's utter cheek.

"Is this true, Aline?" Charlie demanded in a surprisingly hard voice she'd never heard him use before.

She glowered at Sasha, trembling with rage. "Yes. I mean, *no*." She sighed and ran a hand over her face. "After our row yesterday, I came here —"

"To have a row with me," Sasha interjected. He turned to Aline. "Charlie and I have been discussing his accusations against me before you joined us, Finch, by the way. I told him I had nothing to do with his dismissal."

Charlie looked increasingly incensed. "And I told him I don't believe him."

"And I told him I could care less."

Dear God.

She didn't think she could handle much more of this. "What do you want, Charlie?" she demanded. "You made yourself perfectly clear yesterday."

Charlie made another move to reach her side, and Ilya barked, his hackles rising. Charlie gave the dog a murderous look, which he quickly turned on Sasha. "Professor Romanov, if you could call your beast off, and let me have a moment with my fiancée?" he bit out.

Sasha merely crossed his arms and quirked his eyebrow. "I was under the impression you cried off." He looked at Aline. "Did he not cry off, Finch?"

Charlie's murderous expression managed to deepen, and for a moment Aline feared Charlie would try something ridiculous, like challenge Sasha to a duel. A duel he'd have no hope of winning.

"Professor," she said through gritted teeth, "if you would give us a moment, I would be *most* appreciative."

Sasha gave her an odd look. Was that hurt she saw in his eyes? If it was, it was quickly gone as he nodded and crossed the room. "Of course, Finch." He snapped his fingers, and Ilya reluctantly followed after him. As Sasha passed by her, however, he completely disconcerted her by brushing the back of her arm with his fingertip, as if he couldn't resist touching her. She barely restrained her gasp.

Charlie glared at the door once Sasha and Ilya had slipped out. Something dark clouded Charlie's eyes, unsettling Aline even more. But she could hardly blame him. Charlie could be scatter-brained, but he wasn't completely oblivious. He had every reason to hate the Professor.

"I never approved of you working for that man, Aline. I do not like him," he muttered.

She put her hands on her hips and glared at him in exasperation. "Well, I believe you lost the right to have an opinion over my life yesterday. Or did you forget breaking the engagement?"

Charlie's brooding expression turned contrite. He strode over to her and took her hand. "I did not forget. I spoke very harshly, but I've regretted my words ever since. Perhaps I was hasty in breaking things off."

This was the last thing she'd been expecting this morning. God help him, Charlie was such a good man, really, despite the lapse yesterday, and she didn't deserve his apology – *or* a reconciliation – not after last night. "Charlie, I must tell you..."

"No, don't say a word, Aline. I know I mucked it up. I took out my anger on you and it wasn't right. I already have a new sponsor lined up for our Egyptian dig. I believe my plans will work out after all."

"That's good news, Charlie."

Charlie raised her hand and kissed it. "But they won't work out without you, Aline. I don't want to lose you, my dear."

Her heart was sinking. "Oh, Charlie, I don't know."

He caught her shoulders before she could pull away from him. "We are to be wed in a week, Aline. The airship sails in eight days. Tell me you're going to see this through."

"Charlie, after yesterday, the things you said ... the way we both behaved..."

He grasped her shoulders rather too firmly and shook his head earnestly. "My dear, say you can put yesterday behind you. I know I have."

Aline stared up into Charlie's earnest face and felt thoroughly miserable. Even if she'd wanted to, she couldn't possibly consider reconciling with Charlie, not after last night. It was unfair of her to even consider it.

Though technically they had been finished, over and done with, for the duration of the evening.

Technically, she'd not really betrayed him, since they hadn't been engaged. Technically.

Justifying herself just made her feel even worse, and it was pointless anyway. One thing she was certain of was that she couldn't marry Charlie, and it had nothing to do with what happened between her and Sasha. She'd seen a side of Charlie yesterday that he'd hidden from her all of this time. And she hadn't liked it. She thought of all the things she hid from him, and wondered how many other secrets he was keeping from her.

She suspected Charlie was not the steady, dependable character he'd always made himself out to be, and she feared marrying him and enduring a lifetime of unpleasant surprises. She was beginning to think their broken engagement was for the best. She'd been angry with the Professorover his interference, of course, but beneath the anger, she'd been secretly relieved.

She just hadn't anticipated this strange turn of events. How had it come to this? How had she let herself be drawn into Sasha's web so totally? How had she let him seduce her?

No, that wasn't quite fair to Sasha. He had attempted several times to make her leave. *She* had been the aggressor. *She* had wanted him.

God, how she had wanted him, and how she still wanted him! She'd never known such pleasure was possible. Even thinking about the way he'd felt inside of her, the way he'd looked, poised above her, so beautiful and savage, made her ache between her legs.

She couldn't marry another man. She didn't *want* another man.

She faced Charlie, guilt clawing her insides. He must have sensed her mood, for his expression fell. "I'm sorry, Charlie. I can't forget yesterday." *Or last night.*

He dropped his hands from her shoulders. "Will you at least think about it?" he asked.

She opened her mouth to stay firm in her refusal. But something in his eyes, something a bit desperate, a bit frightening – the same look she'd seen yesterday right before he'd thrown that strange fit – made her pause and reconsider her words.

"Of course, Charlie," she said, patting his hand. "I shall think about it."

*W*HEN Aline walked back into the study after sending Charlie off, Sasha was stooped over his desk, as still as a statue. He lifted his head and locked eyes with her, and those strange amber depths shone with an outrage so profound she felt as if he'd slapped her in the face.

She had not expected this.

"Did you just reconcile with the bone-hunter?" he demanded in a hard voice.

His imperious tone raised her hackles. She drew herself up. "What makes you think that is any of your business?" she retorted.

He pointed towards the chair he'd sat in last night. *The* chair.

She blushed crimson, her entire body going hot. "What happened was a mistake. We were drunk. *I* was drunk. You took advantage..."

Something painful flashed over his face. "*I* took advantage? *Liar.* You came to me. You wanted me just as much as I wanted you, *milaya.*"

He was, of course, right, though she didn't want to admit it to herself *or* to him. "Does it matter? Does it change anything?"

"You can't possibly reconcile with Neverfeel!" he cried.

"Why are you so worried?" she asked quietly. "Have your plans changed, Sasha? Do you no longer intend to leave me behind?"

He was taken aback by her bluntness. He just stared at her, as if trying to puzzle something out. She didn't wait for his response. She didn't think she could bear it. "As I thought. Nothing has changed."

"I could stay. For a time..." he began.

She couldn't help but feel stung by his suggestion. Somehow it was worse than him simply leaving. "I won't be your mistress, Sasha. I know what happens to them. You have your secretary break up with them. You'll soon tire of ... this."

His amber eyes darkened. "I'll not tire of you, ever," he said fiercely, pounding his fist so hard on his desk the wood cracked.

She stared at what he'd done so carelessly, so effortlessly, and went cold inside. She kept forgetting what he was. What he was capable of. He'd said himself he felt out of control around her, which was why he was leaving. She finally understood why he thought it necessary. Judging by his broken desk, it took very little to set him off these days. She didn't think he would hurt her, not intentionally. But his secret life was dangerous. Violent. And it scared her.

He'd ripped off a man's head with his bare hands, for God's sake. She could never forget that.

She wondered if she was strong enough to stay by his side at all, if it came to that. But it was fruitless to even consider these things. When he said he'd never tire of her, she yearned for it to be true. Yet she dared not believe it. Their physical attraction was one thing, but letting herself believe that he cared for her was dangerous folly.

Sasha could give her nothing she needed, besides his body. He was too damaged to even think to offer her more. And in the end, despite what he claimed, he would grow bored of her, as he grew bored of all of his women. Even if he didn't, even if this was somehow different for him, not merely a fling, he was *not mortal.* He would remain as he was forever, and she'd age and die. It was an impossible situation.

He looked down at what he had done and winced. Clenching his hands into fists, he came around the edge of his desk, and she could tell he was struggling to hold onto his frayed temper. "I will not let you marry him," he declared.

She was exasperated by his persistence on the subject, but it just proved that all of her racing thoughts were foolish. She doubted a future beyond a short liaison had even entered his thick, male head. "You selfish, arrogant ass! You can't have me, so no one else can, is that it?"

"Yes!"

She recoiled at his brutal honesty and backed away as he stalked towards her.

"I am my father's son," he sneered. "I tried to warn you. I tried to send you away last night. You know what I am. Do you think I shall not have my way?"

She searched his angry eyes. "I know you'd never hurt me, Sasha," she said quietly.

"I don't want to. But I can't seem to help myself," he said.

"You're leaving. Would you have me spend the rest of my life alone? As miserable and ... and soulless as you?"

Something seemed to snap in him at her brutal words. His lips turned up in a snarl, and he seized her by the shoulders. "What do you want of me? What would you have me do? Do you think this feeling between us when we make love is normal?"

Make love. She shivered at his words and shook her head. "I wouldn't know."

His expression softened for a moment. "Of course you wouldn't know, *milaya.*" He kissed her forehead. "But *I* know. It is not normal. It is madness. I've never felt this way before."

"Don't say such things, Sasha."

"It's the truth."

"This must stop," she whispered, pushing him away, her heart pounding with forbidden hope. "Things have gotten out of hand."

"Is that what you call it?" he asked, trailing his long, elegant fingertips over her cheek, down her neck. She caught his hand before it could move any lower, before her defenses were completely shattered by his wicked touch.

"Please, Sasha, listen to me," she entreated.

But he didn't seem to hear her any more. He leaned into her, and she was drowning, suffocating in his intoxicating scent once more. She gasped for air.

"You must break with him," he whispered.

His words brought her out of her momentary stupor. He was like a dog with a bone. She attempted to break away, but he caught her close in his arms and lowered his head. He kissed her passionately, and she was immediately lost to the world in physical rapture, her body melding to his.

She tried to fight it. She'd been fighting it ever since the night he'd tipped her on her desk and kissed her. If that one event hadn't happened, she would have gone her whole life without ever knowing such feeling could exist between two people. She would have married Charlie and have been complacently bored for the rest of her days.

But he *had* kissed her, and she had felt the world as she knew it fragment around her. And it was terrifying, because she knew that more than her body had been surrendered to Sasha. He'd not asked for anything else, and he'd not want anything else, but somewhere along the way, her heart, traitor that it was, had fallen at his feet, filled with foolish love. And she feared he would trample it, no matter what he said now.

Suddenly, she felt suffocated. She broke the kiss and wrenched free of him, gathering her wits. She needed to leave before she made yet another wretched decision. She couldn't seem to help herself when he touched her. And he knew it, the devil.

"Where do you think you're going?" he demanded as she stumbled towards the door.

"I'm leaving. I can't think straight here."

But before she could reach the door, he was there, pulling it closed and turning the lock.

She stopped up short and gaped at the speed with which he'd moved. It was the second time this morning he'd betrayed his inhuman abilities, as if he were beyond caring. For the first time since this strange conversation started, she began to feel truly uneasy.

"We're not finished, *milaya*," he murmured with quiet, deadly intent.

"Yes, we are. Let me out."

"You'll not leave me. Not yet. You're mine. *Mine!*" he breathed hoarsely.

She couldn't believe what she was hearing. "You ... beast!"

He laughed darkly. "Yes, that's what I am. And you like it."

"You are unbelievable! I'm leaving," she cried, trying to push him aside and open the door, but the minute her hand touched his hard torso, she could feel her good sense flying out the window. She snatched her hand back and fumbled for the lock.

He surrounded her from behind, giving her no quarter, his body warm and solid against her back. He moved his lips to the nape of her neck in a whisper of a kiss, causing her breath to seize and the place between her legs to grow damningly hot.

She sank to her knees, and he came with her, catching her wrists in one hand, pulling them away from the lock. He turned her, and his other hand slid over her backside, pushing her hips firmly against his own, so that she could feel the hard prod of his erection at her belly. She gasped in outrage and despair as a tremor of pleasure spiked down to her toes from their glancing bodies.

He tried to kiss her lips, and she arched away. "I'll bite you if you don't let me go this minute," she warned.

This did not act as a deterrent however. He seemed to grow even more against her belly, and his lips curled into a devilish grin that didn't reach his desperate eyes. "Please do."

With that, he released her hands and brought both of his to

the front of her beleaguered dress. With one fluid motion, he ripped the material aside. She gasped as the cool air hit her bare flesh. She struggled to cover herself. He swatted her hands away and lowered his head, taking her left breast into his mouth. He suckled her, pulled her erect nipple taut with his teeth, sending a tremor of lust streaking through her body so fierce, so overwhelming, that the fight in her sputtered out.

She arched against his mouth on instinct, relishing the sensations he provoked, all of her resolve to never succumb to him again flying out of her head.

She felt his hands pushing the remains of her dress and corset down her body, stroking her skin as they went. Then they were under her skirts, tearing at her underclothes. At last his fingers found that perfect spot, already slick with fierce arousal.

They both gasped. He raised his head and met her glance. Lord, he was beautiful, his black hair tumbling over his brow, his clever lips drawn taut with his passion. Color stained his exotic, high cheekbones, and his eyes glittered wickedly at what he felt beneath her skirts, his breath becoming as labored as her own. As if he were as mindless with pleasure as she was.

Suddenly boneless, she fell back against the door, her back grinding against rough wood, and she gasped, more shocked than hurt. Sasha followed her on his knees, dragging himself up her body. He pulled her against him, insinuating himself between her legs, her crinolines and skirts tumbling about them.

The exotic scent of him invaded her senses, making her traitorous body want to melt against him, soak up his scent and his heat inside of her. He reached between them again and ran two fingers between her legs, causing her to quake.

His animal eyes bored into her as he stroked her. "Tell me to stop, *milaya*."

She couldn't form the words. He felt so good, she didn't want him to stop. "Never stop, Sasha."

She felt him shiver at her words, saw his eyes turn nearly translucent with need. He groaned desperately, causing her heart to pound so hard against her chest it hurt. She burned like fire in her belly, arching into his hand, so near the brink already.

With fingers that trembled, he unfastened his trousers, lifting her higher against the door. Then with one stunning thrust of his hips, he was inside of her to the hilt, never taking his eyes off her. They both cried out helplessly, clinging to each other. It felt even better than before. Damn him. She still didn't see how he fit inside of her, but he did, and so perfectly that she wanted to weep.

He dropped his head back, the grimness fleeing his expression, a look of wonder taking its place. That she was responsible for it gave her a fierce, hot throb of satisfaction. He coaxed her hips down on his lap, filling her even more, then he stilled, as if he wanted to freeze them in that moment.

"I've been wanting to be here all morning," he whispered.

She couldn't disagree with that particular desire. Because as much as she'd fought it, she'd wanted much the same ever since she'd awakened to find him gone from the bed.

Her mind floundered as she tried to recall the thousand reasons why she should be anywhere but here, in his arms, joined together in the most inappropriate manner imaginable. She could not recall anything, as his lips were currently covering her face with sweet, hot kisses, as if attempting to memorize her face. He found her mouth and plied it into submission with tender insistence. His tongue tangled with hers.

Quickened desire, hot and incapacitating, stole through her limbs with his kisses. She'd lost her mind. Her body relaxed into his own, taking him further inside, to the edge of her womb. She felt so full of him, but it wasn't enough. She willed him with her hands and hips to move.

Breathing raggedly, as if remembering where he was, he drew back, nearly leaving her, and she whimpered in protest, following with her hips. He stopped her and held her in place as he thrust back inside of her, hard and swift, then did it again. It would have been painful, if it didn't feel so good.

"I can't go slow," he breathed against her neck in anguish. "I want you now. *Now*." Then he licked her from the base of her throat to the tip of her chin, a gesture so erotic she felt the warmth of release already stirring in her blood. She cried out again and pressed closer to him, tilting her hips, opening herself to his thrusts in complete abandon. He drove into her, the power of his ardor slamming her against the door, nearly knocking the breath from her body. But she knew he wouldn't hurt her.

God help her, she liked the power of his body surging against hers, so much stronger, so much bigger. She liked the earth shattering strokes of his manhood within her. He would leave bruises from his hands, from the impact of their bodies coming together, but she didn't care.

"I can't wait. I can't ... Come for me, *milaya*," he whispered, pounding and pounding into her, his breath a frayed torrent against her throat.

She came for him. She fractured into a million, sizzling pieces, and for a moment in time her body and soul ceased to exist. He moaned and clutched her hard against him, shuddering from head to toe, the heated power of his own climax spilling into her.

"My God," she breathed, much later.

He held her close for a moment, caressing her with languid hands. "So sweet," he murmured. "So lovely. You make me feel so good, Aline. So *young*. You make it go away."

"What? What goes away?" she whispered earnestly.

He didn't answer. He buried his nose against her hair and breathed deeply, his arms tightening around her as if he'd never let her go. And she didn't want him to. She didn't think she could ever let *him* go. Not now.

At last, he moved away from her, repairing his clothes, his head bowed. But she could see enough of his expression to start to worry all over again. Their moment of respite had been too short. He looked ... ravaged. A thousand years old.

She shuddered to think what she must look like to his eyes. She looked down at herself. She was falling out of her torn bodice like some Seven Dials tart. She attempted to right herself, but she discovered her hands were shaking too hard.

He let out an anguished sound and reached out to help. She flinched without thinking, hating that he had to see her in such awkward disarray, and she froze, his hand halfway outstretched. When she dared to look at him again, her skin crawled at the pain in his eyes. Such utter horror. Such self-loathing.

She placed her hand in his to reassure him – though it didn't – and he pulled her to her feet, fixing her dress for her in silence, his movements mechanical, as if he didn't truly see what he was doing. She stared at his face, grim-set, anguished, as he set her to rights, every second that ticked by widening the chasm between them.

She wished she hadn't flinched. Somehow she knew that was a critical error. Not making love with him. Not loving him. Never that. But she had flinched, right at the end, as if he'd frightened her, and that had shattered him. She could see it in his eyes.

"I must leave you," he muttered. "I must let you go."

Her heart plummeted. She fisted her hands at her sides to keep them from shaking. "So you are finishing with me? Now? After what just happened? Have you lost your mind?"

He barked out a laugh. It sounded raw, dreadful. "Yes. Utterly." A pause. Another wretched intake of breath. "We both know I can never give you what you need. Go back to your bone-hunter, if that is what you wish."

So he'd finally accepted the fact that he had to leave her, just when *she'd* accepted the fact that she could not leave him. She'd laugh at the irony if it were at all funny. He spun away, rubbing at the scar on his chest. Why had he given up now? *Now*, when she could still feel the imprint of him inside her, the evidence of their love-making still wet on her thighs?

Finally the tears that she'd held back all morning started leaking down her face, all of the shame and frustration she'd tried to squash rising to the fore. She'd had enough of his fickleness.

"Is that it? You've got everything you wanted from me

already?"

He groaned and wrenched her against him. His eyes were blazing with a righteous fury.

"I got nothing I wanted!" he rasped. "I do not want to break you. I do not want to hurt you. But that is all I seem capable of doing. My love is a poison. *I* am poison."

She gazed at him, thunderstruck. She'd known that he cared more than he let on. But this ... this couldn't be true. "Sasha, do you *love* me?"

He didn't even hesitate, which was further shocking. He gave her a fierce, devastating look. "*Yes*, I love you, Finch," he said. "As much as a monster like me can love."

Her heart soared at his words.

"I think I always have," he continued, causing her heart to quake. "And that is why I must go. I can't bear to hurt you any more than I have already. Look at what I just did to you. Against a *door*," he said with self-loathing.

"But it was glorious," she retorted.

He was momentarily speechless. He recovered enough to say, "Don't say such things, Finch. Say you'll be happy when I'm gone."

"I can't," she said through her tears. She drew a ragged breath and continued. She had to say it too. Just once. Just so he'd know. "I can't be happy when you're gone, because I love you too, Sasha. I love you, and I don't want to lose you."

He looked at her as if she were mad. Then he turned away from her and ran an unsteady hand through his black curls. If anything, her confession seemed to upset him even more.

"I'm not marrying Charlie," she said. "I was never going to. How *could* I, when I love you? I was prepared to let you leave, Sasha, because of what you are. How could I bear to be cast aside when you're through with me? Or grow old by your side while you remain unchanged? How could I bear it at all, when I didn't think you even loved me? I can still hardly believe it."

"Why is it so unbelievable?" he demanded. "Do you think that I cannot love? That I am entirely a machine?"

"I don't think that you're a machine at all," she protested. "I just never thought you'd love *me*."

"Well, I tried my damnedest not to," he muttered.

She took a deep breath, her heart filled with trepidation. There was a way to solve all of their problems, if Christiana was to be believed. She wasn't sure she was quite convinced in the wisdom of it, but it was the only thing left to try.

"There is one way, Sasha. Christiana explained everything to me. What you are. What she is."

He grew rigid at her words, and his expression shuttered. "No," he said simply. "I will not Bond you. I will *not* do that to you."

"You'd rather leave me?" she demanded.

"*Yes*, by God. Don't you see? Have you not realized it yet? I hate what I am. I hate never growing old, never dying, seeing everything and everyone I care about wither and die. How could I consign you, or *anyone* for that matter, to such a fate?"

"But we would be together," she said quietly.

Her words seemed to give him pause. But finally he shook his head. "Would you give up everything? The chance of a normal life? Children? A Bonded woman can never have them. You'd be stuck as you are, forever. Stuck with me. *Forever.* Tell me, is that enough?"

She couldn't answer him, because she didn't know if it would be. She could accept never having children. She could accept being stuck with him. Or at least with the man she knew he could be, the teasing, mercurial Professor she'd known and grown to love over the last five years.

But how could she bear a life with a man who hated his very existence? How could she bear an eternity enduring moments like this, when the blight in his soul made him lash out at the world — at *her*?

When she made no response, he sighed, and something crumbled in his eyes, as if he'd held onto some small hope she'd contradict him. "You know it is not. It is precisely because I love you that I could never do that to you. You'd hate me for it, in the end."

Her shoulders slumped. "No, you just don't love me

enough," she said sadly. "And you hate yourself too much to believe you could ever be happy. That *we* could be happy." She sighed. "Perhaps you're right. There is a darkness inside of you that I can never fix, not in a dozen lifetimes. Only *you* can do that."

"It's not so easy," he said.

"All you have to do is forgive yourself, Sasha." She went to him and began to smooth out the wrinkles in his jacket, then reached up to retie his neck cloth, knowing with a bittersweet certainly that it would be the last time. Such an ordinary act after so much tumult. Yet she wished she could tie his neck cloths forever.

He watched her movements, his body tense and wary, as she worked to untangle the knots. "I read my uncle's letters that you kept in your drawer," she began. "I never knew he was in the War. But it explains a lot. Sometimes he would be in the middle of a sentence, and he would just drift away. I always attributed it to his eccentricities, but he'd get this terrible look in his eyes that used to chill me to the bone. I'd never seen that look in anyone else, until I met you. Sometimes at night, I would hear him scream. He had terrible nightmares. Just like you."

She worked the knots free and began to retie it. "And I never understood why he was so driven, so hell-bent on his mission in the stews. But I guess it was his penance, much like your work is to you."

He made a sound of protest, which she ignored. The truth was so glaringly obvious, he'd never convince her otherwise. For a man trained in psychiatry, he was singularly obtuse about his own motivations.

"Whatever happened during the War, whatever role he played, it must have been devastating. Reading his letters to you, he blamed himself for what happened. But you forgave him, didn't you?" She finished with his necktie and glanced up at his grim countenance.

"Yes," he said at last with great reluctance.

"Why can you not forgive yourself? Stop using your past as

an excuse to push people away. You're not your father. The man I've known for five years, the man I just gave my body to, is no monster. Until you realize that, you'll have no peace."

He looked floored by her words, but he shook his head in stubborn denial. "*I* may have forgiven him, but your uncle could never forgive *himself*," he pointed out.

She stepped away from him and started for the door, giving him a sad smile, and one final, lingering glance, her heart breaking. "And look how he ended up. Half-mad in St. Giles. And alone. I *do* love you, Sasha, but you're right. It's better we go our separate ways. I couldn't watch you torment yourself forever. *I'd* go half-mad."

She'd accused him of not loving her enough, but perhaps the horrible truth was *she* just didn't love *him* enough, which was why she was able to walk out the door without a backward glance. Callous as it was, she'd rather believe this than the alternative – that she'd left her heart behind with him in that study, and that she'd never be whole again.

Days after the smashing success of her annual Charity Ball, Lady C— was seen by several witnesses on a certain Mayfair street, engaged in a Shocking Behavior. This author can hardly credit the reports this office has received, as The Most Beautiful Lady In England has always seemed quite incapable of such a Faux Pas. Brace yourselves, readers, when you learn the Scandalous Truth. Lady C— was seen Sprinting down Berkeley Avenue Without a Chaperon...

-from the Society Page of *The London Post-Dispatch*, 1896

11

week later, Aline struggled to finish her belated installment of the *Chronicles* for the *Post-Dispatch* on her new typewriter. Christiana had given it to her, since hers had been destroyed by the wardrobe door the Professor's vampiric brother had thrown that fateful morning in her flat. After all that had happened over the last few weeks, she'd not been able to focus on her writing, or indeed anything useful. Fortunately for her career as a serial novelist, she had a peer of the realm to plead her case for an extension with the editors. She was not about to turn down such a favor, especially when it was because of the Earl and his fellow immortal brethren she was in such straits to begin with.

After a week of wallowing that doubtless rivaled any dramatic fit The Luclair – another victim of the Professor's exotic charm – had ever thrown, Aline had finally had enough of herself. No amount of tears was going to change the basic facts of her existence.

Sasha was leaving any day now. She was not. Plenty of people fell in love without things working out. Romeo and Juliet. Helen and Paris. Marc Antony and Cleopatra. Tristan and Isolde.

Well.

Just because *they* died didn't mean she had to. She may have no experience with such a sophisticated matter as a broken *affaire*, which she felt more than excused her tendency to turn into a watering pot. But she was no wilting violet, whose life was over just because she'd been disappointed in love. She was a modern, independent woman of the Steam Age. And she was British. She'd soldier on.

Though the fact that she was in love with a brooding three hundred forty-two year old Russian Crown Prince masquerading as a criminologist who killed vampires with his bare hands did make her situation uniquely piquant.

She was quite ready to get on with her life. Truly. Even though she was still at Llewellyn House, a virtual prisoner. Since the discovery of the existence of vampires and their proclivity for her blood, the Earl had been loath to let her return to her flat.

Not that she would ever be able to live there again, after what had happened.

She was not exactly thrilled at the thought of vampires lurking about London, thirsting for her blood, either. But she knew she couldn't stay at Llewellyn House forever. She had to start working again, however, if she wanted to find her way to the other side of the ruins of her life.

And that began with the *Chronicles*. If she happened to take the plot line in an unexpected direction, owing to recent events in her own life, she was prepared to forgive herself. The characters in the *Chronicles* were, after all, better versions of their living counterparts. And *they* at least would have their happy ending, damn it. Eventually.

The Misses Eddings and Ridenour would have the vapors when they picked up the next edition of the *Post-Dispatch*.

Christiana entered the drawing room where Aline had set up her desk and peered over her shoulder as she worked. "So what happens next in the *Chronicles*?"

"You shall find out soon enough," she said wryly.

Christiana tsked impatiently. "Tell me. Rowan's out on some dreadful Council business, and I'm bored. It's Miss Wren's wedding day next. Tell me she doesn't marry Standish."

Aline sighed and turned away from her work. "She doesn't marry Standish."

Christiana looked delighted at this plot twist. She settled on the settee opposite for a coze, probably relieved to find Aline without tears coursing down her face for a change. "So, what happens?"

"Augustus appears in his dirigible and whisks Miss Wren away to his lair."

"Really? He kidnaps her? To his *lair?*" Christiana looked devilishly pleased.

"Not so much a kidnapping," Aline admitted. "I believe Miss Wren was quite willing. She has always had a secret *tendre* for her employer."

Christiana gave her a mock-surprised grin. "*Has* she? So you've finally seen what half of England has known for years."

"Something like that," she admitted.

"And so, shall they live happily ever after?" Christiana continued, a bit tentatively now.

She snorted. "How trite. I believe I shall make Augustus do something dreadful and send him into exile first. I won't make it easy for him."

Christiana nodded. "Good for you, Aline." She paused and twisted her fingers together in her lap nervously, clearing her throat. "I hear the Professor leaves tomorrow into *his* exile."

Aline went rigid and sucked in a breath, determined not to let the news bring her low. Which was futile. She felt punched in the stomach, though she knew this day was approaching. Lady Christiana studied her with such sympathy it made her feel even worse. She'd not told her friend all that had transpired between her and the Professor the night she'd spent at his townhouse, but she was sure Christiana had some idea, considering the state she'd been in when she returned to Llewellyn House.

"You're not going to even say goodbye, my dear?" Christiana asked her gently.

She managed to shake her head. "We've already said all there is to say."

"I wonder," Christiana murmured. "I do wish there was some way for him to stay. You were so good for him, Aline."

She gave a bitter laugh. "Hardly. We were at each other's throats."

Christiana quirked a brow. "But you loved it, just like he did. When I first met Sasha in Vienna years ago, he was a different man. As if all the light had been extinguished in his eyes. Who could blame him? But he changed when he came to live in London. You put a spark back into his eyes."

"Well, it wasn't enough. He's leaving, and it's for the best. Please, can we talk of something else?"

Christiana hesitated. "My dear, have you considered..." She faltered, blushing. She grimaced and tried again. "I know this is indelicate of me, but I must ask, is there a chance of a child?"

Aline felt all of the blood drain from her face. She involuntarily raised a hand to her stomach. The possibility had not once crossed her mind, which was stupid of her. She swallowed unsteadily. "Surely not..."

Christiana pursed her beautiful mouth, looking troubled. "I thought as much."

She shook her head. "But is it even possible? With what he is? He said something about your kind not being able to have children."

Christiana looked even grimmer. "That is true. I cannot have a child, according to the Council. But an Elder is well capable of fathering a child, even though, from what I understand, it is not the done thing."

The thought of having Sasha's child terrified her. But deep down, in her innermost heart, the idea was not so dreadful. *How* could she not love a child of his? But she felt that Sasha, on the other hand, would be anything but pleased. "Even if it comes to that, it wouldn't change anything,

221

Christiana," she said with quiet certainty.

"Oh, darling, you *can't* believe that!"

"I wouldn't want him to ever know. I think it would destroy him, after what happened to his wife."

"I don't think you can keep something like that from him," Christiana said, her brow furrowed.

"I can try," she said quietly, feeling suddenly exhausted. Christiana had given her yet one more thing to fret about, perhaps the biggest thing of all. How could she have been so thoughtless of the consequences? How could Sasha?

"Well, hopefully there will be nothing to worry about," Christiana said, moving closer to her side so she could pat her hand. "It was only the once, was it not?"

She looked at Christiana in dismay. Oh, it hadn't been *once*. She'd lost track of how many times Sasha had turned to her that night. She was *still* sore. And she didn't think it mattered if it had been. Once was enough. For all her years, Christiana seemed even less informed on such matters than she was.

Christiana blushed at Aline's unspoken response. "Oh, dear."

"Can we change the subject?"

Christiana looked grateful. "Of course. There is no sense in dwelling on things that may never happen. Though now I quite understand why you refused to reconcile with your Dr. Netherfield."

"That was one reason," she gritted out, her heart sinking even further. She'd forgotten Charlie completely.

"Well, if you must know, I'm glad. There has always been something about that man I cannot like, my dear. And when we visited him in his offices last week and he said such awful things, he made me quite uneasy." Christiana shivered, as if remembering something unpleasant. "He is not the man he appears to be, Aline. I am certain of it."

Aline was about to reply when the butler came into the room to announce a visitor. "Dr. Netherfield to see Miss Finch, my lady," the butler intoned.

Christiana gave her an arch look. "Speak of the devil. Shall I stay, Aline? You don't look like you're up for this."

She shook her head. "I shall be fine."

Christiana looked doubtful, but she left the room. When Charlie entered, Aline immediately wished she'd not sent her friend away. He was looking as desperate as she felt. She'd never seen him in such a state, unshaven, jittery, in clothes she was certain he'd slept in. He stared around the room as if making certain they were alone before he approached her, and his furtive manner did nothing to tamp down her own rising anxiety.

Surely he was not in such a state over her. Perhaps he was still worked up over the Professor's role in his dismissal, though Aline was beginning to have some doubts about Charlie's story altogether. His behavior of late was bizarre.

She struggled to her feet as he took her by the hand. For some reason, she didn't want to be sitting down for what was to come. He gave her an odd, hard smile that didn't reach his eyes, crowding close, squeezing her palm as if he didn't mean to let her go. "My dear, are you feeling better? I was told you've been ill."

She removed her hand from his overly zealous grasp, feeling suddenly suffocated. He was standing far too close to her. She crossed the room and positioned herself behind a chair.

"I am well, Charlie. What do you want?" she asked bluntly. She regretted being impolite, but she'd had about all she could take for the day.

Charlie arched an eyebrow, his smile turning to stone at her tone. "I came to have your answer, my dear. Do you not remember? You gave me hope at our last meeting. As I am departing quite soon for Egypt, I thought I'd have my answer."

Her stomach lurched with guilt and dread. She'd forgotten all about her parting promise to Charlie to reconsider their engagement, given in a moment of weakness. Perhaps he was pining over her, after all.

Though his persistence hardly made sense. He'd always

made it clear that their's was not a love match, and after his behavior at his office, she wondered if he'd ever cared for her full stop.

Uneasy, though she couldn't explain quite why, she considered her response carefully, unwilling to stir the pot. "I wish you well, Charlie, I really do. But you deserve a better match than me. I think it's for the best that we part ways." And in this case, with this man, it was the truth. She only wished it were true for the last man she'd parted ways with. She was afraid she was going to regret letting Sasha go for the rest of her life.

Charlie's smile evaporated. "Are you quite certain, my dear? You do not wish to come with me?"

"I'm afraid we just would not suit in the end, Charlie," she replied, giving him a weak smile.

Charlie gave a beleaguered sigh and pinned her with an impatient look that erased her smile completely.

And then he ... *changed* in the blink of an eye.

Something in his eyes, in the rigid cast of his jaw, made her start back in alarm. She hadn't thought it possible for him to look so hard, so ... mean. He seemed like a different man all of a sudden.

"How tiresome you're being, my dear." Even his voice was different. It had a cadence to it that was not even British at all. The hairs on the back of her neck and arms stood on end. Something was *very* wrong.

"Why can't anything ever be easy?" he mused to himself.

"What are you talking about, Charlie?"

He stalked towards her, moving with a predatory grace that had nothing in common with the stiff, slightly ham-fisted archaeologist she'd known for three years. The horrible gleam in his eyes only seemed to intensify as he drew nearer. "I'm talking about your sudden maudlin attachment to your employer, my dear. It *quite* complicates matters. I counted on his sentimental regard for you, but I never expected you to become his whore."

Her blood froze in her veins at the venom in Charlie's

voice, the sneer on his face. His words were cruel and inexplicable.

He shrugged. "But perhaps it is all to the good. He shall be that much more motivated to give me what I want," he said, reaching into his pocket and extracting a pistol. "You, on the other hand, are giving me a headache. Why could you not simply come with me as you are supposed to?" He leveled the pistol in her direction and motioned for her to walk towards the French doors at the other end of the room.

Feeling as if her legs were made of jelly, she followed his unspoken order. Judging from the insane glint in his eyes, he was quite prepared to use the weapon in his hands. She couldn't quite believe what was happening. "Charlie, what are you doing?" she demanded. "What is going on?"

He reached up and tugged off the Iron Necklace at his throat. Her heart dropped from her throat to her knees when she saw his unmarked neck. The Necklace had been a fake. Like so many of her acquaintances of late, Charlie seemed to have had no need of the breathing implant at all. He cast the disguise aside and glared at her.

"First of all, Charlie is *not* my name. Secondly, what does it look like I'm doing? I'm kidnapping you. If you scream or raise any sort of alarm, I shall shoot you. I'm not *that* keen on keeping you alive."

"But why?" she cried, trying to remain calm, but finding it increasingly impossible.

She was afraid she'd pushed him too far, for he was at her side in the blink of an eye, grabbing her arm and shoving her through the doors and onto the terrace.

"Quiet," he hissed, glancing around the garden. "You've no idea the trouble I've gone through to catch you in a moment when the Earl and his men are absent. Hurry," he demanded, pushing her across the terrace and down into the gardens.

She tripped on the stone stairs and fell to her knees, scuffing her palms. She raised her eyes from her bloody hands and glared at Charlie. He made no move to help her, merely motioned her onwards with impatience. She stumbled to her feet, and he shoved her in the back, nearly sending her to the ground again. She quickened her pace.

She was alarmed, of course, to discover her fiancé was insane, and she was definitely afraid of the gun in his hand, but she was also vastly annoyed. This was the last thing she needed, to be kidnapped at gunpoint by an unbalanced bonehunter – who she was beginning to suspect was not a bonehunter at all.

"You can't want to marry me this badly," she said, rubbing her stinging hands on her skirts, trying to stop the bleeding. "Tell me you aren't a vampire, at least."

He looked disgusted. "Nothing so vulgar, my dear. Unpredictable, violent creatures. They never do what you want them to."

A horrible suspicion began to form in her mind. She skidded to a stop and rounded on him. "You knew that creature who attacked me, didn't you?"

He gave her a dark smile. "Vasily? He and I have been associates for years. Unfortunately, I had to distance myself from him when he became unmanageable. I had not counted on your particular affliction, my dear. It quite drove him mad, your blood, and nearly exposed me. He could not stick to the plan. All he could think about was drinking you dry, I'm afraid. I would have gladly obliged, if he'd but *waited*."

His words made her shudder with dread. *Dear Lord.* He motioned her towards the side of the gardens, leading into the mews. She slowed her pace as much as she dared, stalling for time, searching all around her for some sign of Matthews, or any of the other men who were usually patrolling the residence. Since they'd all thought the threat to her was passed, however, their vigil had been limited. As far as she knew, the Earl and all of his men were off on an urgent matter for this mysterious Council of his. She held out little hope of rescue.

"Don't tell me *you* are responsible for all of those murders," she said. Surely the man she'd known for three years was not so evil.

"Necessary collateral, my dear. Though those women in Whitechapel were all Vasily's doing. As I've said, I lost him to his thirst. Fortunately, the good Inspector and your lover took care of that little problem. Wrapped everything up quite neatly, too. How I would have loved to see the Tsarevich's face when he met his bastard brother for the first time in centuries."

Another unpleasant realization dawned, and her stomach churned anew. "Those hearts at the museum weren't from mummies at all, were they?"

He looked at her as if she were stupid. "Finally figured it out, did you? I was afraid you'd suspect me that day. You quite caught me off guard with your little visit. I had to get rid of you quick, hence our little tiff."

She was certain she would be sick. She clutched her middle. "Why would you ... *keep* them? What sort of disgusting monster are you?"

He just grinned at her. "They are ... trophies, I suppose. Research. I have studied the human heart for centuries, preparing for a time when I finally have what is mine."

As much as she didn't want to hear his sick revelations, she'd keep him talking as long as he could to delay him. He seemed more than happy to linger while he explained himself to her.

"*What* is yours, Charlie? Who are you? What is your connection to Sasha?"

"I am Carlos Salerno," he said, as if it were obvious. "I was to be the thirteenth Elder, alongside my brother. But that *thief* stole my heart," he seethed.

"I don't understand. How could Sasha have stolen the heart?"

He gave her a frustrated look and pushed her onwards, shoving the pistol against her back. "*He* didn't. Leo's damned assistant Fredo stole it and disappeared. It took me half a century to find him rotting in a Russian dungeon. But I was too late. The Tsar had already made Fredo put the heart inside his dying son. The fool couldn't even do it correctly either. Useless creature. I made sure he suffered for his crimes."

She wondered if Fredo hadn't done the world a favor by his theft. Perhaps the man had sensed the rot in Charlie's soul and stolen the heart before it could be implanted. She wished *she* had sensed the rot. "So Sasha was given the heart. Why are you still alive?"

He sneered. "Through the *grace* of my Elder brother. But I shall not be dependent upon his Blood Bond for much longer. He grows suspicious of me, anyway. I can no longer count on his usefulness."

The truth dawned on her. "You want Sasha's heart, don't you?"

He gave her a droll look, as if it were obvious. "It's *my* heart, my dear. It always has been. I thought I could retrieve it from him in Russia, with none the wiser. But I could never get close enough. Ivan Grozny's defenses were impressive, especially around his precious heir. Eventually the Council became aware of Romanov's existence. They weren't pleased, of course, and my brother and others argued my case. But the Duke of bloody Brightlingsea refused to take action to retrieve what was rightfully mine!"

Her heart stuttered to a stop. Bile rose in her throat. She was truly beginning to hate this Council. She suspected these Elders were the cause of a great deal of suffering in the world, with their arrogant belief in their right to play God.

"You mean, the Council actually considered killing Sasha to take back the heart?"

"It was *never his*!" he cried loud enough to echo off the garden walls, forgetting his own demand for discretion. He pounded his fist against his thigh, his temper rising. "The only way they would consider such an idea was if the Tsarevich was proved unredeemable. So I enlisted Vasily's help and set out to change the Council's mind."

"All those murders, for centuries, to implicate Sasha!"

"At first. But the damned Duke never quite believed Ivanovich's guilt. Not enough to take action. So I decided to find a way around the Council altogether."

"I don't understand."

He gave her an impatient look. "Since Fredo's demise, there is only one person left in the world with the skill and knowledge to perform Da Vinci's Vital Regeneration. He is an Elder, and only with Council approval would he agree to the operation. But I no longer need him. I believe I have found a man capable of the surgery. It has taken three centuries, but I shall finally have what is mine."

"You are insane, Charlie!" she breathed.

"Don't call me that. *My*, but I'll be glad to be rid of you when this is through. Three years in this tiresome role as the incredibly boring Charles Netherfield is enough to truly drive me insane. I really don't understand what the Tsarevich sees in you."

They finally reached the gate leading out into the mews. She could see an unmarked steam carriage hovering in the alleyway with a familiar figure at the helm. Professor Hendrix. His daughter, the beauteous Theodora, was watching them approach out of the carriage window. *Well.* She'd thought Theodora was infatuated with Charlie. She never would have guessed the woman was part of Charlie's murderous scheme.

Charlie gave her one last considering look as he threw the gate open. "Whatever the attraction, don't think me ungrateful, my dear. I've waited years for him to find something he'd be willing to die for."

"You plan to use me as ... as bait? Me in exchange for the blasted heart?" she cried, sickened, terrified for Sasha.

"Have you just now realized that? My dear Aline, you are really less clever than I gave you credit for. I admit this was not *always* the plan. I attempted one last time to sway the Council with the Tsarevich's latest rampage, but they have grown too suspicious of me since Vasily's overzealous actions this past month."

Theodora leaned out of the window, signaling at something behind them. She cried out something in Italian, and Charlie cursed.

Aline's stomach bottomed out with dread when she saw Lady Christiana running towards them along the garden path.

Charlie seized her around the waist, pulling her against him and pointing the gun at her head.

"Whatever are you about, Dr. Netherfield?" Christiana called out. "Where are you going with Aline?" She stopped up short when she noticed the gun, her mouth falling open.

"Don't come any closer, Christiana," Aline called out. "He's the true killer. His name is Carlos Salerno, and he's absolutely cracked!"

Charlie didn't like this last bit and cuffed her hard with the butt of the gun on her temple. Her vision went black for a moment, and she collapsed against him. The pain, delayed at first, finally caught up with her, and she sucked in a breath and struggled to remain lucid. When her vision came into focus, Charlie had dragged her to the steam carriage.

Theodora swung open the door, and Aline groaned when she saw the woman's glowing amber eyes and extended incisors. *Another* vampire. Theodora was staring at the blood trickling down Aline's temple as if it were water in the desert.

"Contain yourself, my dear Theodora," Charlie said. "Remember the plan."

Theodora's nostrils flared, and she made a pained sound. "But she smells so good, my love."

"Better than your life?" Charlie asked sharply, shoving Aline inside.

Theodora gave Aline one last longing glance. "I suppose not."

Aline was not comforted in the least by Theodora's reluctant response. She moved as far away from the woman as she could on the bench. Charlie climbed inside after her and began to shut the door. But Christiana suddenly appeared in the doorway, blocking the door.

"Aline!" she called, reaching for her.

"Don't, Christiana!" she warned. "Stay back. He'll kill you."

"I won't leave you!" Christiana cried.

Charlie shoved Christiana away with his boot. Christiana took the carriage door with her as she fell away, and Aline's breath seized. The steam carriage lurched forwards into motion. Unfazed, Christiana regained her feet and trotted alongside of them, attempting to enter the carriage in a show of bravery that was as foolish as it was commendable. Christiana was nothing if not stubborn. Aline cried out when Charlie leveled the pistol at Christiana and pulled the trigger. The bullet clipped her in the side, sending her sprawling to the cobbles.

She did not get back up.

Aline screamed her horror, and Charlie smashed the gun into her head again, sending her into darkness.

HERO OF SEVASTOPOL RESIGNS! Just days after the Duke of Brightlingsea brought the Abominable Russian Army to its knees, ending the dreadful conflict in the Crimea, His Grace returns to Albion's shores to a hero's welcome. After meeting with Her Majesty, His Grace revealed he has resigned as leader of the Allied Troops and plans to retire to his Welsh estate. One wonders what really happened on the Peninsula...

- from *The London Post-Dispatch*, August 1855

12

*S*ASHA decided that his life had definitely hit a new low when Fyodor resorted to pouring a pitcher of water over his head to rouse him from his latest drunken stupor. Sasha jumped up from his seat at his desk, where he'd spent the past several nights, immediately regretting it. His head spun, and he lost his balance, crashing to the floor of his study, wet, bleary-eyed, in the same shirt he'd worn for the last three days, and spoiling for a fight.

When he saw the look on Fyodor's face, however, he remained where he was. Fyodor looked prepared to thrash him, and Sasha suspected he would succeed. He was no match to battle a fly in his present condition, Da Vinci heart or no.

He pushed his damp hair out of his face and glared at his friend. "What the devil are you about?" he demanded in Russian.

Fyodor narrowed his eyes and stalked to the desk. He sorted through the pile of unopened post tubes and empty vodka bottles for something to write with. He found pen and paper and scrawled something. He held it up to Sasha's eyes.

You love her.

Sasha stiffened and felt his stomach drop to his knees. He shook his head in denial.

Fyodor stabbed his finger at his words for emphasis.

Sasha swatted the paper away as he stumbled to his feet. "It doesn't matter, even if I do."

Fyodor wrote something else and held it in front of Sasha's face.

She loves you.

The words still had the power to floor him. Impossible though it was, she *had* claimed to love him.

When he deserved nothing but her condemnation for reducing her life to a shambles. For taking so much from her. Especially that final, drunken night together when he'd taken her like the beast he was. Thrice.

Thrice. Even though he'd been completely off his face and therefore shouldn't have had the wherewithal for a satisfactory once, *especially* in a chair. But as soon as he'd touched her, he'd been gripped by a monumental, aching fever that no amount of vodka could quell.

That night may have been a drunken mistake, but as he'd lain there, holding her in his arms, he'd had the first peaceful night of sleep in decades. How could he let that go? He wanted to throttle her, to kiss her, to chain her to him forever. And it was exactly this outcome of events he'd sought to avoid by leaving this life. Too late.

He'd not wanted her love. He couldn't bear it ... though hadn't that been what he'd been craving from her all of these years? Begging it from her at every turn by his requests, his constant demands that kept her always by his side? Weaving her into the gaping, empty holes of his life without her consent? Feeding off of her wholesomeness like some giant, parasitical monster?

But what choice did he have but to give her up? She was not like Luciana or any of his other women, who could be content as a temporary mistress. And he didn't want her like that. She was not like any woman he'd ever known. He wanted all of her, for the rest of time. Yet he'd taken too much from her already, and he didn't dare ask her for more.

He wasn't even sure if she wanted more from him. She'd made that very clear to him when they parted. Even if he were to consider Bonding her, she'd never agree to it. She thought he was too damaged. And she was right.

Fyodor touched his shoulder and shoved another note onto the desktop.

Don't let her go.

Sasha gave a humorless laugh and shook his head. "I must, Fyodor. I am poison. I'd end up hurting her in the end."

Fyodor crossed his arms and glared at him, as if to say he already had.

"Even more than I have already," he amended wearily.

The bell on the post box blared again as yet another message came in, and Sasha groaned in exasperation. He'd lost control over every facet of his life, so he was not about to let a post box bell lay him low. And he needed to hit something. Hard.

He stalked over to the fireplace and retrieved the poker, then stalked to the post box, raising his weapon. Ilya whimpered from his bed by the empty hearth and fled the room entirely at this sign of impending violence. Fyodor's human eye went wide in alarm when he figured out what Sasha intended. He stepped between the box and Sasha.

Sasha lowered the poker. "Out of my way, Fyodor. If I have to hear that infernal bell go off one more time, I swear I will go down to the Ministry of Correspondence and level it with my bare hands."

Fyodor studied Sasha's face for a moment and decided he was in earnest. He stepped aside. Sasha raised the poker.

"Are we interrupting something?" came Rowan's wry voice from the doorway.

Sasha spun around, nearly losing his balance, and the poker clattered to the ground. There seemed to be quite a few people entering his study. Uninvited. He listed to the side, and Fyodor propped him up.

Rowan turned to a man even taller than the giant Fyodor

with a grim expression. "I told you we'd find him like this. He's in no shape for this, Your Grace."

Sasha felt Fyodor stiffen next to him, which was a considerable feat, considering his friend was nearly entirely made of metal. His vodka haze quickly faded as his heart began to pump adrenaline through his veins. Rowan, Drexler and Lieutenant Matthews were not entirely unwelcome, but the others were. He'd go so far as to call them intruders.

One of them, Franco Salerno, of all people, hovered near the rear of the group, looking as if he'd rather be in Hell. Sasha wanted to scream in frustration. Whenever that man appeared, bad things tended to happen to him. Like spending weeks in a stinking Genoese jail. The other intruder was hardly an improvement, however. The last time Sasha had seen the Duke of Brightlingsea had been after the fall of Sevastopol forty years ago.

It hadn't been long enough.

The Duke was the tall, broad brute of a man standing next to Rowan, dressed completely in black, with hair as black as Sasha's, and a black scowl on his face. Black upon black upon black. Fitting, in Sasha's opinion, for if ever a man was surrounded by darkness, it was the Duke. Sasha had forgiven Alyosius Finch for his role in the Sevastopol genocide, but he could not forgive the Duke.

Brightlingsea had claimed his so-called Solution was the only way to stop the unbeatable Abominable Army from overtaking the continent. Perhaps he'd been right, but the price had been high. The Duke's Solution had laid waste to thousands of square miles of land, from Constantinople to Kiev, ensuring the Abominable Army's defeat. The resulting miasma, officially blamed on the Steam Revolution, had blanketed the whole of Europe for years, suffocating its inhabitants until none could survive without an Iron Necklace.

Brightlingsea had made an impossible decision, one Sasha hadn't envied. But it wasn't for this decision that Sasha blamed him. He probably would have made the same call. It was for the true genocide that came next, when the Duke, in his grief, abandoned his post and left the field to the idiots in the War Office.

He blamed the Duke for turning his back while hundreds of thousands of survivors like Fyodor, unwilling victims of Stieg Ehrengard's lust for power, were slaughtered while they lay helpless in the field. They'd been free of the strange hypnosis Ehrengard had used to compel them to fight, and blameless for what they'd been made to do. But the War Office had declared them less than human and therefore disposable.

Only the Duke could have prevented such a travesty, had he not run away. This was what Sasha had a hard time forgiving.

As far as Sasha knew, the Duke hadn't left his self-imposed exile on his remote Welsh estate in forty years. Seeing him here now was enough to clear the rest of the vodka from his mind. Or very nearly. He reached down for the fire poker, just in case he needed it.

Fyodor had to prop him up again. He shook off Fyodor's arm, attempting to retain a shred of dignity. "Your Grace, finally stirring from your lair after all these years?"

The Duke frowned at him ferociously. "Don't try my patience, Tsarevich," he growled. "I'm not happy about being here either."

"Why *are* you here? We caught the murderer."

"No, we didn't," Rowan said in a grim tone.

Sasha laughed in disbelief. "You can't possibly still believe *I* am the murderer. Rowan, Elijah, you were there. You heard Vasily admit his guilt."

"Your brother *was* involved, but we don't believe he is Osiris," Rowan said.

"Again, *I* didn't do it!" he insisted.

Rowan cringed when Sasha went for the poker once again. "For God's sake, pull yourself together, Sasha. No one believes you did it!" he muttered in exasperation. "Not even Franco."

Sasha studied Franco warily. The man scowled at him, as usual, but the anger that was usually behind the scowl was gone. In its place was something that looked very much like guilt. *That* was new.

"What the hell is going on?" he demanded. "Why don't you think Vasily was the man we were looking for?"

"For one thing, he was a vampire. Did you not wonder how he became one? Who turned him?" Drexler asked with exasperation. "Or have you been drunk for the entire week?"

"I've been drunk for the entire week," he admitted honestly, running a frustrated hand through his hair. Elijah brought up a valid point, one Sasha had briefly wondered about. But he'd been distracted. Badly. He turned his attention back to the Duke. "Did *you* know that London is infested by vampires?"

The Duke gave the Inspector a sidelong glance. "I have been informed of the situation. But that is another matter. I am here to put a final period to this whole infernal business with your heart, Tsarevich."

"I don't see how *that* is any of your business," he said, affronted. "I am leaving London. She has agreed it is for the best."

The Duke's expression went from annoyed to incredulous. "Are you speaking of a woman right now, Tsarevich? The same woman who has reduced you to this ridiculous, drunken state?" He shook his head. "Does it look like I care about your *domestics*? I was speaking of the device that beats in your chest, you idiot."

The others backed up a step at the edge to the Duke's voice, even Fyodor. Brightlingsea wasn't the leader of the most powerful group of men on earth for no reason. But Sasha had never been afraid of him. He'd grown up with Ivan the Terrible for a father, after all. Brightlingsea was a kitten in comparison. He glowered at the Duke. "What about my heart?"

Rowan approached him, put a hand on his shoulder. "You might want to sit down, Sasha. There's a story here you're not going to like."

Sasha shook off Rowan's aid. "Get to the point, then get out. I've had enough of the damned Council to last until eternity."

The Duke summoned Franco forward with a flick of a finger. "I'm thirsty. *You* tell the tale, Salerno, since it's your fault we're in this mire," the Duke said, striding over to Sasha's sideboard and pouring himself a drink uninvited.

Franco sighed unhappily as he faced Sasha. "There were to be thirteen of us originally. The heart that now beats in your chest was stolen by one of Leo's Bonded acolytes, who disappeared without a trace. Then *you* came to our attention a century later. To most on the Council, your existence was unacceptable and illegal. We voted to retrieve the heart and give it to the man it was originally intended for."

Sasha was floored at this revelation, but he didn't know why. He'd always known he couldn't trust the Elders. "You were going to kill me and take back your heart?" he asked.

"I voted against it, Sasha," Rowan said quietly. "And the motion was eventually overruled after the Duke seized control of the Council."

Brightlingsea didn't look pleased at Rowan's interjection. He tossed back his glass of vodka, scowled at the bottom of it, and poured another. "We decided to let you live."

"How magnanimous of you," he muttered.

"Unless you proved unworthy. Then we reserved the option of retrieving the heart," the Duke continued dryly.

"Killing me, you mean," Sasha corrected.

The Duke scowled at him. "It was agreed from the beginning that should any of the Elders be proven guilty of a heinous crime, their hearts would be forfeited and destroyed."

"I wonder *you* are alive, then," Sasha said. "*And* Stieg Ehrengard, after what he did."

The Duke gave Sasha an arctic smile. "Oh, *he* won't be alive much longer, you have my word on that, Tsarevich," he said in a tone that disconcerted even Sasha.

Before Sasha could digest this new intriguing insight into Council politics, Franco began to speak again. "In your case, however, because of your unique situation, the Council agreed that your heart would not be destroyed, should you prove unworthy of it, but rather restored to its original intended owner. My brother. Carlos Salerno. I Bonded him to extend his life as we searched for the missing heart. I've continued to Bond him in the centuries after you were discovered. But I've come to believe *he* may be the one responsible for the murders."

Sasha couldn't believe what he was hearing. He took Rowan's advice and sat on the edge of his desk to absorb this news.

Franco continued, pacing the room: "When the murders began, I was more than happy to believe you responsible. The heart that beats in your chest was my brother's, after all. I never suspected Carlos could have orchestrated the whole thing." Franco shook his head. "But what you said in Genoa made me think of him. We are no longer close, and he's … gone his own way for centuries. I see him only when he wishes to renew our Blood Bond. I knew it broke the covenants to give a Bonded such latitude, but Carlos was supposed to be an Elder like me. I felt guilty, I suppose."

"You've hounded me for three centuries, and you never once stopped to think it was your brother, the man who wanted my heart?" he demanded with barely-restrained fury.

"I love my brother. It is still hard to accept the fact that he may have committed these horrible crimes," Franco cried.

"We believe that somehow Salerno enlisted Vasily in his plan to implicate you in the murders," Rowan continued, sensing Sasha's desire to attack Franco, and hurrying the conversation along to avoid a confrontation.

"I recalled that Carlos made a trip to Russia around the late 16th century when we were hunting for the heart," Franco said after a deep breath. "He must have met Vasily there and turned him in order to use him against you."

"What makes you so sure your brother is behind the murders?" he asked.

"When I followed you to London, I saw him," Franco said.

"You followed me? Of course you did," he growled.

"And he was in the company of a woman who should have been dead a century ago," Franco continued as if he hadn't heard Sasha's snide comment, "which is when I saw Theodora last. I knew *then* that my brother had broken at least one Council law, and I had no choice but to seek out the Duke and relate my suspicions."

Sasha froze at Franco's words, his blood running cold.

Rowan went still as well, demanding, "Did you say *Theodora?* You never mentioned her to me before."

"What does your brother look like?" Sasha urged, rising to his feet, completely sober now as a horrible suspicion began to take root.

Franco had no chance to answer, however, as yet another uninvited guest appeared in the doorway, breathless and clutching her side as a pale Madame Kristeva hovered over her. Lady Christiana pierced Sasha, her brother and the Inspector with a disgusted glare, her bodice heaving. "Does no one ever check the bloody wireless? I've been trying to contact the lot of you for an age!" she declared with exasperation.

"We have urgent business here, Tia," Rowan said with equal exasperation. "Can't you see we've company?" He gestured at the Duke.

Lady Christiana looked unimpressed with the Duke's presence, which raised her considerably in Sasha's estimation.

The Duke, who was finishing off his latest glass of vodka, quirked a brow at Rowan. "Can't *you* see Lady Christiana has been shot?" he retorted mildly.

Sasha finally noticed the blood seeping through Christiana's fingers as she clutched her side. The Inspector started in her direction as if to rush to her aid, but he stopped abruptly and flew to the other side of the room, averting his face. But not before Sasha had seen the glow in his eyes and the glint of his fangs.

That was certainly not a good reaction in a room full of Elders, and the Inspector knew it.

Fortunately for Drexler, Sasha was the only one who seemed to notice his reaction in the ensuing chaos, and Sasha wasn't about to give the Inspector away. He trusted a damned *vampire* more than the Elders.

With a harsh oath, Rowan rushed to Christiana and guided her towards a chair. She attempted to wave off his attentions. "I'm fine. Truly. You know I'll heal shortly," she protested. "It's only bleeding because I had to run here from our townhouse. You really should check your tickertexts!"

"Who the devil shot you?" Rowan cried.

"Charles Netherfield! He's gone mad! He's kidnapped Aline!"

Sasha's heart stopped. Literally stopped for several seconds while he struggled to absorb this news.

He could feel the blood draining from his face, and a horrible pit begin to form in his gut, growing deeper by the second, and filled with dread.

"I think we've found your brother, Franco," Brightlingsea said in a weary tone.

"Netherfield?" Rowan exclaimed. "That stuffy old archaeologist?"

"Who studies ancient Egypt, and the god Osiris," Sasha said grimly. "How could we not realize something so obvious?" He crossed the room and clutched Christiana's shoulder. "Did he say where he was taking her? What he wanted?"

"Aside from shooting me, he didn't make much of an attempt to communicate," she shot back wryly. "The Hendrixes were with him. I think Theodora may be a vampire, by the by." She took the handkerchief Rowan had provided her and clamped it against her side. Her usually beautiful features were taut with unspoken pain. It had to be excruciating, but she was enduring it stoically. "Perhaps if you check your wireless, like I suggested? In case he's tried to contact you. If your *urgent* business can be interrupted, that is," she bit out waspishly.

Everyone in the room, including the Duke, did as told. Sasha pushed aside layers of detritus atop his desk before he unearthed his wireless device. None of the unspooled messages were from the bone-hunter, however. In a fit of frustration and rising terror, he swept the contents of his desk to the floor with a loud curse, startling everyone in the room.

Fyodor was the one to tap him on the shoulder and point urgently at the post box, where the latest tube still lay after its noisy arrival had nearly spurred him to violence. He rushed over, opened up the glass door, and pulled out the tube. He ripped it open and unfolded the note with trembling fingers. His heart sank.

I have your whore. You have my heart. Bring it to me alone, and I'll let her live. We await you at the air docks. Osiris.

He balled up the letter in his fist, reluctant to let the others read its contents. That this psychopath dared to call Finch a whore was the last straw. He would see the bone-hunter dead, if it were the last thing he ever did.

And it might very well be.

Parliament fell in line with the rest of Europe when it passed a bill in both Houses yesterday, banning Dirigibles and Dirigible-like conveyances from Her Majesty's Skies. The agile, swift vehicles, which proved so valuable for Allied Forces during the War, have become a threat to National Security, according to Officials. Dirigibles have been instrumental in the rise of Piracy across the Empire, as well as the recent airborne violence between gangs in Britain's cities ...

-from *The London Post-Dispatch,* 1871

ALINE tested the strength of the ropes binding her wrists to the post of the airship. Charlie – or Salerno – paced the deck, pistol in hand, as they waited for their quarry to arrive. Theodora stood on the other side of Salerno, her attention fixed on Aline to the exclusion of all else. She reminded Aline of a barely leashed wolf, ready to pounce on her prey if given the slightest opportunity.

Salerno had banished Theodora to the opposite side of the ship after she'd nearly succeeded in sinking her fangs into Aline's neck. Salerno hadn't counted on Theodora's thirst for Aline's blood being so strong, and he was clearly annoyed at this added complication to his plans.

"Don't you dare drink her, Theodora," he'd warned after pulling the vampire off of Aline for the third time. "She's no use to me dead. You may have her once I have my heart, not before."

Aline's relief at Salerno's rescue was tempered by the fact that it was only a temporary stay of execution. Once Salerno had what he wanted from the Professor, he planned on throwing her to the vampire. But she didn't think she'd care if she died at that point, since Sasha would be dead. Because of her.

And she would have to watch it all. She turned her attention to Dr. Hendrix, who was preparing for the upcoming surgery. She'd gleaned the fact that Dr. Hendrix was not an archaeologist at all, nor related to Theodora, but rather a medical doctor. He'd been promised eternal life as a Bonded in exchange for his services as a surgeon. It seemed Dr. Hendrix planned to remove Sasha's mechanical heart on top of the table he was preparing.

Aline eyed the ancient, square metal box that was the focus of most of Dr. Hendrix's attention.

According to the voluble Salerno, it was a box specially designed by Da Vinci that would store the heart once it was removed from Sasha's chest.

While he was still alive.

When she'd learned just exactly what Salerno and Dr. Hendrix had planned for the Professor, she'd nearly cast up her accounts.

Theodora darted in Aline's direction once more, unable to restrain herself, and Salerno intercepted her, striking her in the face with the butt of the pistol. Theodora flew backwards and landed against the side of the ship, the ugly tears to her flesh quickly healing. She glared at Salerno, her fangs descended, her eyes glowing with her thirst.

Aline's dread deepened.

"I'll cut your head off, see if I don't," Salerno hissed at her. "Stick to the plan."

"But she smells so good," Theodora whined. "Are you sure he'll come?"

"Oh, yes," Salerno said, throwing a dark look in Aline's direction. "He'll come for his whore. I made sure of his attachment to her."

Aline refused to show her fear, considerable though it was. She raised her chin defiantly and glared at her former fiancé.

"What *does* he see in her?" Theodora sneered. "Those spectacles!"

Aline turned her disdain on Theodora, though her pulse

began to thud in her veins. The vampire scared her more than Salerno, considering her unpredictability, but Aline was fast losing her patience. Was it *really* necessary for Theodora to hurl such personal insults? "*You* seem to see something in me," Aline retorted. "At least in my blood."

Theodora growled her rage and started forward again. Salerno shot her in the arm, once again sending her crashing backwards against the rails. Salerno spun towards Aline with a furious expression. "I suggest keeping your mouth shut, if you want to live."

Aline only barely leashed her bitter retort. He planned on killing her anyway, so it hardly mattered what she said. And she knew in the back of her mind that the best solution for the Professor would be for her to die before he arrived. Salerno would have no leverage against him, and he wouldn't have to trade his life for hers. The thought of her being the cause of Sasha's death was unbearable.

But she couldn't quite work up the courage to tempt Theodora to do her worst. She could only hold onto her hope that somehow they both walked away from this. Surely Sasha would find a way to circumvent Salerno's evil scheme. He had Rowan, Fyodor and the Inspector on his side. *Surely* he would not be stupid enough to walk into Salerno's trap alone.

Or perhaps he would. Out of the corner of her eye, she noticed movement towards the entrance to the ship. She swung her head around, her heart sinking as Sasha came into view. Alone. Wearing nothing but his shirtsleeves, the shadow of a beard on his grim-set face. He looked terrible – he looked absolutely lovely. Despite her deepening terror, she drank in the sight of him.

He was doing the same, his attention focused solely on her as he drew closer.

And she knew in that moment that if they both got out of this alive, *nothing* was going to keep her from his side. How silly she'd been to think she could let him go. But at the moment, she feared their chances of surviving were very slim. What could he *possibly* be thinking? He just walked blithely up to her, ignoring the others, as if he'd no intention of fighting at all.

"Ah, lovely, the Tsarevich has arrived," Salerno said, moving next to her and cocking the pistol against her temple. "Stop where you are, if you please."

Sasha's nostrils flared and his amber eyes flashed with rage at Salerno's actions. He stopped a few lengths from them, his body tense. "I'm here. Let her go, you bastard."

Salerno laughed and signaled in Theodora's direction. The vampire had moved to the helm, and on Salerno's orders began to start the engines of the airship. Aline's stomach bottomed out with dread. If they managed to take to the skies, their chances of rescue were reduced to nil.

"Not yet, Tsarevich. She remains to ensure your cooperation through the procedure."

Sasha pounded his heart with his fist. "You can take the bloody thing, just let her go!" he cried.

"It doesn't work like that, I'm afraid," Salerno said as the motors whirred into life and the airship began to lurch upwards.

"He's going to kill me anyway, Sasha!" she cried out over the engine's roar. "Don't give him your heart!"

Salerno cuffed her on the temple with the pistol to shut her up, and her vision swam. She heard Sasha's anguished cry.

When the dizziness passed, she saw that Sasha had fallen to his knees and held a dagger to his own throat. She cried out in dismay. "Sasha, no!"

He looked at her with desperation and terror, shaking his head. His eyes were filled with unshed tears and fierce resolve. He was prepared to sacrifice himself. "If you spare her life and let her go now, I shall do it myself!" he cried.

Salerno laughed. "Such enthusiasm! Unfortunately, I cannot accept your generous offer. You must be alive for the procedure to work. Otherwise, the device will die with you. Throw aside your weapon, Tsarevich."

Sasha reluctantly cast the dagger away. "I'll do anything you want, just don't hurt her," he said.

Salerno gestured for him to move towards Dr. Hendrix's

table. "This will not take long. Cooperate and I will set her free afterwards."

"Don't believe him, Sasha!" she shouted, struggling against her bonds as the nausea rose in her. Judging from the suddenly sorry state of her stomach, they were entirely airborne. Of all the times to get airsick! But her illness gave her a sudden inspiration to get free of her bonds. "Let me go!" she cried.

"Shut up, you bitch," Salerno muttered, pressing the pistol hard against her skin.

"I'm going to vomit," she retorted, bile rising in her throat. "I get airsick, remember?" She didn't know what she'd do when she was free, but anything was better than remaining bound and helpless. She pretended to convulse, as if about to vomit on Salerno's boots.

Salerno cursed and jerked back.

"Let me loose," she said, "unless you want me to vomit all over you. What am I going to do? Where am I going to go? We're in the sky, Charlie."

He growled at her. "That's *not* my name."

She convulsed again, but Salerno pulled her upright. She felt the ropes come loose behind her, and then he was shoving her towards the side of the airship. This time, she really *was* sick over the railing.

When she finished, Salerno was eyeing her with disgust. Which was a good thing, since he was distracted from the dirigible coming up behind them. She'd noticed it over the side of the railing when she was casting up her accounts, and for the first time all night, she felt a glimmer of hope. She'd recognized Fyodor's familiar bulk on the foredeck of the approaching ship. Sasha had not come unprepared after all.

"Are you through?" Salerno bit out.

"For now," she said, clutching her stomach. She glanced at Sasha. He was sitting on the edge of Dr. Hendrix's table, watching them. Dr. Hendrix hovered at his side, looking a little green about the gills himself and uncertain what to do next.

"Well, get on with it!" Salerno demanded, jerking Aline forwards so he'd have a better view of the proceedings. They stopped near a hatch leading into the bowels of the airship, and he pressed her into the rusty hinges on the edge of the door to keep her still.

If Fyodor and the others planned on stopping this, they'd better arrive soon. The only thing she could do was buy as much time as possible.

"Dr. Hendrix," she cried, "are you really prepared to do this?"

The doctor ignored her, and Salerno laughed. "It's not his first time, my dear Miss Finch. He's been practicing his technique on quite a few ... ah, subjects. Playing upon his conscience is useless."

This time, Aline's nausea wasn't caused by the lurching airship. "The lot of you are mad," she cried. "Sasha, don't do this! He'll kill me. He'll let Theodora drink me dry when he has what he wants."

"He has a gun to your head, *milaya*. What else can I do?" Rowan answered her helplessly.

She suspected he knew help was on the way and was playing along until it arrived, but she could tell by the bleak, determined look in his eyes that he was prepared to play along to the bitter end. Even if it meant lying there while Dr. Hendrix ripped his heart out of his chest, he'd do it. Noble, foolish man.

"Not this," she cried, her own heart breaking, "please don't do this, Sasha. Not for me!"

"I'd do *anything* for you, Aline," he said with a bittersweet twist of his lips, undoing the buttons of his shirt and pulling it apart, revealing the hard ridges of his chest and abdomen, and the long scar over his heart.

"How touching," Salerno sneered. "We'll see how strong your love is when Dr. Hendrix has his knife in you. Strap him down, my love," Salerno commanded, and Theodora flashed to Sasha's side. She took his hand and began to clamp the crudely-made iron restraint dangling off the table around his wrist. The vampire moved with such inhuman speed she'd quickly secured it and moved to the other wrist. But not before casting another hungry glance in Aline's direction.

Suddenly, Aline knew what she had to do before Theodora could restrain Sasha further. It was a risk, but it was her only option. She'd do anything, *anything*, rather than witness Sasha's execution.

Salerno didn't even notice what she was doing until it was too late. She jabbed her arm against the jagged edge of the hatch's hinge and jerked it down, ripping her flesh open. Blood gushed from the wound, running down her arm and dripping onto the deck.

Theodora's body stiffened, her head jerking up from her task. Her nostrils flared, scenting the blood, and her fangs popped out as her eyes began to glow yellow. She held herself back for only a second, then, as if she couldn't help herself, she flashed in Aline's direction, knocking Salerno aside and grabbing Aline by the neck.

In the next second, Theodora's fangs were embedded in her throat. The last thing she saw was Sasha running towards her with a horrified expression on his face. Then everything went black.

*T*HE vampire was so enraptured by its latest meal that Sasha easily overtook it. He knocked the creature away from Aline, blood spurting everywhere, and they both crashed into the airship's railing. Aline slumped to the ground, and Sasha rose to go to her side. The vampire had the same idea, hissing as it scrambled towards Aline's supine form. Sasha's vision went red with fury. He grabbed the creature around its neck in the same manner it had grabbed Aline moments before.

It kicked and clawed at him in its frenzy, nothing left of the glacially beautiful woman Sasha had met at the Llewellyn ball. In her place was a rabid animal, Aline's blood dripping down her chin. He was beyond mercy. He backed the creature up to the railing and hurled it over the side of the airship. Its terrified screams were swallowed by the roar of the airship engine as it fell to earth from thousands of feet.

Salerno roared in anguish and shot off his pistol, clipping Sasha in the shoulder. Sasha staggered back from the blow, and gritted his teeth against the pain. He shook it off and rushed to Aline's side, ignoring Salerno, who still struggled to regain his senses from Theodora's blow.

Sasha took her into his arms, his heart in his throat. She was deathly pale, the cut on her arm and the puncture wounds in her neck gushing blood. He staunched the wounds with his hands and leaned his cheek close to her mouth to feel for a breath. At last, he felt a feeble gust of air, and he nearly sobbed with relief.

"You bastard!" Salerno cried, his features twisted with his rage, as he regained his feet and advanced in their direction. "You killed her!"

Sasha cradled Aline closer, protecting her from Salerno with his body. His heart sank with dread when he noticed the pressure on her wounds did nothing to stop the bleeding. Her lips were nearly as colorless as her cheeks.

God.

"Stay with me, Finch," he murmured, disregarding Salerno's approach, rocking Aline back and forth.

If she died now, he didn't care what happened to him. Foolish, foolish girl, what had she been thinking? How could she have tempted Theodora like that? For *him*?

He raised his head when he felt Salerno's shadow looming over them. He stared at the man through a haze of tears, unwilling to let go of Aline even with Salerno's pistol aimed at his head.

"Kill me now, and you'll never have your damned heart," Sasha bit out.

Salerno lowered the angle of his pistol to Aline. "No, I'll just finish her off," he sneered.

Sasha tensed, but a second later, something hit Salerno from the side, carrying him clear across the deck and into the macabre operating table Hendrix had prepared. Hendrix shrieked and jumped away from the fracas, but not before grabbing up the strange square box that had crashed to the deck. He turned to flee the scene, but ran into the immoveable bulk of Fyodor, who quickly subdued the man, pinning him to the deck with his automaton leg.

Salerno regained his feet and came at his attacker, who turned out to be the Inspector, eyes aglow and fangs out. Drexler easily dodged Salerno's onslaught, then rounded on the man with a speed to rival any Elder, sinking his fangs into Salerno's neck, ripping it open. Salerno clutched at the wound, and Drexler jerked away from the man, spitting out the blood as if it were distasteful.

Salerno, weakened but undeterred, fell to the deck and crawled towards his fallen pistol. Another figure appeared in that moment, kicking the gun farther away from Salerno's grasping hand with the toe of his tall boot. It was the Duke, black cloak swirling about him in the wind and a look of supreme distaste on his austere face.

"About bloody time you arrived," Sasha muttered.

The Duke curled his lip in disdain, as if he found the whole business a dreadful bore, and focused his attention on Salerno, who crouched at his feet, clutching his neck, his eyes wide. Clearly, Salerno had not expected the Duke to appear. "You've made a fool of me, Carlos," the Duke murmured. "A fool of the whole Council. Anything to say for yourself?"

"That heart was supposed to be mine!" he spat out, defiant to the end.

The Duke shook his head. "Fredo always said you didn't deserve it. If only we had listened to him, we could have been spared this unpleasant business," he said, pulling an ancient broadsword from the sheath around his waist. "I hate this part."

Salerno scrambled backwards, but he wasn't quick enough. The Duke raised his sword and brought it down, severing Salerno's head – and the fingers still around his neck – in one smooth motion. An anti-climactic end for three centuries of havoc – but then, the man hardly deserved anything more.

The Duke calmly cleaned his sword on Salerno's waistcoat before sheathing it, and turned to the Inspector, who was still spitting out Salerno's blood, looking quite ill. "What's wrong with you?" he demanded.

"Bonded blood," Elijah muttered. "Not good."

The Duke studied the Inspector with an inscrutable expression, then finally turned his attention back to Sasha. "How is she?"

Sasha clutched Aline tight to his chest, feeling the tears course down his cheeks. She wouldn't stop bleeding. He took a trembling hand away from the cut on her arm and felt her neck for a pulse once more.

He couldn't find one.

"She has a blood condition," he heard Rowan say in a grim tone, though Sasha hadn't seen the man approach. "It doesn't clot. She'll bleed out."

Sasha shook his head, lying Aline's limp body across the deck. There was blood everywhere, dripping from her spectacles, saturating her gown, his shirt, pooling around them. *Oceans* of blood. And she was so still. He ripped aside her bodice and pressed his hand against her sternum, searching for a heartbeat.

"She's alive," he breathed in relief when he felt the barest glimmer of a pulse.

"Not for long," Rowan said above him. "She's *pissing* blood, Sasha. There's only one way you can save her."

Sasha shook his head in disbelief, his heart dropping to his knees.

"Damn it, if *you* won't do it, I will!" Rowan cried, shoving him in the shoulder. "She doesn't deserve such a death."

Sasha shook him off with a growl and stared down at Aline's face, so bloodless, so still. So *dear.* He knew he couldn't just let her die, but there were no guarantees that the transformation would even work, with her damned blood disorder and her current condition. Bonding was not an exact science. And even if it did work, she'd hate him. It was not what she'd wanted, was it? But at least she'd be alive. At least she would not have wasted her life for *him.*

"I'd do it now, Tsarevich," the Duke murmured, "if you're

going to do it at all." He offered Sasha the dagger he'd dropped earlier, and Sasha took it reluctantly.

He ripped his blood-soaked shirt all the way off and gathered Aline once more in his arms. Then he plunged the dagger deep into his chest near his heart, where the wound would remain open the longest before closing up. His acidic, amber Heart's Blood sizzled to the surface, and he pressed Aline's mouth to the wound, allowing it to gush over her lips. It burned her flesh like acid, and he closed his eyes against the sight.

When it was done, he held her close and waited. "Don't leave me, *milaya*. Please, don't leave me," he murmured. His damnable heart felt like it was arresting in his chest at the very thought of losing her. His soul ached as it had when he was still human and watching his wife's life slip away, helpless to do anything to stop it. If she died, he knew he'd die with her. He'd beg the Duke himself to cut out his heart.

But she remained unmoving in his arms, and the last of his hope began to fade.

pilogue

Two months later...

" ARE you quite sure you want to leave us, dearest?" Lady Christiana asked as Aline tightened the last strap of her luggage. Aline sat down gingerly on the bed beside her friend, groaning from the exertions of the morning. She'd remained at Llewellyn House for the last two months since she'd nearly lost her life aboard the airship. Even with Sasha's Blood Bond, it had taken a fortnight for Aline's body to recover completely from its wounds and accept the transformation. The rest of the two months had flown by in a haze.

She'd slept a lot in the last few weeks.

She'd soon discovered the reason why, after she'd begun spending her mornings bent over a chamber pot. Not only had she become quasi-immortal, she'd become a mother as well. Adapting to her new circumstances was not easy. Any time she'd thought of leaving Llewellyn House, a profound weariness of the soul had descended, forcing her to her bed.

And deep down she'd thought that perhaps if she waited long enough, Sasha would come back for her. But he'd left before she'd even awakened from her delirium, and as the weeks passed, it became increasingly clear to her that he was gone for good. Not even Rowan knew where he was.

She'd finally begun to accept that he was not coming back, and that she needed to get on with her life. She touched her middle, feeling the slight bump already forming. *Their* lives, she amended. This impossible turn in her life was overwhelming. But she knew one thing: she would *never* regret the child Sasha had given her.

"It's time," she said as brightly as she could manage. "And you know I have always wanted to see the Continent."

Christiana looked doubtful but squeezed her hand. "I shall come join you soon. I won't leave you to endure your labor alone."

Aline's vision began to blur with tears, and she wiped them away with exasperation. The one thing she *would* change about her condition was her tendency to turn into a watering pot every five minutes.

"Besides," Christiana said, "it shall be the closest I ever get to motherhood myself. You'll grow sick of me, I vow. I plan to be a very overbearing godmother."

Christiana was joking, but Aline could see the real yearning in her friend's eyes. When Christiana had Bonded with the Earl decades ago, she'd given up the possibility of ever having a family. It seemed it was forbidden under Council law, if not impossible anyway.

The discovery of Aline's pregnancy, however, had thrown Council law into question. The Earl had been anything but pleased at the news, and he'd been forced to inform the Duke of Brightlingsea, the Hero of Sevastopol himself, who, as it turned out, was the bloody leader of the Elders. Aline had been mortified to have such a private matter bandied about by strangers. And frightened.

And, in the end, spoiling for a fight. Her anger had trumped all. If these ancient, arrogant men with their ridiculous laws thought that they had any sort of say over her body and the child that she carried, they were wrong. When His Grace summoned her for an audience to inform her that she was "allowed" to keep the baby, since it had been conceived before the Bonding, she'd demanded to know why he thought it was any of his business in the first place.

He was clearly surprised by her defiance, as he was a man few dared to cross. She could see why, as he was the most intimidating man she'd ever met. But she refused to be impressed by his consequence, perhaps as a result of her raging hormones, and harangued him for a good while on his presumption.

At the end of her rant, she'd declared the only way he could have stopped her from having the baby anyway was to kill her, which she didn't think he was prepared to do. *That* had settled the matter permanently.

The Duke, eyes wide, had said cryptically, "Now I understand why he was so drunk," washed his hands of the situation entirely, and retreated to his Welsh estate.

When Christiana had heard what Aline had said to the Duke, she'd been shocked, then secretly delighted. But Aline's unique circumstances had not changed Christiana's. Aline couldn't help but feel guilty that she was having a child when Christiana never could.

But the point was likely moot. Even if it were possible for Christiana to conceive, the only man she seemed interested in was a vampire. Aline didn't even want to attempt to work out the logistics of *that*.

Aline tried to lighten the mood. "One benefit of Bonding is that I no longer get airsick," she said. It was a fact she'd discovered on a short balloon ride the other day. "I mean to take advantage of that, *and* the fact I no longer have to worry about my Unenhanced lungs. I shall be the worst tourist."

Aline had decided on settling in Paris, at least until the baby was born. Paris was, after all, where all of this had begun. She was going to see every sight she'd marked in her Baedeker's this time. With the royalties from the last installment of the *Chronicles*, as well as the unexpected advance from a publisher who wanted to print the first series in a single volume, she could live comfortably for some time. The newspaper didn't want to start the next series of the *Chronicles* until the fall anyway. She had time to gird herself for the task. After losing Sasha, however, she feared it would be nearly impossible to write about Dr. Augustus anymore. It was too painful.

"Now," she said, rising, "if I don't leave soon, I shall miss my departure."

Christiana and the Earl accompanied her to the steam carriage waiting outside. The servants finished loading her things, and she climbed inside, her heart sinking at the long, solitary journey ahead.

"Are you sure, Aline?" Christiana said again. "It is a

terribly far distance to go alone. Perhaps you could at least wait until I can travel with you."

Aline gave her friend a determined smile. "I am quite set on leaving. Don't fret so. I'm hardly the fragile creature I was. I believe I shall manage just fine. In fact, I am looking forward to it."

The Earl, who had never been comfortable around her since learning of her condition, cleared his throat. "My dear Miss Finch, perhaps remaining with us for the time being would be prudent. I am certain I shall run Romanov to ground soon."

Aline tried to contain her exasperation … and heartache. "My Lord, as I have said before, please do not concern yourself. I don't want anyone run to ground. What's done is done. If he doesn't wish to be found, I *certainly* don't wish to find him. We both agreed that this is what is best."

"That was before you were discovered to be in a delicate condition," the Earl pointed out.

She fixed him with a stern glare. "Please stop trying to find him, my Lord. I am perfectly happy as things are."

The Earl was incredulous at this statement, which was quite obviously a lie, but he finally dropped the matter. After a few more parting farewells, the steam carriage pulled out into traffic. She settled into her seat with a sigh.

The old-fashioned Earl meant well, with his dogged mission to locate Sasha. Perhaps a small part of her had secretly hoped Rowan would succeed in finding him, but despite what had happened on the airship and Sasha's decision to Bond her rather than let her die, nothing had changed between them. At least *he* seemed to think so. She was not so sure any more. But if Sasha had gone to such lengths to disappear, she would not seek him out. She didn't want him on those terms.

She was becoming very good at lying to herself.

A familiar profile and the glint of metal on the street corner brought her miserable thoughts to a crashing halt. She pressed her nose to the glass of the carriage window and surveyed the busy intersection. Her heart lurched at the sight of Fyodor staring after the carriage, attempting to look inconspicuous in a bowler hat.

She rapped on the roof, calling out for the driver to stop, and before the vehicle had completely slowed, she'd jumped to the street. By the time she made it to the street corner, however, Fyodor had disappeared into the crowd. She cursed in frustration, struggling to pick up his trail. This was the first hint of hope she'd had in months, and she was not about to give up.

At last, she saw a man with Fyodor's distinctive height and ridiculous bowler hat turn a corner to the right. She pushed her way against the pedestrians, murmuring her excuses. She rounded the same corner she'd seen the man take and stopped up short, frowning her disappointment. She faced an empty alley.

She nearly jumped out of her skin when a hand landed on her shoulder. She spun around and looked up. And then up some more, her heart lightening. She'd never been so glad to see anyone in her life.

She threw her arms around the giant Abominable Soldier, unable to restrain herself. Fyodor stood rigid, awkwardly enduring the moment. When she drew back from him, she saw his human side was scarlet with embarrassment. Remembering his manners, he doffed his hat, as somber as always. But she could detect a glimmer of a smile at the edge of his lip.

"Have you come back with the Professor?" she demanded. His ghost of a smile faded completely and he shook his head.

Aline's hopes plummeted. "Why are you here, then?" But she knew the answer to that. "He sent you to watch over me, didn't he?"

Fyodor nodded unhappily.

Her heart twisted for Sasha. She was furious at him for leaving her, even though she'd agreed to it at their last proper interview, but the fact that he was totally alone now made her worry for him. What was the foolish man thinking?

But sending Fyodor to guard her from afar meant that he was worrying about her too. A part of him couldn't let her go, and that meant all hope was not lost. She felt a hundred pounds lighter already. She'd not known until she saw Fyodor today how heavy of a cloud hovered over her. For the first time in two months, with just this glimmer of hope, she felt alive. Wonderfully, horribly alive. As mad as she was at Sasha, as uncertain of their future together as she was, she knew in that moment she could not run away from the truth any longer.

Sasha may have given *her* up to protect her from himself – stupid, noble, bumbling male – but she'd *let* him go, because she was a coward. She'd been afraid she was not strong enough to love him. But she had been wrong. The truth was she wasn't strong enough to live without him.

She didn't *want* to go to bloody Paris. Not without him.

Not without him.

She wanted him, all of him, with no barriers between them – no stupid words, no secrets, especially no clothes. And she no longer wanted to fix him. She didn't need to. She wanted him as he was: a contradictory, emotionally damaged Russian Prince from the 16th century. Who thought he wasn't good enough for her.

Her!

She looked up at Fyodor, her heart quaking. "I suppose he told you never to tell me where he is."

Fyodor nodded sadly.

"But you're not going to obey him, are you? You were standing on that street corner on purpose, weren't you?"

This time, Fyodor's nod was a bit bashful.

Aline couldn't contain her relief. She tugged on Fyodor's forearm. "Take me to him, Fyodor. I love him, and I mean to have him." She touched her stomach. "*We* mean to have him."

When Fyodor puzzled out what she meant, his eye went wide, and for the first time in their acquaintance, he gave her a true smile.

*W*HEN Aline learned of their destination, she knew she'd made the right decision. Fyodor procured them transportation aboard a slightly-illegal dirigible, the *Lucky Lady*, piloted by a slightly-dissolute privateer with a Welding leg and red kerchief by the name of Thaddeus Fincastle.

Aline learned this was the same man who had picked Sasha up outside of Paris, and piloted the dirigible that had intercepted Salerno's airship. He was every bit the character she had suspected him of being. It appeared Sasha had done him a service long ago, rendering him permanently in Sasha's debt. For the length of their journey north, he regaled Aline with tales of the outlandish places he'd taxied Sasha and Fyodor to over the years.

He'd been baffled by Sasha's current destination.

"Can't figger that one out, Miss," he called out over the whirl of the propeller. He had a wad of American tobacco stuffed into his bottom lip, which caused him to spit with some frequency over the railing into the clouds. Thankfully, it was into the wind. "Been from Borneo to Timbuktu with that man, had tea with the King of bloody Nepal, chased lions across the African bush, but he wants to go to a cold Scottish island, in the middle of bloomin' nowhere."

Aline adjusted her round, glass-lensed traveling goggles against a gust of wind and smiled at the old salt. "Grimsay is where I grew up, Mr. Fincastle."

He raised a bushy brow beneath his goggles and cocked his arms at his hips. "Is that right, Miss F? He's been pining for a woman, has he?" He grinned, his lower lip jutting out over the tobacco. "'Bout time he be laid low by Cupid's bow."

"Oh, I plan on laying him *quite* low when I see him again, Mr. Fincastle. Now, tell me, is it possible to deliver me directly to the old cottage?"

Mr. Fincastle's grin deepened. "Just down the beach from it. Wondered why he bought that old heap with all his blunt. I s'pose that's where you lived?"

Aline's smile wavered a little bit with the force of her emotions. "I never took him for such a maudlin old fool, Mr. Fincastle. I don't know whether to be touched or disgusted." But she *was* touched, down to her toes. Sasha had run away, all right, straight into her past. He couldn't bear to part with her any more than she could part with him.

Aline learned this was the same man who had picked Sasha up outside of Paris and piloted the dirigible that had intercepted Salerno's airship just two months ago. He was every bit the character she had suspected him of being. It appeared Sasha had done him a service long ago, rendering him permanently in Sasha's debt. For the length of their journey north, the privateer regaled Aline with tales of the outlandish places he'd taxied Sasha and Fyodor to over the years.

He'd been baffled by Sasha's current habitation.

"Can't figger *that* one out, Miss," he called out over the whirl of the propeller. He had a wad of American tobacco stuffed into his bottom lip, which caused him to spit with some frequency over the railing into the clouds. Thankfully, it was into the wind. "Been from Borneo to Timbuktu with that man, had tea with the King of bloody Nepal, and chased lions across the African bush, but he wants to go to a cold Scottish island, in the middle of bloomin' nowhere."

Aline adjusted her round, glass-lensed traveling goggles against a gust of wind and smiled at the old salt. "Grimsay is where I grew up, Mr. Fincastle."

He raised a bushy brow beneath his goggles and cocked his arms at his hips. "Is that right, Miss F? He's been pining for a woman, has he?" He grinned, his lower lip jutting out over the tobacco. "'Bout time he be laid low by Cupid's bow."

"Oh, I plan on laying him *quite* low when I see him again, Mr. Fincastle. Now, tell me, is it possible to deliver me directly to the old cottage?"

Mr. Fincastle's grin deepened. "Just down the beach from it. Wondered why he bought that old heap with all his blunt. I s'pose that's where you lived?"

Aline's smile wavered a little bit with the force of her emotions. "I never took him for such a maudlin old fool, Mr. Fincastle. I don't know whether to be touched or disgusted." But she *was* touched, down to her toes. Sasha had run away, all right, straight into her past. He couldn't bear to part with her any more than she could part with him.

When they at last arrived at the small island she'd called

home for twelve years, she had Fincastle put her down a short walk up the beach from the cottage in which she'd grown up. She'd sent the old pirate and Fyodor back to the mainland with orders not to come back for a week. She wasn't certain how long it was going to take to convince Sasha she belonged by his side, but she wasn't giving him any quick escape routes. He'd have to swim the sea if he wanted to escape her.

Her stomach filled with butterflies as she walked along the familiar path across the cliff's edge. She wasn't about to give up on him. How could she, when imagining any life without him filled her with despair? Her chances of succeeding were perhaps very slim, considering Sasha was as stubborn as she was. But she had to try.

She'd always loved long odds, after all.

The roses her mother had planted were in full, riotous bloom in the garden behind the cottage, a small ramshackle structure a few hundred meters up from the cliff's edge. The sun beat down from a rare blue, cloudless sky, dappling the ground with patches of light through the thick boughs of the old trees that stood sentinel over the garden.

The air was so thick with the sea air and the fragrance of the roses and wild mint that had overgrown everything else, that it could have been cut with a knife. Insects buzzed, and pollen danced like little fairies in the twinkling sunlight.

It was even more beautiful than she remembered. And empty.

She picked her way through the garden, her heart growing heavier with every footstep she took.

Fyodor and Fincastle assured her he was here, but there was no sign of human occupation anywhere. Perhaps he had left the island somehow without a word to his friends, which meant she could be farther away than ever from finding him, not closer.

She cursed, then swatted a bee away from her face, which had broken out into a very untidy sweat.

She didn't remember Grimsay ever being so hot. Perhaps it wasn't so beautiful here after all.

She sighed and turned back to retrace her steps, perhaps

peek inside the cottage, but she froze, catching sight of
something out of the corner of her eye. She trudged through a
patch of mint and looked over a wall of roses. Her breath
caught in her throat at what she saw, and silly tears pricked the
back of her eyes. He was here, after all, spread out before her
like some enchanted prince in a fairy tale.

Well, he *was* an enchanted prince. And he was all hers. He
was in his shirtsleeves and waistcoat, reclining on his jacket,
napping among the roses. Sunlight shifted over his dusky
complexion, catching in his long, thick black lashes. He looked
young in his slumber, and at peace. And so delicious she
wanted to eat him up. Or lick him. Perhaps both at once.

She couldn't speak. She didn't want to break this strange
spell. He had always been in a near perpetual state of
movement over the past five years of her employment. In
retrospect, she suspected he'd spent the better part of his long
life in such a state, always running from the demons that
chased him. That he was now so relaxed, so at his ease, filled
her heart with even more joy. The battle she'd expected to face
was already half-won, in her opinion.

Carefully gathering up her courage, she started to climb
over the roses.

Familiar growling stopped her cold. She hadn't awakened
her prince, but she had awakened the dragon that guarded him.
She heard rustling in the foliage coming at her. She dropped
her skirts and turned to flee, but it was too late. Before she
could draw her next breath, she was on her back, staring up
through the trees, being licked to death by a hellhound.

"Oh, for heaven's sake!" she cried, trying to push Ilya's head
away.

Then she heard a sharp command, and Ilya bounded away
with a few excited barks. Her heart felt near to bursting at the
sound of that familiar, arrogant voice. She squeezed her eyes
shut, then slowly opened them again as a shadow fell over her.
Sasha loomed above, his black curls at sixes and sevens,
frowning, his lovely amber eyes glittering in the sunlight.

She struggled to sit up. "Hello," she said, trying to contain
her grin, since she was certain she'd frighten him away with its

brilliance.

"What are you doing here?" he demanded.

Well, at least he was talking to her. And despite his frown, he was drinking in the sight of her with his eyes. "At the moment, rutting around in the dirt." She held out her hand, but he looked reluctant to touch her.

She took that as another positive sign, but she'd make him pay later for leaving his pregnant lover in the dirt. She clambered to her feet and dusted her hands off.

"How did you get here?" he barked.

"Mr. Fincastle graciously gave me a lift."

He crossed his arms over his chest, glaring at her. "You rode in a dirigible with a notorious pirate?"

"He claims to be a privateer, and he's your friend. And one of the lovely benefits of my transformation is that I no longer get airsick. The trip was lovely, thanks for asking."

He'd grown pale at the mention of her Bonding. "I shall kill that old man. And Fyodor. He sent you here, didn't he?" he growled and stalked away, back towards his jacket.

She followed after him. He was not going to make this easy. He stooped to retrieve his wireless from the pocket of his coat and began to tap out an urgent message, jaw tight. She decided to put an end to this problem immediately.

"Oh, my God, Sasha! It's a vampire!" she cried, pointing to the right.

Sasha tensed and turned towards the imaginary threat. While he was distracted, she ripped the device out of his hand, threw it on the ground, and stomped it with her boot heel.

He stared at her, jaw slack. When his initial shock wore off, anger suffused his features. "Have you gone mad, Finch? What are you about?"

"I still have *my* wireless, Sasha," she said, patting her pocket. "But if you want it, you'll have to *touch me*."

His expression darkened, and he tensed, as if restraining himself from pouncing on her. She smiled as sweetly as she could. "I wouldn't *mind* if you touched me, Sasha."

Something hot flashed over his face, which he tried to quell with a frown and a growl. But she'd seen it. "Stop this, Aline."

"Never. I've been waiting two bloody months for you. I'm *not* waiting any longer."

He clenched his hands into fists and averted his glance. "There was no reason for you to wait. I thought I'd made myself perfectly clear to you. I don't want you hanging about me, Finch. I Bonded you to save your life. That's it. Nothing has changed."

"Everything has changed," she said, refusing to be hurt by his words. She tipped her chin at its most stubborn angle and stared him down. "I've changed. I was scared of my love for you. But I refuse to be a coward any longer. You're trying to push me away, because you think that's what's best. But it's not. I wasn't ready before, but I'm ready now. You're stuck with me, Professor Romanov."

"But I don't want you," he said, bowing his head, miserable and defiant all at once. The liar.

She snorted. "You can't even look at me when you say it, you impossible man. And do you want to know why? Because you're a bloody coward too."

He shook his head and turned away. "You need to leave, Aline."

"Not until you see reason. You think there is something monstrous inside of you, that you can never be what I need, but that's not true."

"You're wrong," he grit out.

"I'm not. And I'm not going anywhere," she said, sitting down on top of his jacket, and crossing her arms over her burgeoning belly – which he'd yet to notice, oblivious male. She stared him down.

He broke first. He turned on his heel and stalked away. "I'm leaving, since it doesn't appear *you're* going anywhere," he said bitterly.

"Shall you swim to the mainland, then?" she asked.

"If I must," he muttered.

"Coward," she called after him. He paused to glower at her over his shoulder. "I'll wager you a hundred pounds you'll be back in less than five minutes."

"You're not serious."

She fished around in her skirt pocket for her timepiece and set it in her lap just to prove how serious she was. She arched an eyebrow at him in challenge. "I've not wagered in months, since you blackballed me. I'm overdue for a win. The odds are in my favor, after all, Sasha. You're on Grimsay, taking a nap in my mother's roses, for heaven's sake. This is pretty damning evidence that you can't completely leave me behind."

He groaned in exasperation and took off through the garden.

Aline's confidence fled her when he was gone. *That* hadn't gone well at all. For some idiotic reason — perhaps because of his true age — she'd not expected him to act like an eight-year-old child who stormed off when he didn't get his way. What if he didn't come back? He was just stubborn enough to attempt the swim to the mainland, and he was just stubborn enough to make it, leaving her here to rot. But he wouldn't. He *couldn't.* For the same reason he had come here and fallen asleep in her mother's roses.

She reclined on her elbows and waited. And waited.

But not for very long. She heard him tearing his way through the undergrowth before she saw him, and her heart leapt from her chest, clear across the garden, and landed at his feet. He came into view, trampling the roses and scowling at her like a displeased Russian martyr. He stalked all the way to her feet, dropped to his knees, and began jerking his jacket from beneath her.

"Forgot my coat," he growled, not meeting her eyes.

"For your swim?" she asked sardonically, digging her heels into the soft earth as she held onto the edges of his jacket for all she was worth. He may have superhuman strength, but it was hard to use when he avoided touching her as if she had the plague.

Stupid, stupid man.

She took the opening when it presented itself. She had seduced him once before, and she was prepared to do so again. As he strained backwards, tugging on a sleeve, she suddenly released her hold. The jacket ripped, and he tumbled into the mint.

She quickly scrambled forwards, straddling him. He stared up at her in shock as she pinned his shoulders and leaned forward, until they were nose to nose.

"You owe me a hundred pounds," she whispered, winded from the struggle, her blood burning in her veins. He was so wonderfully warm and hard beneath her. She'd never thought to see him again, much less feel him, and she savored every moment of it. His breath was harsh against her lips, his Da Vinci heart scrambling in his chest.

"You little demon," he rasped. "I should..."

She kissed him before he could say another word, and his whole body went rigid beneath her, resisting. But she had nowhere else to go and nothing else to do but change his stubborn mind as best she could. So she kissed him and kissed him until his rigid lips opened to her, and he kissed her back, capitulating. His hand snaked up through her tangled hair, pressing her closer, and the tension drained out of his body.

After a gratifyingly long interval, he tore his mouth away from her and gazed up at her, looking muddled and mussed and nothing like the sophisticated intellectual she'd always known.

"I don't want to leave you. I *never* wanted to," he murmured.

"What *do* you want, Sasha?" she demanded.

He shut his eyes, tried to shake his head. "I don't know," he cried. "But you are all that keeps me from drowning. You. And your love. I can't lose it, but it shouldn't belong to me. How abominably I have treated you. Yet I can't let you go. I try and I try." He pressed his hand against his racing heart. "My heart ... my heart *aches*. It is supposed to be invincible, yet I feel I can't breathe."

Aline wanted to sob with relief. His words were heart wrenching, but they filled her with more hope than she'd ever had before. She reached down and covered his hand with her own. She could feel that magic device beating furiously against his ribs, as furiously as her own. But she wanted to banish his pain and confusion once and for all.

"Well, that could be because I am sitting on you," she said wryly.

He barked out a laugh. "Yes, that could explain it. You do like to have me at your mercy, don't you?"

She wriggled on top of him, causing him to gasp with pleasure.

"Yes, I rather think I do," she said, brushing his black curls back from his forehead. She gave him a victorious smile. She liked the fact she had the power to stir this ancient, beautiful man's desire with so very little effort.

He did not return it. He stared at her, memorizing her face, it seemed, with an agony of expression that told her he was waging an internal struggle with himself. But at last, he seemed to reach a decision – and that decision was decidedly in her favor. Something shifted behind his eyes, as if a curtain was sliding away, revealing the full, blinding force of his emotion. She caught her breath at the sight of his love-struck expression. He'd never let himself reveal so much.

At last.

But it seemed that with his decision to love her came a more carnal imperative. His agonized expression grew heated as his hand trailed down her cheek, to the edge of her spectacles, which she still wore out of habit. He didn't remove them, however, just traced the golden rim with one elegant fingertip, his lips curving with a wicked smile.

"You're wearing these still to drive me mad, aren't you?" he murmured. "I dream of you in your spectacles. And nothing else."

Dear God.

His hand continued over her throat, to the edge of her bodice, his eyes following in a predatory manner that made her blush down to her toes. His fingers toyed with a bit of brown lace just above one breast.

"Finch," he murmured. "This has to be the ugliest dress I've ever seen. Will your wardrobe *never* improve?"

"Perhaps I should take it off," she replied, feeling her cheeks heat at her own daring. She bit her lip.

His hand fell away. His gaze darkened. "No."

She was supremely disappointed at his continual resistance. What did she have to do to defeat this man?

"*No?*" she huffed. "In case you hadn't noticed, Professor, I am trying to seduce..."

Suddenly, without warning, she was on her back in the mint, the words knocked out of her, and Sasha had rolled on top of her. He pinned her with a hungry, wild look as his hands went to the front of her dress, ripping buttons and lace as he tugged the material off her shoulders.

"*I* shall take it off," he said firmly, his mouth following the progress of her gown down her body.

She wanted to shout in triumph. It hadn't been so hard to break him after all. Not even an hour's work.

He seemed to become distracted when he reached her breasts, his tongue gliding over the thin silk of her chemise so that her suddenly taut, suddenly aching nipples clung to the wet fabric. They were twice as sensitive as before. Pleasure spiked through her with every stroke of his greedy mouth, and she threaded her hands through his thick hair, pulling him closer to her.

She marveled how quickly she descended into madness at his touch, and how wonderful that madness was. He had taught her desire so well she would never need another teacher.

As if she would ever want another.

Magician that he was, he'd removed her dress and her muddy boots before she even realized they were gone, and divested himself of his waistcoat and shirt in a few lightning-quick movements. Then they were tangled together in the itchy weeds, half-clothed and desperate for each other.

He rested his forehead against her, struggling for breath as he ran his large hands over the swells of her breasts, cupping their weight. She could feel the wonderfully large, rigid length of him behind his trousers, pressing against her belly, but he remained where he was, stroking her breasts.

"You make me want you too much," he whispered against her ear. "You make me lose all of my finesse. All I want to do is take you like an animal, as quick and as hard as I can."

"That sounds fine with me," she said, thrilling at his words.

He groaned, burying his head in the crook of her neck. "Your breasts are ... they're even lovelier than I recalled."

"Well, they *have* gotten larger, if that's what you mean," she said rather shyly, her face heating.

He stilled, raising his head. "What?" he asked in a befuddled whisper, only half-hearing her through his haze of passion.

She frowned. She'd not addressed this particular subject yet. She'd become sidetracked by her mission to seduce him. She sighed and covered his hands with her own over her breasts, determined to settle matters between them once and for all before they completely lost their heads. "Sasha, I love you. And I don't care that you think yourself a villain. I've always known you were."

A slow, wolfish grin curved his mouth.

"From the moment I met you, I could see you were a tyrant. An imperious, controlling, arrogant, selfish, insufferable..."

His grin faded. "I think I get the point."

"Well, you *are*. And you come with some extremely inconvenient baggage. Three centuries' worth, I might add. I'm marrying you anyway," she continued, feeling rather bold, all things considered. "If you'll say yes, of course. But I'm warning you, I'm not getting down on one knee to ask you." She paused. "I'm not *that* desperate."

He snorted.

She scowled at him and ran her hands down his naked back, feeling every delicious ridge and angle. She reached his trousers and continued her journey beneath them, until she was very boldly, very wickedly, squeezing his backside. She arched her hips and stroked his straining erection with her body, and he growled a curse against her throat.

"Or don't marry me," she said with a devious smile. "I think the point is moot. But know this, Prince Ivan Alexander Romanovna Ivanovich, you are mine. And I am most definitely and forever yours."

He kissed her ferociously, as if would make her surrender to him. But that was a futile battle, because she already had, long ago. When he realized this, he at long last surrendered to her, body and heart. "You shall marry me, Finch," he said between kisses. "Aline. *Milaya.* My sweet little bird. I'll not let you fly away from me. I'll bind you to me if I must. For a thousand years."

"If you must," she said nonchalantly. Seemingly satisfied, he reached between them and began to unbutton his trousers, but she put her hands over his, stopping him, bring them back up to her breasts. "But I want one thing clear between us, Sasha."

"What is that?" he demanded, his body now thrumming with impatience.

"No more opera singers. Or dancers. Or audience members."

He looked mortally wounded. "How can you even think I would be unfaithful?"

She gave him her driest look.

"Fine. I'll agree to your little stipulation. If you promise to give up bone-hunters," he growled.

She scowled at him. "That was low, Sasha!"

He silenced her with a kiss, then gazed down at her with such tenderness he took her breath away. "Just to make things perfectly clear to you, I could *never* be with another woman, Finch. How could I, when you're all I could ever need? For the rest of our long life together, I am yours. I love you," he tore out. "I love you."

Her happiness was complete. Almost. She knew the centuries-long pain he'd suffered for his lost child, and the risk she ran now. But she had to trust his love was enough to overcome his fear. "Even when I'm fat?"

"You, fat? Finch, you weigh less than a feather."

"Not for long," she murmured. She moved one of his hands down to her gently-swelling stomach. "I'm already expanding after two months. I shall be the size of this cottage in a few more."

It took him a few moments, but the truth finally dawned on him as he felt her stomach through the thin linen of her chemise. He sucked in his breath and pulled back from her with wide, incredulous eyes. He couldn't seem to speak.

She propped herself on her elbows, watching him tentatively. She could not tell what he was feeling. "Apparently, it is something of a miracle, Sasha. The Duke of Brightlingsea himself said nothing like this has ever happened. As none of the Elders' ridiculous laws cover such an occurrence, the Duke has given us his blessing. I told him we didn't need it, and that we'd have as many children as we want. It's the least he can grant you after the way the Council has treated you for the past three centuries. I gave him quite an earful, you may rest assured."

She paused, trying to gauge his mood. He was still staring at her in shock, holding her belly. "That is, if you want children..." she began again. "Besides this one. You're quite stuck with him, you know," she said, her voice rising a little as panic began to set in.

He frowned, stroking her belly. At last he spoke. "The Duke of bloody Brightlingsea knew you were carrying my child before I did?" he bit out, furious.

Well, this was an unexpected reaction. She had been prepared for an epic existential meltdown. Savoring his ridiculous anger, she said in her most reasonable tone, "You abandoned me, Sasha. You disappeared to this damned island to sulk. Of course he found out."

"I wasn't sulking, I was *pining*," he insisted. Then, after a pause, "You gave the Duke an earful, did you?" he asked, his tone softening.

"I don't know why everyone's so surprised by that," she muttered.

He ran the backs of his fingers over the swell of her belly. "You think it's a boy, do you?" he asked in a strange, dumbfounded whisper.

Her panic faded. She felt a warm glow spreading through her body, the warm glow of complete happiness. "I hope so," she whispered fiercely. "A boy with black hair and a devil's grin."

He gave her *his* devil's grin. "I hope it's a tiny little girl with fawn-colored hair and chocolate eyes. I hope she wears spectacles she doesn't need, just like her mother."

"Sasha," she whispered, "are you glad? Will it be all right?"

He laughed wildly, kissing her soundly. "Well, let me see," he murmured. And then, as if unable to contain himself a moment more, he took her chemise and ripped it down the middle. She gasped as he gazed down at her naked body, the swollen shape of her breasts, the rise of her belly.

At first she was mortified that he should see her in her current condition, but at the look on his face, her embarrassment quickly disappeared. He drank in the sight of her, running his hands over her skin, testing the new contours of her body as if he would never have enough of touching her.

Then he turned them on their sides, pulling her near, holding her tight so there was no space left between them. He kissed her nose, her eyes, the smile on her lips. "I didn't think I could ever be this happy. Or love you any more."

"Sasha," she moaned, embracing him with arms and legs, wanting to melt into his flesh and never leave.

"It must have started the first time you came to my office, five years ago," he mused. "You stumbled over the pups, and your spectacles went flying. That's when I knew…"

"So long ago," she murmured.

"And when I knew for sure," he said, nipping her bottom lip. "The day I spied on you, singing to *Aida* in my study. You sounded like a drowned cat. It was appalling."

She scowled at him. "I think that is *quite* enough," she said, arching her hips to meet the gentle undulations of his body.

He chuckled and reached between them to the fastenings of his trousers. "I knew, but I did not understand what it was. But now I do."

"So do I."

He hesitated. "I'll not be easy to endure, Finch."

She snorted. Didn't she know? "Neither will I, Professor. And you'll learn that soon enough if you don't get on with it."

He laughed and rolled over her once more. "I am yours, *milaya*. Forever."

THE END

If you enjoyed this title, read on for an excerpt from
Margaret Foxe's next book in the series:
A Dark Heart: The Elders and Welders Chronicles Bk. 2

Prologue

London, 1888

LADY Christiana Harker couldn't count the number of times she'd awakened with the image of Elijah Drexler's brilliant sapphire eye still gleaming in her mind, a remnant of her never-ending dreams of him. The number was embarrassingly incalculable. She'd loved Elijah since she was seventeen and he was a wounded, feral boy of eight. And she'd been *in* love with him since she'd returned to London six years ago and met the man he'd become. She hadn't been able to help herself. The moment she'd seen him again, she'd lost her heart – and the tormenting dreams had begun.

Impossible dreams, for so many reasons. He didn't even know she was Ana, the sick girl from his past, a girl who was supposed to have died over twenty years ago. He, like everyone else, thought she was her younger sister. And she was forbidden from telling him the truth.

Though she doubted it would change anything between them. She might be hopelessly in love with him, but he'd never shown signs of suffering the same affliction. He didn't even seem to *like* her – went out of his way to avoid her, in fact. And she knew it was because of her resemblance to the dead girl he'd once adored. So she'd endured her case of unrequited love without attempting to interfere in his life, just as she was destined – and bound by an oath – to do.

But then, last week, she'd followed Elijah into Whitechapel, and everything had changed. She'd more than ignored Rowan's rules. She'd shattered them ... and she'd not seen Elijah since.

Until now. This time the sapphire eye peering down at her wasn't part of a lingering dream. She was quite awake, for she could feel the cold spring breeze from the open casement window caressing her exposed skin, and the hot, uneven breaths from the man hovering above her against her cheek. The sensations were too real to be a dream. *He* was too real.

He'd come to her. *At last.* Moonlight made the deep blue of his left eye glimmer, just like in her dreams. And just like in her dreams, he was much too close, the heat of his trembling body like a furnace and just inches from her own. So close, but never close enough.

But this very real, very angry, wild-eyed man was hardly the tender lover of her foolish dreams. So she lay still beneath him, afraid to move, her own breath growing labored as he studied her with feral intensity.

Her body was on fire from his proximity, and her mind raced with a thousand questions. She'd been so worried, wondering where he'd been since he'd run away from her a week ago in that alley in Whitechapel. Wondering if he was even alive. But despite the chaos of her thoughts and her uncomfortably feminine response to his nearness, she finally latched onto one significant fact. Elijah Drexler had two eyes. Two real, human eyes. Which wasn't possible.

He'd lost his right eye when he was eight years old, in the same fire that had given him the razor-like scar streaking down his cheek and the limp in his right leg. In an act of charity, her father had taken in the half-dead East End urchin after he'd been discovered by the Metropolitan Police in the ruins of a burnt-out slum. The old Earl had given Elijah a brass-fitted, goggle-like Welding eye to replace the one he'd lost, and a Welding brace to support his crushed leg. Christiana, herself an invalid at the time, had helped nurse the lad back to health. She'd *seen* his ruined eye before the Welder had come to fix it.

But now...

She couldn't restrain herself any longer, despite the warning in his expression. She sat up abruptly, the bedcovers falling to her waist, and raised a hand towards his left cheek to draw him near. He dodged her with a hiss, leaning just out of her reach. As if her touch were unbearable.

His rejection stung, as always, though she refused to show it. She reached over to her nightstand and turned up the gas lamp instead.

He glared at her with stony defiance as she studied the miracle before her in the warm glow of the lamp. The strange scar on his cheek remained, but he had a new, perfectly formed eye, fringed with beautiful long, sooty black lashes to match the other one. And it wasn't sapphire. It was the color of amber fire.

The color of Rowan's eyes.

Her blood ran cold, and she clutched the bedsheets around her lap to keep from reaching for him. She'd imagined a thousand consequences to her actions that night, but not this. He'd *regrown* an eye – an *immortal's* eye, judging by its unnatural color. And somehow she suspected that was not all that had changed.

"What did you do to me?" he rasped.

She shook her head, unable to speak through her shock. He scowled at her silence and impatiently jerked the collar of his loose white shirt apart, revealing a throat untouched by a Welder's blade. She sucked in a sharp breath, her unease growing. The Iron Necklace, a breathing device everyone of his generation had implanted in order to survive the years of the Great Fog, was gone. Not even a scar remained as evidence of its existence.

She trailed her eyes back up to his face, the stark, ruined beauty of his features obscured by the shadows dancing through the room and the thick stubble on his jaw. He looked as if he'd not slept in a week, and his fever-bright, mismatched eyes were filled with such confusion, such *accusation*, she flinched. And then she flinched again when, in an abrupt move she didn't see coming, he reached out and jerked the Iron Necklace from her own neck, snapping the metal clasp in the back as if it were made of air. Had the device been real, he would have ripped her throat out with the force of his action. But it wasn't real, and her neck was as untouched as his own, a fact that he'd obviously deduced.

At least, she hoped he had, before he'd torn the device off of her so violently.

He tossed the false necklace aside with a look of disgust and crouched further from her at the end of the bed, watching her, waiting, his body literally thrumming with his fury.

She clutched her exposed throat reflexively, her mind whirling. She knew she owed him answers, though she didn't have very many. "Your leg?"

He growled – literally *growled* – his response. "Healed. What did you *do* to me?" he repeated, gritting every word out.

Her mind raced back to last week's debacle. Elijah had been one breath away from his last that night, after the Ripper had left him for dead. If she hadn't been there, watching from the shadows, he would have died. As she'd held him in her arms, she'd *felt* the life leeching from him. She'd reacted purely on instinct, unable to bear the thought of losing him, not knowing if what she did would even work. But she'd had to try something – even if that something was forbidden.

"I didn't even know if it would work, but I couldn't lose you, Eli. I couldn't let you die."

When the nickname she'd called him as a boy slipped from her lips, unbidden, she knew she'd made things even worse. He froze and fixed her with a look that took the last of her breath away. The fury was still there, but alongside that was a quiet devastation.

As if she'd broken his heart.

"You're her," he whispered. In anguish.

Her heart sank, and she hated herself for causing the pain she heard in his voice.

"You're Ana. Somehow ... you're *her*," he continued.

"Eli ..."

"Tell me the truth, damn you!" he breathed. "You're Ana. Not her *sister*."

She could do nothing but nod, and, coward that she was, stare at her trembling hands, unable to meet his accusatory stare any longer.

He cursed under his breath, and, even with the distance

between them, she could feel the tension in his body coil even tighter.

"I should have known, the moment I saw you six years ago ... I *knew*, but I couldn't believe ... How is it possible?" he cried. "How is any of this possible?"

She sighed and threw back the covers, sliding her feet to the ground, unable to remain where she was a moment longer. She felt too ... vulnerable, tucked up in her bed while he raged at her.

But at her movement, he leapt from the bed all the way across the room in the blink of an eye, pinning himself against a wall and gazing at her in horror. "What are you doing? Stay where you are!" he breathed, his lungs working as if he'd run clear across the city.

She froze halfway to her feet, her stomach turning over. She'd never seen anyone move as fast as Elijah had, save for Rowan and the other Elders.

Oh, this was not good, not good at all. But she refused to panic. Elijah was doing enough of that for the both of them, crouching against the wall and following her every movement like a cornered animal. She feared he was a breath away from shattering completely.

She tried to remain calm as she stepped across the room and fetched her silk wrap from the back of a Queen Anne chair. It was flimsy, but it blocked the chill in the air. And it gave her time to gather her wits. She approached him, but he held up a hand, averting his head, nostrils flaring.

"Don't come any closer," he gritted out with such agony in his tone that she stopped, though her instinct was to wrap him in her arms and hold him close to her heart forever. "Just tell me what is happening to me," he demanded. "Tell you aren't a monster like me!"

Her dread deepened at the word. "You're not a monster, Elijah. I'm not a monster either. You remember how sick I was when you were a boy. I was dying, and Rowan healed me."

His eyes widened at the mention of the Earl. "Healed you? He did more than heal you," he bit out.

She nodded weakly. "I don't age. And I don't get sick, and if I'm hurt, I heal ... very quickly. I know it's difficult to believe. But Rowan is ... well, he's immortal."

But Elijah was hardly listening to her any longer. He just slumped against the wall, shaking his head. "You never died. *Ana* never died."

She clenched her hands at the horror in his voice, resisting the growing urge to go to him. "To the world, that sick girl *did* die. It was a necessary fiction, since the truth is ... impossible."

"A necessary fiction," he repeated in a dead voice.

"I'm sorry, Eli," she said softly. "You were my dearest friend, and I had to lie to you."

"Friend," he spat, the broken expression quickly replaced by anger. "You let me believe you died. You're not my friend. And I certainly as hell am not yours. You've no idea..." He paced the room at an alarmingly inhuman speed, running his hands through his unkempt, coal-black hair in agitation. "Why did you come back at all? Why have you tormented me for *six years*? Every time I looked at you, I saw *her*."

She shrugged helplessly. "I couldn't stay away. Father was dying, and he needed me. It was easy enough to become Lady Christiana, and for Rowan to become the brother I'd lost. So many years had passed, no one cared. And I wanted to see *you*..."

"Don't," he warned, cutting her off. He covered his face with his hands again, as if blocking out the world. "God, how I wish this were a nightmare, how I wish I didn't believe every ludicrous thing you just told me! The Earl is an *immortal*, and you ... I don't know *what* the devil you are. Bloody hell! I'd rather be insane than have this be real. Tell me what you did to me!"

He was nearly shouting now, and she flinched at the rage vibrating through his whole body.

"I ... I gave you my blood," she said. "It was the only thing I could think to do to save you. I thought that, perhaps, since Rowan's blood had saved me, mine could save you. And it did."

He laughed wildly, humorlessly. "You've no idea what you've done, do you?"

"No, not really," she admitted, biting her bottom lip. "What I did is forbidden, against the laws that govern our kind."

"Your *kind*," he sneered. "Didn't you ever think there was a good reason it was forbidden?"

"I didn't think. I just didn't want you to die, Eli."

"Don't call me that. Never call me that," he said quietly, his breathing once again growing ragged as he glowered at her.

"You'll always be Eli to me, that little boy who was so dear to me," she answered defiantly, stepping towards him once more, and into a beam of moonlight. "And I'll never regret saving you—"

She broke off with a gasp when she saw the change come over him. One moment he was scowling at her, the next moment both of his eyes glowed with amber fire, and two long, sharp, metallic blades seemed to descend from his mouth, curving slightly over his bottom lip. She had a hard time believing what she was seeing, but the ocular evidence was fairly conclusive.

Elijah had fangs. Metal fangs.

And now *two* glowing amber eyes. Even the whites of his eyes were filled with the strange fire.

And he looked a hair's breadth away from pouncing on her, if his flaring nostrils and clenched fists were any indication.

"What in heaven's name..." she began.

"Damn you, Lady Christiana," he growled in a deep, animal voice she hardly recognized. "Move out of the moonlight before I do something I'll regret."

But she remained where she was, too stunned to process what was happening, much less move. "What?"

He tried to turn his head to hide his transformation – she could see his struggle – but he couldn't seem to tear his eyes away from her. An inhuman sound issued from deep in his chest, and he took a step towards her, as if he couldn't help himself. "The moonlight ... I can see *everything* through your robe," he hissed.

It took another long moment before his meaning finally penetrated through her shock. "Oh!" Her cheeks turned crimson, and she quickly retreated back into the shadows, wrapping her arms around her breasts, pulling her robe even tighter around her waist.

Some of the tension seemed to leave his body, but only a little. His eyes continued their eerie glow, and his fangs – his *fangs!* – remained extended, glinting silver in the moonlight. And he continued to track every movement she made with a predatory intensity that was both alarming and ... strangely arousing.

Her cheeks – her entire body – still burned, but it was no longer solely from embarrassment. It was from something primal inside of her responding to something primal inside of him. He looked like he wanted to eat her. And she didn't think she would mind all that much if he did.

Dear God. What was happening? What had she done to him?

For a long time, all they could do was stare at each other, their heavy breaths the only sounds in the room, aside from the ticking of the old ormolu clock over the hearth. She attempted to rein in the dark and confusing urges coursing through her body, desperately trying to focus on their most immediate concerns.

Namely his eyes. And his fangs.

She took a deep breath and slowly approached him, careful to avoid the direct moonlight again. He tensed and backed away a few steps, still breathing heavily. But no matter his dire warning, or the mounting desperation in his expression, she knew he'd never hurt her, so she continued towards him until an arm's length separated them and stared up into his transformed face.

Her breath caught in her throat as a fresh wave of heat passed through her, low and deep. She was a tall woman, but standing so close to his towering height had always made her feel petite, delicate. Now his proximity made her whole body sizzle. She'd always been madly attracted to him, but this ... *this* was new. And she realized that it was because he was no longer looking at her with studied indifference, as he had for the past six years. He was looking at her with barely leashed, desperate hunger.

"What am I?" he whispered, his glowing eyes burning her to her soul. "What have you made me?"

"I don't know," she whispered back.

"I can't die," he continued, anguished. "I've tried a hundred times this past week."

She reeled with horror, her strange arousal suddenly doused by his stark words. "Elijah, no! No!" She reached out to him, but he shied away.

"I've stabbed myself through the heart. I've jumped from the tallest buildings in the city. I've shot myself here, again and again," he said, pointing to his temple. "But I always wake up."

Her stomach roiled with every horrifying revelation he made, her eyes pricking with tears.

"I always wake up," he repeated, "and I'm always the same. A monster."

"You're not a monster. I must have made you immortal, like me..."

"*Not like you*," he insisted. "I crave blood, Lady Christiana. Human blood. The night you ... *turned* me and I ran away, there was this fire in my blood, growing and growing. And all I could think about was finding you again, *taking* you and drinking you dry."

She swallowed, her throat suddenly dry. "Taking me..." It spoke to her rising hysteria that she focused on *that* part of his speech, rather than the part about drinking her dry.

His eyes pulsed even brighter. "I tried to resist, but in the end I couldn't. I returned to the alley where you'd found me. You weren't there. But the body of that woman was."

Christiana nodded numbly, remembering the woman that night. One of the Ripper's victims, who Elijah had been too late to save. Her stomach sank. She had a bad feeling about what he would say next.

"She was cut open. Dead. But the blood ... The blood was

everywhere, and the moment I scented it, I couldn't control myself. The thirst was too much." He paused and looked away, unable to meet her eyes a moment longer. "I found out that night that the best tasting blood in a corpse is in the liver and the heart."

She couldn't help it. The tears flowed down her cheeks, and her heart felt as if had been mortally bruised. What had she done?

"And the next night, when I had my fangs buried deep in the neck of someone *living*, I discovered that I liked the taste of it fresh and warm even better," he finished bleakly.

"No!" she cried, "Tell me you didn't..."

The dark look he gave her made it impossible for her to continue. Sobbing, she took his face between her hands, made him focus on her despite his attempts to look away. And as if he couldn't help himself, he leaned in close, so close their foreheads were almost touching. She could see the dark stubble on his chin, the deep groove of the mysterious scar on his cheek that hadn't healed, and the way his nostrils flared, as if he were absorbing her scent into his blood.

And she could see the fangs, glinting like silver in the moonlight. Long, thin and metallic, they weren't of the natural world. She just didn't understand how it was possible, how her blood could change him so profoundly.

"My God, Elijah, I'm sorry," she murmured, sliding her hand towards a fang. She couldn't seem to help herself.

She gasped as the skin on her finger ripped apart at the barest touch against the razor sharp edge. She pulled her hand away, or at least she tried to. But she wasn't fast enough.

With lightning-quick speed, he caught her by the wrist with one hand, and with the other hand jerked her body tight against his own. Something dangerous flashed over his glowing eyes. Then, with a moan, he took her bleeding finger into his mouth and sucked the blood from it.

Shocked and more aroused than she'd ever been before, she slumped helplessly against him. She couldn't take her eyes off the sight of her finger between his lips. She couldn't stop the slow, delicious burn deep in her core at the feel of his hot, wet mouth against her skin, his hard, lean body pressed against her own.

Then he slowly released her finger from its prison, his tongue snaking out to lap up the last drops of her blood from her rapidly-healing cut. "So sweet," he murmured, and she moaned in response as he rolled his hips against her own.

Dear God, she could feel him. *All* of him.

When the wound was no more, healed as if it never was, he released her wrist and gripped the back of her head. Holding her tight to him – too tight – he tilted her boneless body back, lowering his head towards her neck, his entire body shuddering against her. And in the last corner of her mind not overcome with the fog of desire, she knew that she should start to worry. She was fairly certain he was going to bite her with his fangs.

And she was going to let him.

"All the blood I've had this week, and still it's not enough," he murmured against her throat, each glance of his lips against her skin sending gooseflesh all over her body. "I want more. I want *yours*, more than my next breath." He pressed his hips against her own again, sending a shockwave of sensation through her lower body. "I want to strip you bare and come inside you, again and again, as I suck you dry," he whispered against her ear.

She didn't know whether to be aroused or horrified by his words. She was a confusing mix of both as she lay helpless in his arms.

But she had to believe one thing of him, for if she didn't, if she *couldn't*, she might as well let him do his worst there and then. She'd turned him into a dangerous, unpredictable creature she'd not even begun to understand, but he was still Elijah. He was still the little boy she'd befriended a lifetime ago. He was still the man she loved.

"You'd never hurt me, Elijah," she said softly.

And – this time at least – he proved her right. With an anguished whimper, he released her, tracing in the blink of an eye to the other side of the room.

She reeled in place for a moment, regaining her equilibrium, before she turned to face him again. He was thrumming with tension, his broad shoulders heaving beneath his shirt, his eyes burning her down to her toes.

"Don't tell me I'm not a monster," he hissed, still trembling, still on a knife's edge. "You did this to me. You made me into this ... *thing*. This craving, horrible, deathless *thing*. Make it stop. *Please*."

"I don't know how," she whispered through her tears. "Rowan must..."

"They'll kill you! If Rowan and the others know what I've done, they'll kill you!"

"Good. Then there *is* a way," he said, relieved, and he actually started towards her bedroom door, as if prepared to seek out Rowan immediately – to seek his death. And after everything he'd told her, she knew he would.

She'd never been so terrified – for him, for herself. She had to stop him, and she could think of only one way to do so, though she knew he would hate her even more for it.

"They'll kill *me*!" she cried.

He stopped in his tracks and slowly, reluctantly, turned back to her. The fangs were gone, and his eyes were no longer glowing. He looked as if he'd been kicked in the gut.

"Tell me this is another of your lies," he breathed.

She shook her head. "I made an oath when Rowan bonded me, and breaking it is punishable by death."

"I don't believe you," he whispered. "How can I believe a word out of your lying mouth?"

She wished she *was* lying. As much as Rowan loved her, as much as she loved him, she knew that his duties as an Elder would force his hand. Now that she saw with her own eyes the horrifying consequences of her actions, she knew deep in her bones that Rowan and the Elder Council wouldn't let this betrayal slide.

"I would not lie about this. Rowan would have no choice. He's a powerful man, but there are others like him who are even more powerful. They'll kill you, and they'll kill me."

He believed her. She could see it in the complete bleakness in his expression, the sudden stillness of his body. As if she'd snatched the last of his hope away. The sight of his defeat was soul-wrenching.

He truly wanted to die, but he couldn't condemn her to the same fate. And it destroyed him.

It nearly destroyed her.

He drifted away from the door and towards the open casement window as if in a fog. She followed him, careful to not touch him. She suspected that if she did so now, he wouldn't be able to control himself.

"We'll figure this out. We'll find a way to fix this," she said, cringing at the ridiculous inanity of her words. There was no way out of this nightmare, and they both knew it.

He stopped, gripping the edge of the sill until his knuckles were white with the strain, his head bowed. "There is no *fixing* me. And there is no *we*, my Lady," he said coldly. "You've done quite enough. Stay far away from me. I've restrained myself tonight ... God knows how. I cannot guarantee I will do so again." He leapt upon the windowsill, his massive body blocking out the moonlight, his white shirt billowing in the wind.

"I just wanted you to live," she murmured to his back.

He shook his head. "Bloody *hell*, you're selfish, just as you were all those years ago. You and your bloody father, wanting to *save me*. You never stopped to ask me if I *wanted* to be saved. Because I didn't." He shot her a look over his shoulder, and she wanted to die at the anguish blazing in his eyes. "I wanted to die then. And I wanted to die last week, and I'll hate you forever for not letting me."

Then he jumped from her window, at least thirty feet above the back garden, and disappeared into the deep, impenetrable darkness of London as if he was no more than a shadow.

And all she could think for the longest time as she stared into the black gloom, freezing and hopeless, was that he should have just tossed her out the window with him, alongside her shattered heart.

About the Author

Margaret Foxe is a professional musician from Tennessee. She has lived in several countries and travelled from Costa Rica to Cairo. Her crowning transcontinental glory was ascending Jebel Toubkal in the High Atlas Mountains with her best friend, a mule, a Berber guide named Omar, a bota bag, and lots and lots of orange Fanta.

She also writes witty historical romance under the name Maggie Fenton. You can follow her literary(ish) escapades on her blogs on Goodreads, Wordpress, Amazon, and Facebook. Send her a Tweet @FoxeSteampunk. She loves hearing from her   fans.

CPSIA information can be obtained
at www.ICGtesting.com
Printed in the USA
FSOW02n0117310516
20952FS